In HIS Eyes

A Parallel Of Putting Down The Flesh

Peggy Sue Miller

In HIS Eyes
Written by: Peggy Sue Miller
Copyright © 2016
Published 2017 by P. S. Miller

The friends that made this book possible are:

Lynn Miller, for his constant love and patience and for being the one to smooth out this book's rough edges.

Editor- Mac Campbell, Assistant Editors- Joy Renee Clavell and Katrina Lubbecke

Proofreading and Encouragement - Polly Bainbridge and Liorah Norris.

And Chronological Order - Melissa McGhee

Thank you all so much!

Table of content:

In HIS Eyes

A Parallel Of Putting Down The Flesh

Peggy Sue Miller

Prologue

*"And God will wipe away every tear from their eyes;
there shall be no more death, nor sorrow, nor crying.
There shall be no more pain,
for old things have passed away."*
Revelation 21:4 NKJV

"I'm sorry Joe, there really isn't anything more I can do for you. It's just a matter of time now. Get your affairs in…" The doctor stopped speaking. The words seemed so empty. He laid his hand on Joe's shoulder and with compassion said, "You have been a real blessing to me. The last couple of days have been eye opening. You've given me a lot to think about. My way of thinking has definitely been challenged. Thank you!" He stopped again and sighed. "It won't be long before you see the God you love so much, face to face. May He bless you, Joe."

The doctor smiled as he patted him on the shoulder and walked back to talk to Joe's best friend Mike, before leaving the room.

Joe's son, Cody, walked up to his father's bedside and moved in close to speak quietly, "Dad, you have to fight this. You can't just give up now."

"Cody, the Word says, 'It is appointed every man once to die' and it seems it's my time. I know it's hard, but you need to let me go."

Cody wasn't ready to hear those words from his father. "*Why is God doing this to me?*" he thought as he paced a step this way, then that, running his fingers through his crazy blond hair that seemed to reflect the conflict that raged within him.

With a trembling hand Joe reached out for his son. Cody encircled it and held it to his chest.

Joe asked, "Cody, how many six-thousand-year-old men do you see walking around these days?"

"What?" Cody responded impatiently.

Joe raised an eyebrow and paused, waiting for his question to sink in.

Cody knew he couldn't win an argument with his father's big picture logic, so he changed his tactic, wiping away the tears that ran down his face. Calmer now, he spoke; "Dad, you have to get well. Who's going to take care of your garden this year? The weeds are going to take over and you haven't planted anything. You're going to need to get started soon." He knew it sounded ridiculous but he was desperate, and grasping for anything he could come up with to make his father fight harder to live.

"Well, that's not true." The corners of Joe's mouth showed a slight smile. "I planted some bird seed, but I haven't seen any birds come up yet." He rolled his eyes to emphasize his mock disgust with the bad seeds.

Cody smiled as, again a tear slid down his cheek. He was going to miss his Dad's lighthearted humor and quick comebacks. His Dad had always been one to light up the room when he entered it, no matter where he went, people would gravitate towards him.

Taking a deep breath, Cody attempted to make the conversation a bit lighter, trying a clever response. "Dad, if you wanted birds, shouldn't you have planted eggs?"

"No, I tried that last year and all I got was eggplant, and you know how I dislike eggplant. I ended up giving them all to Egger and Birdy."

Cody had to laugh out loud despite the pain gripping his heart. He heard Mike laughing as he stepped up next to him by the bed.

As the laughter subsided, Mike spoke quietly. "Joe, the doctor thinks you should rest now."

"Oh nonsense! I'll get all the rest I need when I enter God's kingdom. I'm running out of time here and I won't waste the little time I have left sleeping, if I can help it."

There was a moment of silence between the two men as Joe's brow drew up into a plea. "Mike, I need you to make me a promise."

"Anything, Joe."

"Promise me you'll take care of my boy."

Cody's head snapped up, not ready to concede to what he viewed as defeat. He seized his father's frail hand again and appealed, "Dad, no!"

Joe gave his son a look that Cody knew all to well. A look that said, 'Be still boy.' He had heard those words and seen that look countless times throughout his thirty-one years. But 'being still' had never been as difficult for him as it was right now. He swallowed hard as the tears of despair continued to run down his face. He knew his father's request wasn't about him needing a daddy, although right now he couldn't help feeling like he did. No, this was more about a dying man appointing a counselor, a mentor, for his son. Someone his son could run to when things got hard. It was about his father being at peace knowing his son would still have someone to stand beside him.

So, Cody took a step back and sat in the chair near the window, dropped his head and let the tears flow. His body language suggested a surrendering to the idea his dad wasn't going to be there for him anymore.

Although Mike could never take his dad's place, Cody couldn't think of anyone that could come closer to filling his dad's shoes than Mike. He couldn't remember a time when Mike hadn't been a part of his life: school and church plays, Cub Scout ceremonies, graduations, Birthdays, Cody's wedding, family barbecues, camping trips and game nights. Mike had been there for every mile marker and every season throughout his life.

Mike spoke quietly, his voice broken by the emotions he tried to hold in check. He laid one hand on Joe's forearm and turned to lay the other on the base of Cody's neck, as if he were about to take an oath. "I promise Joe, rest assured, I will be there for him, I prom-" Mike's voice cracked as he tried to regain control.

Tears fell freely from Cody's eyes and off the tip of his nose onto his lap, where his hand lay limp with resignation. The warm sun peaked through the swaying branches of a tree near the window, and it's light danced across Cody's lap, spilling off onto the floor. The broken sunlight flashed across his lap, highlighting the limp hand that lay there. Through his tears he could see his hand looked like the hand of Adam as depicted on the ceiling of the Sistine Chapel. His tears landed on his hand, and ran into his palm. As they pooled there he reflected on *Psalm 56:8,* where it says, *"When we cry out to God, He catches our tears and saves them, putting them into a bottle; keeping record of them in His book."*

Cody believed those words, and it brought him comfort and peace as he was reminded that God knows his pain and would someday wipe away all his tears.

1
Gully Wash

...I am trusting in you, O Lord, saying
"You are my God!"
My future is in your hands. Rescue me
from those who hunt me down relentlessly.
Psalm 31: 14-15 NLT

Five years later
Twilight – At a remote campsite in the Appalachians

The sound of gunfire rang out, echoing off the river, making the shots seem as if they were coming from all directions. The sound charged the air surrounding the small camp with a fearful energy. Cody bolted out of his tent, followed closely by his wife Shelly.

The other couple with them was already up and standing, frozen, facing the sounds. Mike stood holding an armload of sticks while his wife, Holly, dropped a carton of eggs that now lay broken at her feet.

They stood rigid, taking in shallow breaths as they listened intently to the sound of men yelling at each other in the distance.

Shelly whispered as she came up behind Mike, "Can you hear what they're saying?"

"One of them shouted out 'Shut up' just before the shots rang out."

"That doesn't sound good."

"No, it doesn't."

"Should we go see what's going on?" Cody said, barely audibly.

Mike answered him, "Yeah, maybe. But we don't want to just walk in on them. We need to check it out, without drawing attention to ourselves."

Holly gasped, "There's a gully wash that starts up at the top, just to the left of the trail head."

"Yeah, I saw it too. It comes out over there." Cody pointed down the trail towards the river. "I passed it last night when I came back from the river. Shel, you and Holly stay right here; we'll be right back. Let's go Mike, follow me." Cody slapped him on the shoulder as he started to run, causing Mike to drop the load of sticks he still held.

The men ran to where the gully washed into the river during the wet season. The gully was clear of debris and the surface had been washed smooth. A large crack ran down the center of it where the stream of water had gotten smaller and smaller, cutting its way through the soft mud until it too dried up, forming an even deeper crack in the side of the mountain.

The sun was just beginning to warm the sky with a deep blue glow that faintly lit the men's way. A damp mist filled the air, falling in waves around them, licking and cooling their faces as they moved quickly up the gully. The black shadowed trees loomed over them, watching as the men ascended, whispering above their heads secrets that only the trees knew.

Clambering up the gully Cody put his hand on a shoe and wondered to himself, "Why is it there's always a lone shoe wherever you go?" Then he saw the owner of the missing shoe. The man's limbs were broken and twisted, wrapped around the gnarled roots of a tree as they grew over the gully. Cody let out a high-pitched scream when he saw the two bullet holes in his chest. And when he saw the man's dead eyes staring straight at him, he screamed again.

"Shhhhhhh! Be quiet!"

"Is he dead?"

Mike pushed past him to check for a pulse, placing his hand on the man's neck. "Yeah, he's definitely dead." The cold touch of death lingered on his fingertips as he held his hand out away from his body.

"What do we do?"

"I don't know, but we need to report this as soon as we can."

"How? Holly's phone has no reception out here."

The whole time the two men spoke, they stared at the dead man, and he stared unseeing back at them, as if his deep blue eyes were calling to them to join the dead! Finally, Mike reached over and closed the dead man's eyes, then frantically wiped his hand on his jeans. "I think we've seen enough. We better get back to the girls." Turning to go back down, he continued with, "Those men know we're out here now so we need to get out of here before they come looking for us."

"What? How do they know we're out here?" Cody slipped on the smooth surface of the dried mud as they climbed back down the gully.

Mike stopped and turned to look at him in disbelief, as Cody's feet skidded forward and he landed on his butt, sliding into Mike's feet, causing Mike to catch himself before saying in a hushed but coarse tone, "Cody, are you serious? You screamed like a little girl back there, twice!"

Cody's mouth dropped open as he realized what he had done. He had always had a tendency to scream whenever he was caught off guard or frightened. 'Now I've done it!' Panic struck him as he thought of the men with guns coming after them.

Mike broke into his thoughts. "It'll be faster if we slide down the rest of the way on our backsides."

"Right, we're going to end up on our butts anyway. Let's go."

Mike turned and sat back, sliding down the steep incline with Cody close behind.

When they reached the bottom they scrambled to their feet and ran back to their camp.

Holly turned to stare at them as they ran into the clearing. She looked at them with fear as she pointed at the trailhead that went up to the parking spaces above. And with a trembling voice she said, "Shel."

When the women heard Cody's screams, Shelly seized her bow and ran up the path as fast as she could go. The path was steep, and she had almost reached the top when she realized she couldn't take even one more step before catching her breath. She struggled to quiet her breathing, but her body needed massive amounts of oxygen. She leaned over with her hands on her knees and took slow, deep, steady breaths. Her lungs felt like they might burst, but she knew she couldn't afford to be heard by the men as they spoke in the parking area above her.

"Before this is over you'll shoot someone or I'll shoot you, you got that?"

"Yeah, that sounds about right."

"Ok then, let's go find them folks."

Shelly gasped as fear surged through her veins. Standing frozen she heard a still small voice say to her, 'RUN!' So, even though she knew better than to run down a steep incline, she ran, praying as she went. 'Lord keep my feet under me somehow.' She went faster and faster. Still she stayed upright. As she approached the end of the trail she could see rocks where the trail turned. She knew she wouldn't be able to turn or to stop unless someone or something stopped her, so her prayers became more fervent. "Lord, he-lp me, Lo-rd help me!" the pounding of her feet broke her words as they slammed down on the hard path.

Right then Mike and Cody ran round the bend and reached out to catch her, just in time to prevent her from crashing into the rocks. She hit the two of them with such force that they all three teetered around like bowling pins that struggled to stay upright as they regained their balance.

She spoke with starts and stops as she tried to catch her breath. "They're - Coming! - Right Now! - We Have! – To Go!"

As the men and Shel came running back into camp, Holly was crawling from Cody and Shel's tent, dragging their backpacks behind her. She screamed as she stood, "Let's go!" They each grabbed their own pack and ran down the small mud trail to the water's edge, where the rubber rafts that Mike had blown up the night before stood waiting for them by the river.

Without hesitating, the men jumped in, taking up the oars. After pushing the rafts into the river, their wives jumped in to face their husbands. The men feverishly began to stir and slap at the still dark water as they pulled away from shore and moved into the current, sliding smoothly downstream over the waters troubled surface.

They could hear the men behind them, cursing and shouting. "Hey! Get back here!" A shot rang out and the bullet hit the water, sending up a spray behind them, missing them by several feet.

Cody made an attempt to pray out loud, "Lord, Lord, Lord!" He didn't seem to be able to get past the word 'Lord' to say anything else.

Mike picked up the prayer, speaking loud enough for all four of them to hear as he rowed frantically, trying to match the speed of the younger man. "Lord, give us wisdom and insight. Save us, protect us, bring us out of this safely somehow. Provide for us Lord!"

They all struggled in thought as they traveled in

silence down the river for what seemed like forever. They hadn't had any breakfast and now, with the unexpected strenuous workout and adrenaline rushes, they were each feeling exhausted and weak. They had lost their shelters, most of their food, and they had no idea where they were headed. But still, they somehow managed to keep moving.

Despair settled in around each of them in their weakness and silently they began to question God in their own ways.

'Why is this happening?'

'Why did You let us come here, if You knew this was going to happen?'

'Lord, what have I done leading my friends out here to die? I should have prayed more about this trip, this is all my fault.'

'Help us to hold to our faith Lord, please keep Your promise to us, to work all things for the good, for those that love You, Lord. We do love You Lord, You know that right?"

As they neared a bridge their eyes and ears were aware of every movement and sound, but all they saw was a family of opossum along the riverbank. There was no sign of the men anywhere as they continued to row closer and closer to the bridge. The rafts slid under it, then out again on the other side. Not wanting to get caught anywhere close to the bridge they rowed again as fast as their tired arms could go. Behind them they could hear an old pickup truck rumbling to a stop, on the bridge.

Chuck and Leroy jumped out of the pickup, and when they saw the rafts slipping away, they began to curse loudly again. Chuck fired his gun and the bullets hit the water near the rafts, but not close enough, sending up a spray that spattered the woman and man in the raft closest to them, causing them both to jolt away with a surge of fear. Both men pulled even stronger on the oars, rowing once again out of range of Chuck and his gun.

The couples in the rafts could hear every vile word that came out of the men's mouths. The morning light shimmered across the clear, dark water beneath them. The black-silhouetted trees held up their hands, trying to warm their cold fingers. While the rays of sunlight made their way through the almost bare branches to the dense dew-covered floor of the forest below. Everything that was touched by the sun's morning light sparkled like glitter. It looked like a fine work of art, but its beauty was lost to those that ran for their lives, as the curses cut through the air like a dull knife, ripping gaping holes in the canvas of the masterpiece that stood before them.

Mike took in a deep breath and let it all back out again as they rounded a bend in the river. Looking over at Cody he said, "Your dad used to say, 'The man who fills in the blanks of his vocabulary with curse words is showing his lack of intelligence'."

Cody gave a wry half smile, "I think he may have been right."

Everyone was quiet as they rowed on. None of them spoke about what had happened only hours ago. They all needed to process it, to wrap their heads around the fact that someone actually wanted to kill them.

For Mike and Cody though, it was a little more than that. They had seen the dead man and they couldn't blink their eyes without seeing his dead eyes staring back at them.

Mike tried to focus on the way he had closed the dead man's eyes and that seemed to comfort him somewhat. Maybe he had found some kind of closure in the act. He didn't know. Still, as they rowed along, he kept dipping his hand in the cool water to wash it free of the death he felt lingered on his fingertips.

Cody had always thought closing the eyes of the dead was about respect for the dead person, but now he realized it was more likely that the living didn't want the eyes of the dead looking back at them from death. Even if that wasn't possible, that's the way it felt to him.

But the weaker he got, the more the eyes seemed to follow him, being everywhere, he sought a reprieve. He felt a cool breeze and a shiver ran through his body as if it were the dead man's cold breath blowing down his sweaty, tense neck. As he rowed he looked up to find that the eyes were still following him down the river, to a place where there would be no rest for him tonight.

2
Walking the Goat

*Nevertheless let each one of you in particular
so love his own wife as himself,
and let the wife see that she respects her husband.
Ephesians 5: 33 NKJV*

Three days earlier in Northwest Ohio

When Cody got home from work he picked his newspaper up off the porch, entered the kitchen and poured himself a glass of cold milk, then took a package of stale cookies from the cabinet. Walking into the living room, he kicked off his shoes, leaving on his stinking socks, making a wordless comment of how he felt about his surroundings. He sat down on his recliner to read the paper, wagging his feet back and forth, feeling the air dry his sweaty socks.

Shel never looked up from her computer. Their supper dishes from last night were still sitting in the sink, and the house was in desperate need of a good cleaning. All day she had told herself she needed to get up and clean it, but she never did. She sighed again, and tried to justify herself with the thought of *'What's the point? It isn't like Cody is going to notice, so why try?'* But the conversation she had with herself brought her no comfort; still each day she said it to herself over and over again, like a chant, trying to convince herself that this time it would bring her peace.

Today was no different than any other day. Once again, she couldn't motivate herself to do what needed to be done. She didn't even attempt to change out of her frumpy pajamas. And so there she sat, rumpled and dirty with her greasy hair pulled back in a messy ponytail.

All the while Cody said nothing to her, not seeming to notice her as he was quietly reading his paper.

She felt angry inside; angry with herself and angry with Cody as she glanced over at him, then back to her computer. She thought to herself, *'if he would just notice me, if he would just say, "Hi babe, how was your day?" like he used to do, if he really loved me unconditionally, no matter what the house and I looked like, if he did that, all would be well in our marriage once again'*.

After a while she began to talk, cutting in on Cody's quiet time. "What time do you want to go then?"

"What? Go where?" He snapped, irritated with the interruption as he laid the paper on his lap. He scratched his dirty head, stirring his blond hair around with his hand, making it stand on end. This, along with his five o'clock shadow, his dirty work clothes, his stocking feet, and the sour expression on his face, made him look a little crazed.

"We're going to Mike and Holly's tonight for dinner. You haven't forgotten have you? Have you and Mike decided where we'll be camping yet? Have you written any list? You and Mike have a lot to get done you know. Holly and I still need to plan the meals and figure out who's getting what. It's been so long since we've gone camping, I can't remember half the things I'd like to. And I want to take healthy alternatives to the usual s'mores and hot dogs so I can put it on the list?" She made a disgusted face and shivered. "Do you have any suggestions for what you'd like to have?"

Cody mumbled under his breath, "s'mores and hot dogs."

Her sentences ran together, with no pauses, she only had time to take a breath before prattling on.

Cody sighed heavily and cut in with, "Yes, I'd like to have some quiet so I can read my paper!" His dark blue eyes narrowed with irritation.

Shel's posture became rigid and the air was thick with tension. "Oh, I'm so sorry!" She threw the words at him like darts. "I didn't mean to interrupt your latest 'Local-drunk-beats-his-goat' report." Her eyes flashed and her chin jutted out defiantly, with each word clipped and dripping with sarcasm.

"He doesn't beat his goat every day, only when he's trying to walk the dumb thing."

"How do you know that's the only time he beats it? You're such a moron Cody, how stupid can you get?" She turned back to her computer, tapping the keys harder than necessary, raising herself up a little to turn on her printer.

"Whatever," he said as his newspaper snapped back up and he began to read again, pointedly turning his body away from his wife.

After only a minute of silence, she grumbled to herself as if talking to her monitor. "Who keeps a goat in their house as a pet anyway?"

It was true, Cody and Shel lived in a small town and the reports were humorous at times. Still, he just liked the lightness of the local news stories as a way to wind down in the evening, '*and what was wrong with that?*' He thought to himself. '*Especially if it gives me a chuckle or even a hearty laugh, right? Anyhow, she doesn't know that the man keeps the goat in the house with him, where'd she get a goofy idea like that?*' But Cody kept his thoughts to himself, even though it made him mad that she had just taken the humor out of his occasional goat reports.

He tried to go back to his reading, but it was no

use. So, he left the paper on his chair and went to change out of his work clothes.

When he had finished, he entered the living room again. "Ok, I'm ready." He sat back down in his chair, the leather making groaning sounds as he settled back into it. Now, if Shel would just get ready to go, he would have a few guaranteed minutes to himself to read the rest of his story. He may even have time to read another one before she finished, or started chattering from the other room.

She turned away from her computer to face him, "Oh, why didn't you say something? You got ready to go and didn't tell me?"

"How's it my fault you can't get off your lazy butt?"

"I told you WE needed to get ready, you moron! What'd you think 'We' meant?"

"I'm not taking a shower with you!"

A sad expression passed over her face briefly as she thought of a time when they used to take showers together. She brushed the thought aside as a fond but very distant memory. "Still, there's a lot more to getting ready then just changing your clothes."

"So, Go! Do it then! And leave me alone!"

Shel snorted and ended the conversation for the time being. Then she picked up her phone, looked at the time and called Holly. Facing Cody she made sure to speak loudly in rebellion to his request for silence.

"Hi Holly," she said in a perfectly pleasant voice. "What time do you want us to come over? --- Ok, it'll take us probably a half hour, maybe forty-five minutes --- Good, do you need me to bring anything? ---- Did you get your list done? -- Oh good, I think mine's done too. --- Yeah, I've been online looking up things all day, and I went out yesterday and bought some stuff, but I still have to hit the sporting goods store to get a lot more. Oh, and there's a couple of things I want to ask you about, but I'll save it until we get there. Also, I have some things to show you. I'm so excited, I can't wait to go, we're going to have so much fun! ----- Ok, yeah I'll bring it along. ---- All right, we'll be there shortly then. I still have to get a quick shower and get ready, but it won't take me long. – See you in a little bit--- Bye-bye!"

By the time she hung up, Cody was glaring at her with teeth clenched. He had never been good at reading with sounds and/or conversations going on around him. "I'm trying to read here!" he said before asking her, "Couldn't you have taken your conversation somewhere else?" He was already irritated with her, so this just added to his stress level as he braced himself for her next attack.

But instead she turned and started to chatter happily, seemingly oblivious to his marked irritation. "Ok, they want us over as soon as we can get there. I have to get a shower quick, I never got one all day, can you believe it? So I still have to do that. I can't believe I've been sitting here all day. The day has just flown by. Don't you think it has? And you need to put your shoes and socks on still. And not those dirty work shoes either. And for crying out loud, would you comb your hair!"

"What's the point? This is what my hair looks like whether I comb it or not." Cody's hair had always taken on a life of its own, going this way and that. Combing it did very little to change that fact, even if he combed it while it was wet and pressed it down in place.

"Just do it!" She demanded.

"Ok, Shellyyyy," Cody drug out the last syllable as he combed his fingers through his hair.

"The name is Shel if you don't mind! You know I don't like Shelly! So, Stop Calling Me SHELLY!" She screamed back in reply.

But he ignored her, picked up his paper, his cookies and milk, and left the room. Opening the front door, he went out onto the front porch to finish reading his story, alone.

As soon as she heard the door close, the steam that was coming out of her ears condensed and turned into tears that ran down her face.

Cody knew how to push her buttons, and she was ashamed that it always seemed to work. She had never liked the name Shelly. Even as a child she had asked people to refer to her simply as 'Shel'. Why did she let that get to her every time? She didn't have time to think about that right now, she had to get ready to go.

She stopped and looked in the mirror hanging in the hall on her way to the bedroom. She didn't want puffy red eyes when she got to Mike and Holly's house, so she did her best to swallow her tears. And after taking some deep breaths, she gathered some clean clothes and went off to take her shower.

Inwardly, Shel knew she was as much to blame for the conflict as Cody was. She purposely did everything she could to provoke him. Seeing the signs of his irritation, she would push him until he blew up every time. It made her feel happy, *No- not happy?* She couldn't call the feeling happiness, because happiness was clearly not close to the way it made her feel. But still, she did it. She didn't know why, and she didn't care either.

Shel turned her thoughts away from what was happening and made herself think about the upcoming camping trip. She knew it was going to be fun, but she was having a hard time imagining her and Cody having a good time on any camping trip together. But, even if it meant ignoring and avoiding him the whole time, she was determined to do it. That shouldn't be too hard to do. It was, after all, the way they lived most days. The trick would be in convincing their friends and mentors that they were madly in love, while they did everything they could to stay away from each other.

'It would be so much easier if Cody would just get

sick and have to stay home, alone.' Shel prayed as she worked, frustrated with the situation. 'Oh Lord, why can't he just, just?' She couldn't finish saying what she was thinking as tears began to run down her face again.

❖ ❖ ❖ ❖ ❖

Cody knew calling his wife Shelly was the one thing that would send her over the edge and end the argument, and possibly giving him the silent treatment for days. He had found over time he could at least live with that better than hearing her constantly tearing him down. So, whenever they were having one of their arguments and he couldn't take any more, he never failed to use it against her. It was the only weapon he had after all. He certainly didn't have the talent Shel had of battering him with her sharp tongue.

He was so frustrated, he hated coming home to a messy house; he hated it when Shel didn't even try to take care of herself, and he hated it when she called him a moron and worse. All these things in his eyes were indicators of a lack of respect and respect was more important to him as a man, than love.

Sadly in his own home, he had no respect. 'If Shel would only clean up and take care of herself for me. If she would meet me at the door with a 'How was your day honey?' like she used to do. If she would stop calling me degrading names. If she respected me, if she did that, all would be well in our marriage once again.'

Cody's mind began to wander as he thought about a woman he worked with and how she always treated him civilly and with respect. "Why can't Shel treat me like Julie does?" He was shocked to hear himself say the words out loud, "Take your thoughts captive Cody." Then he turned his mind back to his paper, working harder at concentrating on each word but ultimately, failing.

After Shel finished getting ready, she stood jiggling her keys nervously in her hand, trying to remember if she had forgotten anything. She stuck her list in her pocket and pulled a sweater from the hook by the front door. She would lock the door as she left.

She expected to see Cody sitting on the porch with his shoes on, ready to go. But instead she walked out to see him absentmindedly picking lint from between his toes and dropping it on the porch next to his dirty socks.

"Gross! Can't you at least try not to be so disgusting?" She snarled in a vicious whisper so the neighbors wouldn't hear her. "Where are your shoes? Why aren't you ready to go? What have you been doing all this time? Can't we ever be on time anywhere?"

"Which question do you want me to answer first?" He glared at her with one eyebrow raised.

"What do you mean, which question?" Her eyes flared, "All of them and none of them. Can we go now?"

"Yes, we can go now." He got up with his things and walked into the house, closing the door behind him.

Shel stormed out to wait for him in the car, crawling into the passenger seat then slamming the door. She took several deep breaths to fight the tension that relentlessly gripped at her skull like a vice.

Shel loved to talk, but she was determined not to say another word to Cody. She knew if she said anything at all it wouldn't be good and she needed to calm down. So she sat silently staring out the side window of the car, rubbing the stress from her forehead as she told herself to *'just breathe'*.

3
Zombie Eyes

Be kindly affectionate to one another
with brotherly love, in honor
giving preference to one another; not lagging
in diligence, fervent in spirit, serving the Lord.
Romans 12: 10-11 NKJV

Shel pulled the pale pink sweater around herself, folding her arms over her breast. Peeking out of the top of the sweater was the scalloped collar of the sky blue blouse she wore underneath. The pink and the soft blue complemented the long gold strands of her hair, still damp, lying limp over her shoulders. The edges of her hazel blue eyes were more blue tonight than green.

The cold night air rushed into the car and bit Shel as Cody got in and closed the door behind him. A shiver trembled through her as she pulled her pink sweater tighter yet.

Cody looked over at his wife and thought to himself how beautiful she looked, but he certainly wasn't about to tell her that.

It had been a lovely warm Fall day, but now as the sun sank low in the sky a cool breeze began to blow the leaves from their homes in the trees, sending them sailing, raining down over the car. Spinning around as they fell, sliding across the road, looking like so many baseball players making a slide for home plate. The

21

beauty that surrounded the couple went unnoticed as they drove from their home in the suburbs of their small town and into the country in silence.

When Mike got home from work he came through the front door where Holly, his wife, had been waiting for him. She stood on the bottom step of the stairs that led to the second floor so she might be closer to his height. She threw her arms up and around his neck as Mike wrapped his arms around her waist and squeezed a little too hard, just to hear her squeal.

"Mike, stop, you're going to crush me!"

"I can't stop," he said as he ran the side of his finger down the curve of her face and gently lifted her chin to kiss her full rosy lips. "I love you too much."

"I love you, too." She kissed him back.

"Oh, really!" He snapped his head back and his big brown eyes got even bigger as a goofy smile spread across his face and froze there. His eyes looked her up and down in rapid succession, ending with them rolling around in his head, as he waited for her response of protest.

She pushed her way out of his arms and let out a little scream. Her red corkscrew hair bounced as she jumped down and her green eyes twinkled as she let out a little giggle. She had seen that look before and knew full well what it meant. "Mike no, not now! Cody and Shel will be here any minute!"

The goofy face remained, as he tilted his head slowly from side to side and stared at her like a Zombie looking at its next meal.

Holly let out another little scream and ran to the kitchen. "I have to finish supper."

Mike quietly followed her and slowly peeked his head around the corner, his face still holding the smiling Zombie pose.

"Mike, stop it! You're creeping me out," she said

with a nervous giggle in her voice, as she tried to keep a straight face. He walked towards her with his arms out zombie style. His eyes growing ever bigger and more animated with her every protest.

"Mike, stop! Stop! I mean it! Stop!" She slapped at his hands.

His face transformed from Zombie to sad puppy as he dropped his arms in resignation. When she turned to finish fixing their evening meal, he slowly wrapped his arms around her waist, pulling her close. He kissed her neck, causing her to giggle once again and he finished the kiss with his teeth rested against her skin as if he may at any moment bite her neck.

She screamed and turned to push him off. "You're terrible, can't you wait until later?" She said fighting a smile as she tried to look threatening.

His face fell into a playful pout but he wasn't truly worried. Mike was a happy man, sure of his wife's love and willing to wait for her affection, if he had to. Even so he gave her his pouty lip and sad puppy eyes as she pushed him again.

"Oh Puppy, go on, get out of here!" Holly made a brushing motion with her hands, as if she was brushing him out of the room. He left the room as she, with a lingering smile, turned to finish snapping the green beans. She really did love that man, even if he was a nut case. "What a goof ball!" She said quietly to herself.

After cleaning up, Mike came back into the kitchen. He took a cookie out of the cookie jar and quickly shoved it into his mouth before Holly could say anything to him about waiting until after supper. He sat back against the counter and began to talk, "Cody seemed irritated about something today, but then again he's been acting that way for a while now." Holly stopped humming and listened as Mike continued, "I get the feeling that their marriage is going down the tubes fast."

Holly turned around and picked up a towel to wipe her hands. "Puppy, I think we're going to have to cover this trip with a lot of prayer, don't you?"

"Yeah, I think you're right." Mike stepped over and took her in his arms.

She reached up and wiped away the chocolate smudge from the corner of his lips, noting the evidence that convicted him of the crime of sneaking a chocolate chip cookie on the sly. All she said was, "You!" in a scolding tone. His pouty lip shot back out as he looked at her with his big sad puppy dog eyes.

"Oh, stop it!" She laughed, wrapping her arms around his middle and laying her head on his chest.

He pressed his lips against her ear and began to pray softly.

❖ ❖ ❖ ❖ ❖

Shel had always loved going to Mike and Holly's old farmhouse in the country. She loved its big front porch with its gingerbread trim and the cute white picket fence that encircled its front yard.

The smells and sounds of the country had always called to her. The birds sang in the trees as the leaves rustled in the wind, mimicking the sound of a gentle rain. The last rays of remaining daylight shining on the pale yellow house caused it to look like an extension of the sun's setting. The house looked happy somehow, at peace with where it sat on a hill, amongst green bushes with fading flowers and a backdrop of green, yellow and red leaves that still hung on to their respective trees. A crisp and gentle breeze blew the scent of moist soil and decaying leaves, along with the distinct smell of burning brush as the leaves gently fell to the ground to rest.

The sight of the house and the smells of fall should have brought Shel a refreshing peace, but instead, when the old farmhouse came into view she braced herself for the show that they were about to put on.

The stage was set and the two of them put on their best smiles. Anyone who saw them would have believed they had the best marriage ever, or so the two of them thought.

The truth was, they weren't kidding anyone. Their marriage had been struggling for some time now. While some days were ok, others were not. If they chose to, they could still be civil with each other but, more and more they chose to be less than civil.

Now they were on their best behavior as they walked up to Mike and Holly's house with plastic smiles plastered across their faces, like clowns at a circus pretending that all was well, when clearly all was not well.

Stepping up onto the front porch together Shel rang the doorbell then took a step back to stand next to Cody her husband.

When the door opened, Mike welcomed them both in a warm embrace and offered to take their wraps.

Holly's red hair bounced just above her shoulders as she sprang around the corner to meet them. She took Shel's sweater and hung it on the hall tree that had been setting in the same spot since Mike's grandparents had bought the house in 1946. Walking into the house made one feel like they were stepping back in time, and Shel loved it.

She took a deep breath, smelling the meal that was cooking in the kitchen and her mouth began to water in anticipation. She started talking about her plans for their upcoming camping trip, and Holly's face lit up with interest as they walked around the corner and into the kitchen.

"How you doing buddy?" Mike asked as he studied Cody's face.

It always seemed to Cody as if Mike's dark eyes were looking right through him. So, when Mike released him he said, "I'm doing great," unconsciously shaking his head 'no' as he unnecessarily wiped his shoes on a small rug by the door.

Mike ran his hand over his damp graying brown hair thoughtfully as he watched Cody. He knew that Cody was hurting and felt compelled to say something, but what? So instead he turned without saying a word and went into the dining room with Cody following close behind.

The night had not gone well, and Cody and Shel didn't talk most of the way home. Instead, Shel stared blankly out the passenger side window while Cody kept his eyes fixed straight ahead. But, just before they pulled into their driveway Shel said with tears in her voice, "Cody, when are we going to start working at our marriage again?"

Those words stung, Cody hadn't ever thought of it as him not working on their marriage.

"I don't know?" He managed to say as he thought to himself, *'How's it my fault?'*

If it hadn't been for the tears in her voice and the fact that he was too tired to fight anymore, he would have corrected her right there and then. But instead, those words, *'When are WE going to start working on our marriage again?'* ate at him, churning over and over in his mind, all night and then into the next day.

4
Out to Lunch

And do not be conformed to this world,
but be transformed by the renewing of your mind,
that you may prove what is that good and
acceptable and perfect will of God.
Romans 12: 2 NKJV

As Cody took his lunch bag and headed for the cafeteria, a coworker stopped him to ask a favor.

"Hey Cody, do you think you could swap hours with me tomorrow? I'm scheduled to work swing shift but something's come up."

"Yeah, well maybe? I'm not sure. We're going camping this weekend so I'll have to check with The Boss. She might have something else she NEEDS me to do." His eyes flared then rolled with disgust.

"Yeah, I get that, I have to take the old ball and chain to the airport so she can go and visit her MOTHER," the man said rolling his eyes in agreement.

"Alright, well, I'll let you know, ok?"

"Yeah, Ok, thanks buddy." He slapped Cody on the shoulder as he walked away.

As Cody approached the corner of the cafeteria, Mike shook his head slightly and watched him with a disapproving expression on his face.

"What?" Cody snapped, as he slid in on the bench seat across from him.

"Why do you go along with that kind of talk?"

"What do you mean?"

"You just called Shel 'The Boss'."

"So?"

"So, do you think that kind of talk lines up with what you're supposed to do as a Christian husband? Aren't you supposed to love and honor her?"

Just then Evan, one of the regulars in their weekly Bible study, walked over to the bench to sit next to Cody. "What are we talking about today?" He asked, as he opened his lunch bag and pulled out its contents. Mark and Brent followed him, sliding in to sit next to Mike and momentarily stopping the conversation that Mike and Cody were having.

"We're talking about conforming to this world in the way we talk about our wives and our mother-in-law's." Mike sent a meaningful glance at Cody then continued with, "for instance saying, 'The Boss', 'The old ball and chain', 'The old lady', 'bat' or 'bag', dishonoring remarks that tear down."

Evan's face was grave. "Wow, I was just praying about that on my way in to work this morning. I made 'The old ball and chain' comment on the phone last night to a friend and Mary ran off to the bedroom crying. Now she won't even talk to me."

Mike pulled out his Bible and opened it to Ephesians 5:33. "Would you read this to us?" He asked as he slid his Bible across the table to him.

"*Nevertheless let each one of you in particular so love his own wife as himself,*" Evan paused and then thoughtfully continued, "*and let the wife see that she respects her husband.*"

"Would you feel respected if your wife called you a name like 'The old ball and chain'?"

The men around the table guffawed.

"How about 'moron'?" Cody injected, bitterness present in his voice.

They all turned and looked at him confused, as

Evan answered, "No?" not sure if the question required an answer.

"Would you feel loved?" Mike continued.

"No, I guess I wouldn't." He turned back to look at Mike.

"Neither does she." He pointed to the scripture and tapped his finger up and down on the page to make his point. "She needs love from you, and you need respect from her. That's pretty much all there is to it, *'Doing unto others as you would HAVE them do unto you'*. It's a simple concept but so hard to do. Still, that's what a happy marriage is all about, 'hard work'. Anyone who tells you differently is lying."

"When you speak to your wife, your words should always honor her, and honoring means to lift her up. What you did last night was tear her down, humiliating her, making her feel unloved. No one gets a perfect marriage. You build a perfect marriage, one brick at a time."

Evan sat quietly, staring at his half-eaten sandwich for a moment. "Wow, no wonder she's mad."

"She's not really mad, she's wounded. It looks the same, and if you let it fester, it may turn to deep resentment and anger."

Evan slipped out and walked away, leaving his half eaten lunch behind, digging through his pocket for his phone as he left.

"So that's it? If you do that you'll have a happy marriage?"

"There are no guarantees, Mark. God gives us all the formula to make a good marriage and the free will to make choices. But it's really up to us. If a husband and wife are willing to work at their marriage, then this is the key that will help to unlock that door."

"Ok, you said something about mothers-in-law?" Mark stated as a question. "That one's hard for me to swallow."

"Well Mark, have you ever done any gardening?"

"Yeah, I hoe and water our garden every year."

"Perfect! Ok then, how do you kill the unwanted plants in your garden?"

Mark gave him an impatient look as if to say what does this have to do with my mother-in-law? "I pull them out or cut them off at ground level, then go after the root to cut it to bits."

"That's what you're doing to your wife when you cut your mother-in-law to bits. You can't separate the root from the plant without killing the plant."

"What do you mean?"

"You can't cut your wife's root away without doing damage to her, Mark. Even if your wife claims not to like her mom, it still hurts her to hear you cut at her roots, her life source. Families are complicated, their roots go deep."

Cody had heard enough. He had heard Mike preach this all before and he knew what was coming next. He would say that he had seen divorced couples, after learning love and respect, honoring each other and not tearing at the others roots, being happily married once again.

He knew it was true, he had seen it himself, but he just didn't want to hear it again. He had given up on applying these principles to his marriage long ago and couldn't see himself trying to make a go of his marriage now. He had hardened his heart towards Shel. He didn't care anymore, or at least that's what he told himself. So feeling rebellious and angry, Cody stood and abruptly walked away from the table, scanning the cafeteria until he saw who he was looking for.

Julie Salamon was a married woman and a little older than Cody, but he didn't care. She was a pretty and petite woman, an overall sweet and happy person. He had known Julie and her husband Will, for years. But his interest in her changed when he started spending time with her at lunch, talking to her more and more every day as it gradually turned into something more than just friendship.

He imagined that she was enjoying the attention he was giving her. He believed she understood his intentions and was on the same page. So, when he saw her, he found himself headed her way.

He was ready for more than just flirting today. He looked at her figure, as she stood with her back to him in a secluded corner of the cafeteria.

Standing at a vending machine, Julie's candy bar fell into the slot and as she leaned to get it, Cody said, "That's what I want." But there was something in his voice that brought her back up before she could get a hold of her candy bar. She stood fast and as she turned she fell back against the vending machine. He brought his hand down to rest on the candy machine behind her, then moving in close, he looked her up and down as his eyebrows bounced he said, in a low and husky voice, "I want some of that."

She was stricken with fear as her eyes got big and her face turned white.

"What's the matter?" He chuckled with a slight smile, raising one eyebrow. She ducked under his arm that still rested on the vending machine and practically ran, leaving him standing there alone.

Cody's head spun with questions, 'What's this game she's playing now? Does she want me to follow her or something? Maybe she's having a bad day,' he concluded. 'I didn't do anything wrong after all.'

He turned and looked around, becoming suddenly very conscious of the other people in the cafeteria. 'I hope no one saw me. Well, it's her word against mine.' He was nervously scanning the faces around the room, but people were careful to avoid eye contact with him. He thought that meant no one had seen him make a pass at Julie, but the truth was his reputation would be stained for the rest of his life because of his one indiscretion. Some would never forgive him, even those that called themselves brothers-in-the-Lord. And many would point a finger at Julie and say that somehow it was her fault.

"What if she tells Will what I did?" he mumbled under his breath as a rush of fear shook him. The disgrace of it was more than he wanted to deal with. "Well Will, it was like this," he said to himself as he turned back towards the vending machine, "she just misunderstood me. I was just trying to get a candy bar, that's all." He reached down and picked up the candy bar that Julie had left behind. Maybe he would believe that. He tore the wrapper open with his teeth then took a bite. 'I'll just convince him it was a misunderstanding.'

The sweetness of the candy bar melted in his mouth and mixed with the bitterness of the lies he told himself. He wanted to spit it out but opted to swallow the bite instead. Throwing the rest of the candy bar away he left the cafeteria, no longer hungry.

It didn't seem to matter what Cody told himself, deep down he knew he was wrong. He knew he would have to spend his life trying to justify his sin or face it head on. Someday he would have to decide what he was going to do; someday soon, someday very soon.

5
Distraught

But in my distress I cried out to the Lord;
Yes, I prayed to my God for help.
He heard me from his sanctuary;
my cry to him reached his ears.
Psalm 18: 6 NLT

Julie walked through the plant as quickly as she could to clock out. She couldn't stay another minute pretending all was well. She felt sick and needed to get away to think and cry. She tried to avoid her friend, May, when she passed her workstation, but her perceptive friend glanced up and started after her.

"Girl, what's the matter?"

"I'm sick."

"You were fine twenty minutes ago."

Julie tried to slip by, but May held her arms out to stop her. "No Jul, I'm not buying it, this is way more than 'I'm sick'. I can tell you're upset about something."

Julie looked down. "I can't talk about it right now, I have to go home."

"What happened Sweetie?" Her voice softened.

"Please May, just let me go, I'll tell you ..." Her voice cracked.

"Ok Jul, but I'm calling you tonight!" She pulled her friend in for a hug, kissing her on the top of the head. "You take care of yourself. Ya hear?" May scrunched down, tilting her head sideways to get a peek at her hidden face, brushing Julie's black curtain of hair to one side and tucking it behind her left ear. "I'll call you tonight then, ok?"

Julie could feel the tears welling in her eyes and knew if she looked up she would burst out crying. She felt like running but managed to say, "Ok, we'll talk tonight." She moved around her friend, feeling May's eyes watching her as she quickly walked away.

Once she got to the parking lot she ran to her car. When inside she locked the door and laid her head on the steering wheel, taking deep breaths, still feeling like she was suffocating. She consciously tried to quiet the panic she felt by forcing herself to think about other things. Her hands trembled as she pulled her grocery list out of her purse and tried to concentrate on the things she needed to get today.

"Ok, I can do this." But when she reached for her keys, panic rose once again as she realized they weren't in her purse. '*Did I leave them on the table with my lunch pail?*' Thinking of going back to the cafeteria made her feel sick, and she scrambled to remember where she had left them.

"Think, Julie, think," she muttered to herself as she sat her purse down on the seat next to her and began to search through her pockets. There they were in the pocket of her jacket. She took another deep breath and slid the key into the ignition. Pulling out of the parking lot she drove away.

As Julie walked through the grocery store, she could hardly see the list she held in her hand through the tears that filled her eyes. She prayed silently, '*Lord, please don't let me run into anyone I know right now. Help me to keep it together.*' She knew all it would take was a kind '*How are you doing?*' from a friend for the dam to burst right there in the middle of the produce aisle. Her tears were just waiting for the moment they would be set free to race down her face.

She began to scan the check out clerks for the one lady that she knew was all business. Rarely did the woman say a word to the people who came through her line, other than to say, *'Hello'*, *'That will be - a blank amount of money'* and *'Have a nice day.'* Julie allowed her bangs to drop down over her eyes as she moved through the line. She pretended to scan her list for any forgotten items.

Nearing her car the tears began to spill out. She put on a pretend smile and let the tears flow as she drove out of the parking lot and made her way home. She hoped no one would notice her. When she got home she ran inside as quickly as she could to avoid any neighbor's greeting her.

Julie pulled a casserole out of the refrigerator, put it into the oven and set the timer. She could still see Cody's eyes and felt as if his lust had burned through her clothing leaving her exposed; she felt dirty, naked, hurt and betrayed by a friend. She walked into the living room and laid down on the couch as she put her hands over her face and cried out to God, *'Why? Why God, why?'*

Julie was putting on some makeup to cover up the evidence of her crying, when Will came up behind her. "Hello beautiful!" He towered over her as he kissed the back of her neck. Wrapping his arms around her waist, his dark face held a bright smile as his black eyes sparkled at her in the mirror.

Julie was a pretty woman with fine straight black hair that was cut in a short pixie style. Her skin was a smooth honey tone. Her lips were more than usually red and her almond shaped eyes were a dark chocolate color, except now they also had a tint of red around their puffy edges.

"What's wrong Sweetheart?" Will said, with concern in his voice.

"Please don't ask me right now." She looked down with shame. "I'll tell you later, ok?"

Will nodded, knowing she needed some time to think, and he trusted she would tell him when she was ready.

"Alright Sweetheart, I'm going to change out of my work clothes. When I'm done I'll come down and help you get supper on. That is, if you need my help." Will had learned years ago that Julie saw his helping her in the kitchen as being romantic.

"I would love some help but...."

He stopped her words with a kiss. Then turned and went to get some clean clothes out of the bedroom.

"There's really not that much to do. I made a casserole last night, it's already in the oven."

From the bedroom Will said, "What'd you say?"

"Oh nothing, just that I love you!"

As he stepped back into the room, he patted her on the bottom as he walked by. "I love you too, Sweetie."

She slapped his hand away in mock disgust. "Oh, you!"

❖ ❖ ❖ ❖ ❖

When Will came into the kitchen he began pulling the dishes out of the cabinet to set the table. "Do you want salad dishes?"

"Yes please," Julie said, as she pulled the casserole out of the oven and sat it on the stovetop. She picked up an avocado, cut it in two and removed the pit.

"Alright, the table's set. Can I do anything else for you?"

"Could you wash the tomato and cut it up?"

"Yep!"

"Oh, I knew you loved me!" She threw Will a sweet

smile and a coy smile was returned. She focused again on the avocado, scooping it out with a teaspoon and dropping it into the salad bowl. She faltered and her smile vanished. *'Lord, how can I ever tell Will about Cody?'* She whispered, "Help me."

"I am helping you!" Will said as he stood by her at the sink.

"Oh thank you..." Julie's mouth smiled softly but her eyes did not.

Will dried his hands and came close to her turning her towards him. He lifted her and sat her on the counter-top in front of him. He stepped between her knees and turned her chin up to face him. "Julie, please tell me what's going on?"

She fell forward and buried her face in his chest as she started to sob. She told him that Cody had made a pass at her and how it made her feel. She had always dressed modestly; therefore she didn't understand how anyone could misunderstand her intentions. She went on to say, "I'm sure it's my fault somehow. I gave him some of my leftover cake once. I didn't know why he wanted to talk to me all the time. I didn't know Will, I honestly didn't know!" She pleaded as she continued sobbing.

Her husband watched her quietly until she was done. Then he lifted her face to his again and kissed her swollen eyes. "It's not your fault Cody has a dirty mind. I don't know what's going on with him lately, but clearly something's not right. But, I do know this is not your fault. Do you hear me?" He tensed all over as his anger built. "A Christian man is to treat a sister in the faith as his..." he paused before he spat out the word, "sister," then finished with, "protecting and honoring her, but instead Cody...!" Stopping abruptly, he turned from Julie and walked away to let off some steam.

Will circled the small kitchen with his muscular arms rigid and his hands drawn into fists. Then he walked over to the window, the setting sun shone through the glass and reflected brightly across his hard face, making him look like a statue cut from onyx stone. He stood completely still for a while, then he came back and gently looked Julie directly in the face. Brushing her fine hair out of her eyes he said, "It's going to be alright Sweetie. I'll take care of this."

"Will, please don't..."

He gently pressed a finger to her lips, "Shhh," then he lifted her down from the counter and pulled her head into his chest. "Don't worry Honey, I'll pray about it before I beat him to a pulp."

Julie drew her head back and looked up at his face as he gave her a little smile. "Oh you!" She said, as she gave him a shove. "Don't beat him too hard, remember, he IS a friend."

"Hmm!" Will grunted, then leaned down and kissed his wife. Then he repeated, "It's going to be alright Sweetie, I promise you. Now, how about we eat our supper before it gets cold? It smells good!"

6
Meatloaf

O my God, I am utterly ashamed;
I blush to lift up my face to You,
for our sins are piled higher then our heads,
and our guilt has reached to the heavens.
Ezra 9:6 NLT

Mike sat in his SUV waiting impatiently for Cody, who had carpooled with him today. Grimly he watched as Cody slowly walked across the parking lot, got in the car, and settled in the seat next to him. "You know Cody, I saw you make a pass at Julie today."

"Boy, you don't pull any punches do you?" Cody growled defensively. "Aren't you going to ask me how my day went, before you start accusing me of something? No, not you, you just go straight for the jugular vein, don't ya?"

Mike didn't back down as he continued, "What's going on? What do you think you're doing?" He pulled the SUV out of the parking lot and onto the road.

"Nothing, nothing's going on, it's none of your business anyways. I have it under control, so don't worry about it! No one saw me, no one knows about it but you!"

"Oh, is that right!"

Cody snarled, "She started it. It wasn't my fault!"

Mike turned his steering wheel hard to the right and pulled off the road into the parking lot of an old abandoned building. His SUV skidded through the gravel and slid around to the back of the building as gravel pelted the concrete block wall. He turned off the engine then spun to his right to face Cody. "Look Cody, Will and Julie have been in love since they were kids, so don't tell me how she came on to you. Look at yourself. You're just a pup. She's not interested in you sexually. Women don't have the same sex-driven imagination that men do, so it was your fault! Own up to it and face it like a man!"

All of a sudden Julie's shocked and hurt look flashed through his mind. He knew that Mike was right, but he wasn't ready to admit it yet. So he sat there with his teeth clenched and his chin out. Neither of them spoke for a few seconds as they stared each other down. Mike took a deep breath and softened his voice.

"Cody, what's going on with you and Shel? Something's not...." His words trailed off, leaving them in silence again.

Several moments passed between them as Mike waited for Cody's response.

"I don't know. I just don't care anymore." He turned and stared out the windshield at the gray block wall, which seemed to reflect the way he felt right now. It was as if Cody had come to a dead end. He was quiet for a minute longer as the feelings of frustration and anger built up inside him.

Then he exploded, "Shel wants to be the boss! I can't ever plan anything without checking her calendar first! And I hate meatloaf! But she makes it for me every week!" Cody would never have mentioned the meatloaf, if he hadn't been dreading the fact that he was going home to it tonight.

The edges of Mike's mouth began to turn up slightly, but he didn't laugh. "Have you told her you don't like her meatloaf?"

"No! She'll say 'You hurt my feelings'," he said with

a high-pitched mocking voice. "And then she'll cry or get mad. I can't stand it when she cries and I can't win when she gets mad."

"So, you just make snide remarks about her cooking, and you don't think that hurts her feelings?"

"Sure it does!" He said, nodding his head as he turned back to face Mike. "But, she doesn't cry and throw a fit in front of others."

"Cody, did Shel tell you she wanted to be the boss?"

"No! But she's always planning everything before I can say anything. Look, it's like this - she asks me what I want to do about something and she gets me thinking about it. Then before I have a chance to tell her what I think, she already has it figured out. Everything's planned and written in red ink on her calendar, like she enjoys rubbing it in my face."

"Did you tell her that?"

"Did I tell her what?"

"Did you tell her that's the way it makes you feel?"

"No! She doesn't want to know, she doesn't care!"

"No Cody, she thinks because you don't say anything right away, that you don't care!"

"I CARE! I CARE! Tonight's meatloaf night, believe me, I CARE!"

"Ok, ok, calm down buddy before you blow a gasket!" Mike paused before adding, "Cody, are you telling me this is all about meatloaf?"

"No, I don't understand her, why can't she just tell me what she wants?"

The corners of Mike's mouth turned up again.

"WHAT'S SO FUNNY?" Cody yelled.

"I'm sorry, I just find that humorous. You don't tell her things because you don't think she wants to know, but you expect her to tell you things. You have to admit it sounds a little funny. Did you ever think maybe she thinks you don't want to know too?"

Cody turned away. Mike leaned forward trying to

catch his eye, but Cody just stared straight ahead.

"Ok Cody, when God handed out the curses for Adam and Eve's sins, He did tell the woman that she would have a desire for her husband. Now that doesn't sound like too bad of a curse if you're thinking it means 'Ha Cha Cha!' But what he was referring to was that she would want her husband's position of headship over the home and in most homes today that is the case."

"Shel has been raised in a Bible-teaching church, Cody. She knows her weakness to fall in that area and I think when she asks you for your advice, she wants you to take that position of headship. But, when you don't respond to her, she doesn't think you care. She sees a void and she fills it, making the decision for you. Cody, she wants you to care. She wants your input. Have you ever thought of telling her you would like to pray about it before you make a decision? That you'll get back with her on what ever she's asking you about in a couple of days?"

Cody said nothing, but stared at the button on the glove box with such anger that it should have melted.

"Cody?"

He started to turn to look at Mike, but caught himself and went back to staring at the button.

"Cody, call Shel and tell her you're taking her out to eat tonight. And for crying out loud, tell her you don't like meatloaf! Get her some cooking classes if you don't like the way she cooks. Or, you could even take a class with her. Help the girl out a little! It won't kill you, ya know? Anyway, I think you'll find that she likes it when you work side-by-side with her."

He could hear a little laugh rising in Mike's throat as he talked. "THAT'S IT!" Cody yelled as he threw open the door of the SUV so hard that he thought it might break off its hinges, then slammed it with the same fervor. The gravel crunching under his feet brought Cody some satisfaction, but that was little-to-no consolation for having to listen to the painful truth.

He was so humiliated that Mike and who knows how many others had seen the way he had come on to Julie. He was angry with himself for being so stupid and blind, especially since he thought he had been so discreet with keeping his sin concealed.

He felt so ashamed that Julie had seen his lust for her and ran away. Would she tell Will? Would he admit his sin and repent or would he try and hide it to save face? He could see what Mike had said was true about finding a woman to blame for his sins. The first thing he thought of when Julie ran off was how she had encouraged him and how she was acting all offended about something he thought she had started.

Now realizing she had only treated him as a friend twisted his stomach with shame. Humiliated, he said out loud, "Lord, help me to know what I should do now."

When he heard Mike's SUV coming up behind him he tensed until it passed. He was glad he hadn't stopped.

He was about twenty minutes from home, fifteen if he didn't pace himself. So Cody slowed down and took some deep breaths. He needed that extra five minutes to think and pray.

The afternoons were cooler now that the sun had been going down earlier every night. It had been an unusually long and hot summer. Cody found the cool air refreshing. Taking a deep breath and letting it all back out again, he released some of the tension that had built up throughout the day.

Eating out did sound good, especially since he knew what awaited him at home. He would tell Shel he really didn't like meatloaf and hopefully he would never have to eat it again. He really didn't know why he hadn't told her before this. Maybe it was because it was the only night of the week that she attempted to please him anymore. He liked that. He missed that in their marriage.

He would also have to tell her about Julie before someone else did. It would be easier to tell her now, without having to explain someone else's exaggerated version of what they saw or just heard.

As he thought about what Mike had said he knew he was right. He also knew he couldn't stay mad at him for long. He would have to resolve this issue soon, but not yet. Cody would be working swing tomorrow; so it would have to be Friday morning as they packed up for their camping trip together. "That's alright, make him squirm a little longer," he mumbled.

He pulled his phone out of his pocket and called Shel to tell her he decided to walk home and would be there soon. "Get ready to go out to eat, I have some things I want to talk to you about."

With no questions or comebacks, Shel simply said, "Ok."

"Alright, I'll be there in a bit then."

Shel sat at the pizza parlor with a blank expression on her face. "You don't like my meatloaf? How long have you not liked my meatloaf?"

"Oh, pretty much forever."

"Why didn't you ever say anything?"

"I didn't want to hurt your feelings."

"My feelings are pretty much hurt now, to think you didn't trust me enough to know that all I wanted to do at first was to make you happy. You always made yummy sounds like it was your most favorite meal ever." She was leaning over the table yelling at Cody in a clipped whisper.

It was true. He had been noticing that about himself lately. Whenever he was uncomfortable or nervous about something he would either try to cover it up with acting overjoyed or by becoming sarcastic. In this case, it was with his 'yummy sounds,' while inside he was undetectably being sarcastic.

"I thought Meatloaf Wednesday's were the only thing left holding our marriage together anymore. The one thing I was still doing just to make you happy! And It All Was Just A Lie!?"

"Mike says I have to start being more honest with you."

"Ya think???" Her voice raised a little as her eyes flashed with anger. Then she looked around to see if anyone had noticed.

Cody sat looking at her, not knowing what to say as she went on.

"Mike knows you don't like my meatloaf? What else does Mike know about us that I don't?"

"No! Mike didn't know, not until I told him just now, on our way home."

"I thought you said you walked home?"

"I did part way. I needed to think over some things Mike told me. Shel, I need to tell you about something that has been going on at work. I have been...."

Just then Shel's phone rang.

Cody breathed a sigh of relief and thought to himself 'saved by the bell!' Which was followed immediately by the thought, 'What if it's someone who wants to tell her what I did today?' Cody started to sweat and take rapid, shallow breaths as Shel said with irritation, "Who could that be now?" Then she answered her phone with a pleasant voice.

"Hello-. Oh, hi Holly. Yeah, I got all the stuff I needed for those today. No, oh, that's right! I'll get that tomorrow if you'll get the food. Apparently I don't know what the guys like." She turned and glared at Cody. "Oh yeah... All right... I'll talk to you tomorrow then, bye."

Cody relaxed a little then started again, "Shel I..."

Shel threw her hand up to stop him. "I don't want to hear anymore. I know I'm not the best cook in the world, but I do try." She started to tear up. "So, what can I do?" Her shoulders went up with her plea.

"Mike said you should take cooking classes."

"Oh did he really!" She shrieked not even trying to whisper as she stood up abruptly and stormed out of the restaurant. Everyone in the place got out of her way as she charged on by and out the door, then she climbed into the car to wait for Cody.

He knew she had gone to the car because he could hear the resonant slam of the car door from inside the now silent restaurant.

'Well I guess I deserved that,' he thought to himself. *'Now she's mad at me and Mike, and I'm mad at Mike. What's next?'* Cody thought about last night's dinner date at the Hilbert's and how uncomfortable they had all been. *'How are we going to survive two whole weeks with each other?'*

Cody got a box for their mostly uneaten pizza, aware of the stares and whispers around him, and walked out, pizza in tow, mumbling to himself as he went, "Lord please help me, I'm face down and drowning here."

7
Borrowing a Tent

*Those who have been born into God's family
do not make a practice of sinning,
because God's life is in them.
1 John 3:9a NLT*

At home the next morning, Cody could clearly see
Shel was still irritated with him. He tried to talk to
her, but she would only say, "We'll have two weeks to
sort things out... or not!" She glared at him. "Now
leave me alone so I can pack."

"Alright." He was fine with that, because it meant
she would be leaving him alone, too. She would also
be quiet, which was something rare in their house. He
could catch up on the things he wanted to get done
without being disturbed.

He raked the leaves and mowed the lawn for what
he hoped was the last time this year. He put yard and
garden things away and straightened up the garage.
When he finished sweeping the floor of the garage he
felt good about what he had achieved. He was glad
that he had some much-needed time alone to pray and
think.

When the paperboy came, he thanked him and sat
down on the porch swing to read. He read
distractedly, not comprehending much because his
mind kept drifting angrily to what he imagined Shel
would say if she saw him just sitting there. *'What are*

you doing? Have you done anything...?'

When he was finished he sat there waiting to prove the point that she would eventually put some kind of demand on him. As time passed he became irritated that she hadn't come out and he hadn't enjoyed reading his paper at all, not one word.

When Shel looked out on the front porch she grumbled under her breath, "What a worthless bum I married." But then she opened the door and came out and with a perfectly pleasant voice said, "Cody, would you swing over and get the tent we're borrowing from the Salamon's on your way to work?"

"Will and Julie?" He growled in response.

"What other Salamon's do we know?" She snapped back, her unyielding bitterness now showing.

When Cody heard the obvious change in her voice he softened his tone, "Shel, I'm sorry, but I have to talk to you about something first."

"Just go!" She snarled and gritted her teeth as she slammed the door.

Cody felt sick on the way to Will and Julie's. *'I'm sorry, Julie. Please forgive me, it will never happen again,'* seemed to be the hardest thing he would ever have to say.

The feeling reminded him of stealing a pack of gum from the store when he was young and when his dad found out, he drug him back to the store and made him apologize. Cody's dad then paid for the gum and Cody got to keep it, but his dad made him work off that stolen gum with a month of slave labor!

Admitting that he had stolen that gum was the hardest thing he ever had to do, up to that point in his life. But, he never stole again after that, and he absolutely hates gum to this day.

If he was ever to be free of his sin he knew he would have to repent. He could almost hear his dad saying, *'without repentance there is no forgiveness in*

God's kingdom. We might be able to hide our sins from others but we can't hide them from God.'

As he drove to the Salamon's he practiced it over and over and over again. "I'm sorry Julie, please forgive me, it will never happen again. I'm sorry Julie, please forgive me, it will never happen again..." It was only a ten minute drive from his house to the Salamon's but in that ten minutes, he felt like he had said that painful line a couple hundred times. He questioned whether he should use the words 'for making a pass at you', but the sound of them twisted at his stomach, bringing the taste of bile up in his mouth.

When Will opened the door, he glared at Cody, "What do you want?"

Cody was struck dumb with Will's appearance at the door. His mouth hung open as he looked up at him for what seemed an eternity.

Finally he managed to blurt out, "I'm sorry Julie, please forgive me, it'll never happen again! I mean Will, I mean please tell Julie, I mean - I'm sorry?"

Will threw up a hand to stop him. "I'll tell her, alright?"

The two men stared blankly at each other for some time. Will was clearly upset with Cody, but his countenance had noticeably softened. He had to think about what had just happened. He never thought Cody would come right out and confess. He promised Julie he wouldn't hit him but every scenario he imagined ended with him slugging Cody in the face. He didn't know what to do now, how could he even think about slugging a guy that just openly confessed and repented?

When the silence between the two men became unbearably uncomfortable, Will finally said, "Sooo, is there anything else?"

"Uhhh, Shel sent me to get, to get ahhh ...the tent!" He suddenly remembered.

"The tent? Oh, all right, it's out in the garage. Follow me."

Will stepped out of the house, opened the garage door and they went in together. Everything in the garage was neat and clean. Shelves were stacked and cabinets lined the back wall. Leading Cody to what appeared to be his camping corner Will said "There, grab those two small green bags," he pointed to a top shelf that Cody could barely reach.

Cody imagined that Will was smiling behind his back as he stretched to get the bags. He pulled down a small bag of tent stakes, which dislodged the longer bag of tent poles and brought them nearly down on his head. Cody straightened himself and the bags before turning casually.

Will turned away and easily pulled down the bag that held the tent, not saying a word. "Ok, that's it. Is there anything else?"

"No that's all she told me to borrow. I think she must have talked to Julie about this." Cody picked up his two bags and led the way back out of the garage and to his car. He opened the trunk and put the small bags in as Will began to talk.

"You know Cody, there aren't a lot of men that would just come right out and confess the way you did. That took a lot of guts. No pointing a finger, no excuses, and I respect you for that. It was very well done."

"Good – I mean – thank you! I'm glad to get it off my chest. But shouldn't I talk to Julie?"

"No, you need to give her a little more time. I'll talk to her and tell her what you said though."

"Thanks, I'd appreciate that."

Pushing the smaller bags aside, Will fit in the tent, then Cody closed the trunk.

"Where have you guys decided to go camping?" Will asked.

"Some walk-in campgrounds Mike and my Dad

went to when they graduated from high school. It's up in the Appalachian Mountains, I think."

"Aw, that sounds like fun!" Will became quiet as he stood thinking for a second then continued, "You know Cody, I miss your dad sometimes, too. He was a good man." He stood silent for a moment in thought then smiled and added, "Did you know they used to call your dad and Mike, 'Pete and Repeat' in school?"

" 'Pete and Repeat'?"

"Yeah, that's what everyone called them. I was five years behind them in school, but everyone knew who 'Pete and Repeat' were."

Cody smiled to himself at the thought of it.

" 'Pete and Repeat', huh? That's funny!"

"Everyone stopped calling them that after your dad and Mike each got married."

"Which one was which?"

"The names were interchangeable I think. They were always together, so..." He brought his shoulders up.

"My dad never told me that before and Mike..." Cody rolled his eyes, then said, "I think we might be in trouble. I don't think Mike remembers exactly where this campsite is that we're supposed to be going to. I think he's just planning on driving along until he recognizes something."

"Does he think he can find it after all this time?"

"He's determined to try, anyway he seems pretty sure he can find it."

"Well, if Mike wants to go back that bad, they must have had a lot of fun there. Are you planning on hunting or fishing?"

"We're going to do a little fishing, relaxing, maybe some hiking. Shel bought a bow and arrows and she's been practicing in the back yard."

"Wow, she's really into it then."

"You don't know the half of it; she has found us all backpacks and filled them with everything we would need if for some reason we had to survive." Cody made quotation marks in the air with his fingers and rolled his eyes, to make the point that he thought it was ridiculous.

"It's too bad I only get one vacation a year. Julie and I have been talking about camping in the mountains for years. When are you coming back then?"

"In a little less than two weeks, Mike and I decided we wanted more than just the weekend to relax and get settled back in before going back to work that Monday."

"That sounds about right. Hey, maybe Julie and I can swing by when you get home that night. You could talk to her then about what happened between you and apologize to her in person. Two weeks will give us all some time to pray, and after your apology, we can put this all behind us. We'd love to hear how your trip turns out and maybe go with you next year, if you plan on going again."

"Yeah, that sounds great," Cody said, surprised that Will would even make a suggestion like that after what he had done to his wife.

"You all have lots of fun and God bless."

"Yeah, thanks. Take it easy."

Will threw a hand up in a wave and backed away from the car as Cody drove off.

Cody took a deep breath and thanked the Lord for His help. He was thankful that Will hadn't hit him, even though he knew he deserved it. He was amazed that Will had actually forgiven him. And, last of all, he thanked the Lord that it could now be put behind him.

He knew his dad would've been proud of him today. It had been quite some time since he had done something that he knew his dad would have been proud of. It also felt very good to know he had done what his Father in heaven expected of him.

8
Scarecrow

Let us search out and examine our ways,
And turn back to the Lord.
Lamentations 3:40 NKJV

The alarm clock went off near Cody's head, rousing him from a sound sleep. He squinted, moving in close to look at the clock in the dark, his glasses still on the nightstand. He flopped his head back down on his pillow. "Tell me it's not four o'clock in the morning."

"It's not four o'clock in the morning," Shel mumbled as she lay next to him in the bed.

"It's not? What time is it then?"

"It's four o'clock in the morning."

"What? I thought you said it wasn't four o'clock in the morning."

She rolled on to her back, "I thought you said to tell you it wasn't four o'clock in the morning."

"Oh very funny!" Cody could tell that Shel was still angry with him. "And why are we getting up at four in the morning?" he moaned.

"Mike wants to leave no later than six. It's a long drive."

"Ok, then let's get going."

But neither of them moved.

Cody woke with a start as Shel jumped up and out of bed.

"We overslept! It's a quarter after five. Cody, we're late!"

He jumped up and threw on the clothes Shel had laid out for him the night before. He put on a pair of black denim jeans along with the old black t-shirt that both had lost their blackness long ago. Then he picked up the blue-and-black plaid flannel shirt, thrust his arms into the sleeves and quickly buttoned it. This shirt had once been his favorite because it matched his blue eyes, but it now was faded as well. Even though he was well coordinated, he felt a little like a scarecrow, and looking into the mirror he found he was right.

His golden straw like hair was standing up all over his head. He had buttoned his shirt up wrong with one side tucked in while the other hung out. His fly was open and his feet were bare. As his eyes flashed big in the mirror through the magnification of his glasses, he asked himself, "Now where'd ya put y'ur straw hat and corn cob pipe?" He ran his hands through his unruly hair, trying to comb it down. Then he waved a hand at the mirror as if to say, "Ah, who cares?"

Shel stuck her head out of the shower. "What'd you say?"

"Ah nothin', just trying on my field clothes. They comes out every year 'bout this time," he said, still looking at himself in the mirror. Then putting his thumbs under his imaginary suspenders he pulled them out as far as he could and let them go, to snap on his chest. "Ow, now that there hurt!"

Shel mumbled something as she turned off the shower and grabbed a towel.

❖ ❖ ❖ ❖ ❖

Cody packed the car with everything except what Shel would be using that morning.

Shel hurriedly got dressed and then ran out to the car, quickly throwing the last bags into the backseat while Cody locked the front door. The two of them jumped in and headed off down the road, without breakfast.

When they reached Mike and Holly's house, Mike was packing their camping gear into the back of his SUV. Cody hurried to join him, hauling his gear over and laid it on the ground in a pile to be packed in by Mike. Shel went into the house to see how she could help Holly. They all worked together in silence and somehow managed to hit the road just after six o'clock, without pausing to pray. In any case, God would be less than interested in such prayers while their unresolved anger hung in the air like a black curtain, dividing them from each other and distancing them from Him.

As they drove, Shel, who was normally chatty, was deep in thought. When she and Cody were first married, she felt as if they would be the one couple in the history of the world that would never have any problems. Shel sighed. She wanted to believe that all the trouble they were having was all Cody's fault, but she knew that wasn't true. That by being consistently disrespectful to him she had cut him deep, ripping out his manhood and trampling it under foot. She knew it was wrong, but now it was too late, she felt that too many things had been done and said, that there was no coming back from. She was determined to continue on as she was rebelling against everything that Cody did or said, although her bitterness brought her no happiness. She knew that the Bible talked about rebellion being as witchcraft, but she didn't care anymore. She would repent when it was all over.

Holly, who was usually pretty quiet, was nervously chattering non-stop. They drove for hours listening to her tell every childhood camping trip story she could recall. She told them about running along a warm beach dodging waves, running through the campgrounds over roots that rolled across the surface of the ground like small mountain ranges. And how she and her brothers found a gully wash and they slid down on their bums, going faster and faster, ducking under a fallen tree and then on again until they reached the bottom. Turning and pulling themselves back up the side of the hill by holding onto branches and roots, only to slide back down again and again, until the bums of their jeans were worn clear through.

As Holly told her stories, they could almost see her as a little girl, her red hair bobbing up and down as she ran, climbing up then sliding back down that gully wash. Her bright eyes only a jolly slit from laughing, her rosy cheeks surrounding her mouth as it opened to let out shrill childish squeals of joy.

Holly had put on a bubbly childlike personality today, because she wanted to make those who shared her day, happy. She wanted to make peace where there was no peace. She didn't know who had a problem with whom, but it was clear that some or all of the other passengers in the vehicle were angry at each other. It made her very nervous. She felt like she had somehow done something wrong and that it was her job to fix it, whatever it might be. So, as the day went on, she became louder and more animated to fill the deafening silence. She was trying so very hard to get them all to laugh, to break through the invisible tension in the air, but with little success.

Of course, none of the others in the vehicle could see what they were putting her through. All morning, Mike and Cody never said a word to each other. And Shel only responded whenever Holly needed a response.

Both Cody and Shel were hungry and hoping that they would stop somewhere soon to eat. But Mike didn't know that, since neither one of them had spoken to him or to each other.

Cody knew Shel wouldn't say anything to Mike unless it was a biting snide remark. He knew that the hungrier she got, the more irritated she would be. And he knew he had to find a way to keep that from happening.

Just then Holly said, "Wow, I'm really hungry! Aren't you guys hungry? I think we should stop and have a second breakfast. Mike, aren't you hungry?" Mike just brought his shoulders up but said nothing as he glanced over at Cody. Holly had hoped for more of a response from him than that, so she turned and looked at Shel. "Well, what do you think?"

"Yeah, I'm hungry, maybe we should stop somewhere and I can whip us all up some of my world famous meatloaf," she said, glaring first at Cody, then at the back of Mike's head.

OK, it was time for Cody to say something before things got any uglier. "Yes, I think we should stop," Cody said, "but maybe pancakes would be a better choice since we never had breakfast this morning."

Shel snapped her face towards the window in a huff.

"Oh, why didn't you say something?" Mike said, "Second breakfast it is then!" He shot a timid smile at Cody.

Cody reluctantly smiled back as Mike took in a deep breath and let it back out slowly, releasing some of the tension he felt.

Within a short time they found a Denny's and pulled in.

"Mike, just order Shel and me each a 'Grand Slam', if you would please. We're going to take a quick walk," Cody said as he clutched Shel's hand and pulled her in the opposite direction of the restaurant.

She trudged along behind him, secretly thrilled that he was taking control of the situation. She didn't know what he was going to say to her but it made her feel good to know that he cared enough to take her aside and say something, anything.

The two of them walked down the street towards a city park, passing a motel and stopping in front of a bench beside the road. They didn't sit down but instead Cody turned her towards him and said, "Shel, stop it."

"Stop what?"

"Being so angry at Mike, that's what! Mike didn't say 'maybe you should get cooking lessons' because he doesn't like your cooking, he said it because I was complaining about your meatloaf. He was just trying to make a suggestion to help me. Your cooking wasn't even the subject we were discussing."

"Oh really, then what was the subject of your discussion?" She asked with disbelief.

"I tried to tell you in the pizza place and then again at home yesterday, but nooo, you have to wait until now to want to hear it."

"So, let's hear it then!"

"We don't have time right now, I'll tell you later."

"So, what's the big secret?"

"It's not a secret, I said I'll tell you later didn't I?"

"Ok fine, but I'm not the only one mad at someone. I noticed you weren't talking to Mike either."

"You're right, but that's something I have to work out with him. The advice he gave me was good and I got my back up about it, that's all." He turned her to look him in the face. "Shel, please forgive me. Because of what Mike said to me the other day, I'm determined to work harder on our marriage and work harder at seeing your value. I want," his jaw began to work as he struggled with his next words, "to concentrate on falling in love with you again. We lost that somewhere down the line and I," his jaw worked once more, "I miss it."

At that, she began to cry and threw herself into his arms. "That's what I want too." She was amazed at her own transformation from a few moments ago.

Cody held her in his arms for a few seconds as the traffic buzzed by. He put a hand on the side of her head and drew it towards his lips, kissing her hair near her ear. He took in the smell of her shampoo mixed with car exhaust.

He stepped aside, moving her with him as a dog ran past with a man holding his leash jogging close behind.

"Babe, are you ready to go back and eat yet?" He asked softly.

"Oh, yes please, I'm starved."

As they walked back, Cody took her hand in his. She turned and looked at him with surprise on her face. He smiled at her and she smiled back. Then he leaned towards her and kissed her as she raised her face to welcome it. The look on her face reminded him of how she had always loved it whenever he held her hand in the past. So, he gave it a little squeeze and held it affectionately as they continued their walk back to the restaurant.

When they reached the swinging doors of the restaurant, he graciously opened one of them for her as she stepped inside.

Holly let out a sigh of relief and sat back when she saw them smiling contentedly at each other.

Cody patted Mike on the back before he slid into the booth next to Shel. Mike looked across the table at him and smiled. The meals had just arrived, so they prayed over them and then over their trip. As they ate walls came down and they all talked as if nothing bad had happened.

When they finished eating, Mike and Cody went to pay their bills.

"Mike, my Dad asked you to be there for me, and you always have been. Thank you." He paused as a smile crept across his face. "Thanks for being my Dad's repeat."

"His 'Repeat'? Are you talking about our

nicknames in school 'Pete and Repeat'?" He asked in surprise.

"Yeah!"

"I thought I had lived that one down long ago, how'd you hear about it?"

"Will told me," he said nonchalantly, walking up to the register and pulling out his debit card.

"When did he tell you that?" Mike pulled some bills out of his wallet.

"Yesterday." Cody stated, smiling at the cashier as he handed her his card.

Mike's eyes got big as his head jerked around to look at Cody. "What, you talked to Will yesterday?"

The cashier remained silent, being caught in the middle of their conversation.

"I'll tell you about it later, but just so you know, all is well." Cody nodded his head as he spoke, taking back his card from the cashier.

Mike turned and looked at the cashier and smiled.

"Was everything alright?" She asked the pair of them with a smile.

"Oh, yes everything was and is just wonderful, thank you!"

9
The Prophet

"And it shall come to pass in the last days, says God,
That I will pour out My Spirit on all flesh;
Your sons and your daughters shall prophesy,..."
Acts 2:17a NKJV

At three in the afternoon they drove into a small town named Ponder.

"Can we take a break and get an ice cream to hold us over until we stop?" Holly asked.

A resounding, "Ohhhh, ice cream!" was the only reply she got from the rest of them.

Mike turned the SUV around to backtrack to a diner with 'Ice Cream Parlor' written on one of its picture windows. The sign over the door simply read 'McClure's Diner and Ice Cream.'

Together the four of them walked into the old-fashioned diner they took in a breath of surprise. The place had been built in the 1930's and was well maintained. Under their feet, the tile was laid out in a black and white checkerboard pattern. The benches that lined both sides of the parlor seemed to have been replaced with a burgundy vinyl sometime in the last twenty years. The table tops and counters had a dusty mauve Formica from the 1980's, most likely, in an attempt to replace the 1930's pale pink. The nostalgia of the place was like a bridge into the past.

They spun around looking at everything, enjoying the ambiance.

At the end of the long room stood an old jukebox, just waiting for someone to come along and drop in a dime for a song and start dancing. Inside it were the original 45's, ranging from the early 1950's to mid 60's. Mike walked the length of the room, followed by Holly, and dropped his quarter in carefully selecting three songs. When the first song began to play, Mike took Holly's hand and snapped her up with one step into his arms, the two moving in harmony from side to side, ever so slowly. Mike, lowering his cheek to rest on his wife's, turned his lips in for a kiss as he spoke sweet words that only Holly could hear as she giggled at some long ago memory.

Just then an old lady came out from the back of the shop and walked up to the counter. Like the building she owned, she too looked as if she had been made in the 1930's.

"Can I help ya folks?" She spoke, exposing a toothless grin. She had a comfortable, well-worn smile that drew her wrinkles up almost burying her eyes in the folds. She looked like a cute version of an apple-head granny doll, all you wanted to do was take her home and sit her up on a shelf.

Shel smiled in response to the old woman's contagious grin as she stepped up to the counter and said, "We'd like some ice cream, please."

"Y'all from up north somewheres?" She didn't wait for an answer. "Kate, these folks want themselves some ice cream!" She yelled to the back room as she slipped onto a stool that gave her a good view of the entire room.

A tall, pretty looking young woman stepped out. She was in her mid-thirties with long, dark, wavy hair pulled back into a ponytail. "Can I help you?" She said with a smile that somehow matched the smile of the old lady, except with teeth.

"Y'all know of any nice young Christian fellers for my granddaughter here?" The old lady began to ask.

"Oh Granny, please don't do that!"

"Now Kate, you're not getting any younger and the only fellers buzzin' around here, well, they ain't good enough for ya, or they ain't exactly lookin' ta get hitched."

"Granny, you're going to scare these nice folks away," she said as she shuffled around self-consciously, embarrassed by her Grandmother.

The old lady then turned to watch Mike and Holly dancing for a second and a tear seeped from the corner of her eye and slid down her old cheek, getting lost somewhere in amongst her wrinkles.

Watching the couple dancing cheek-to-cheek, she looked over at Cody and Shel and said, "Now ya young folks need to take note from them two." She pointed at the dancers. "Life don't last long and ya ain't got time for none of this," she pointed at them both with her index fingers and drew two circles in the air over their chests, as she spat out, "discord!" As if it tasted bad in her mouth.

"Granny, you don't even know these folks! Don't go telling them how to live their lives like you do!"

"Hush Kate, the Lord's dealing with these young folks." She scolded Kate then turned back and continued with, "Now you kids are goin' ta have some hard times to go through here real soon like, and you're gonna need ta be a-relyin' on each others strengths ta get ya on through it."

Cody and Shel stood with their mouths hanging open. Shel turned and looked over at Cody, waiting for him to say something but he kept his eyes glued on the old lady and said nothing.

The things she was saying frightened him, burning him inside and he wanted to run away. But his feet seemed to be glued to the floor and he couldn't say a word. This woman, without knowing them, had pinned them both down. Somehow he knew he was hearing from the Lord, so he swallowed his pride and listened intently. Shel on the other hand, responded with resistance to what was being said.

"Now y'all just listen ta old Granny McClure." She continued, "you're always gonna feel like you're still young in here," she tapped on her heart with one of her boney old fingers. "But your body, it just keeps gettin' older till it wears out, then it's done carryin' ya around."

"Granny, stop it!" Kate interjected.

Cody put his hand up to stop Kate. "Go on," he said as he nodded for the old woman to continue, determined to hear her out.

"Well, ya just ain't got time for that there rot that's goin' on in there." She slid off her stool and tapped hard on Cody's chest. He imagined he could feel the bone of her old finger cutting through his flesh and into the 'rot', as she called it. He almost expected her finger to come back out with some nasty green slime hanging off the end of it. It was a shock to Cody that this old woman could see the darkness of his heart. It made him feel exposed and vulnerable, but still all he could manage to say was, "Thank you."

As Mike and Holly finished their dance they joined the others at the counter. Holly said, "Did ya order yet?"

Shel closed her mouth and turned back to Kate to order. "I'd like a double scoop of tin roof sundae, please."

They took turns ordering, and then sat down with the biggest double scoop ice cream cones they had ever seen. While they ate the music continued to play in the background.

Mike leaned over the table and whispered, "So what's going on guys?" But no one answered him as their attentions were being diverted by what was being said behind the counter.

Granny continued with, "Now Kate, why can't ya find yourself a nice young feller like that un?" she pointed at Cody. Then the old lady slid around the corner and into the back room.

Shel half expected her to come back around the corner to perform a 'shotgun wedding' right there, so she scooted up under Cody's arm to make the point that he was hers.

Kate came over to the table. "Can I get you anything else?"

"No, this is more than enough," Mike said as he looked at the half gallon of ice cream that teetered on top of his tiny cone.

Kate turned to Cody, "I'm so sorry, sir, about my Granny. She fancies herself some kind of prophet or something." She rolled her eyes. "She just can't seem to understand that people just want to eat something or have ice cream when they come in. They don't want the answers to all of life's problems in one easy installment."

"No, she was right. I have actually seen in my life some of the 'rot' she was talking about, rearing its ugly head. I appreciated her frankness. There aren't a lot of people who will tell you the truth like that."

"You're right about that," she rolled her eyes again. "I'm sorry to you, too, ma'am, for her bluntness about me marrying someone like your husband and all, she doesn't mean no harm," Kate said, as she looked at Shel.

"The funny thing is," she looked back at Cody, "you do look a lot like the guy that folks think is my beau. But she..." Kate nodded towards the back room where her Granny had gone, "doesn't like him. He's not a Christian, not yet anyhow, I'm still working on him. Well, you all enjoy your ice cream," she said as she went back to the counter and began to clean up.

Holly leaned in, "Ok, explain to us what we missed?"

The bell over the door jingled loudly announcing the arrival of two men. Kate stood and eyed them tensely as they approached the counter.

"Now Chuck, I told you I'm not ever going to be your girlfriend. You might just as well face it."

The auburn-haired man leaned over the counter to talk quietly to her while the other leaned back against the small bar with his elbows up on the counter and focused on the two couples, tossing his fine black hair back with a jerk of his head, only to have it fall back over one of his dark eyes.

"You folks new around here?" He said staring almost entirely at Shel.

"Just passing through," Cody said in response. Feeling threatened, he laid his hand on Shel's lap and she took it up.

"Can we go now?" Shel asked quietly.

"Yeah, we have to get going," Mike said, from across the table as he slid a tip out onto its surface.

The visitors slipped out the door with their half-eaten ice cream cones still in their hands as the dark-haired man watched.

After getting back into the SUV and starting down the road, Mike turned to Cody, who was now driving, "So, what was that all about?"

"I don't know, but I hope that she doesn't think I look like that skinny, auburn-haired guy."

"No, it sounded to me like this guy was a boyfriend wannabe. Didn't you hear her say she'd never be his girlfriend?" Holly went on, "She didn't seem to want that guy anywhere near her."

"True," Mike concluded.

There was a moment before Shel started again with, "Cody, tell them about the old lady that was all up in our business!"

"Shel, that's not fair. What did she say that wasn't

true?"

"She may have been right, but who asked her anyway?" Shel said with anger now flashing in her eyes, as her tongue snapped like a whip.

"Well, I thought it was refreshing to hear someone who doesn't dance around the truth. I felt like the Lord was using her to speak to me. Who knows, maybe she is a prophet?"

Mike spoke up, "Well Shel, I don't know what she said or did, but if she was right, she may have been a prophet, like her granddaughter said. The way you're acting says to me that she hit a nerve with you. Think about it, how many of the prophets were popular people? How many of the prophets didn't get killed for speaking for the Lord? Maybe you need to allow what she said to sink in. The truth often does hurt and we usually don't want to hear it but that doesn't mean that it isn't the truth and that the prophet is wrong."

"You don't know what she said!" Shel spat out with frustration.

"No, but being able to listen and hear what the Lord has to say without getting defensive, is a strength that I can see Cody is better at than you."

Shel's anger melted slowly as she got quiet for a moment; deep in thought she turned and looked at Cody while he drove. "Yeah, I was shocked that Cody just stood there and took it. I was actually watching him more than the old lady and seeing his cool reaction confused me. Maybe you're right, maybe it was a good thing." Anger still scored her forehead, but now it was joined by resignation.

"Look Kate, I told you a thousand times that you're my gal and you ARE my gal! You got that?" Chuck said in hushed tones as he leaned over the counter to talk to her. His coarse auburn waves holding their position as he nodded his head to make his point.

"No Chuck, I am not your girl, and I'm never going to be. You've always been trouble and I'm not going to follow you around and do whatever you say, whenever you say it, like your boy there." She nodded her head towards Leroy, who had just turned around from saying 'hello' to some folks who were passing through town.

When the newcomers got up and left, Leroy followed them out and sat on the bench out front. He watched their dark SUV as it disappeared down the road and out of town.

As Kate continued to argue with Chuck, her Granny stepped into the parlor from the back. "What ya doin' here Chuck Atteberry? Ya get outta here! Ya got no business a buzzin' round my granddaughter. Now ya get!" She made brushing motions with her hands as if to sweep him out of her parlor but he didn't move.

"Get back, you old goat! Kate should of put you away a long time ago."

"Oh Lord, may the words he speaks fall back on him." She seized a wet mop, came around the counter again and started to push him out the door with its dirty, dripping head. As he smacked the mop head aside, she was knocked off balance and started to fall.

Kate caught her before she hit the floor, letting her down gently. Then Kate rose in a rage, saying, "You get out of here right now Chuck! And I don't ever want to see you again! Now get!"

"Kate, you're going to be sorry," he spat, putting his finger in her face. "Anyone that comes between me and you is going to be feeling a world of hurt."

Chuck strode out the door slugging Leroy in the shoulder as he passed him sitting on the bench out front. "Let's go!"

Leroy got up and started to follow Chuck down the street just as   Chief Burt came running across the road.

"Have you boys been behavin' yourselves? I got a report that there was some kind of ruckus goin' on over here."

"Ruckus? No ruckus here," Chuck said smoothly, as he and Leroy kept on walking. "You best be careful chief, or you'll have a heart attack. And I'd be real sad if that happened, just before your retirement and all."

"Atteberry, I'm warnin' ya! Ya better not be makin' any trouble. 'Cause I'll be more than happy ta take ya in, if I find ya are!" Chief Burt shouted down the street at the retreating men as he rounded the door of the diner.

When the chief was out of sight Chuck and Leroy ran to Chuck's pickup and sped away, laughing as they went.

10
In the Mist

A gentle answer deflects anger,
but harsh words make tempers flare.
The tongue of the wise makes knowledge appealing,
but the mouth of a fool belches out foolishness.
Proverbs 15: 1-2 NLT

"How much farther is it?" Cody asked.

"I don't know. I know your Dad and I came this way, but it's been about forty years ago now. I guess a lot has changed in that amount of time. I've just been thinking it'll be around the next bend, but still nothing looks familiar."

The ice cream they had eaten hadn't lasted very long, leaving a gaping hole in its place. They had been driving all day and they all felt like they needed to stop for the night.

"I really don't know where we are!" Mike muttered in frustration.

"Why don't we just pull off at the next spot and check it out?" Cody suggested.

"Sounds good to me," the women said in unison.

"Anyhow, it's going to start getting dark in a little bit." Cody turned to look at Mike for his response.

"Ok, pull off up there," Mike answered pointing to an opening in the undergrowth up ahead.

Cody pulled off into the clearing and found there

were two parking spaces divided by a bank of trees and bushes. He pulled into the farthest parking space from the road, behind the bushes. They all got out, moaning, bending and stretching, taking some deep breaths of the fresh mountain air.

"This is amazing!" Shel spun around excitedly like a wild animal being released from its cage. "Let's go!"

Mike rubbed his lower back. "Cool your jets girly, give us old folks a minute."

So Shel went off to explore alone, with Holly trailing slowly and stiffly behind. A path to the right of the parking space went down into the valley below. Shel couldn't tell where it went, but she was determined to find some sort of a clearing where they could at least set up camp for one night. A nice fire and something to eat sounded really good to her right now.

When the girls heard the doors to the SUV slam, they rushed back to help the guys bring some things down. After finding a nice place to set up camp, the men would come back to get the rest.

Shel insisted that everyone carried their survival backpacks. Mike was already wearing his hunting knife on his belt, and Shel slung her new bow and quiver across her back while also carrying her backpack in her hand.

Cody was watching her as she walked beside him. She wore a pretty olive green sweater that changed her blue-hazel eyes to green. The sun coming through the trees kissed her skin with its pale light and made her eyes twinkle as if a flame lived inside. Her long blonde hair rose and fell on her back as she walked down the path and a slight smile played across her pink lips. It had been a long time since Cody had seen that sparkle in her eyes and he missed it.

The mountains were beautiful this time of year. The leaves were ablaze with the most beautiful shades of red, yellow and orange. A mist rose from the valley floor and the clouds hung low. The rays from the lowering sun cut through the clouds giving their surroundings a mystical appearance. The trail ended down by a river where they found Mike exploring the area.

"There are some nice level spots here for the tents and we can build a fire here," he explained as he led them around a big clearing that lead away from the path about forty feet. They agreed it was an ideal place to camp, so ideal that they talked about staying there the whole two weeks of their vacation.

While the others went back to get the rest of their camping gear, Holly collected firewood, stacking it teepee-style on top of crumpled up balls of newspaper. By the time the others returned, she had the fire blazing.

Shel checked Holly's phone to see if it had reception, but there was none. *'Maybe at the top by the SUV'*, she thought, as she stuck it back in Holly's backpack. *'She's never going to check this phone, but then again we did come out here to get away.'*

The rest of them had left their electrical devices at home so they would not be tempted to use them and defeat the whole purpose of getting away. Since Holly seldom used her phone, it was highly unlikely that anyone would try to call them on it, so it was designated the emergency phone.

The men started to set up their tents while there was still daylight, then they could all relax and eat without having to worry about stumbling around in the dark. Holly had already thrown the corn on the cob and potatoes wrapped in foil into the now hot coals. A batch of orange peel brownies sat waiting on an old wooden picnic table that now wore a red-and-white checkered tablecloth.

"Wow," Cody said as he saw all the foil packages full of food. "When did you do all this?"

"Shel came over yesterday when you were at work.

She mixed up the brownie batter from scratch and put it in the orange peels," Holly said as she glanced over at Cody to see his response. A look of panic passed over his face but she just smiled and put the BBQ chicken on the grill to cook. "You're in for a surprise!"

"Oh yeah! We're gonna eat good tonight!" Mike almost sang as he banged another tent stake into the ground.

After the tents were set up, the women quickly moved everything inside.

Mike went off to pump up the rafts by the river for the next day. He wanted the rafts to be ready so they could do some fishing in the cool of the morning.

Cody replenished the fire and sat back poking it with a stick. Meanwhile Shel inspected the plants around their camp. Cody was irritated because in his view she was just wasting her time looking at weeds.

"What are you doing?" He snapped at her.

"I'm looking at the plants, but it's hard to identify some of them this time of year because there are no flowers or buds, and some don't even have their leaves anymore."

"You're such a hippy!" He said with disgust.

"Well, I'm so sorry!" she snapped back, "How could anyone possibly enjoy something you don't?" Shel stormed away, walking over to where Holly was working in her tent. As she watched she saw that Holly was zipping her and Mike's sleeping bags together, making them into one big sleeping bag.

"I didn't know you could zip two sleeping bags together like that!"

"Well, you can if you have two of the same kind with the same type of zipper. This is the way we've always done it," Holly grinned as she continued working.

❖ ❖ ❖ ❖ ❖

Cody sat half listening to the girl conversation and half focusing on the fire when Mike came back from pumping up the rafts.

"What is the matter with you buddy?" Mike asked quietly.

"What do you mean, what's the matter with me?" He answered back with an irritated whisper.

"Why does it bother you so much that Shel's looking at the plants around the camp?"

"I don't know, it just makes me angry that she's having fun looking at stupid weeds!"

"Why, don't you want her to have fun? She's making the most of this trip and she likes that kind of thing. Is that so wrong?"

"I don't know."

"Well Cody, if it is, then it's wrong for you to collect model airplanes and know everything there is to know about them. It's the same thing."

"No it isn't," Cody hissed.

"How's it different?"

"I don't know, it just is. Why can't she act like a normal person instead of acting like a freak? Why can't she just come and sit down with me and watch the fire? Would that be so bad?"

"Oh I see, you want her to come sit with you. Did you ask her to come and sit with you?"

"No, she should just want to sit by the fire. That's what people do when they're camping, that's what you're supposed to do. She'd have known that if she was normal."

"Are you serious Cody?" Then added with, "You growl at her in hopes that she'll come running to spend time with you? How's that working for ya buddy?" He said with sarcasm and a slightly raised voice.

With that Cody got up and walked away from Mike and the fire. Coming up on the girl's conversation, he listened as they sat together on the sleeping bags that lay on the floor of Mike and Holly's tent.

"I wish we lived in the country like you guys do,"

Shel said.

"Yeah, I can see you with braids in your hair chasing chickens around a farm," Holly said with a giggle as she laid back.

Shel said, "I'd love to garden, I'd hang herbs to dry in my kitchen," as she held some dry weed over her head. "Maybe we could get some sheep or a goat or something?"

As the girls talked, Cody thought to himself he could see Shel doing those things too. She would love it, but...

Holly sat up suddenly and looked at Cody, bringing him into the conversation. "There's a house about a mile down the road from us that just went on the market yesterday."

Cody's mouth fell open as she caught him off guard.

"We would love to have you two as neighbors!" She continued.

Cody caught his breath then said, "Neighbors? Are you kidding me? How can we be neighbors, a mile away?"

Holly ignored him and continued talking to Shel.

"Anyway, it's a light blue farm house with a cute white picket fence. It has a nice barn and a couple of acres. I think you'd really love it! Even your 'City Boy' there would love it if he just gave it half a chance." Holly glanced back over at Cody, giving him a nod.

"Oh Cody, I want to go look at it when we get back home."

"Maybe, I'll pray about it," he said as he quickly walked away. Working his way down to the river's edge he grumbled to himself. "I thought this was supposed to be a vacation. Looks like I'm in the classroom again Lord, what is it you want me to learn now?"

Cody spent some time watching the water glistening from the remaining light of the sun as it dropped in the sky. A mist slipped from between the trees, sliding out onto the shimmering surface. Bugs danced across the water making delicate ripples, as fish jumped up and out to swallow the unsuspecting bugs, then vanishing as they dropped back into the water's depths. The crickets had started to warm up for their nightly concert and Cody could hear a flock of geese flying over, off in the distance. "Forgive me for grumbling, Lord. This place is so beautiful. Thank You."

❖ ❖ ❖ ❖ ❖

When their supper was ready they ate it, savoring each bite. They talked and laughed well into the night. By the time they were ready to go to bed they were completely worn out.

Shel yawned, "I'm so tired, I can hardly keep my eyes open."

"Well then," Mike said, "let's pray together before we go to bed." Holly sat up from laying her head on Mike's chest and they all lowered their heads as he prayed.

"Lord, thank you for blessing us today. Thanks for providing such a beautiful place for us to spend some time alone. Bless us with a good night's sleep; protect and keep us, go before us each day so that we can go back home refreshed and changed, in Jesus' name, amen."

Cody crawled into his and Shel's tent, noticing that even though she knew she could zip the sleeping bags together, she had not done so. He wanted to put his arm around her but knew she would just slap him away. So he laid on his back, staring at the ceiling of the tent, listening to the night sounds, until he fell asleep.

11
Them Bad Guys

Wrath is cruel and anger a torrent,
But who is able to stand before jealousy?
Proverbs 27: 4 NKJV

The blue grass band played quieter than it had been earlier that evening. It was about closing time at the only bar and nightclub on the outskirts of town and some of the band members had already drifted home.

Chuck and Leroy were usually the last people to leave on Friday and Saturday nights. Chuck was always looking for trouble by the end of the night and expecting Leroy to back him up. Tonight was no different than any other night at the bar, except that Kate was there. He couldn't remember her ever coming into the bar before. In fact she had told him repeatedly she would never be caught dead in a bar. Chuck had always been obsessed with Kate, asking her to be his girlfriend over and over again since they were small; but she would never agree to it. "No Chuck, you're a heathen!" She had said to him when they were children. That phrase stuck with him through the years as pent up hurt and irritation that challenged him to try harder to win her over.

Kate had deep Christian roots and Chuck's goal was to prove to her, finally, once and for all that there was no God. But first he would have to be nice to her, so as to lure her in. He was certain he could do this by pretending he was okay with her faith, even acting as if he were a Christian himself, in front of her, just short of going to church. That was the one place he would 'never be caught dead in'.

He could not stand to think of Kate with anyone other than himself and tonight she was with the man that Chuck hated the most in town, Mac Ferrell. As Chuck watched them he saw Mac with his head down and his hands wrapped around a glass of hard drink. Mac looked up at Kate and mumbled something to her as she scooted closer to sit next to him. She took his hands off of the glass then sat holding them in hers as she spoke to him quietly. Too quiet for Chuck to make out what they were talking about, but it seemed to him as if she was anxiously trying to get him to go home with her.

Chuck had a hard time just sitting there watching her make eyes at Mac. He drank one beer after another, all the while getting madder and madder until Mac and Kate got up and left the bar together.

Suddenly Chuck drove his fist down in anger hard on the bar, cursing, "What can she possibly see in that drunken loser?"

"Let's just go home," Leroy said, thinking that he knew what was coming next.

"No, we're not going home yet!" He ordered a shot of whiskey and slammed it down as he threw his head back hard and swallowed. "We're going to follow them to Kate's house and when Mac comes back out, we're going to jump him."

Leroy winced knowing that when Chuck said 'we', what he really meant was 'you'. "Oh, come on, let's just go home," he pleaded.

Chuck jumped up, shoved his fist up under Leroy's nose and growled, "I said we're going to Kate's and waiting for Mac to come back out, and that's what we're doing! You got that?"

"Ok Chuck, we're going to Kate's!"

Chuck sat back down; content with the power he had over his large friend. They had been friends since childhood and Chuck had once bloodied Leroy's nose to establish his dominant role. Even though Leroy was now much bigger than Chuck, the dominant role had never been challenged again.

"But, he may not come out until morning," Leroy whined. "I'm tired."

He snapped his head around to face his large friend and growled again. "We're Going! You Got That?"

"OK!" He threw his hands up in surrender.

Chuck stood to go, catching himself on the stool next to him to keep from falling. They both stumbled out of the bar and towards Chuck's old blue Ford pickup. The blue paint was barely visible through the rust and mud that spattered its scratched and banged up surface. Crawling into the pickup they started down the road, closely following the red tail lights of Mac's car.

As Chuck and Leroy pulled into a long driveway that led up to a small gray house in the country Leroy said, "I wonder whose house this is? I haven't ever been here before."

Chuck turned off his headlights and continued down the driveway, "I don't know, but it looks like there's some kind of party going on." He turned off the driveway and pulled in behind a tree just out of view of the house but, misjudging the distance, rammed the right side of the front bumper into the tree trunk. The back axle lifted up off the ground and swung slightly to the left before slamming back down, causing them both to fly forward and then thrown back against their seats.

Leroy was stopped by his seat belt, but Chuck's chin smacked into the steering wheel.

"Oww!" He howled as he held his chin.

"Why aren't you wearing your seat belt?"

"Cause I'm a good driver!"

"That's what everyone thinks when they're drunk."

"I'm not drunk!" Chuck opened his door and stepped out and kicked the tree to pay it back for getting in his way. Then he got back in the truck with a slight limp. Closing the door he said, "Give me another one of them beers."

Leroy reached around behind Chuck's seat and picked up two beers. He pulled one off and handed it to Chuck then sat the last beer back down, dangling from the plastic rings, on the floor next to the last six-pack.

"So, why didn't you drive if you thought I was drunk?"

"I'm not going to be responsible for wrecking your truck. Besides, I'm drunk too."

"I'm not drunk, I told you! You better not say I am again, and I mean it! You got that?"

Chuck laid his head back on his seat and was soon snoring with his mouth hanging wide open. Leroy also decided to get some sleep, secretly hoping that Mac would make his escape while they both slept.

When Mac finally came out of the house early in the morning, Chuck backhanded Leroy across the chest to wake him.

"He's coming," he whispered hoarsely.

Leroy clumsily sat up and rubbed his neck as he yawned. All but one other car had left, including Kate's.

"Party's over buddy," Chuck said as he opened his door and started to step out of his truck. When he did the empty beer cans that lay at his feet fell out onto the ground. They clanged into each other as they fell and he stepped on one of them, making a loud crunching sound.

Mac looked up and saw him kicking the cans and cursing under his breath. He jumped into his car and sped past Chuck and Leroy down the driveway.

Chuck cursed even louder, jumping back into the drivers seat. Pulling out around the tree, he took off after him, scattering gravel as his truck fishtailed from side-to-side.

As Mac reached the end of the drive he turned in the opposite direction of town, hoping to throw Chuck off of his trail. It may have worked if he had turned off his lights and drove into the dim morning light, but he didn't think of that until it was too late.

Chuck followed Mac at a distance matching his speed. They swerved this way and that, just missing trees on one side and avoiding the drop off on the other.

"Look at him," Chuck laughed. "He's a worse driver than I am!"

Leroy turned and looked at him in disbelief as he clutched the dashboard for dear life.

"Chuck, slow down!"

"Are you kidding? I'm not stopping until he's dead!"

"Or we are," Leroy said under his breath.

They chased Mac for about twenty miles before they came around a corner and saw his car parked alongside the road. He had run out of gas and was now on foot running as fast as he could. When Mac saw them coming he disappeared into a turnoff encircled with trees. He scuttled around, looking every which way for a good place to hide, but he didn't have enough time.

Chuck managed to pull off the road without crashing. He and Leroy got out of the pickup and ran into the clearing where Mac stood with his hands out in front of him in a stop gesture.

"Now Chuck, she's not your gal," Mac said. "You have no right to be mad at me."

"SHUT UP!" Chuck screamed, pulling out a gun that Leroy didn't know he had.

"Chuck, NO! Stop! What are you doing?" Leroy protested.

Mac began to talk fast. "Chuck, now I'm sorry, I promise I won't go near Kate again, I promise, ok?"

"You're right, you won't."

Mac pleaded, "Come on Chuck, don't do it, please!" He turned and looked at Leroy, "Leroy, stop him! Please!"

But before Leroy could say another word, Chuck had fired two shots into Mac's chest. Leroy stood with his mouth hanging open as Mac's knees buckled under him and he fell to the ground, shaking and twitching as he laid on the dirt and gravel. His blood was pumping out of the two holes with each beat of his heart, getting slower and slower until he stopped moving and the bleeding stopped.

Chuck stepped up next to him and looked into his dead eyes and spat in his face. "I said, shut up!"

Leroy finally yelled, "NO! Chuck! What did you do?!"

Chuck turned and looked at him coldly, and then walked back to his truck to drink his last beer as Leroy followed.

"Chuck, what are we going to do now?" Not really expecting an answer, he crawled into the pickup and sat staring out the windshield.

"First, we're going to push his car the rest of the way off the road. Then we'll get rid of the body." Chuck said as he finished off his beer, giving Leroy a stern look. "Now let's go!"

Leroy obediently got out of the truck and together he and Chuck pushed the car over the edge of the embankment until it slammed down on its nose, making it all but invisible from the road.

"No one will ever find this car now," Chuck said with satisfaction, dropping some dry brush over the taillights. He turned and started back to the parking space where Mac lay dead.

Suddenly they heard a car coming. Leroy gasped, "Chuck! What do we do now?"

"Calm down and just take a piss."

"What do you mean?"

Chuck turned towards the edge of the road by a tree and unzipped his pants and Leroy did the same, fumbling nervously at his zipper as the car passed by behind him. All that the people in the car had seen were two guys casually watering a tree.

As soon as the car was out of sight they zipped up and walked to the clearing to deal with Mac's body. Mac lay flat on his back with his legs folded under him in an uncomfortable looking position. His eyes were wide open and Chuck's spittle ran down one cheek.

"Shouldn't we close his eyes or something?" Leroy said as he stared at Mac in horror.

"No, I want him to see what's coming next. Get his shoulders."

They picked him up and looked for a place to throw him over the side.

"There. That gully," Chuck thrust his chin in the direction he wanted Leroy to go. "Let's throw him down there. That'll give him one last thrill."

The dead man's shoulders slipped out of Leroy's hands and as the body dropped to the ground, its feet pushed Chuck over, causing him to fall backwards through a bank of bushes, his head hitting a green SUV on the other side. He stood up and began to curse, crashing through the bushes like a lion fighting off a contender that was after his kill. Through clenched teeth he snarled as he shoved the body hard with his foot sending him sailing down the gully.

Mac's body spun around, tumbling this way and that, sending up a cloud of dust as his lifeless form crashed into the sides of the gully and bounced back for more; snapping bones and branches alike as he slid out of sight.

When they couldn't see him any more Chuck screamed down after him. "And now I NEVER have to see your ugly mug again!"

"I'm sick!" Leroy moaned as he turned and bent over with his hands on his knees before throwing up.

Chuck pushed his way back through the bushes to investigate the SUV he had banged his head into. He cupped his hands on the window and peered in. "Wow, this is a real nice truck." He tried all the doors to see if any were unlocked. Then he cupped his hands again, "Wow, just look at..."

Just then they heard a scream, then another louder scream. Leroy stood and Chuck joined him in looking over the gully's edge where they had just discarded Mac's body.

"Was that Mac?" Leroy asked, holding his mouth as if he might just throw up again.

"No you idiot! It looks like we have some company. Probably campers, sticking their noses in where they don't belong.." He pointed towards the SUV. "Someone that wants to join Mac," Chuck said with a sly smile.

"Now, just a minute, I don't want to be any part of killing anyone else, Chuck, No! I'm tired of being the bad guys! I'm done!"

"Look, you're already part of this, like it or not. And if you don't help me and I'm caught, I'm going to tell them you planned the whole thing from beginning to end."

Chuck laid his hand on Leroy's shoulder and stepped in close to speak. He then looked from side to side as if he was going to tell a secret he didn't want anyone to hear and yelled in Leroy's face, "Before this is over, YA WILL shoot one of them, or I'll SHOOT YOU!"

Patting Leroy on the chest he whispered, "You got that?" As he stepped back he looked at Leroy with determination burning in his eyes.

"Yeah, that sounds about right to me."

"Ok then, let's go find them snoops."

As the two men walked quickly down the dusty trail they saw a lot of shoe prints going up and down with long scuff marks over top, as if someone had tried running down the steep trail. When they turned a corner near the bottom, they saw two rafts pulling out into the current of the river as they closed the gap between them and the river's edge. Inside each raft was a couple.

Chuck began to curse and yell. "HEY! Get Back Here!" he hollered, as he pulled out his gun and began to fire at the rafters. "You get back here right now, you're not getting away. YOU-GOT-THAT!" His face turned red and his veins popped out of his neck as he screamed.

"Chuck, just let them go, they don't know who we are and we'll be..."

But Chuck swung around and stuck his gun in Leroy's face before he could finish his statement. "We're going after them folks and when we catch them, you're going to kill them all! You got that?"

Even though Leroy thought the gun might be empty, his eyes got big with fear. He threw his hands up and took several steps backwards. He had seen Chuck angry plenty of times before but this was different, in fact everything about this incident had been different. As if Chuck's obsession for Kate had finally driven him mad.

"Whoa- whoa- whoa, come on Chuck, calm down! We'll find them folks all right. We just need to go back to your pickup and get ourselves down to the next bridge, that's all."

The flames that shot from Chuck's flaring eyes, gave way to a narrowing, as a snide smile spread across his face. "That's right; they'll come right to us!" He snickered.

12
Marshmallows

Knowing this that our old man was crucified with Him,
that the body of sin might be done away with,
that we should no longer be slaves of sin.
Romans 6:6 NKJV

As the two couples rowed out of view they heard the gunfire cease and the pickup speeding away.

"They're probably trying to get ahead of us so they can find a good place to pick us off."

"Stop!" Cody yelled. "Stop stop!" "We need to backtrack, to go back just before this bridge."

"What?"

"You're right Mike; if we keep going we're likely to get picked off. And, if we stop here, they'll come back and find us. Either way we're dead! But they won't go back any farther than where they saw us last. So we need to backtrack a ways to be safe."

"That's probably true," Mike said. "We'll be able to get out of the water and rest, knowing that they're not going to be sneaking up on us."

"What if we go back to camp?" Shel asked.

"No," Holly said. "I'll be lucky if I can make it a mile."

"You and me both dear, I think a mile will be more than enough for me today, too."

Rowing back against the current was harder than they expected. They moved slowly at first and then went towards the shallower water that gave them less resistance. After passing under the bridge again, they continued to press on with trembling arms. Finally they decided to stop, and after pulling their rafts up and away from the river's edge, they managed to hide them from view.

Pulling their packs and sleeping bags out of the rafts, they hiked inland a ways until Shel took hold of a sapling to see how far it would bend. "Let's stop here. These three saplings will work really well to make a shelter, don't you think?" She looked to the others for some response, putting on a smile to try and lighten the mood.

Mike and Cody just looked at each other, bringing their shoulders and eyebrows up. And Cody mumbled under his breath, "Hippie."

Holly turned to look at Cody in disbelief, letting out a sigh and shaking her head, she went to help Shel with whatever she had in mind.

Her silent comment of disgust stung Cody and he realized that he had been nurturing an attitude of superiority over Shel, belittling her, tearing her down instead of building her up. He stood and watched his wife as she moved quickly, knowing exactly what needed to be done and how to do it.

"Are we going to cut these down?" Holly pulled on one of the saplings as she spoke.

"No, they're anchored to the ground now better than we could ever manage and when we're done here, we can just untie them and let them continue to grow." She then pulled the tops of the saplings down one by one tying a rope to each. "First we need some stakes to hold these down to the ground." She pulled one of the saplings by the rope, bending it until she held its top above the ground to demonstrate what she meant. "Then we'll need some long green branches to tie on top, going across the saplings, to form a grid." She spoke with her hands as she explained, "and after that we'll need some smaller branches, with leaves or needles. We'll start from the bottom, weaving them in and work our way up."

Cody asked, "Like you would if you were laying shingles on a roof?"

"Yeah, I guess?" Shel paused to think, and then said, "Cody, I think the hatchet is in your bag."

Cody took off his bag and rummaged through it. "Wow, there's food in here!" He looked at Holly with amazement.

"Yeah, I put as much food in our bags as I could fit, but it isn't much, the survival packs were already pretty full."

After Cody found the hatchet, he held it out in front of him and thought to himself, *'maybe the Lord was directing Shel with all her hippiness all along."*

The men started cutting branches and brought them back to the women. Mike used his hunting knife to cut the smaller branches, while Cody used the hatchet to cut the heavier ones.

When they had enough branches, they joined the women in finishing the shelter. It was actually kind of fun; even though they would all have rather been sitting down and resting their tired arms.

The minute the shelter was finished Holly pulled a sleeping bag inside and laid down as Shel showed Cody how to make a water filter.

First, using three sticks she tied them together at the top, making a small Teepee type frame. Second, she tied a triangle shaped piece of fabric inside the frame by its corners, one corner to each stick, forming a small hammock. Then she tied two more pieces of fabric on the same way, each piece being progressively smaller; hanging one above the other, forming a three-tier filter system. In the top tiny hammock she put some grass, in the next level down she put sand, saying, "When it's safe to light a fire and we have cooled charcoals, we'll crush them and put them in the bottom hammock, then pour water into the top filter with the grass. The grass will filter out any big things that are in the water, the sand will take out the smaller particles and the charcoal will kill any contaminates. By the time the water runs through all three levels, it should be safe for us to drink." She slid a pan under the teepee to demonstrate how they would catch the water when they were ready to try it out.

All of them sat for hours staring into space, shocked at the turn of events that had shattered their ideals of a perfect camping trip of peace and relaxation.

As a fog began to pull itself towards them, Mike lit a fire then started to pull food out of the backpacks. He was curious to see what Holly had managed to shove in amongst their tightly packed survival gear. He soon gave an appreciative chuckle. There were a few potatoes, a couple of cans of baked beans along with a can-opener, and even four beautiful steaks wrapped in foil, that just this morning had been frozen solid. "Oh, I do love my wife!" he said, to no one in particular. Continuing to rummage he found a chocolate bar and a very smashed bag of marshmallows. He asked, "Marshmallows? What was she thinking?"

Holly sat up and said, "Well puppy, I was just thinking they're lightweight, they'll keep virtually forever and they're comfort food, and we might need some of that. And, I don't know about you, but I could use some comfort right now!" She crawled out of the shelter, dragging her sleeping bag over and snuggled in next to Mike, overlooking the fire.

Mike handed her the bag of marshmallows and she opened it with her teeth and popped one in her mouth. Then she held the bag out for him and he shook his head as he made a face of disgust. "I'll just have a chunk of the chocolate, thank you."

Mike had never been a fan of marshmallows. The only way they were even palatable to him was burnt over a campfire. After burning it, he would then eat the fragile black crust and put it back in the fire to burn again and again until the white slimy center was completely reduced to ash. Even though that did sound good right now, he didn't have the energy to get up and find a stick.

So he put his arm around his wife and pulled her in close instead, whispering in her ear, "It's alright dear." And after a moment longer he added, "You really put a lot of thought into the food you packed this morning."

"I didn't have a lot of time to think this morning, so I'm sure in a little bit I'll be hearing about something I forgot," she said grinning at him with a wink, then snuggled back on his chest.

He smiled back, saying, "I'm still happy about the food you packed, especially the steaks! But, how are we going to cook them?"

"Just hold them over the fire on a stick, like a hot dog."

"Really?"

"Sure, why not!"

"I guess that'll work."

"Did I hear that we have steaks?" Cody asked as he dropped another load of sticks by the fire.

"Yep!" Mike answered as he flashed Cody a big animated smile.

"I'm ready for mine now!"

Shel dropped another load of sticks, then went and sat by Holly, taking a marshmallow for herself. "You didn't perhaps happen to bring any hot chocolate did you?"

"As a matter of fact I put some packets in the front zipper pouch of one of the bags." She brought her shoulders up to indicate she didn't know which one.

Shel leaned over and kissed her on the cheek. "Thank you!" Then she laid her head in Holly's lap as she popped another marshmallow in her mouth.

"No, thank you!" Holly said as she brushed Shel's fine blonde hair out of her eyes, gently combing the knots out with her fingers.

They were weary in body and their minds spun with the question of what might happen next.

At about 7 o'clock Cody and Shel crawled into the shelter then into the now zipped together sleeping bags. They had only escaped with two sleeping bags so they would take shifts, one couple standing watch in case they had to run for their lives, while the other couple slept.

Cody scooted in behind Shel and he could feel the tension leave her body as he put his arm around his bride and whispered, "Everything's going to be all right, babe." His Mom had told him repeatedly when he was growing up, "there's only one thing a woman needs to hear from her husband when she's upset, 'It's going to be alright'," and she had been right. Even in the terrifying trouble they now found themselves in, it seemed to bring Shel comfort, just to hear those words.

Shel felt a release of tension as he whispered in her ear. Even if she wasn't sure what he said was true, she still needed to hear it. Plus she always loved it when he called her 'babe'. It made her feel so loved and that was good right now. She sighed deeply as she felt God's covering for her through Cody, the way God had always intended it to be. She felt content just to lie in his arms with no demands on her; just a oneness, a peace as she drifted off to sleep.

Cody lay there listening to Shel's soft breathing and the crackling of the fire as his dear friends' calm and quiet conversation rolled softly through the air outside the shelter. The wind blew gently in the treetops, making a shushing sound, like a mother trying to quiet her child. As Cody listened, he slowly drifted off into a much-needed sleep.

Cody woke with a jerk as Mike gently shook his foot from outside the shelter. "Sorry buddy, but it's your turn to stand watch."

Cody and Shel groggily crawled out of the shelter and sat by the fire with their backs against a rock, using their backpacks for padding. They were lumpy, but after pulling out the dishes and some other hard tools, they were better than the rock alone.

The fire's orange glow and the snap of its small flares filled the air. It was warm and they sat transfixed staring into the blaze. As its light flashed against the blackness of the night, it cast a shadow that danced amongst the trees. The crickets sang a comforting song, their singing being broken only by the occasional hoot of an owl.

Shel was talking excessively about snares and traps, and about things they could eat. Cody patiently listened knowing she just needed to go over it in her mind so she wouldn't forget anything. After awhile he interrupted, "Shel, thanks for listening to the Lord about all this survival stuff. I know that the Lord has a plan for us, that even the things we can't see are working for our good, according to His Word."

She was quiet for a moment then said, "Thank you, I know God's looking out for us, directing our paths, because if all the things this morning hadn't happened just as they had, we probably wouldn't be alive right now." She shivered from the cold and scooted into Cody's arms, laying her head back on his chest, she sighed. "But still I can't help but feel like I have learned all this 'survival stuff' as you put it, for some reason. What if I forget something and we all die because of me?"

"Shel, God's not going to leave us alone, to see if you're going to pass or fail some cosmic survival test."

Shel was quiet again, and Cody thought maybe she had fallen back to sleep. Then she simply said, "true," with another sigh.

After a while, Cody began to share with her, "I can't seem to get that dead man's eyes out of my head."

"Why do you think they killed that man?" Shel asked.

"I don't know, maybe he drank their beer."

She laughed, "No, he probably kicked their truck."

It felt good to laugh together once again, even about something as frightening as this. He wasn't sure that Shel would be lying in his arms, snuggling in like he was her safe place, if something like this hadn't happened.

"Cody," she asked, "do you think we lost them?"

"For tonight, I think we did."

"Do you think they'll keep looking for us?"

"I don't know. Maybe they'll just take the body and bury it somewhere. We never saw them so there wouldn't be anything we could do but report a dead man that no one could find."

"Yeah, but they don't know we didn't see them, do they?"

"I guess not."

They sat quietly for a while, when Shel said, "Running away from men with guns is the last thing I ever thought I would have to do."

"I know just what you mean." Cody sat transfixed, staring into the fire. And there too, were the eyes of the dead man; eyes much like his own, staring blankly back at him, snapping and flashing along with the flames that encircled them, imprisoning him with their gaze.

13
Turtle and Shel

Two are better than one,
because they have a good reward for their labor.
For if they fall, one will lift up his companion.
But woe to him who is alone when he falls,
for he has no one to help him up.
Ecclesiastes 4:9-10 NKJV

Holly got up at about seven-thirty. "Good morning," she said waving at the couple sitting sleepily by the fire. Stepping into the bushes, Holly began to whistle. Her whistling this morning wasn't as much about the song that had been playing in her head as it was about Mike knowing where she was. It was a kind of marker, a way to make sure she didn't go too far off in the wrong direction. Having absolutely no sense of direction whatsoever, Holly had a tendency to get confused and lost. So, her whistling was an unspoken but understood precautionary measure that she and Mike had set up to keep her safe.

"Oh!" She exclaimed, stumbling to avoid kicking a box turtle as it slowly crossed her path. "Wait a minute there, speedy." She knelt down and carefully lifted it from the ground by the sides of its shell. As she lifted it, it longingly stretched out its neck towards the ground and began to run in midair; its stubby legs swimming out to the sides of its shell as it feverishly tried to escape from whatever it was that had suspended it above the solid ground that it knew and loved.

"Are you doing anything this morning? I'd like to invite you over for breakfast," Holly said, in a childlike voice, as she looked him in the eye. "We're having turtle soup, we'd really like it if you'd come!" She rounded the bushes with the turtle grasped between her hands, holding it with only her fingertips as if it might give her cooties. She was proud of herself for being brave enough to pick up a turtle. "Look what I found!"

Shel jumped up and ran over to take the turtle from her. "Oh, isn't he cute!?" She cooed. "What are you doing out here, big fella?"

"Shel, don't talk to it," Cody half whispered, looking very uncomfortable.

"Why not?" She looked up at Cody, then at Holly and her face fell. A shiver passed through her as if the morning chill had just reached her bones.

Mike crawled out of the shelter and stood up. "What's all the commotion about?" He asked, stopping abruptly when he saw the turtle in the midst of the three friends. Conflicting expressions of horror and concern held them motionless as they faced each other. "What's going on guys?"

"I found a turtle and sheee..." Holly said looking over at Shel.

"Give it to me." Mike said gently prying Shel's fingers from the turtle, "Turtles are good eatin'."

"NO!" Shel screamed and ran off into the woods. Holly hesitated then began to follow, carrying the pan that Cody quickly handed her, mouthing 'Water' as she turned to leave.

Shel stopped at a stream and sat down hard on the shore, wrapping her arms around her legs and burying her face in her knees.

Coming up behind her Holly asked, "Shel, are you

ok?" as she dropped to her knees and placed her arm around Shel's shoulder.

"I guess I have to be," she mumbled into her knees, then looked up. "I just never thought I would have to eat a turtle. It's horrible! This is the trip of 'everything I Never thought I'd Ever have to do'," she said as she shook her hands out in front of her to emphasize every word.

"Yeah, I know what you mean." she said no more. Silence passed between them as the sound and sight of the water trickling down the stream soothed their frayed nerves. After a moment Shel took off her shoes and wiggled her toes in the water, squealing at its coldness. Mischievously she flicked a foot up, splashing Holly. Within seconds the two women were splashing each other and shivering together in the cool morning air as they giggled like children playing in a mud puddle.

By the time the women returned, Mike had killed and was cooking the turtle in its shell amongst the hot coals. Cody had collected more firewood and was doing his best to cover the turtle so Shel wouldn't see it as it cooked.

The women were laughing and wet when they came into camp with a pan full of something, exclaiming, "Look what we found!"

Gazing into the pan they could see several crayfish, crawling over each other as they tried to climb up the steep sides of the pan, then falling back down only to right themselves and try again.

"Not bad!" Mike said as he took the pan and eagerly hung it over the fire. "You girls are good at this whole hunting and gathering thing,"

Holly groaned in disgust. "Aren't you going to at least clean them first?"

Mike reasoned, "They're easier to clean after

they've been cooked."

But the expression of disgust stayed on her face.

"Oh, ok, I'll clean them," Mike said taking the pan, then returning with it a few minutes later, the crayfish no longer struggling to get away.

Holly cut up the last two potatoes and dropped them into the pan, kissing Mike on the cheek in thanks as she re-hung the pan over the fire.

"Ok, I think it's time for us to talk before we take off this morning." They all sat down around the fire facing each other while Mike continued, "As I see it, we have only two choices, we can either go back or go forward."

"Well", Cody said, "I don't see how we can go back. We don't know how many men there are. We don't know what they're up to. Plus, they could have our camp site cleared away, or they may even possibly be guarding it."

"That's true," Mike nodded thoughtfully.

"I think we have to go on," Cody continued, "we need to do what they won't be expecting us to do. Walking back into our old camp only to have someone jump out of the bushes to shoot us doesn't sound like a good plan to me."

"Ok, do we all agree then?" Mike asked and everyone reluctantly nodded. "Where do we go then, and how?"

Now Shel spoke. "We need to stay near a water source. The river will lead us to a town or at least people. If we go any other way, we could roam around in circles forever and never get out. And if we follow a road, we may end up going away from our water source and possibly deeper into the wilderness. Also those men will have an easier time of picking us off if we're walking down some road."

Mike rubbed his forehead, "That's right. And we need to remember; we are in forested mountains. Not a lot of people just hang out up here, unless they live here somewhere," he paused to look around and shrugged his shoulders as he shook his head. "Or they're on vacation like us. And, the reason we came here in the off-season was so we wouldn't see a bunch of other campers. So now our goal is to find the people we were trying to avoid." Mike ran his fingers through his thick graying hair as he sighed and shook his head slightly.

Shel spoke again, "We also need to keep in mind we're in bear country, so I think we need to find some way to defend ourselves, some sort of weapon. Maybe long strong sticks that we can sharpen on one end to fend them off if we need to."

"We're going to kill a bear?" Holly said fearfully.

"No, just poke them in or around the face if they come at us. It might make them want to find easier prey. It could be a lame idea, I don't know? But still, it's something we can do. I think we're going to be fine if we stick together either way. Not running off by ourselves, like I did a while ago. That wasn't very smart of me. Running through the woods alone is a good way to attract predators who are looking for something to eat. And if we're going to make it out of this alive, we're going to have to be smarter than..." she paused for a second.

"The average bear!" Holly put in with a chuckle.

"Well yeah, and smarter than those men, too," Shel finished.

"Ok, now should we take our rafts or walk?"

"Well, we're back to what are they expecting us to do?" Cody said, "I think they're probably expecting us to use the rafts, so we should walk maybe for the next couple of days, until we know it's safe to use them again."

"No, I think one day will be enough," Shel argued. "If they don't see us on the water today, they'll try looking somewhere else tomorrow."

"We Can't Take That Chance," Cody raised his

voice. "We need to stay out of the water and out of sight of anyone looking for us on the river."

"WHAT MAKES YOUR OPINION BETTER THAN MINE?" She cut him off.

"BECAUSE I'M RIGHT, THAT'S WHAT!"

"Ok, ok, ok!" Mike put his hands between them to stop the argument. "How about we worry about today?" Mike continued to say as he got up, "Well, Cody, let's go deflate those rafts and cut some long sticks, while the ladies finish cleaning up here. Does that sound good to you all?"

They all nodded in agreement but Cody and Shel were still glaring at each other. Mike clasped Cody's arm and gave it a tug to get him started in the right direction, pulling him away from camp. "We'll be right back then!" Mike said.

The men returned to camp with the rafts ready to pack. Tying them onto their backpacks, and putting the lighter sleeping bags on the women's packs.

Sitting down and ate the chowder that Holly had made and even though it was a little flat, it tasted surprisingly good.

Cody pulled the turtle out of the now cooling coals and wrapped it up for later, stuffing it in a paper bag that had held the potatoes the day before, while Mike sat and sharpened the sticks, making the points off to one side.

"Why don't you sharpen the point into the middle?" Holly asked.

"Because the outside of the stick, just under the bark is stronger than the soft core of the stick," Mike said as he finished all the sticks, then handed everyone their own.

They started walking back into the trees, away from the river, keeping to the shadows. When they reached the road they crossed it quickly, avoiding a bridge and any clearings where they might be spotted. They tripped, stumbled, slipped, and crawled over fallen trees, climbed down crevices and over rocks as they traveled throughout the morning.

At about noon, they came across a small stream that flowed into the river. They could hear falling water coming from somewhere up above, so they turned away from the river and followed the stream up to the most amazing waterfall they had ever seen.

The falls towered over their heads as it flowed over a steep cliff. Walking out onto a massive tree that had fallen long ago they all sat down to survey their surroundings. The log that they sat on extended the whole length of the clearing where the stream ran through. Everything was covered with a thick layer of lush moss and ferns that sprang up in groupings, everywhere. A spray rose up in waves from the crashing waterfalls watering all the plants generously, while it kissed their skin with its cool lips. The mist filled the air, casting a rainbow as it fell gently around them.

Glistening leaves drifted amongst the trees, as the warm sun shone through them, turning them like pinwheels as they found their way onto the lush green carpet below. Beyond the valley a cloud lay across the mountain peaks. It looked like a soft white cotton blanket under a brisk baby blue sky that spread out beyond its fringes.

Holly said with a sigh, "Can we just stay here forever? It's so beautiful!"

Cody answered, "Well let's eat something while we rest for a little bit."

After a while Holly spoke again. "This place makes me feel so small, like we're some kind of little people in a great big world."

Then Shel exclaimed, "Look Holly, mushrooms!" They looked at each other and laughed as they slid off of their seats and ran over to collect Morel mushrooms. Morels were the only mushroom that Shel knew were safe to eat for sure. So she and Holly picked all they could find growing up through the moss.

Taking advantage of the women being busy, Mike pulled out the turtle and cut it into small unrecognizable pieces. Cody heard Mike praying to himself as he cut up the meat, "Lord, please help Shel and Holly to eat this turtle; we may have to go for days without finding any other meat."

Cody said, "Amen," with a smile, as Mike turned and smiled back at him.

When the women came back, Shel had the bottom of her shirt pulled up holding the morel mushrooms that they had collected, exposing her slender belly. Fishing a clean white undershirt from Cody's bag, she knelt down and gently poured them out, wrapping them up for their breakfast. She gently placed them in the front pouch of her backpack, so they wouldn't get crushed.

Even Shel ate the turtle meat without any trouble, talking and laughing like it was no big deal. And after taking care of their stomachs they sat nursing their scrapes and bruises with some herbs Shel said were good as a natural antibacterial agent, along with some Band-Aids she had packed.

After spending maybe an hour there, resting and talking, Mike finally said, "Ok, we need to be moving on." They all groaned, but they got up and went obediently.

The birds were singing all around them and as they listened, Cody started to imitate their songs. The birds would call then he would do his best to call back. When the birds were quiet he called louder and in the distance they could hear the birds responses, either because they could hear him or more likely because they couldn't hear him.

"You're a born natural Cody," Holly smiled

sarcastically, the corners of her smile pulling down, and they all laughed. While they were still laughing they heard men's voices and froze. *Could the men be following them or was there someone else on the river?* They all put down their packs and cautiously worked their way through the bushes towards the voices. Mike and Cody stopped near the river's edge, behind some rocks as the women moved in close behind them.

Mike said as he cautiously pointed at the bridge. "They're back where we crossed the road earlier."

Cody sighed, "Is that the bridge we crossed? I thought we'd gone a lot farther today than this!"

"Shh!" Mike whispered.

They could see two men standing on the bridge. The man standing next to the open door of a pickup truck started yelling at the other man, "BUT WHAT!"

The other man raised his voice to defend himself, "I heard some weird soundin' birds out here and..."

"Do ya think we're lookin' for BIRDS?"

"No, but..."

"BUT NOTHIN'! If ya go shootin' at birds, you'll scare off that family and they'll be putting nails in our coffins instead of us putting bullets in their heads. You got that?"

"But..."

"Save your dumb buts!" The door to the pickup truck slammed before it peeled out and sped away, leaving the other man still on the bridge to watch.

Mike tapped Cody on the shoulder and nodded his head to the side indicating he wanted them to move away from the river and talk. They all moved back from the river as Mike spoke in hushed tones. "It's pretty clear that we're not as invisible as we think we are. We have to be quieter and make better time too."

Shel said, "We need to find a game trail, even if

that means it's going to take us close to the water at times where we might be watched by predators. It's going to make it easier to walk and faster than this stumbling along over stumps and holes."

"I'd rather have predators than those men with an agenda following us," Mike said in agreement.

Holly's fear was renewed by the angry man's statement, '*Find that family and put bullets in their heads!*' She said nothing as the others spoke. Her green eyes looked like they might just roll out as she took in rapid shallow breaths.

When Mike noticed her he took her hand, "Let's go, Sweetie. I think we crossed a game trail when we came over this way." They followed Mike, retrieving their packs, then found the trail. At times it swept down to the water's edge but they were soon moving faster than they had all day. They crouched down low as they carefully skirted the river, hopefully being hidden from view.

Throughout the day they all felt as though they were being watched. Each of them felt compelled to turn around from time to time, to see if something or someone might be following them. They tried to reason with themselves that it was the eyes of predators that Shel had mentioned or maybe it was just the suggestion of predators that had set them all on edge. Still they were more concerned that it was the men that were following them. The thought of men intent on murder was more frightening than any animal could possibly ever be. To think about a gun being pointed at one's head and that you could be shot dead at any moment was unnerving. It was more than any of them wanted to think about, but think about it they did.

14
LOST

But certainly God has heard me;
He has attended to the voice of my prayer.
Psalm 66:19 NKJV

The sky was growing dark and thunder was rumbling off in the distance. The land around them was becoming increasingly rocky and they were hoping to find a cave or someplace dry to hide before the rains came. After awhile, they found a rock overhang that was big enough for them all to fit under. It would be a tight squeeze but they had no choice and no time to waste.

The men hurriedly began cutting branches for a lean-to, to cover the front of the overhang. They worked quickly, cutting and gathering the same as they had done the night before.

The women worked on putting the lean-to together and tying it down, hammering heavy sticks into the ground to secure the frame, while the top was tied off to roots that stuck out of the rocks around the overhang. Then they gathered as many dry leaves as they could find to make a soft bed to lay their sleeping bags on, while the men collected pieces of firewood and small logs, stuffing the small space set aside for that purpose.

Once they were all finished, Shel and Mike ran off

in opposite directions to set some snares as Cody started on the fire, pulling the rest of the wood into the overhang as he worked.

"Holly, would you run down to the river and get us some water quick? Try and get it as clear as you can. We're going to have to boil it because we don't have time to build a water filter, and the water will be easier to drink if it doesn't look like mud." Not hearing a response, Cody turned to look at Holly and saw her staring at him, with her mouth hanging open. "Well?"

"Me?"

"Why not you, you're not doing anything are you?"

"I might get lost," she said timidly.

"How are you going to get lost? We just came from the river, its right through those trees." He pointed impatiently. "It's easy, anyone can do it. Now hurry, that storm's coming up fast!"

She stared at him with big eyes a second longer, then picked up the empty canteens and started off towards the river. As she walked away, Cody could hear her saying to herself, "I can do this, it's easy, anyone can do it," before beginning to whistle a shaky tune.

The fire was roaring when Shel, then Mike, came back into camp. Shel moved in under the overhang and sat down by the fire, next to Cody. But Mike seemed to be listening for something. It was only a few seconds before he turned with a start, "Where's Holly?" He asked, looking at Cody. "Is she changing or something?"

"No, I sent her to get some water," Cody said casually with his eyes still on the fire. "I don't know what's taking her so long."

Shel jumped up, banging her head as she stood. "Are you kidding me?" She said rubbing her head.

"How long ago?" Not waiting for an answer, Mike ran towards the river with Shel at his heels. Cody could hear them calling, "Holly! - Holly! - Holly!" the sound of their voices fading as they got farther and farther away.

'What in the world's that about?' Cody said to himself as he sat there, not knowing if he should go running through the woods waving his arms, screaming Holly's name, or just stay and wait for her to come back. 'She'll be back any second now then she'll want to know where those two are.' He chuckled a little as he thought of her running off into the woods yelling their names. It was getting darker and with that storm coming in, there wasn't time for this silly game they were playing.

After a while Shel came running back into camp.

"Ok, what's going on? Did you find her? What are you looking for?" Cody questioned her impatiently as she frantically dug through their backpacks, one after the other.

"I'm looking for the flashlights."

"Where'd she go?" Cody questioned.

"Cody, you're a moron! She has no sense of direction. She gets lost in town when there's a detour and she's lived there her whole life!"

"Oh, come on. Anyone can walk down to the river and back."

"Is that what you told her to get her to go?" She snapped, "'anyone can do it?' Sorry to sound like a broken record Cody, but you're a moron!" Finally she threw down the last backpack in frustration, "WHERE ARE THEY?"

"What?"

"The FLASHLIGHTS!" She screamed impatiently.

Cody leaned back and pulled them out from behind the sleeping bag and handed them to her. "I put them back there so we could get to them easily tonight."

"You could have given them to me when I asked for them the first time, couldn't you? You knew what I was looking for, didn't you!?"

"Yeah I guess, but I still don't see what the big deal is."

"Do You See Holly Anywhere?" She threw her arms out and looked both directions.

"No!"

She practically whispered, leaning in as if she were talking to a child, "Neither do Mike and I, that's what the big deal is!"

Getting down to the river wasn't hard, but it was farther than Holly remembered. "That wasn't so bad," she said to herself, "I can do this." She filled up all the canteens and started walking back. As she went around some rocks and up the bank, she unknowingly veered slightly to the left. She was feeling good about how it had worked out so far, so when she heard something in the bushes to the left she turned towards it and continued on until she came to an opening in the bushes.

"I did it!" She said, feeling proud of herself, but instead of her finding Cody sitting there working on the fire, she found a family of raccoons. Freezing in her tracks, fear filled her as the largest of the raccoons stood on its back legs and hissed at her, showing its sharp yellow teeth.

'Run!' Adrenaline rushed her as she turned around and ran as fast as she could without a clear idea of what direction she was heading.

Every tree and every rock looked exactly the same to her in the growing gloom. As she ran she remembered and could almost hear Shel saying, *'Running through the woods will attract predators that are looking for something to chase.'* She tripped over a root and fell to the ground, landing amongst dried leaves that were now pressing into the soft mud below her. She sat up quickly, swinging this way and that, looking for the imaginary predator that was ready to pounce. Seeing all manner of fearful shapes in the shadows below the canopy of trees, amongst the undergrowth. A scurrying of leaves flew past her being driven by the heavy wind.

She didn't get up, but lay back down. Curling up she began to cry- "Lord please, don't leave me out here alone to die!" She pleaded with the Lord, and then quoted scripture to herself, " 'Be still my soul and know that he is God'." She stood to her feet, "Ok Holly, think, how do you get back?" she began to yell as loud as she could, "MIKE! - Cody! - SHEL!" pausing with every name to listen for a response, but she heard nothing - just the howling of the wind.

Tears filled her eyes again and ran freely down her face. "If we follow the river downstream we will come to a town and people," she heard Shel's voice again. "We're traveling downstream," she said to herself. She quieted her breathing, trying to hear the river. She listened for a long time, then, faintly off in the distance she could hear the sound of water. She turned towards the sound and walked a few steps, then stopped to listen again.

It was getting dark, but she knew she had to stay calm. She started tripping over things in the growing darkness, but managed to stay upright as she kept moving as best she could towards the river.

When she could hear the water clearly she moved quicker, no longer needing to stop to listen. Soon she was standing, looking directly at it. She could see reflection from the remaining light on the shimmering water, making it look like it was glowing slightly in the darkness among the black silhouettes of the trees and mountains.

Shel brought the flashlights back to Mike who was still frantically searching the shore for any sign of Holly being there.

"What took you so long?" He growled.

"Oh, Cody decided to move the flashlights and

didn't tell me. You know, he told her to go get the water, that 'anyone could do it'."

"What!" Mike yelled, snapping his head towards her. Then seeing the look of shock on her face, he said no more as he turned away and began to swing his flashlight back and forth along the ground.

"I'm going to move inland a little ways in case she wandered off in that direction," added Shel.

Mike said nothing more as she walked back into the woods.

When she saw Mike's angry reaction, she felt terrible about sharing with him what Cody had said. It was the very same reaction, which she only minutes ago, had displayed. Why was it, when she reacted badly to someone; somehow it seemed to be right? But, when she saw someone else do the same thing, it looked so much uglier than she thought she had looked.

"Lord, help me to not lash out at my husband, help me to be a peaceful place for him to come to. Help me be someone who can help him, not harm him. And please, don't let Mike kill him because of something I said. Lord, we really need to find Holly. She's out here all alone. And Mike's angry, Cody's confused, and Holly's afraid. I may be the only one praying. I'm so sorry about that. Please hear the cries of our hearts, Lord and help us to find Holly, before it's too late."

Holly paused by the water trying to decide if she had been running up stream or down? If she turned the wrong way, she would go farther from camp. After a moment she began following the water downstream, hoping that God was guiding her steps.

Her ankles kept turning on the rocks as she walked as fast as she could in the dark. The spirals of her corkscrew hair caught in branches that reached out to scratch her face, claw at her, catch on her clothes, and refusing to let her pass in peace.

She knew Mike would be out looking for her soon, so she tried to listen for his voice amongst the night sounds that seemed to be getting louder every second. Frogs, crickets, the water rushing to somewhere she didn't know and the sound of the wind whistling through the trees. "Could someone turn down the ambiance, please?" She yelled out into the night.

Lightning flashed in the distance, bouncing off of the water's surface. The thunder rolled, pulling a black curtain across the sky as the storm drew ever closer. Darkness surrounded her, so she stopped and prayed fervently with every breath. When the lightning flashed she could see out in front of her enough to take only a couple of steps safely, before stopping again in darkness, awaiting the next strike.

Amid the night sounds, faintly, far away, she thought she could hear someone calling her name, "Holly! - Holly!" She turned and looked upstream, then down, but couldn't figure out what direction it was coming from? Now her tears became a flood that poured down her face as her sobs shook her violently. She tried to cry out, but her tears choked out her voice. As she turned to face back downstream, she could see a single point of light now swinging back and forth as it came closer to her. She then realized that some of the flashing lights she had been seeing on the water's surface were from the flashlights.

She could see Mike coming ever closer and finally as his light stopped on her face, their eyes met and her mouth moved mournfully and silently, saying his name, "Mike!"

❖ ❖ ❖ ❖ ❖

It had been about forty-five minutes since Shel and Mike took off looking for Holly. Cody was very worried as he paced back and forth, his thoughts rolled over him, pressing him down. How could he live with himself if something happened to Holly?

Would any of them be able to make it back before the storm hit? What if they all got lost? Suddenly he felt very alone. "Lord, please bring them all back safely, we all just have to come out of this alive and well. Please."

As he sat there his only companion seemed to be the dead man's eyes that still dogged him. Cody sat rigid as every flash of the fire lit the eyes of the dead man staring at him from around every tree. The sound of the crickets seemed to be disguising the sound of branches snapping as he came creeping ever closer. And the hoot of an owl, 'Hoo, Hoo' seemed to say, "Who are you? Come with me!"

When Cody heard hushed voices, he froze and then jumped up as his companions pushed their way through the bushes. He took a deep breath of relief and smiled when he saw that all three of them were there but it was short lived.

Mike made a beeline for him, pushing his face into Cody's, almost touching noses as he snarled, "How would you like it if Michelangelo told you 'get up here and help me paint this ceiling, ANYONE CAN DO IT!' Or Miles handed you a four barrel carburetor, 'Here Cody, I need this by tomorrow morning, FIX IT-ANYONE CAN DO IT!' Or Pattie in accounting, 'I'm going on vacation Cody; you do the payroll this month. ANYONE'..."

Shel pushed in between Mike and Cody. "Mike, it's ok, he didn't know." She put her hand on his chest.

He continued to talk over her head as she gradually pushed him away from Cody. "You don't just belittle people because something comes easy to you!"

"You're right. I'm sorry, Mike. I'm sorry, Holly, I swear I didn't know!"

Holly answered with, "It's alright, Cody. I forgive you," as she took Mike's arm and pulled him away.

Smoke was still coming out of Mike's ears and his

eyes were snapping along with the fire that now seemed to be burning brighter because of the darkness that surrounded it.

As the first raindrops started to fall, Mike's anger shifted gears, dragging sadness in alongside it. When he finally managed to say, "I almost lost her," his voice cracked and he walked away, staring off into the darkness.

As the rain came down hard, Mike's tears were overtaken before they had the chance to get away. The women crawled into the shelter as Cody stood and watched Mike a little longer, before saying, "Mike I'm sorry, I'm sorry."

Lightning struck somewhere close and Holly screamed as the sky lit up and the crash shook the ground. "Mike, please!" He turned and looked at her; the rain was running down her face as she sat half in and half out of the shelter, poised and ready to race towards him at any moment. He came to her, crawling in beside her, holding her close in his arms, speaking soft words of love and comfort for her ears alone.

Even with the fire and the lean-to that covered the opening, the damp cold air cut through them all like knives. With all the tension in the atmosphere, both from the storm and from Mike's unrelenting anger, it proved to be a cold and miserable night.

Mike was still mad, that was quite clear. Cody couldn't really blame him. He felt like he was the moron that Shel had called him. He had been so arrogant about the whole thing and now he was paying for it. Twice this last week he had seen Mike truly mad, and he never wanted to see it again.

They ate the last of the cold turtle meat as the storm raged on. The wind got stronger and the lightning with its thunder louder as the night went on. At about three in the morning, half of the lean-to ripped off and blew away allowing the rain to come pounding in, completely soaking them. All efforts to get dry and stay warm were lost. They all sat up and pressed their backs against the cold rock wall to wait out the long night. Shivering and cold, they huddled together and shielded themselves with their wet sleeping bags, waiting for morning, and hopefully an end to the miserable rain.

15
Mud Wrestling

*A single rebuke does more for a person of
understanding
than a hundred lashes on the back of a fool.
Proverbs 17: 10 NLT*

It was still raining lightly the next morning as the four sat under the overhang looking out at the gloom. They were wet, cold, and sleep-deprived; huddling around a small fire as a cool mist rudely came in, without an invitation. The fire threw sparks that seemingly ignited the vapor that surrounded them and turned it into a white veil that moved translucently but couldn't be penetrated by the naked eye.

"Oh, what I wouldn't give for a hot steaming cup of coffee!" Cody said lightheartedly, glancing over at Mike to see his response.

The women hummed in agreement as Shel began to babble on about coffee and how good it would taste right now. But Mike remained silent, his dark hair and brown eyes made even darker by his mood.

Holly closed her eyes and took another sip from her small tin cup, trying to imagine the steaming liquid as being hot coffee rather than just being water. But try as she might, she could not imagine the smooth, strong, bitter flavor, so she gave up and instead wrapped her fingers tightly around her cup and allowed it to warm her cold fingers as she sipped, thankful for warmth, even though it held no flavor.

Mike was clearly still angry with Cody, who was being overly gracious to make up for the offense of the night before. Everyone but Mike talked loudly, laughing at the most stupid of jokes in order to cover up being uncomfortable with Mike's silence.

But Mike was unmoved by their attempts to lift his spirits. At every response he was required to give, he snapped and growled like a rabid dog until eventually they all left him alone.

Shel brought out the mushrooms that she had collected the day before and laid them out in front of them all. They each took a couple and skewered them onto the ends of small sticks, before hanging them over the fire to roast.

Holly handed her stick to Mike, then pulled out the cans of baked beans and, after opening them, sat them in the hot coals to heat. The labels on the cans burned off right away, the ashes rising and falling into the cans as they burned but no one seemed to care. It didn't take long before the beans were bubbling hot, sending up little puffs of steam as they cooked.

Holly picked up one of the cans with a makeshift hot pad made from a thick sock and began to share her can of beans with Mike, while Cody took up the other can using the sock's mate and shared its contents with Shel. The beans and hot water made them feel a little warmer. And as they huddled closer to the fire it began to dry their clothes, sending up a steam that mixed with the smoke, then rose and rolled out over their heads and into the light of day.

The clouds eventually lifted, so the couples packed up and they quickly moved on. The sun broke through the gray sky, at times throughout the day, as they slogged along. The rain had made the way muddy and slippery, but with each other's help and the long sticks, they managed to stay on their feet somehow.

They moved fast as if to escape the tension they all felt. The anger hung heavier in the air than the fog. The up side was that they made really good time.

By noon they were all exhausted, so they agreed to find a nice place to rest where they could lay out their wet things to dry.

When they finally stopped, Holly took hold of Mike's hand and dragged him out of earshot of the others to talk. "What's the matter with you? Cody said he was sorry, can't you just let it go?"

"Why should I let it go? You would have died in the woods last night if we hadn't found you; died alone from exposure or of being torn apart by wild animals. His stupidity almost took you from me and I couldn't..." he stopped, realizing how selfish he sounded.

"Alright, I understand that Mike, but what about your statement 'Anger is like a sawed-off shotgun. You take careful aim, but everyone that is standing close gets shot as well'. I don't know how many times I've heard you say that to others! And now we're all getting shot, by you, because you're angry and not willing to forgive."

"I don't care. He has to pay for what he did!"

"Is that who you think is paying for YOUR anger? Cody's uncomfortable around you, to be sure, we all are, but you - you're being consumed by it, you're drowning in hatred." She looked at him mournfully then added, "I don't even know who you are right now." She walked away, leaving him standing alone.

Mike wandered off for a while before coming back into camp to find Cody. "Let's go down to the river to see if we can see any signs of civilization. We can check to see if those men are still around while we're at it."

Cody hesitated, then got up and followed him into the woods.

As they walked towards the river, Mike stopped

suddenly and blurted out, "Cody, I'm sorry, I don't know what got into me – well, that's not true, I know what it was but I'm not proud of it." He paused as Cody watched him, waiting for Mike to gather his thoughts before adding, "Holly's always been a soft spot for me. I feel like it's my job to protect her."

"It *IS* your job to protect her Mike! And I'm the one that's sorry. You were right, I guess; we all think, 'if it's easy for me, it must be simple for everyone else'. That's arrogance or ignorance, I guess. And I didn't know she had a problem with getting lost, seriously. I'm more sorry then I can say." He put his right hand out for Mike to take. "Please?"

Mike snatched his hand and pulled him into a bear hug. They held each other for only a second then slapped each others backs twice, before stepping back a respectable distance.

"Ok, good." Mike patted Cody on the shoulder again, as they turned and continued down to the river. "I'm glad to clear the air. We can't afford to be angry at each other if we plan on getting out of this hair-raising experience alive. We need each other's strengths."

Approaching the river cautiously, the two men looked upstream seeing the sun now glaring off the water, causing the water to glimmer like a thousand smaller suns.

Turning and looking downstream they could make out the small faint shape of another bridge, masked by a mist that still hung stubbornly over the water.

"Do you think they're watching that bridge, too?" Mike asked.

"I hope so."

"What?" Mike turned to look at him. "Why do you hope so?"

"Well, because that would mean we're going in the right direction. They wouldn't be standing in our way, if they knew we were headed in the wrong direction and would be dead, soon enough, on our own."

"True. Ok, here's another question for you. Do you think it has even dawned on them that they could track us? I mean, we've been making some pretty serious tracks in this mud today." He raised one foot to show what he was talking about.

They both laughed, as they looked at their shoes, caked with about two to three inches of mud on all sides. The tracks that they had been making looked more like Big Foot tracks than that of humans. And their tracks would, without question, have been easy to follow.

"I guess they're not real bright, or maybe they're just lazy. Of course in all fairness, we have only been making these monstrous tracks today."

Cody sat down on a big rock overlooking the water and thought for a few moments before commenting, "It's hard for me sometimes to think about God loving them too. I mean, that God can be giving them opportunities to repent. At the same time, He's working in my life to teach me about forgiveness. Prompting me to pray for them and thank Him for the trials they're putting me through. That's the hardest part, thanking Him for the trials as I'm going through them."

Mike was struck dumb for some time before he said, "True. You know, I have been questioning the Lord, feeling sorry for myself. I've been thinking only about why He might be doing this to us? I guess it's a matter of seeing the whole picture. What you said is so true; those men do need the Lord. Thanks for putting this whole situation into perspective for me."

Cody smiled in gratitude of Mike's respect. He desired and needed that respect. It was good to know that Mike thought of him as an adult. Even though he was well into his thirties, he had known Mike since he was a baby and still felt like he was just a boy and Mike was the grown man. "Thanks," Cody said with a smile, and then he slapped his hands down on his knees, pushing himself up.

"Ok, buddy, enough of this sappy slobbery stuff, I'm starving. Let's see if we can find something to eat around here."

Kicking off their shoes, they waded into the river and began turning over small rocks on the bottom, near the shore. Mike decided to pull up his shirt to hold the crayfish they found, like Shel had done yesterday while collecting mushrooms.

Cody took note that Mike's belly wasn't sexy like Shel's had been. Her image flashed before his eyes - exciting him - for a moment before leaving him to stare at Mike's belly, that in contrast, was hanging out over his belt, not a lot mind you, but just enough to say, 'Hey, I'm over fifty, give me a break!'

When they got back to their women, Holly was crying and Shel was trying to comfort her without much success.

Seeing the men coming back, Shel jumped up, slightly relieved, and said, "We're going to find something to eat," as she took Cody's hand and pulled him through the trees.

He said, as he looked back, "Is she ok? It's not because of what happened last night is it?"

"Yes and no, it's just catching up with her all of a sudden, the tension, the lack of sleep, being hungry and cold. She's taking this whole 'men are chasing us, trying to kill us' thing pretty hard. She'll be alright; Mike has the cure for what ails her." Beginning to search the trees and undergrowth, Shel responded, "It's fall, so there's not a lot of things to eat out here right now, that I can identify, that is. We may have to eat inner bark."

"What, we're going to eat bark?"

"Oh, not exactly; here let me show you." Finding a

White Pine tree she took out her knife and reached up to the lowest branch on the sunny side of the tree. Taking her knife she laid the blade flat against the bark, then tilted it slightly to cut into and peel away a patch of the rough outer bark. She scored with the point of her knife the white inner bark, cutting out a rectangle shape. She then put the tip of the blade under a corner of what she had just scored and peeled out a creamy white colored piece of pulp.

"Here, chew on this," she said.

Cody reluctantly put it in his mouth as she continued to talk.

"It's full of protein, fat, carbohydrates, vitamins and minerals. The Adirondack Indians used to live through droughts and hard winters on this stuff. People used to call them..." she lowered her voice, "the 'people who eat trees'. I know, it doesn't taste like much, but it will keep you alive and it's healthier than a Big Mac."

"I'll take the Big Mac any day, thank you!"

Shel ignored him and went on. "We'll get some cattail too, to help fill our stomachs."

"You're kidding now, right?"

"Nope!"

They walked toward a marshy area by a stream where Shel stopped to take off her mud caked shoes and stepped barefoot into the water.

As she took hold of one of the cattail stems and pulled, it slipped out of the stalk smoothly, just above the leaves. "I've had some of this before in a salad, it's crisp like a cucumber but it doesn't taste like much; it was cut like a green onion." Then she took a bite. "Oh, it's tough and stringy. That's because it's fall, in the spring it's tender, but that doesn't do us any good now does it?"

She held some out to her husband and he took it reluctantly. After taking a bite he said, "It tastes like eating grass, it needs salt." And with an expression of disgust on his face he spat the fibrous glob out of his mouth.

"Oh well, forget that. Let's try the roots instead." Shel leaned over and started to pull out the roots. Cody watched her intently as she leaned over, just enjoying the view, not even hearing what she was saying anymore.

"What we want are the roots that go out sideways. We can cut them up and eat them like potatoes." She pulled up several and as they released from the mud they made a sucking sound and she slipped, almost falling over backwards. Regaining her balance she then started again with another. And as she pulled up her fifth root, down she went, flat on her back with the mud splashing up around her body as she went into the shallow water. Somehow she managed to hold her head up high enough that the murky water didn't go in her nose or mouth.

When Cody went over to try and help her up, his feet slipped out from under him. Down he went on his backside, his glasses landing on his lap in the mud. He picked them up with two fingers, folded them carefully and stuck them in his shirt pocket. "There has to be a better way of doing this, Babe," he remarked dryly, shaking the mud from his fingertips.

"Nope, this is it. We're muddy now. We might just as well get what we can." She turned onto her hands and knees, putting her bottom in the air before standing with her arms out like a tight rope artist, trying to keep her balance. Cody watched her every move from where he sat. She was dripping muddy water from her shoulders to her toes. Her jeans and top clung to her every curve and as the wind was blowing; she got a chill. Even though his vision was blurry, Cody had no problem envisioning what was happening in front of him.

Shel stopped and looked at him while a slight smile began to play across her lips. She put her hands on her hips and said, with mock disgust, "And what are you looking at, mister?"

"Oh, only the most beeauutifulll woman I've ever seen," he said, in a singsong voice.

"You can't even see me without your glasses!"

"Oh, I can see well enough."

She leaned forward to playfully punch him in the shoulder, but as she did her feet went out from under her again and she landed in his arms. Face to face, he looked her in the eyes and said, "Oh, there you are!"

The fire was the first thing they saw; a welcome sight to the wet, younger couple that needed a dry place to warm themselves. Cody carried with him an armload of cattail root washed and dripping.

When they came around the bushes, they found Mike with his arms wrapped around his wife as they warmed themselves by the fire.

When Holly saw them, she sat up, "What'd you get? Is it something to eat?"

Shel walked over to her and gave her the handful of white pine inner bark. "Here chew on a piece of this Sweetie, it will help you feel better."

Mike stood and took the cattail roots from Cody. "You two are soaked! We can't afford to be wet all night again. You need to get changed, before you get sick. You can tell us what we're supposed to do with these when you get back." He said it with a questioning expression as he looked down at the armload of wet and crazy looking roots, sprawling out in all directions.

They pulled some semi-dry clothes off of the surrounding bushes and the two of them ducked behind the brush to change.

While they had been off on their cattail excursion, Mike had built a fire, and started heating a pot of water for the crayfish that he and Cody had caught earlier. The water started to boil as Shel returned to explain how to prepare cattail root like potatoes.

Holly peeled and cut them up, then dropped them into the boiling water along with the crayfish, making the same chowder they had already had once before. It was good, but they were all looking forward to something more substantial, something bigger, something different, something other than crayfish.

After eating, Shel went off to set some snares, hoping to catch something; whatever it might be. Then they all sat around the campfire chewing on the white pine inner bark. It wasn't a bad flavor, just different. It did seem to help them have some energy and to think more clearly but it wasn't filling at all.

No one seemed to want to go any farther today so they took turns throughout the rest of the afternoon napping.

The men took their time cutting branches and they all helped to build a shelter. It was getting easier and with all of them working on it, the shelter went together nicely.

Night crept up without them noticing as they sat staring sleepily at the fire.

Mike yawned, then said, "Ok guys, its time for me and my bride to go to bed. You young folks have the first watch." He stood, holding his hand out to Holly, helping her up from the ground. "Good night," they both said while walking towards the shelter, each scooping up a damp sleeping bag as they went. Only the thinnest of things they had laid out earlier that afternoon, had actually dried. So, with difficulty they zipped the damp sleeping bags together and then slid inside, snuggling to keep warm.

It had been a long day and they were very tired, but how would they sleep, and what would tomorrow hold for them?

16
The Cavern

*Give your burdens to the LORD,
and he will take care of you.
Psalm 55: 22 NLT*

As they started out on the fifth day, Holly said as she chewed on a piece of the inner bark, "Mike, I think you need to start praying that the Lord blesses the food to our bodies again, we need all the blessings we can get right now. Oh yeah, and while you're at it, could you pray that this stuff would taste like a steak dinner with a baked potato and a green salad on the side, please?"

"What?" Mike raised his eyebrows and turned to see an ornery smile spreading across her face. Seeing that she was feeling a little better he smiled back.

"Just saying!" She said with big eyes as they all began to laugh.

Getting back on the game trail they began walking more easily, using the long sticks that Mike had sharpened as walking sticks, with their points in the air. As they trudged along they moved away from the water and onto slightly less muddy ground, easier walking made Holly feel almost happy, like they were old-time adventurers. So much so that she started to sing,

♪ 'Valer-ie! Val-er-ah! Valer-ie!
124

Val-er-ah-ha-ha-ha-ha-ha.' ♪

"That's a perfect hiking song!" Mike said as they all joined in:

♪ "As I go a wandering, along the mountain path,
And as I go, I love to sing,
with my knapsack on my back!
Valerie! Valer-ah!
Valer-ie! Valer-ah-ha-ha-ha-ha-ha
Valerie! Val-er-aah!
With my knapsack on my back!" ♪

It felt good to be laughing again, even if it was just in the song lyrics. They only sang for a short time as none of them had the strength to keep it up for very long.

As they went along their way, they saw tracks that looked like little human handprints with splayed fingers.

"What is that?" Holly asked.

"Oh, it's either a skunk, an opossum, or maybe a raccoon," Mike stated. "Judging by their size, I'd say it's a raccoon."

Shel stated, "Opossum are nasty, rat-like looking things and raccoons are just creepy, don't you think? I don't know why, maybe it's because I don't like hairy animals that much. I actually always thought if I were to have a hairy pet at all, it would have to be a skunk. I knew someone who had one as a pet once, and it was soft and gentle."

The others stared, curling their noses in disbelief.

Finally Mike said bitterly. "I don't really know about skunks or opossums but I agree with you about raccoons. They are creepy; they're like great big rats," "People that live in town don't want them around destroying their properties, digging through their garbage cans, chewing on their sheds, porches and so forth. They don't see them as a pest but instead of dealing with it, they go: 'oh they're cute'!" He made a high pitched mocking voice, then continued, "So, they trap the nasty things 'humanely' and dump them out in the country, where they become our problem instead. I'm not sure how humane or cute it is when we find thirty chickens killed in one night by a single raccoon. Then it only eats half of one and leaves the rest to rot. No, you're right, they are creepy," he spat out again.

Cody cut in before Mike could say another word. "Alright Mike, I think we get the idea."

"Mike honey, I know you loved your chickens but you're going to have to let that one go. It's not doing you any good. And like you always tell me, 'The seed of bitterness produces like seed'."

"Sorry, I'm just starving to death and I'd eat one of those nasty vermin right now if I could get ahold of one. Shoot! I'd eat thirty of them, maybe with a little help from my friends."

"I'd help you for sure, sounds like everyone would profit from it, especially your chickens," Cody said sarcastically.

"This wet sleeping bag is so heavy, strapped on my back," Shel said, "and my clothes are only semi-dry. Everything I have has mud or sweat on it, or both. We have to find a way to at least dry these sleeping bags out some before we have to sleep in them again."

"There has to be a clothes dryer out here somewhere," Holly said cheerfully.

"Here, let me trade you backpacks. The raft I'm carrying can't be as heavy as that wet thing," Cody said, sliding his backpack to the ground and lifting hers.

"No, sorry babe, the wet backpack still weighs less than the rubber raft."

"I think you're right about finding a dryer out here somewhere honey, I don't think I can stand sleeping in that wet thing again tonight."

But they couldn't stop now; wanting to get past the bridge that lay a short distance ahead of them. Hopefully, they could get far enough past it by mid-afternoon, to be able to start an inconspicuous fire tonight. However, the bridge was actually farther away than it looked. As they grew closer to the bridge they could make out a man standing in the middle of it. He seemed almost as if he wanted to be seen by them.

They had been walking on solid rock for some time now and as they walked the dry mud fell off their shoes in massive chunks, leaving a clear trail that anyone could have followed, if they knew where to start looking.

They kept moving among the trees, trying to stay in the shadows as they crossed the road, taking only a few short breaks throughout the day.

As the day drew to an end it started to look like they were going to be sleeping in damp bags once again, and this time without a fire to keep them warm.

It was getting dark quickly and they were all stumbling, both from the encroaching darkness and shear exhaustion. When it seemed they could go no farther, Mike said, "We should have been praying for the Lord's guidance today, we have to stop somewhere and soon."

Cody stepped up beside Shel and took her hand as they continued to walk and began to pray out loud, "Lord help us to..."

Just then he felt Shel's hand tearing out of his, pulling him down to his knees before he lost his grip on her. He could hear her screaming quietly as she slid away from him and then the screaming stopped.

"Shel!" He yelled quietly into the dark hole he hadn't seen before, the hole that Shel had disappeared into. Trying to be mindful of the man on the bridge, less than a mile away, he yelled again quietly, "Shel!"

Mike and Holly pushed in close beside him.

"Shel! Are you alright?" Holly yelled with a harsh whisper as she leaned into the large round hole, "Shel?"

Shel's answer came from somewhere beneath them, "I'm ok. It's a cave. But I can't see anything, I need a flashlight."

Holly quickly rummaged through her bag and pulled out one of the flashlights. She pointed it down the hole and turned it on. She sat it inside, sliding it down the smooth steep slope. The flashlight spun around and around, showing the insides of a large cavern as it slid to where Shel stood at the bottom.

Shel quickly picked it up and started to look around. "This is it guys," she said, "this is the answer to our prayer! We'll need some firewood, plus a way to get back out of here though." She turned and looked back up at the others above.

"The rope!" Cody said, as he slipped off his backpack and undid the strap that held the rope to it.

The men turned and started to look for anything that would burn. They moved as quickly as they could in the fading light. They couldn't chance using the other flashlight or the hatchet, so they did the best they could with the little remaining sunlight. Then they carried the firewood to the opening and sent it hurtling down as Shel cleared it away at the bottom.

Holly tied the rope to a tree that had grown out of the rock near the opening of the cave and carefully slid their backpacks down, one at a time. Lastly, she slid down herself, squealing with delight as she did.

Mike and Cody finished gathering the wood, then concealed the rope from clear view before sliding down to join their wives.

The cavern was perfect. Using the flashlight, they could see that on the right side of it was a natural shelf that was raised up slightly off the main floor. It traveled the length of the chamber and was about thirty feet long and ten feet deep.

Shel had started to build a fire on the shelf floor and the fire was now sending out sputtering light as she struggled to keep it lit. Their backpacks sat next to her, some of the contents spilling out onto the dry ground. "This will be a perfect place to set up camp," she said to herself. "We'll be warm and dry here. Now if we can only find something to eat." As the small fire began to burn well on it's own, she sat back and looked at her surroundings.

The floor below the shelf tilted towards the middle of the chamber and into a channel that ran towards the back of the cavern, disappearing through an opening in the wall. Clearly during the wet season the cave had a steady stream of water running through it, as it made its way down to the river.

Once the men finished stacking the wood, they decided to explore what seemed to be two more chambers. The first had steam rolling out of its cool entrance. As they entered it they saw a pool of water that was bubbling from somewhere underneath the surface.

"It's a hot spring! We have a hot tub!" Holly squealed as she looked in over the men's shoulders. "I can't wait to take a bath!" She had seen all she needed to see and so she ran back to tell Shel all about it.

"It is a hot springs! Oh, the Lord is good!" Mike said as he pointed the flashlight to where the bubbles and steam were coming up out of the water. "I'd be careful not to get too close to that if I were you, it could be pretty hot. Who knows how far that water had to travel through volcanic rock to get here?"

They pulled their shoes off and slowly tested the shallow edge of the pool.

"Oh man, I so need this!" Cody said, as he waded in and wiggled his cold, pruned toes and just stood there, in the hot steaming water.

The room was filled with a wonderful warm mist

that smelled of earth. The water in the pool gradually got deeper going towards its bubbling center. About two-feet up on the wall of the pool was a small crack, where the water funneled out into the next chamber. They felt as if they could stand there in that wonderful warm water forever. But, being men, they moved on to explore further.

Exiting the hot tub section, they entered the next chamber. The opening was narrow and shaped a little like an umbrella lying on its side to dry. The men squeezed through the narrow opening and found a clear pond inside the biggest of the three chambers. It measured approximately sixty feet, in every direction.

As they stepped down onto the rocks, which worked like uneven steps, they noticed that even though the water was cool it wasn't cold. They knew of at least one hot spring that fed into the pond and they could now see that there were more spots where bubbles came up, sending out steam, keeping the pond semi-warm.

From the ceiling hung five large white uneven stalactites as water streamed down the walls from various cracks and crevices, it was like standing in the mouth of a huge drooling monster. At the far end of the pond was a round opening where the water poured out, as if it were running down the monster's dark throat.

The water was absolutely clear, making it impossible to tell how deep it actually was. But it was obvious that the center was much deeper than where they both now stood on the edge of the pond.

The light of the flashlight danced off the surface of the water like it was one big diamond, showing off its many facets, throwing flashes of light that reflected off the wet ceiling and walls. They stood there and admired the beauty of it for what seemed a long time before continuing on.

Moving deeper into the chamber, they waded

along the edge so they could look down the monster's throat. The water began to push them from behind, and as they got closer to the throat it forced them forward against the small opening as they stood in the water's way of escape. Looking out of the hole like a window, they could see what remained of the sunlight reflecting off the river below. The water rushed around them, then fell four to six feet straight down from the opening, cascading over the steep wall, to form a waterfall.

"Perfect," Mike said, "we could hang fish hooks out and maybe catch us some breakfast. We may have to make a hook out of a pin or something, unless Shel brought some fishing gear in one of the packs."

"Aren't there any fish in here?" Cody asked.

"I don't know; there might be. Did you see any?"

"No, but there certainly could be. I've seen on nature shows where they found blind fish in some cave."

"True, but I'd rather hang the hooks where I know for sure there are fish. I think we would all rather eat a fish we recognize than some kind of albino cave creature, with no eyes!"

"Yeah, I guess."

Turning around, they pushed their way back against the current to return to where they had left the women in the first chamber.

The fire was burning strong now and the women had tied a clothesline near it, where they had the sleeping bags hanging to dry. They were all very grateful that they each would get to take a hot bath tonight.

Shel had filled their canteens with water she had gotten from a small waterfall coming out of the cave's wall. She and Holly had already drunk all the cool fresh water they could hold without bursting. It filled their shrunken stomachs, easing their hunger, but also made them feel colder, sending them closer to the fire.

Holly had cut up the cattail root and put it in a pan of water over the fire to boil. As she dropped the roots in, she thought how inadequate it looked for their dinner. She sat and stared at the pot as it began to boil, then prayed to herself, "Lord please, this can't be all we have to eat, we need our strength to keep going, please Lord." She then poked at the fire and said nothing more, her head filled with doubts and fear.

When the men came back dripping wet Mike said, "Shel, did you pack any fishing gear?"

She looked at him with a slight sneer that said 'are you kidding me?' Then grabbed his backpack and pulled out a small plastic box full of fishing line and hooks. "There you go!" She said as she handed it back to him.

"Oh, that's what that box is!" He said as he examined the contents of the kit. "Ok, thanks!" And off he went with a flashlight and the fishing kit. Mike needed to wade through the water one more time before attempting to get dry for the night, so he slid quickly through the opening and disappeared inside.

Cody started to tell the women about the hot tub and the pond as he stood dripping beside the fire. Stepping behind the hanging sleeping bags with his pack, he began to remove his wet clothes. "This cave is amazing!" He continued, after wrestling his wet shirt up over his head, knocking his glasses off in the process. He sat on the floor of the cave and pulled his pants inside out in an attempt to free himself from their manic grip. His pants had taken on a life of their own, making a sucking sound as they fought to hang on to his legs with every dripping ounce of life they had in them, only to release his feet one-by-one to fly out in front of him, kicking.

Cody pulled one of the damp sleeping bags off the line and wrapped himself in it, then stepping over to the fire, he sat down next to Shel. His dirty wet clothes were still lying on the ground, needing to be washed.

Holly was coming back from washing her and Mike's clothes, when the three of them heard a growl from the opening of the cave. Cody turned and seized the stick that Shel had been poking the fire with while Shel dove for her bow; quickly nocked an arrow and drew back the bowstring. Cody stepped forward with the flaming stick extended out in front of him. Holly just stood back with her mouth hanging open as her armload of dripping laundry dropped at her bare feet, making a loud smacking sound as it hit the stone floor.

All three stood quietly and listened at what must have been a bear as it seemingly paced back and forth, grumbling to itself. Then growled low and long, one last time before leaving.

As Cody turned to look at the women, he thought of the classic picture of the three monkeys sitting in a row. Holly's eyes were big as she held her hands over her mouth. Shel had the bowstring pulled back covering her ear; and Cody was blinded from the flame he had been trying to stare through.

"How's that old saying go?" He said after rubbing his eyes, he put his glasses back on, "Monkey hear, monkey speak, monkey sees? It's something like that, right?"

Shel and Holly just turned and stared at him as if he was crazy. "What?"

17
Twenty-Two Snakes

Whenever you stand praying,
if you have anything against anyone,
forgive him, that your Father in heaven may also
forgive you your trespasses.   Mark 11:25 NKJV

The fire lit up the water particles that hung in the air, giving the chamber a warm and peaceful glow. Mike was humming as he came back from setting out the fishing lines.

"Look what I caught!" He said as he held up a good-sized brown trout. "I was stringing out the lines one by one and dropping them in the water and before I could lower the last hook, I caught this fish on the first hook I let down!"

They all turned to look at him, "What's the matter now?" He stopped, noticing their expressions, Cody was blinking hard, Shel was holding her bow at her side and Holly was picking up the wet laundry she had dropped on the floor.

"Wait, this isn't one of Shel's friends too, is it?" He looked down at the fish hungrily.

"NO! We just heard a bear at the opening of the cave," Shel said and added, slightly annoyed, "It's a nice looking fish but- it's Not My Friend!"

"You heard a bear?" He exclaimed, missing her little speech.

The three of them began to talk at once. Cody

growled, imitating the bear and the cave reverberated with the sound, making Cody's first attempt at a bear calling, satisfying, so he smiled.

But Holly, instead of being pleased, covered her ears and began to cry. "Please stop!" and with that, she ran away, escaping into the small hot springs chamber.

Cody just looked at Mike, "I'm sorry Mike, I was just showing you how it sounded."

"I know. It's fine," Mike said as he handed him the fish. "Save half of that for us, go ahead and eat." Then he turned to follow his wife into the hot tub chamber.

When Mike entered, he was engulfed by the steam and found Holly sitting with her back against the wall, her knees drawn up.

"I'm sorry Mike, I don't know what got into me," she said as she shook with a tearful tremor. "I just don't know how much of this I can take, while the rest of you seem to be fine."

"Shh," he put his finger to her lips, "it's ok, you just need some down time Sweetheart, let's make this a spa night." He then pulled off his clothes and stepped into the pool, and sat with his arms resting on either side as he waited for his bride.

The flashing fire in the next chamber lit the cave slightly with a faint flickering light similar to a candle burning. Holly slowly took off her clothes; the dark walls behind her silhouetting her rounded pale curves. She stepped through the mist and her lips pursed with an "Ohhhh," as her cold toes gingerly touched the pool of hot bubbling water. Her eyes closed as she drew her head back slowly and took in a long, deep breath. Her red spiraled hair began to grow heavy with the vapor that hung in the air, clinging to her mist-kissed shoulders.

With each step she took, the water welcomed her in, wrapping itself around her legs and working its way up her body, until she laid her head back on her husband's broad chest. A contented smile rested on her lips as she sighed.

Mike took it all in with longing eyes before he made his move to steal a kiss; a kiss that eagerly welcomed her.

Mike and Holly talked low and quietly; words of love, encouragement, comfort and prayer. It was good to be in love, to have someone to walk with into utter danger then, hopefully, walk back out again. They sat and talked for over an hour, wrapped in each other's arms, before they decided it was time to get out.

They came back with tight red skin and wet hair, feeling very refreshed.

Holly approached Cody and said, "I think I'm probably going to be saying it a lot until we get out of this predicament, but I'm sorry Cody."

"It's alright. I understand. I wouldn't have been as nice as you were about it if I had to deal with someone as irritating as I am."

"Amen to that!" Shel threw in.

"Hey!"

"Ok you two," Mike jumped in before things got ugly. "Can we eat now? We're starved."

He and Holly sat down to eat what Cody and Shel had left for them. Mike had never been a fan of fish, but this particular piece of fish, on a bed of boiled cattail root, was among the most amazing meals he had ever eaten. He decided it could have something to do with the fact that his stomach had made up its own language, in translation the gurgling said, 'Oh yeah, that's good!'

After a long silence spent staring into the fire, Shel began to speak, "Mike, I can't believe you thought that fish were my friends! What's that supposed to mean anyhow?" She snapped, making it more than clear that she was a little irritated.

"Oh, I'm sorry Shel, I didn't mean to hurt your

feelings. I thought that the fish was kind of pretty myself."

"How did that whole 'Shel's friends' thing get started anyways?" Cody asked no one in particular as his eyes stayed on the fire, his glasses reflecting the flames as they licked at the air.

"I don't know..." Mike said, turning back to the fire.

"Oh I might have started it," Holly said. "Sorry!" She flinched in Shel's direction.

"Ok, how about you tell us what animals are your friend... your favorites; well, maybe your friends?" Mike was making fun of her now so she hauled off and slapped him on the arm while everyone laughed. "Oww!" Mike howled.

"Oh, you Sooo deserved that," she said smiling in mock revenge.

"Yeah, you most definitely did Mike," Cody added, supportively.

"Oww - I thought we guys could stick together."

"What! - And take the chance of getting slapped myself? No thanks."

They all chuckled. It felt nice to laugh again, as they went back to gazing into the fire.

After a few quiet minutes, Holly said, "Oh Shel, tell us that snake story you told me the other day. That was funny!"

"Snakes are your friends?" Mike asked as he moved quickly out of her range. But she just glared at him as the corners of her mouth turned up into a sneer.

"What snake story?" Cody asked. "Have I heard the snake story?"

"No, but Holly was telling one of her childhood stories and it reminded me of the time Drew and I caught some snakes and got in big trouble for it."

"You got in trouble for it?" Cody asked.

"Well, you have to tell us the story now," Mike

said. "I like to hear stories about friends."

Shel ignored his taunt and sat quietly thinking for a second, before beginning. "When I was little, my Dad used to worked at a place where they made farm equipment. You know, livestock watering troughs and feeders and things, like hand water pumps; they even made those miniature windmills. The kind that you see standing in people's yards, I know you've seen them."

"Well, one day he brought home a big round watering trough, probably eight to nine foot across, for us kids to swim in. There were five of us siblings, along with three neighbor kids who liked to swim too. Day after day, the pool was always crowded, and we had a lot of arguments about who should move their feet and it's my turn to swim around everybody, you know, things like that."

"Until one day my brother Drew and I got the bright idea to put snakes in the pool. Since neither of us were afraid of snakes and everyone else hated them, we thought we'd have the pool to ourselves."

"We eagerly started looking for snakes early the next morning and then dropped them into the pool. The kids in the pool screamed as they fell over themselves trying to get out and every time we'd put another snake in, more protest went up from the kids that stood watching. We knew we were being bad, but we kept on doing it anyway, getting some kind of perverse pleasure out of it, you know, laughing at the other kids torment."

"All day long we worked diligently, keeping count as we went. We looked in the garden, in the yard, under rocks and in the fields surrounding our property. By the time our Dad got home, we had twenty-two snakes in the pool! Big ones, small ones, even little baby snakes no bigger than a large earthworm."

"We knew somewhere inside we had done wrong,

but we wanted our Dad's stamp of approval just the same. We told ourselves he would be proud of us for being diligent, for sticking to the task at hand. We thought he would laugh with us about how funny the whole thing was."

"When we saw him coming, we ran over to him and grabbed his hands, pulling him over to the pool to look at what we had spent our entire day doing. We thought he would be happy but he wasn't happy at all! Instead, he looked around to see the sad and crying faces of the other kids. We tried to drown them out with our arguments but our excuses were flimsy."

"'Why'd you do this?' He said thoughtfully, 'what were you thinking?' Taking us aside, he sat us down and explained gently and calmly what we had actually done. 'You were being selfish about the pool,' he explained, 'you wanted to be in control of who swam in it, so you made it so that not only could the others not enjoy it, but you didn't have time to enjoy it either. Even if you had gone swimming, those snakes you professed to like probably would have bitten you. You know I just cleaned that pool out last night, and now you two are going to get in the pool and get all those snakes out! Then you're going to completely clean the pool again with soap and water. And tomorrow, you're going to watch as the other kids enjoy the pool and you will not be allowed to go in. Do you understand why?' We both nodded yes, then we received the spanking we knew full well we deserved."

Shel then began to reflect, "I think that we spend a lot of time in life thinking we're doing good. We reach out to the world, we go to the prisons, we witness to our neighbors and on the street. But we ignore that God tells us to 'Love one another', 'To love our brothers as ourselves' and 'That the world will know us by our love one for another'. The church seems to be suffering from a lack of love on the inside, and the world knows it. And it's not interested in what we have, because what we have is shallow."

"I wonder if when God looks into the 'pool of our lives', will He find that we have blessed our brothers and sisters in Christ? Will He see them basking in the Son, splashing in the water of the Word? Or, will He find instead that we have filled our pools with backbiting, gossip and unforgiveness, reflecting that serpent that is our enemy. Have we made our brothers and sisters stand on the outside crying, because we won't let them in? Have we spent our time here deciding who we think gets to enter into our Father's pool?"

"I think we each need to examine how we treat our brothers and sisters in the Lord. Then, once we have made things right in the church, then we can go witness to the world and they will see the truth of Christ's love in us. If we don't do that first, we're simply spinning our wheels. And how then can we expect God to come to us and say, 'Well done, good and faithful servant'!"

"Wow," Mike pulled on the short beard that had started growing on his face. "That's a cool analogy, it sounds like Mark 11:25, that says, '*Whenever you stand praying, if you have anything against anyone forgive him, that your Father in heaven may also forgive you your sins*'."

"You didn't tell me your whole allegory thing on this story the other day," Holly said.

"Well, I've had an awful lot of time to think lately, with the absence of electronic devices beeping, ringing and demanding my attention, it's amazing the time I have to reflect on things now."

Holly curled her nose as she asked, "That's a lot of snakes, isn't it?"

"Yeah, but I grew up just outside of the black swamp area of Ohio. It seemed normal to us and they were just garter snakes."

Cody smiled, "That was good, Babe, that was very

good!"

Mike wailed with a head splitting yawn. He had been looking like he would fall over at any second for some time now and Holly looked about the same, adding her own almost silent yawn.

"You and Holly need to go to bed. Shel and I will take the first watch."

"Sounds good to me, I couldn't make it much longer anyhow," Mike said as he and Holly got up and climbed into their warm dry sleeping bags. Before long he could be heard snoring quietly while she breathed deeply.

Cody and Shel sat quietly for a long time, watching the fire as it burned down, until finally Shel asked, "So, what was it you wanted to tell me later? It's later."

"Oh Shel," Cody said, "promise me you won't start yelling at me, that you'll listen to the whole story before you react?"

Shel's face became grave as her eyes narrowed. "Oh... Kay?" She said slowly.

"Alright, here goes, I had been flirting at work with Julie Salamon for a long time, but last Wednesday I made a pass at her and Mike said a lot of people saw it. So on the way home he let me have it. I tried to change the subject by talking about your meatloaf, but Mike didn't fall for it. He corrected me on a number of different levels; I got mad and jumped out of his SUV and walked home. There it is, you know the rest," he abruptly finished.

Shel sat with her mouth hanging open then questioned him with, "Julie? Why Julie?" Her eyes flared with jealousy.

"What do you mean?"

"What Do You Mean 'what do I mean'? You moron!" She raised her voice as she hurled the words at him.

"Shel, you said you wouldn't yell at me!"

"Well, I lied I guess, Just Like You!"

"How'd I lie? I told you everything!"

"And how long had you been flirting before you decided to tell me everything? How can I trust that you don't have another hidden secret?"

Cody expected Shel to get mad and he expected this conversation to be hard, but now he could feel his blood starting to boil and he screamed, "THAT'S IT! STOP!"

"You made a pass at Julie Salamon and because you scream 'STOP!' This conversation's supposed to be over, are you serious?"

Cody walked away, staring into the darkness, his arms folded over his chest. Then, dropping his arms, he took a deep breath and came back. He sat down and was quiet for a moment as his expression melted from anger to sorrow. "Shel, I'm sorry, it won't happen again, I promise you!" He took his glasses off and slipped them into his shirt pocket. He began to massage his forehead with his fingertips. Cody had told himself he wouldn't let his flesh get the upper hand again. But, he had failed once more. He took a deep breath and let it all out. "Shel, please forgive me!" he said as he lowered his hands.

Shel's voice softened. "You know Cody, if it hadn't been Julie you were talking about, or if I didn't know her as well as I do, you would've had to sign that promise with blood. But as it is, if Will finds out, he's going to punch your lights out! I might just get that blood sacrifice after all."

"He knows- and he forgave me."

"What? You talked to him about it?"

"Yeah, when you sent me over to get the tent."

A smile began to turn up the corners of her mouth. "No wonder you were trying to get out of going over there." She covered her mouth and began to laugh uncontrollably.

It irritated Cody at first. He swallowed hard trying

to control his anger but then realized that their dispute was over. And, he began to laugh too, as relief washed over him.

Mike then said, as he lay in his sleeping bag, not fifteen feet away from the arguing couple, "Ok guys, that's great, now do you think you two can hold it down a little so we can get some sleep here?"

"Mike!" Holly scolded. "Shhhhhh!"

Cody and Shel tried hard to suppress their laughter as they stoked the fire and burned the fish bones. They didn't want to take the chance of that bear coming back, even though they couldn't see how the bear could get down to them, short of sliding down on its bottom like they had had to do. And the picture of a bulky bear sliding down the slope brought them both to tears, as they laughed some more.

18
Bear Claw

Rebellion is as witchcraft,
and stubbornness as bad as worshiping idols.
1 Samuel 15: 23 NLT

Cody awoke to Mike kicking his foot and the sound of voices outside the cave.

Mike had a finger to his lips and when Cody's eyes met his, Mike nodded towards the back of the cavern to indicate that they needed to move farther back.

Their wood supply had run out long ago, so all that was left of the fire were hot red coals. Shel was already awake, when Cody shook off his sleeping bag and put on his clean dry clothes. Holly poured a pan of water over the red embers and the coals hissed as steam rose into the air. The ash then floated gently back down to the floor of the cave as the smoke and steam mingled with the mist from the hot springs and together they rolled out of the entrance above.

Mike and Holly quickly scooped up all of their belongings and moved them to the back of the cavern while Shel stood poised, bow drawn, ready to shoot the first man that dared to come through the opening. Still the voices got louder as the men grew ever closer.

"I saw a weird light thingy and the bear right about

here," Leroy said. "Look, see, isn't that bear tracks? I told you I saw a bear."

"I don't see any tracks, this here's rock," Chuck said, stamping his foot down to prove his point. "How can you see tracks on rock?"

"Look right there, that's mud! And I say that's a bear track."

"Ok, there was a bear here, so what? This is bear country you know. That track could have been there for months."

"Or hours."

"Sure, but that doesn't prove anything. You said you saw 'twinkling lights in the trees out this way, too', where do you think we are, 'Disneyland'?" Chuck said while throwing his hands up and wiggling all his fingers to show mock excitement. "Now, what does a bear have to do with twinkling lights?" He swung around looking in all directions for the hidden amusement park.

"I know what I saw! Wait, look there's some kind of a cave, it's probably a bear cave!" Leroy said as he walked over to investigate it.

"Nope the openings too small," Chuck said and rolled his eyes.

"Well, then maybe it's a small bear? Look- there's a shoe print!" Just then they heard what sounded like a bear growl coming from inside the cave. "Oh man, let's get out of here!" Leroy said, jumping from the opening.

"No, wait a minute, let's shoot it," Chuck said pulling his gun out from the back of his pants and stepping closer to the cave opening.

"Are you crazy? If you don't kill him with the first shot, it'll kill us both! And chances aren't good you'll be able to kill him with that little handgun of yours!"

"What about those flashing lights you said you saw?" He mocked again. "Don't you want to find out what they were?"

"It's not worth getting killed over! I'm getting out of here." He turned and walked away leaving Chuck poking around the opening of the cave, his gun drawn.

As Chuck moved closer to the opening of the cave he heard a sudden swishing sound. He fell backwards, yelling in pain, screaming, and grabbing at his leg. There was a cut in his pant leg, and blood was wetting his calf. "What the...!" He jumped up, turning all the way around, looking for the invisible claws that had swiped at him. Another growl came from inside the cave, louder and angrier sounding this time. He jumped away again, almost falling over a stump as he yelled. When the bear growled yet again, he decided he had had enough, stumbling and yelling he ran back down the path. Then turning and looking back to see if he was being chased, he then SMACKED hard into a tree, knocking himself unconscious. As he fell to the ground, his gun went off with a loud KA-BANG!

Leroy, hearing Chuck's scream and his gun firing, started to run away as fast as he could. He jumped into the truck and waited for Chuck for a few seconds but when he didn't show, he started the pick up and peeled out, burning rubber and leaving a trail of blue smoke as it fishtailed down the road, vanishing into the mountain mist.

Shel stood with her bow drawn while a man stood as a dark silhouette, with a gun in his hand, looking down into their cave. Behind her Cody let out a growl.

"Stop that, you moron!" Shel hissed as the taut bowstring pulled free of her numb fingers, sending the arrow flying up and out of the opening of the cave. She took in a breath of surprise and looked with shock at Cody.

One of the men yelled and Shel stepped back deeper into the cave. The thought that she may have shot one of them, or have given their position away, made her feel sick.

Filled with nervous energy, Cody stepped forward and let out another growl, even fiercer than the first one. The man at the top of the cave yelled again, the sound of it fading as he obviously ran away.

Still listening intently, they heard the sound of a single gunshot off in the distance!

"What happened?" Mike asked as he stepped up with an arm still wrapped around Holly.

Cody said with a horse voice, "I have no idea, but I think God just did a miracle for us, at least I hope so!"

Shel stared up at the morning light that streamed into the cave from above and she began to nervously chatter, "My arrow slipped out of my fingers and..." she paused for a second before finishing with, "I don't know if it hit him but when Cody growled again, he just turned and ran away. He must not have been hurt too badly, right?" She turned to study their faces for confirmation, distress frozen on her face.

"Maybe that bear got them," Holly said, burying her face in Mike's chest, and then whispered for his ears alone, "Hold me, Puppy."

Cody said, "I don't think we should spend any more time down here. They could come back at any time and we don't want to be here if they do. I'm going up to look around, and if it's safe we need to go. I'll be right back."

"Be careful," Shel said clasping his arm.

"I will, Babe." He kissed her forehead, and then, pulling away he climbed up through the opening with the help of the concealed rope.

Cody followed a small blood trail leading away from the entrance of the cave. Stuck in the soft mud beyond the rock he found Shel's arrow, with a streak of blood on one side. Not seeing the men anywhere, he stuck his head back into the cave opening. "All's clear, let's get going." They tied their bags to the rope and Cody pulled them up. Then he helped each of his companions as they crawled up and out of the cavern.

After they had been traveling for a couple of hours they stopped for a short break where Holly pulled Shel aside.

"What's up?"

"I just thought I should remind you that, you as a Christian woman, should treat your husband with respect. And you're not showing him respect when you call him names like moron."

"I'll respect him when he deserves to be respected."

Holly stood with her mouth hanging open. "Ok, question. Do you think that he should love you unconditionally?"

"Of course," she said impatiently as if the concept was elementary.

"But you're only going to respect him when he earns it? Is that what I'm hearing?"

Flames shot from Shel's eyes as she snapped back, "Who asked you? Mind your own business." Then she turned and stormed off.

"That's a double standard Shel! Come on, just pray about it! Shel, please!" She called after her, but she had already moved out of earshot.

There was a wall between the two women throughout the day and Shel avoided speaking to Holly altogether. Down deep she knew that Holly was right, but still she was steaming mad. She had indeed assumed that Cody should give her unconditional love while he had to deserve her respect. The more she thought about it, the madder she got. Finally though, she began to whisper a prayer, "Help me Lord to see what I should do and what You expect of me."

Suddenly everything became clear to her. She had been moving through her and Cody's marriage in rebellion to him, bucking against the authority that God had given to him to lead. A scripture came to mind that said that 'rebellion was as witch craft'. She didn't know where that scripture was or what it was talking about exactly, but she knew it was the word that the Lord wanted to speak to her right here, right now. So she began to calm herself and allowed it to speak to her.

"I don't want to be in rebellion to You Lord, or Your will for my life. Please help me to be respectful to Cody." She had a hard time even whispering the prayer, so she added, "Lord, I'm doing this for you as a sacrifice of love, in obedience to your word."

Throughout the day Holly blamed herself for the tension between the two of them. "Maybe I should've kept my mouth shut. I should have just lived as an example of a submissive wife before Shel. She'll never come to me now for anything." Holly had worked so hard to be more than pleasant and accommodating towards Shel, with no response other than her turning farther and farther away from Holly's overwhelming kindness. She felt like crying to think she had lost a friend, a dear friend. She thought their friendship would never be the same again, and Holly needed her friend right now more than ever.

Despair swept over her and she was about to start crying, when Shel stepped up beside her and gave her hand a squeeze, a warm tear ran down Holly's cheek as if somehow it had been sent forth by the squeezing of her hand. A smile passed between the two women. And without a word, they were friends once again.

19
Grub Worms

Be anxious for nothing,
but in everything by prayer and supplication,
with thanksgiving,
let your requests be made known to God;
Philippians 4:6 NKJV

The fog was beginning to lift just after noon when they all stopped for another break. Since there wasn't anything to eat, Shel decided to go off alone to look for something. But the ground was steep and rocky and all she could find among the evergreens were some old overly mature mountain mint, buried under the fallen leaves of the hardwood trees.

'*I won't be finding any cattail around here,*' she thought to herself. She had her bow with her but all she could see to hunt was an occasional spray of birds that sprang up in front of her as she walked.

"Too small and too fast," she muttered in a defeated tone. She felt so alone, even abandoned as she pleaded, "Lord, I know You love us but I just can't see You right now. I'm so discouraged; please don't let us starve to death out here."

She sat down on a rock and began to clear away the dead leaves that stuck in a patch of mint. Picking out what hadn't been eaten by bugs, fallen to the ground or had simply dried on the branch. In the end what she held in her hand wasn't even enough to make a good cup of tea. She threw it in frustration only to watch as the leaves flitted through the air and floated to the ground bringing her no satisfaction for the energy she had spent.

"If you're trying to humble me Lord, it's working! Consider me humbled. I feel so stupid, like I don't know anything. You are our provider, Lord. Forgive me for being so proud. Please don't forsake us because of my arrogance."

She knew that wasn't the way God worked but she had no more energy to give, she was ready to give up when she heard a still small voice saying, "I will never leave you nor forsake you."

"Thank You Lord," she said, a tear rolled down her face as she stooped to collect the mint back up and started out again. While walking back to the others she noticed an old decaying stump speckled with large holes. She stopped and stared at it thoughtfully.

"Oh, why not?" she said giving it a forceful kick. The stump split in two while several smaller pieces flew in the air. There they were, grub worms, the stars of most survival shows. Shel loved to watch that kind of show, but hated seeing people biting into those nasty worms. She thought that they put those scenes in for their shock factor, in her hunger though, she may need to reconsider. "Maybe they really aren't that bad, maybe this is the way the Lord is providing for us?" She thought about that for a second longer then said, "No, He can do better than this!"

Still, desperation drove her to her knees. She began to search her pockets for something to put the worms in, and found an old zip-lock sandwich bag she had stuffed in her jacket pocket a month or so ago when she couldn't find a trash can. She then took a deep breath and started to pick up the worms and, one by one, began to put them into the baggie.

"Eeewww, you guys are nasty!" They squirmed between her fingers as she lifted them; their short fat bodies giving way to the gentle pressure of her fingers, writhing around in circles trying with everything they had in them to wiggle out of the grasp of whatever held them in midair, still fighting to get away as she dropped them into her baggie.

"Oh, no you don't," she said as one of them tried to disappear into a hole in what remained of the stump. She quickly seized it by its backside before it had the chance of escaping. She had expected it to come out of the hole easily, but instead she had applied a little too much pressure and it burst its nasty yellowy-green insides out onto her fingers. "Aaahhh!" She yelled in sudden disgust as she flew backwards trying to shake it off. She wiped her hand on some dry leaves then zipped the bag shut. She could endure a lot of things that other more squeamish women, would run from, but dealing with BUGS or rather WORMS wasn't one of them.

"That's enough," she said rising to go back. Cooked or raw, she knew full well there was no way she could eat those nasty things. "Yuk! I don't do bugs!" A shiver ran through her as she felt her empty and now sick stomach turn over.

When she got back she showed the others the grub worms as if they were something to be excited about. She opened the baggie and dropped them into the small pan. Their fat bloated bodies made a dull thumping sound as they hit the bottom of the thin tin pan.

"They're supposed to be really good for you if you cook them; they couldn't be all that bad, could they?" She chattered on, not allowing any of them to say what she knew they were thinking.

But her overly cheerful chatter convinced no one. Holly turned pale and just stared at the worms as they squirmed in the pan. Cody kept looking back and forth at her and the pan to see if she was serious, and Mike just looked at her as if any minute now he might just pick up the pan and throw its contents at her. Shel avoided eye contact for a while, but the silence eventually got her attention. What was she doing? She didn't even believe what she was saying herself, so how could she expect to convince them?

"Ok, that's a no," she said as she walked off with the pan and dumped the worms in the bushes. "I knew that couldn't be God providing for us," she muttered to herself.

Mike got up and put his hand out to help Holly up as well. "We're going to go and have some alone time. We'll be at the small waterfalls we passed a little ways back. We won't be long." They picked up their backpacks and walked off towards the river.

"Mike, was she serious about us eating those worms?" Holly asked as they left the other couple.

"No, she's just frustrated because she knows they'd be safe to eat. She's just trying to feed us, that's all."

"She's trying so hard Mike, I feel bad that I wasn't even willing to at least..." she stopped mid-sentence, then continued, "did you see her face? She was just as disgusted at the thought of eating them as we were. Can we pray for her, Puppy?" She took his hand.

Mike stopped and pulled her into his arms. "Lord, be with Shel, as You give her a peace that passes all understanding. Help her to know that You are our provider. Help the rest of us to step up and find ways we can help to find food. We want to be able to take some of the pressure off her as she feels it's her job to carry us all. It's too much weight for one little lady. Also Lord, give us a reason to hope, to look forward to another day. Please provide for us Lord." He paused for a moment before saying, "Amen." He held his wife a little longer, just breathing deeply, then sighed.

Holly looked up at him and kissed him. She felt so at home in his arms. His embrace gave her peace and made everything on the outside of their embrace seem small.

"Thank you, Mike."

"For what?"

"Oh, just taking time to hold me. I can't tell you how important it is for me to feel..." she paused for a while to think before saying, "I don't know - complete, loved, covered, protected. I don't think there's a word for how it makes me feel. I just know it's the way God made me, to need this closeness from you."

Their lips met in a mutual tender kiss that only happens between two people who have dedicated their whole lives to one another and have earned each other's complete trust.

The waterfall was beautiful and sparkling as the sun smiled down on it. Mike and Holly ran through its cascade, laughing and squealing like children running in a water sprinkler on a hot summer's day.

When they had exhausted themselves they retreated to a calm shallow area along the side of the stream where the water rested before traveling down to the river.

The sun warmed them and felt wonderful after the coldness of the waterfall. It's light glistened off their wet bodies as they basked on the edge of the shallow water.

After a while Mike stated, "We should be getting back before they come looking for us."

Holly sat up suddenly and clasped her things to her chest. "Do you think they'd really come looking for us?" She said as she frantically put her clothes back on.

"They might. We need to cover more ground today so we probably ought to get going soon." He stood and walked slowly over to the rock that had his clothes draped over it, while Holly had already sat to put her socks and shoes on.

"Mike, what do you think that gold bubbly-looking stuff in the water is?"

"Where?"

"Right there."

She pointed to a spot near the shore amongst some small pebbles.

"Oh!" Mike said as he zipped up his pants and walked shirtless and barefoot over to where she had pointed, his belly no longer hanging over his belt. "It's fish eggs!" He said with astonishment.

"Fish eggs?"

"Caviar!" He turned to look at her response.

"Oh! That's wonderful! What'll we need to collect them?"

She grabbed her backpack and took it over to where he was standing, looking down at their find.

"Let's see, give me that shirt, we'll wrap them in that."

They scooped up the eggs with the shirt, coaxing the eggs to go in with their fingertips. Then Holly pulled up the sides and tied it shut with the sleeves and gently carried their treasure back. On the way, Mike picked some blue flowers and then tucked them in her hair behind her ears. Taking her chin in his hand, he turned her head to admire the indigo flowers against her wet red hair and her sun-kissed ivory skin.

"You're so beautiful."

He lifted her chin and kissed her once more before they walked back to where they had left the others.

When they came into sight Shel saw the blue flowers in Holly's hair and jumped up, exclaiming, "Where'd you get those?"

Holly took a step back and asked, "The flowers?" She reached up to touch them, looking as if she thought maybe Shel was thinking of ripping them out of her hair and eating them.

"Yes, the flowers. Those are Chicory flowers!" Shel

said.

Holly just stood frozen in place, with one hand gently touching the flowers in her hair until Mike spoke up.

"She doesn't want your flowers honey." He turned to Shel, saying, "I picked them on our way back from the falls. There aren't any more of the flowers, but I'll show you where the plants are."

"Look what else we found!" Holly declared awkwardly, remembering their booty.

She laid the shirt down on a flat rock, untying it to expose the tiny golden jelly-like pearls that glistened in the sun. They all, without ceremony, moved in and without saying a word, hungrily took a handful and sucked them down. They each managed three handfuls before the eggs were all gone. Holly then picked up her shirt and sucked the remaining eggs off of it as they sparkled like glitter in the sunshine.

When they were done, Shel turned to Mike. "Well, let's go find that Chicory plant."

They walked off into the trees as Holly went and sat down across from Cody.

"She probably wants us to eat the leaves or roots or something," Cody said.

She gave him a little smile and reached up and touched her flowers once again. "I would have had to chew her arm off if she went for my flowers."

Cody knew she was just trying to sound tough and he smiled, not believing a word she said.

When Mike and Shel returned they brought back the washed roots from the Chicory plant.

"We're going to have coffee in the morning!" Mike said excitedly as they entered camp.

"Coffee?! Did you say coffee?" Cody exclaimed. "How are we going to have coffee?"

"It's not really coffee," Shel began to explain, "but

it can be used as a coffee substitute, you may have heard of Chicory coffee?" She held up the roots. "It has a mild coffee-like flavor when it's roasted, it's quite good! You can use Dandelion root too, I'm told, to get a similar tasting drink."

"We'll have to drink it black, won't we?" Holly turned to Shel to inquire as it dawned on her that the Chicory might not be black. "Does come in black?"

"I don't really know. I've never done this before."

Holly finished her thought in jest, "Unless we happen to find a cow wandering around out here! Oh, and we'll of course need some sugar cane." Seriousness snapped on her face, "Stevia! - That's a green leafy plant, right?" She was so excited that she turned to look for the leaves she had so often seen pictured on stevia packets.

"No Sweetie, stevia grows only in South America, sorry."

"So, we have coffee but no cream and sugar?" Cody's face twisted.

"Sorry, it will just have to be black."

"Come on guys, give her a break," Mike scolded. "It'll be good to have coffee again, no matter what it has in it or doesn't have in it."

"Sorry Shel, I didn't mean to make trouble," Holly said.

"It's okay Sweetie, don't worry about it."

"Sorry Babe." Cody kissed her on the cheek.

"Really guys, it's OK, I like a little milk in my coffee too, so I do understand." She wrapped and tucked the roots into her backpack. She would have to whittle it into small shavings and roast it later, after they stopped for the night.

"Ok, let's get going." Mike slipped on his backpack and picked up his long stick, stepping forward to take the lead.

20
Followed

*And we know that all things work together
for the good to those who love God,
to those who are called according to His purpose.
Romans 8:28 NKJV*

As they moved throughout the day they all felt as if they were being watched. No one seemed able to shake the feeling as they, being nervous, pushed themselves on, trying desperately to get away from whomever or whatever it was that was watching them.

It was mid-afternoon and the extra weight of the rafts and the backpacks were becoming too much. They were slowing down now and stumbling so that when they found a small game trail, they turned onto it. The animals who made the trails only went down to the water occasionally so at times the couples lost the sound of the water altogether. They knew that the trail would eventually bring them back to water at some point, but they never thought it might not be a different body of water.

They climbed gradually as they moved away from the river and soon found themselves looking at a cliff that declined sharply about fifty feet.

Looking over the edge of the cliff, they could see a trail winding down the steep rock wall to the bottom where the ground leveled off again. Taking off their backpacks, they all sat down to relax before Cody and

Shel decided to explore the path descending the narrow cliff.

Leaving their packs at the top, they began to work their way along the narrow deer trail. About ten feet down, they found a small shelf that extended back into a cave, which was big enough that they could all fit inside comfortably along with a fire. If they stayed here they would be out of sight, plus the climb had proven to be easier than it had looked from the top.

"This would be a good place to hide for a while," Cody said as they climbed back up to tell Mike and Holly what they had discovered.

When they reached the top, Shel said without taking a breath, "We found a small cave. Do we want to stop here for the night? I know it's still early, but I'm exhausted from moving so fast for the last couple of hours, aren't you?" She looked from one to the other, hoping that they would also agree with her reasoning.

Mike said hesitantly, after looking around one last time, "Yeah let's drop out of sight for a while." On each of their faces they wore fear, exhaustion and hunger. They were all getting thinner by the day. Both Mike and Cody had a week's worth of stubble growing on their faces and were starting to look more like grungy old-time trappers than modern, clean-shaven men. Mike's beard was getting full and bushy, with more gray than dark brown to match his hair. While Cody's beard was red and neat, lying down nicely along the contour of his face, in contrast to his crazy blonde hair that looked like he had combed it with a wildcat.

They worked their way down the narrow trail with Mike bringing up the rear, clinging to the side as they went. When they finally ducked inside they all took a deep breath at the same time just as if they had practiced their timing.

Holly threw the sleeping bags down, one on top of

the other against the back wall of the cave, then she dropped down onto them. Balling up her sweatshirt for a pillow, she laid down. Mike, crawling in behind her, wrapped his arm around her waist as he tucked his other arm under his head. Within moments they were both fast asleep.

Cody began diligently collecting firewood to burn later, pulling dry branches up off the side of the rock face while Shel got out the snares she had tucked away in her backpack. Sitting down she began to untangle the lines as she prayed quietly to herself: "Lord, I think I'm about done with this whole 'survive in the wild' thing. Can we just go home now?"

When Cody heard her mumbling, he stopped working and came over and sat be side her, putting his arm around her. "It's ok, Babe. We're going to get home all right."

She took some comfort in his words but still she had questions that couldn't be answered by such a generic statement. "Where is He Cody? Where is God? And why haven't we found our way out of here by now? It's been a week, for crying out loud. How can we still be lost?" She threw her hands over her face and began to sob.

Cody pulled her into his chest and said, "I don't know? I thought we would have been home by now too, but obviously God has other plans for us. Maybe what we were feeling today was God watching over us."

"Yeah, right!" She snapped, pulling away from him and shaking her head in disgust and disbelief. "Sometimes Cody, I just don't know about you!" She walked over to the entrance of the cave and looked out, her hands resting one on either side of the opening. "It's not Him we were feeling." She took a deep breath and sighed. "It's just getting harder and harder to believe He's out here with us at all. Why has He forsaken us? Why doesn't He see us struggling?

Don't we matter to Him anymore? I just keep praying, but my prayers keep bouncing off some invisible ceiling." She seethed, throwing her hands up over her head as if she were trying to break through an invisible barrier.

Cody came up behind her and wrapped his arms around her waist. He pressed his lips into her hair and whispered, "Shel, Sweetheart, it's going to be alright. I promise you, He hears us, and He has a plan. We don't and can't know all that He's doing, not yet anyhow. But you know He works all things for the good, for those that love Him and are called according to His purpose. We do love Him, so that promise applies to us. God hasn't been caught off guard by what is happening to us, He knows exactly where we are and He has a plan to use what we're going through, for our good."

She sighed heavily and turned towards him, wrapping her arms around his waist and resting her head on his chest. "Just hold me for a while, Cody." She took another deep breath then asked, "How many days have we been out here?"

"It will be seven days tomorrow. We have five more days after that until we're supposed to be home, plus four more days until we're missed at church. One more after that, until Mike and I are expected to be back at work."

She drew her head back and looked at him with wide eyes. "So what you're telling me is that no one's truly expecting us back for nine or ten more days?"

"Someone will notice that we're not back and send out a search party before that."

"No one's going to send out a search party until they know for sure something's wrong. And how will anyone find us? WE don't even know where we are!"

"Shh, it's going to be alright Shel. We just need to do our best everyday and wait on the Lord to do the rest. Just one day at a time Babe, just one day at a time."

She buried her face in his chest and cried. She wanted to believe everything was going to be all right. So she took a trembling breath and let the thought 'just one day at a time' flood over the desperation that she felt, hoping that it would drown out the helplessness of the situation and wash away her doubts.

Standing in the mouth of the cave in the late afternoon a brisk wind began to blow across the sides of their faces. The sun, dropping lower in the sky, began to peek at them through the trees. But the trees shook and bent to stand in the sun's way and refused to let it see them standing there together.

They had two, maybe three hours, before it would be too dark to go up or down the trail. So Cody brushed the hair back off of Shel's tear stained face and said, "Shel, let's go set those snares before it gets too dark, ok?"

"Ok," she said as she brought her face up for a kiss.

He brushed her hair out of her eyes again and with one hand on the back of her head, held her mouth firmly against his lips. A gust of wind blew her hair up and across both of their cheeks, wrapping itself around the back of Cody's head, gently concealing them in a secret kiss.

They walked single-file up the path then through the trees side-by-side. Shel set the snares while Cody collected more firewood. When she was finished, Cody gave her the bundle that he had been collecting and picked up a few good-sized logs as they walked back through the trees. Just as they were going to take the narrow climb down, they heard a high-pitched distress screech.

"It's a rabbit!" Shel said dropping her load of wood and running toward the sound with Cody at her heels.

She stopped and gasped when she saw two rabbits instead of one, caught in the same snare, one with the cord around its neck and the other by its hind leg, up around its thigh. The one caught by its leg was frantically kicking to free itself, so Shel pulled out her knife and plunged it through the back. Its leg had just slipped out of the noose and it would have escaped if she hadn't moved fast. She then picked up the other rabbit by its ears as it kicked at her with its powerful back legs, and slit its throat, then picked up and slit the throat of the other as well.

Cody just stood and watched in horror as his wife's need to survive caused her to move with deadly determination. "I'm glad I'm not a bunny!" He muttered to himself.

She spun around, holding her limp trophies, one in each hand. "We have two! We have twooooo...", her voice trailed off as she looked up over Cody's head, her eyes big as her smile fell abruptly.

Cody turned sharply and took a step backward, throwing his arms out at his sides. He had been caught off guard and he now was the only thing standing between the biggest bear he had ever seen and his wife, whose hands were covered in blood.

The bear stood, towering over them with its arms out in front of it as if it wanted a hug. (A bear hug!). Its breath, as it rushed over their heads, smelled of strong fish. They both stood frozen in their tracks.

"Don't look it in the eyes," he heard Shel whisper from behind him, so he quickly looked down.

Slowly he reached behind him without turning around. "Give me a rabbit."

Shel laid one of the rabbits gently in his hand and he squatted, being careful not to move too quickly, and laid the rabbit at the bear's feet. Then slowly he backed away from the bear putting his hand behind him to get Shel to do the same.

The bear looked down at the rabbit and then at

Cody, tilting its head. Finally, it leaned over and picked up the rabbit in its paw, like a child with a rag doll. It looked at the two of them a long moment more before placing the rabbit in its mouth. Then dropping down on all fours he turned and walked away, his great weight shifting with each step.

They waited until the bear was nearly out of sight, then Cody clutched Shel's free hand and they ran back, bypassing the wood they had collected and moved down the narrow path as fast as they could move.

When they scrambled back into the cave panting for breath, Mike jumped up from building the fire. "What's wrong?!"

Cody and Shel both leaned over with their hands resting on their knees, still trying to catch their breath. Normally, running such a short distance wouldn't have caused them to be so out of breath; but running, mixed with fear, panic, fatigue and the lack of food, made all the difference and they could hardly speak.

"Are you guys ok?" Mike asked.

All Cody could get out was, "Bear."

"You saw a bear?"

Holly jumped up and repeated the question. "You saw a bear? Is it coming?"

"No, no." Cody put his hand up to calm the fear that he had caused, although fear was still surging through his veins.

Shel laid the rabbit by the fire, and then took up a hand full of dirt, rubbing it like soap on her trembling hands to dry off the blood. The only thing she could do now was lay down on the sleeping bags that Mike and Holly had just abandoned. Her lips were moving as she prayed in silence.

Cody slowly told the story, as Mike and Holly's eyes got bigger. When he was finished, Holly said, "Do you think he can get down here?"

"No Sweetheart," Mike said as he stepped over to her and took her in his arms. "The path is too narrow; we had to turn sideways in a few spots ourselves to get down here. We're completely safe here."

It was quiet for a moment as everyone tried to process what had happened.

"Well," Holly said, "I knew that rabbits could multiply but I didn't know that bears knew how to divide!"

Everyone chuckled in spite of the situation. Mike picked up the rabbit and took it out of the cave to clean it, dropping the entrails and skin over the side of the cliff.

He could see dark clouds rolling in over the already darkening sky and heard the sound of thunder off in the distance. He looked down the path and then up, wondering if they would be able to get out in the morning if it rained without slipping in the mud and falling to their deaths. He took a deep breath and tried to swallow his fear. "It's where we are," he told himself, "there's no place safer we can go tonight."

Cody felt like he needed to be alone for a while so, he said, "I think I'll try climbing down to the bottom and see if I can find some water and more firewood."

Shel sat up, her eyes big with fear. "Cody!"

"It's OK, Babe- I'm descending, so I'll be able to see everything that's down there before I get there."

That seemed to comfort her a little.

"Besides, we need water and it'll be dark soon. It's now or never."

Still, Shel went to the edge of the cliff and watched as he worked his way down to the valley below.

When he got to the bottom, he looked up and saw her watching him. He prayed to himself as he filled their canteens in a stream, "Lord, I'm trying to be a man of faith, to be strong for Shel, help me to believe the things I told her earlier. I need strength God to get me through this. Please, Lord, don't leave us out here alone like Shel said you were doing. Show yourself real to us, Lord."

The sky lit up with a flash, followed by a roll of thunder. Cody finished what he was doing and moved back up to the cave, handing the canteens to Shel, then went back down to get some firewood to last them through the night. Shel followed him back to wash in the stream and helped him get the wood in. When they finished they ducked inside just in time, missing a torrent of rain that pounded down from the blackened sky. Their narrow path quickly turned into a stream that ran along the side of the cliff, meeting the bigger stream below.

When they got inside they were met by the smell of rabbit cooking. It's aroma was so rich they could hardly keep themselves from snatching it off the makeshift spit and eating it half-cooked.

Once it was finally finished, they divided and devoured every bit of the meat and then chewed on the bones, not wanting to admit to themselves that the meat was gone.

Shel got the Chicory out and cut it into tiny pieces, putting them in a pan and setting it over the fire to roast. "I've seen this online done by spreading the Chicory out on a cookie sheet and putting it in an oven to roast, but this will have to do. We'll just have to keep stirring it every few minutes to keep it from burning."

"Wouldn't it taste better if it was a little burnt?" Mike asked.

Shel laughed, "That's what some coffee places think! Well, I hope that it does taste good burnt, because I have a feeling that that's the way it's going to be, no matter how often we stir it." The rabbit had filled their stomachs and made them feel content for the time being. But, the thought of having fresh coffee in the morning made them all look forward to a new day.

21
Double Portion

The ravens brought him bread and meat in the
morning,
and bread and meat in the evening;
and he drank from the brook.   1 Kings 17: 6 NKJV

The fire was down to red coals when Cody and Shel woke the next morning. The storm the night before had only lasted an hour or two, leaving everything wet or damp. The fog waited outside the cave, slipping its toe in as if wanting to come in and wrap its cold damp arms around their already chilled shoulders.

Someone would eventually have to go out and get more firewood if they were going to stay warm and if they wanted to have their chicory coffee at some point this morning. They had been anticipating it all night long, as they smelled it slowly roasting near the fire.

Cody decided that he would be the one to brave the cold damp morning; so, throwing off the sleeping bag that he and Shel had wrapped themselves up in, he stepped out of the cave. The heavy fog engulfed him, making it almost impossible to see. He knew that even though he couldn't see more than a couple of inches in front of his face, the alternative would be to wait, shivering and cold, until the fog lifted.

Knowing that the wood that he and Shel had collected yesterday was still at the top of the cliff, he began working his way up the path slowly, shuffling his feet as he went, being careful not to fall over any rocks or roots along the way.

The fog began to thin as he went up, until he came out at the top where the fog swirled around his knees. It was a beautiful clear, crisp day above the clouds. Cody took a moment to lift his face and take a deep breath as the sun touched his skin with its gentle early morning glow.

When he had closed the gap between himself and the firewood, he looked down. There on top of the woodpile lay a dead piglet. It was just deep enough in the mist that Cody thought he was seeing things. He looked around questioning how it had gotten there when off in the distance he saw the bear, standing up with its arms dangling out to its sides. Staring in disbelief he watched as it lifted one paw in the air as if it were waving to him. Cody had the strangest urge to wave back but he was afraid the bear would see it as a challenge. The bear then dropped down on all fours and turned and walked away.

Cody looked back down at the piglet. "Oh Lord, you are looking out for us! The ravens fed Elijah and now a bear is bringing food to us." He leaned over and poked the piglet with one finger to make sure he wasn't just having another food dream. "It's still warm! Oh, thank you Lord!" He said as he picked it up and carried it along with the smaller bundle of wood, stepping back down into the fog once again.

As he entered the cave he dropped the sticks and raised the little piglet in his hands saying, "Praise God, look what He's provided for our breakfast... bacon!"

They all gasped with astonishment as Cody told them about what had just happened with the bear.

When they had eaten their fill of the meat, Holly carefully wrapped up the rest, making sure to collect every morsel for later. The size and quality of this meal more than made up for the scrawny little rabbit that they had given up to the bear and Holly smiled to herself at the Lord's provision.

"What! You left me lying out there unconscious by myself?" Chuck yelled as Leroy confessed about what he had done the day before.

"I came right back to get you, didn't I?"

"It's a good thing you did, or I would have caught up with you and shot you too!"

"If it were you, you would've left me out there for sure!" Leroy spat back. "Except you probably wouldn't of come back for me. Anyhow, I tried to tell you not to mess with that bear."

"I don't think it was a bear!" Chuck exclaimed.

"Well, what was it then?"

"I don't know, but it wasn't a bear."

"Well, what do you think scratched your leg then?" Leroy asked sarcastically.

"I only got one cut, there'd be more than one if a bear had swiped at me, wouldn't there? They have four or five claws on each paw, for sure."

"I'd rather not go poking my nose back around that cave, just the same," Leroy mumbled hesitantly.

"I say we're going. You got that?" Chuck snarled.

They pulled off the road by the bridge, got out of the truck and started walking along the river. As they neared the cave, they slowed down and listened quietly, but they didn't hear anything. So they began to look around.

"Did you bring that flashlight out of my truck?" Chuck asked, reaching back to retrieve it from him, as he already knew the answer to the question.

"Yeah, I did – here."

Chuck took the flashlight and shone it down into the cave.

"Well looky there, they stayed in here all right," he said as he pointed the light at the charred remains of a campfire. "I'd guess they took off after we left yesterday. That puts them a day ahead of us, so we need to get going."

"I told you I saw twinkling light coming from over here! It must of been their firelight reflecting on the mist coming out of this here hole." Leroy waited for a response or a pat on the back, but he didn't get either.

Chuck set a fast pace with his long, skinny legs. After a few hours, just when he was sure they would be catching up with their prey soon, a bear appeared in the path in front of them. It was about 30 feet away, standing upright with both paws up in a threatening pose, making it look ever bigger than it really was. The two men froze dead in their tracks, their eyes popping with fear.

"Don't, don't run," Leroy whispered as the bear growled, showing its teeth while slobber flew.

Spinning around, they both ran as fast as they could, while Leroy yelled "DON'T RUN! DON'T RUN!! DON'T RUN!!!" But their legs just wouldn't listen. After several yards they realized that the bear hadn't chased them, so they stopped and turned around. Chuck was determined to catch those folks, so slowly they began working their way through the trees hoping to slip past the bear. Finding themselves again face-to-face with the bear, it repeated its actions as did Chuck and Leroy. Still, once again they turned back around, picking a different way through the trees. When they came face-to-face with the bear yet again, Chuck thought to himself, "Well, the third time's the charm." So deciding to out-stare the bear; he looked directly into it's small eyes. Suddenly the bear charged, and the men turned and ran, yelling as they went. Stopping when they couldn't hear the bear chasing them any longer, they stood, frozen in place, waiting in fear for the bear to come crashing through the bushes, but it never did.

"What was that all about?" Chuck managed to blurt out as he sucked in another painful breath.

"I don't know, but it sure looked like that bear didn't want us to go that way."

"Oh, I see, you think he was trying to stop us from following them folks, don't you? Doing the work of God, is that it?" He said sarcastically.

"Well, it sure enough looked that way to me."

"Leroy, you're crazier than a dang lizard being chased by a dozen chickens!"

They sat quietly for a while, still trying to catch their breath.

Leroy finally asked. "So what do we do now?"

"We'll go back to the bridge and cross over to the other side. We can drive down the River Road and if we see them again, then we can get in the canoe and paddle across. I'm getting mighty fired up about this whole thing and I'm looking forward to shooting them folks dead and being done with it."

Leroy asked, "Even if they didn't see anything?"

"I don't care if they did or they didn't, we aren't taking any chances, and when we're done dealing with them folks, I'm going back and getting me that fancy truck of theirs and keeping it for myself. I deserve me a nice truck like that; after all I've been put through with them folks."

"You're kidding right?"

"NO, I AM NOT! And I'm going to get it painted a pretty red, too. YOU GOT THAT?"

It was still early in the day and the couples were moving along the river once again. They had all decided to cross over in their rafts at some point today and hide themselves from view on the other side, hoping that the men wouldn't figure out that they had crossed over. They were making good time and didn't want to stop to blow up their rafts until later in the day, but the ground became rockier and the river grew narrower and more turbulent with large rocks jutting out of it's surface.

"If we don't cross now, we may have to carry these stupid rafts for another day or even two until the water calms down again," Cody said. "I would really like to find some place to dump these rafts after we cross. I just don't have the strength to carry this dead elephant anymore."

"You know," Holly said, "the backpack must be a very old torture device invented for the residents of Neanderthal. My shoulders hurt so badly from a lack of circulation and I swear my arms are getting longer. Not to mention what this is doing for my posture."

Cody agreed, finishing her analogy, "Carry this around all day with rocks in it and if you don't like it, invent the wheel."

Stopping by the water's edge, they dropped their backpacks. The men removed the rafts from their packs and began to inflate them with their mouths, taking much longer then any of them thought it would. When Mike and Holly's raft was full, Shel took it and tied it off on the bank as the rest took turns blowing up Cody and Shel's raft.

The rafts were small, only big enough for two persons each. They weren't the best quality, but then again they had only planned on fishing a little, not rafting the rapids. One raft was older, a bright red and the other a golden yellow, both standing out against the pale sand and dark water.

The women removed the sleeping bags from their packs and tied them on the men's backpacks before loading them into the rafts. When both the rafts were in the water, they all crawled in and shoved off with Cody leading the way.

Approaching the opposite shore they scanned the bank for the best place to pull out of the water.

Cody and Shel's oar had just scraped through sand on the bottom near the shore when shots rang out, nearly missing Cody's oar, sending up a spray of water that made both of them flinch. Looking towards the sound they saw two men running to intercept them, one man firing a handgun as he ran.

"Turn, turn, turn!" Mike started yelling, shaking them from their frozen horror. They all flew into action, rowing wildly, as they tried to turn around. But the flat bottom rafts fought them, moving slowly, dragging through the water with very little response to their frantic awkward movements. Cody and Shel put all their strength into it and soon had turned and were beginning to move back the way they had come. But Mike and Holly, who were about twenty years older, were having a harder time making the turn.

Passing them on the right, Cody helped Mike to finish his turn by pushing the nose of his raft into Mike's, encouraging it to turn as he slid by.

The shots kept coming, but luckily for them, they all missed. The man shooting at them was shouting and cursing as he fired the handgun. "GET BACK HERE!"

Cody and Shel had pulled far ahead of the other raft and the shots were clearly now being aimed at Mike and Holly. A shot whizzed past Holly's head and very nearly hit her, so she dropped to the bottom of the raft. Their raft had drifted downstream quite a ways since they had started to cross. The river wasn't wide at this point but the current was very strong and now they were being sucked into the rapids.

"What can we do?" Cody shouted to Shel who sat in back of him. She thought of the rope that was still tied to the front of Mike and Holly's raft and yelled back to them to throw it to her. Holly sat back up and even though the sound of the rushing water roared in her ears and seemingly ate Shel's words, somehow she heard her, or understood her by the waving of her arms.

"Mike, the rope! Throw it!" The rope flew into the air hitting Shel's fingertips before falling in the water and quickly drifted away, while Shel caught herself from falling in after it.

Holly struggled at the oars but still drifted farther and farther downstream, while the roar of the water got louder.

Shel screamed, "Mike! Throw it again!"

Mike wrapped the rope in a loose ball before throwing it with all his might once again.

This time Shel caught the rope as it slapped against her arm, tying it to the handle on the side of their raft. Then picking up the oar she drove it deep into the water and rowed along with Cody, and even though Cody's muscles were already burning with exertion, he pulled the oars even harder until their raft started to pull the other towards shore.

All the while the gunshots rang out as the man with the gun now stood taking careful aim.

Mike and Holly's raft began to bump and bounce off of rocks, as it turned sideways from being pulled by the other raft.

Cody felt sand under their raft, so he jumped out and began to pull it towards the bank. The water was just above his knees as Shel jumped out and together they pulled to bring the others ashore.

Another shot rang out and this time Holly screamed, falling back onto the floor. Mike's face went pale but he continued to row with new strength. His raft was losing air now, making it even harder to row.

Cody and Shel pulled with all their might and finally brought the others up and out of the water. Holly lay limp in the bottom as a pool of crimson blood pooled next to her, spilling out onto the bright yellow rubber floor of the deflating raft.

22
Blood Trail

When my soul fainted within me,
I remembered the Lord;
And my prayer went up to You,
into Your holy temple.
Jonah 2:7 NKJV

As soon as the bottom of the raft began to rub across the sand, Mike jumped out. Then he and Shel lifted Holly from the raft and hid themselves behind some bushes to get out of sight of the men across the way.

Cody pulled the backpacks out of the rafts then pushed the rafts back into the current, still connected by the rope between, pushing and pulling on each other as they drifted downstream.

Holly was still passed out lying limp on the sand. Her pale pink sweatshirt was stained red. The tips of her red hair were dipped in the even redder blood. And her round face was pale and peaceful as she lay across the coarse sand and pebbles.

"Is she - alive?" Cody asked as he came up behind them.

"Yes, she's alive," Shel said, as she carefully looked Holly over. Finding a small hole in Holly's shoulder she gently shifted her up and gave a sigh as she saw a matching hole going out the back. She cut Holly's sweatshirt away from the wound, then rummaged through her bag for some of the herbs she had brought for cuts and bruises or even sprains. Treating a gunshot wound was going to be another thing she'd need to add to the growing list of things she never thought she'd have to do.

She pulled a small plastic bag marked 'cayenne pepper' out of a pouch that was filled with other labeled bags of dried herbs.

Mike took a sharp breath in as he read the label.

Shel said, "It's okay Mike, it'll stop the bleeding."

He looked doubtful, with his hands out in front of him, his fingers tensely splayed, ready to grab and pull Shel's hands away from his loving wife at the first sign of pain.

"It won't hurt her Mike, I promise, it's alright." She quickly cleaned the wound then pressed a piece of gauze with the cayenne pepper onto each side of the wound. Then getting Mike to hold the pieces in place, she wrapped a bandage tightly around Holly's shoulder. When Holly winced from the pressure she let up a little to avoid both hurting her dear friend and being tackled by Mike.

Cody peered out from behind the bushes to see if the men were following them. The men had run back to their pickup and were pulling a canoe out of the back. Cody darted back to the others exclaiming, "We have to go now, they're putting a canoe in the water and they'll be here soon!"

Mike stood up rigid and he looked pale while Cody helped him get his backpack on.

"Snap out of it buddy, we have to go!" He slapped Mike hard on the shoulder twice, then handed Shel her pack and began to help Mike pick up Holly.

Mike squatted down beside Holly, raising her right arm up over his shoulder and Cody did the same with her wounded shoulder, then they both lifted her. Her head fell forward and her feet lifted off the ground as they moved quickly away from the water.

Shel led the way with both her and Holly's packs as she said, "Try to stay on the rock so we don't leave tracks. I think we need to backtrack like we did before. Maybe they'll get sucked downstream and miss us again." She instructed as she tried to pick the easiest trail she could without being too predictable, staying on the small rocks.

Hearing voices they ducked behind some bushes where they could see the men's canoe sliding through the water smoothly like a hot knife through butter. Cutting into the sand as it came up on shore, it made a scraping sound as it severed and pushed the tracks of the friends from each other, leaving Mike's tracks standing alone, amongst the blood of his wife.

Mike shivered as he looked down, seeing his hands covered with his wife's blood as she hung limp between him and Cody.

The voices of the men following them began to get softer as they moved along the riverbank, heading downstream.

Still listening quietly, the three of them heard Holly whisper, "I think it worked."

With smiles, Cody and Shel looked on as Mike kissed her cheek while tears of joy slid down his face.

Shel whispered, "Welcome back. How would you feel about a little rest?"

"Sounds good to me. Do we get our own luxury suite?" She smiled weakly at Mike.

"We'll have to look into that. We need to find a place to stop for the night. If those men keep going downstream, that's good; but if they come back we need to be as hidden from them as possible."

They turned away from the river and began to climb the steep incline again. A large boulder stood a ways back from the top and as they approached it, it grew bigger until the huge rock stood as tall as a house in front of them. Thrusting up out of the ground, it leaned sideways, looking as if it might fall over. They walked up and around the backside and found that it had an opening where the base of the rock had worn away. Shel went over and pushed on it to see if it was solid and found that, barring an act of God, it wouldn't be moving anytime soon.

"This looks like a good place to camp." Dropping Holly's pack and removing the sleeping bag, Shel rolled it out on the ground under the overhang of the huge rock.

Mike and Cody lowered Holly onto the sleeping bag, noticing that her blood had spilled down her side.

Shel began to remove Holly's bandages as Mike held her in a sitting position.

"We need to let you rest for a while before we go dragging you up and down all over creation, Sweetie." Shel spoke calmly as she worked quickly to unwrap the gunshot wound. She applied new balls of gauze on each side of the wound then wrapped it tightly this time with no mercy. She and Mike then laid her back onto the bandage on her back, which caused her to cry out. Shel just applied more pressure to the top of the wound and held her other hand up to warn Mike not to intervene.

"I'm sorry Sweetie, but this is going to hurt a little, you're not going to get better if this bleeding doesn't stop. Don't worry now. This should do the trick. You just lay back and let us serve you for a while. Lucky you," she taunted- "room service, manicure, pedicure, you get to catch up on some much needed sleep. I'd love to do that myself!" Shel chattered on for the next twenty minutes, talking to Holly as if there was nothing at all to worry about. But her actions betrayed her true state of mind, as the very air around them was charged with a sense of fear.

Thoughts passed with mere glances between the men without a word being said. But Shel kept her eyes on Holly and rambled on; not making eye contact with the men for fear that her eyes might give away something she wasn't yet ready to say out loud.

"Cody, we're going to need some water to boil for later and to fill the canteens. Could you get us some please? And if there's any water left in any of the canteens now, Holly could use a drink before you go."

"I am thirsty," Holly said weakly. "And I'm cold."

Mike ran to get the other sleeping bag to cover her, then continued to stand and stare at his wife with shock and concern on his face.

"Mike," Shel said. But he didn't move. "Mike, would you collect some firewood? - MIKE?"

He shook himself free and ran off into the woods with the hatchet.

Cody brought over a canteen and handed it to Shel, helping her lift Holly up enough to drink as she cheerfully said, "Now I want you to drink as much of this as you can, then you need to sleep for a while, ok?"

"It'd be easier if I could get warm," she mumbled.

"Well, we're working on that Sweetie," as she wiped a stray curl of hair out of Holly's eyes and tucked the sleeping bag in around her again. Then she reached in under the end and began to rub her legs and feet, pulling off her damp shoes and socks.

Cody moved through the trees, following the same path they had taken coming up from the river. It was easy to retrace their tracks since Holly's blood had splattered on almost every rock along the way. They had been so careful to stay on the rocks so as not to leave tracks in the mud and now he easily followed the blood trail almost all the way down to the river.

"What was the point in that?" He said to himself, "if those men had looked around even a little, they would have found us within seconds." He prayed, "Oh Lord, thank you for somehow covering our tracks or trail I should say."

As he got closer to the river he moved slower, listening and watching as he crept down to the water's edge. In the sand he could see the men's foot prints as they had pulled their canoe out of the water, then picked it up and took it with them, leaving tracks that followed one after the other as they moved down river.

In the water, downstream, Cody could see their rafts still tied together by the rope. Mike's limp yellow raft had wrapped itself around some big rocks that stood in the middle of the river, while Cody's old red raft had slid up on the big rock where it flipped over and over again, causing the rope between the two rafts to roll up on itself, pulling the red raft ever closer to the big rocks, until it was forced up onto its end, where it now waved back and forth, like the tail of a huge fish trying to free itself from its hook, smacking its tail against the rocks in violent protest of being caught.

Cody moved quickly, filling the canteens as he said to himself, "It's a good thing they took their canoe with them, maybe they won't come back this way."

When he got back Cody busied himself with pouring the water through the three-tiered water filter, keeping what he saw to himself.

After Holly fell asleep Shel pulled the men aside. "She's lost an awful lot of blood guys; we have to get her to drink as much water as we can, whenever she'll drink it, and keep her still." She put her hand on her mouth as she thought, looking over at the sleeping woman who looked as if she was made of translucent wax. "I don't know, maybe the bullet hit an artery or something," she now allowed the fear to etch deep furrows between her eyes. "I just don't know what else I can do. I think I may have finally gotten the bleeding stopped." She looked back at the men. "But, I can't see how it's going to be possible for us to leave here before she's had at least a couple days to rest and that's being optimistic."

"Well," Cody said, "you better be right. When I went down to the river to get water, I saw that we left a clear blood trail. It was like looking at the dotted line on a pirate's map leading to the treasure and we're sitting smack dab on the big red X that marks the spot. It's only by the grace of God those men went downstream instead of up, or they would've found our trail for sure. We're going to have to keep our eyes open for a safer place to camp. And we have to move her as soon as possible, even if we have to carry her. To be wise, we have to assume those men will come back and when they do, we're sunk if we're still sitting here exposed."

Mike said nothing as his eyes banked with tears he wouldn't let go of.

Cody slid his hand over his friend's shoulder and took Shel's hand with his other. "Let's pray; Lord, we thank You for Your blessings; just this morning You showed us that You were..." he stopped and changed his phrasing, "that You are with us and that You love us. Lord, please don't take Holly from us. Give Shel wisdom in what to do for her. Be with us Lord, especially Mike here, help him through this trial." He slapped Mike's shoulder once then grasped onto it with his hand. Continuing, "touch and heal Holly, and cover us all as she heals. Hide us from those men Lord and continue to lead them in the wrong direction." He paused for an awkward moment, wondering what else he could say to move the Lord's hand, and then he simply sighed and ended with, "Amen."

Mike moved out from under his arm and walked away. Shel wanted to follow him, to tell him that everything would be all right, but she doubted that it actually would be.

Mike stared into the woods for some time, saying

nothing, his eyes growing moist as each breath became more and more painful. He walked off alone to collect firewood for whenever they decided it was safe to build a fire. After he had collected enough wood to build a small cabin, Holly woke up. She had been sleeping for hours. Mike sat down beside her, giving her everything she needed, being very persistent about her drinking water every time he could get her to take a swallow.

Shel had been out setting snares and looking for fresh herbs, anything that she thought might be useful for Holly's healing. Cody had gone along with her, his focus being on finding something more to eat but they both came back empty-handed.

They still had a little of the piglet left over from this morning's feast; one of the back legs, complete with its small ham on down to it's tiny hoof. They would eat the cold roasted pork today; then Shel would boil the bones tonight to make a broth that Holly could drink. The white pine inner bark would be good for nutrition but Holly was too weak now to chew it.

She was sleeping again with Mike lying in behind her, propped up on one elbow, his other hand resting on her waist. When he saw Cody and Shel coming he became alert and said, with distress in his voice, "I think she has a fever."

"It's alright Mike, in fact that's good," Shel said.

"It is?"

"Yes, a fever is the body's way of killing off bacteria or viruses. She hasn't ever had a brain infection, has she?"

"A brain infection?" Mike's eyes got big.

"Yeah, you know-meningitis, encephalitis?"

His eyes darted back and forth as if he were trying to remember if she had.

"No!" His eyes snapped back to look at her.

"How about heat stroke?"

"No?" He didn't seem as sure.

"Then she'll be fine, the body won't allow the fever to go high enough to cause damage to the brain unless the..." She paused and studied Mike's worried, confused face, then continued with, "unless the built-in thermostat in her brain had already been damaged in some way." She paused again, "It's normal for the body to react with a fever Mike, after a wound like this. It's good, because I can't clean the inside of the wound so the fever will do the work for me instead. Do you understand?"

When Mike didn't say anything but sat with a look of complete confusion and horror on his face, she added a simple, "I'll watch her tonight, though, to make sure she doesn't get too hot, ok?" Shel knelt down and felt her head. "She'll be fine Mike, really. It's alright."

The degree of concern in Mike's face took a small step back as he took comfort in Shel's confidence. Shel checked Holly's shoulder again. Then, instead of cayenne pepper, she soaked some dried comfrey leaves and put them on the wound. She carefully wrapped it so the comfrey stayed on the wound, covering both sides of her shoulder and again applied pressure, to make sure it didn't start to bleed again.

Sitting next to Holly they ate the rest of the pork, letting Holly eat as much as she had the strength to. When she had finished eating, Mike encouraged her to drink some more water, and then she drifted back to sleep.

It was getting dark when Mike crawled in behind Holly again, wrapping his arm around her, and began snoring. Cody and Shel sat up talking as a mist crept in around them, making it feel colder than it was. At about ten o'clock they decided the danger of being found by the men had past, so they lit a fire for the night.

It was early in the morning and the sky was turning a deep shade of royal blue as the sun found its way back into another day.

Shel came and sat down across from Mike after feeling Holly's head again. "She's going to be alright Mike; she's going to be alright," she said, unconsciously shaking her head 'no' as she turned and stared into the fire, not wanting to make eye contact with him because she didn't know if she really believed what she had just been saying.

23
Sacrifice Paid

He himself is the sacrifice that atones for our sins-
1 John 2: 2a NLT

The next morning the three of them worked hard to keep busy, feeling nervous about just sitting there. Cody stoked the fire lightly one last time for the day while Mike halfheartedly collected more sticks, suspecting every sound of being someone coming through the trees to shoot his wife again. Meanwhile, Shel was getting ready to go and check her snares.

All night long Holly had run a fever and they had all taken turns making sure that she had plenty of water to drink. That, combined with a cool evening breeze and the ensuing cold mist, all played a part in Holly not getting much sleep. She quivered and shook all night with chattering teeth. Her fever finally broke early that morning and she was able to sleep soundly.

"She'll probably sleep for quite awhile," Shel spoke to Mike as he nervously worked stacking the sticks he had just collected while looking over at Holly every few seconds.

Then all of a sudden Holly screamed and jumped up and out of the overhang, banging her head as she did. She ran towards the fire and lowered herself down gingerly as she felt faint and weak. She rubbed her head as she lay back on the ground, staring back at the overhang.

Mike jumped up as he turned to watch in horror. "Are you alright?" He questioned as he moved in beside her and lifted her head onto his lap.

"Something moved in my sleeping bag!" She said, as she seemed to melt weakly.

Cody grabbed his walking stick and, slipped it cautiously under her sleeping bag, slowly lifted it. A three-foot snake came sliding out of the bag and coiled on the ground.

"What kind of snake is this Shel? Are we going to eat it?" Now Cody had watched enough of Shel's 'surviving in the wild' shows to know the answer to the question, even before it made it out of his mouth, he regretted asking it. His stomach also knew the answer as it made a sick flip-flop sound.

He slid his stick under the snake and picked it up to examine it. It hung there for a few seconds, its tongue lashing out like a whip tasting the air that surrounded it, before it slipped off the stick and began to slither away.

It had barely touched the ground before Shel was on it, striking with speed like a... well - like a viper, matching speed for speed, picking it up by the back of its head with her fingers before it had the chance to escape. Then she took out her knife and walked off into the bushes with the snake wrapping around her arm.

When she emerged again from the bushes, she handed Cody a stick with the snake skewered on it, lengthwise. He swallowed hard as he took it from her. "Thank you," he said with a look of disgust on his face as he hung the snake over the fire to cook.

Shel then walked down to the river to wash the blood off, deciding to also try and clean up a little while she was there. She had never felt so filthy. The water alone did very little to improve her condition. "What I wouldn't give for a bar of soap," she said silently, feeling defeated about her efforts to clean up.

She dried her face with a sky-blue bandana that up until now, had been stuck in her bag, then tied it in her greasy blond hair. The pale blue fabric made her cheeks glow pink, and brought out the blue green in her eyes. She looked sweet and innocent with her sun-kissed cheeks, making her look very young. It would have been hard for anyone to believe that she had just skinned and gutted a snake.

Giving up on her attempts at getting clean, Shel stepped back into camp. "I have to go check the snares now," she said as she picked up her walking stick and headed out once more.

"I'll go with you," Mike said. He turned to Cody, "Would you take care of Holly for me?" nodding in her direction.

"Yeah, sure!"

Cody shook the sleeping bag violently, then laid it down beside the fire and helped Holly to get up onto it. "Are you alright?"

"You mean besides being shot through, freezing all night, starving all day, and nearly giving myself a concussion? Oh yes, and I'm also preparing to eat my good friend 'Stretch' there." She pointed at the snake lying over the fire then continued with, "and to think I had just begun to feel so close to him!"

Cody laughed so hard that his stomach hurt, for the first time in days, from something other than hunger. "So, you feel fine then?" He finally managed to ask.

"Oh, sure, I feel just fiiiiine!" She drew out the last word as she rolled her eyes and they laughed together again. "Oh, Oww that hurts!" She said, "Stop, Stop!"

"I didn't say it, you did!" He laughed some more. Cody couldn't remember spending any time with Holly alone before. She had always seemed hard to get to know, quiet even. But he could now see why when Shel spent the day with her, she would always come home happy.

❖ ❖ ❖ ❖ ❖

When Mike and Shel returned with plants in their hands, Cody asked, "Are we going to eat those weeds?"

"Yes and no," Shel began. "Plantain herb to most people is a weed, but to the naturalist or herbalist it has healing properties, it is antibacterial and anti-inflammatory. Right now Holly needs both of those things. And yes, to answer your question, we are going to try and eat them, because they're also full of the vitamins we need to survive. The reason I say try is because they're old, very old in fact, and out of season. We can steam them, but they still might be bitter and tough. If nothing else, we can make a kind of tea out of them for Holly to drink."

"Oh, lucky me!" Holly grinned up at her.

Cody held up a leaf of the plantain and said, "This grows in the cracks of the sidewalk at home. Why would anyone look at this ugly leaf and say 'Oh, I think I'll try to eat this'?" He said with a high mocking voice.

"You have eaten them before Cody," Shel said casually as she sat down and began to wash the leaves. "When the leaves are young and tender in the spring, I put them in our salads. They're good! In fact I've even put them in salads when we've had company over and had our guests rave about how good the salad was. Salad is one of the things I make that you seem to like. At least I think you like it, but I don't know anymore." She slyly glanced up at him, then back down, to clean the rest of the plantain.

"Wait a minute; you have to tell a guy when you're feeding him some 'alien' food!"

"People have been eating plantain for ages and none of them have turned green and grown antennas, yet!"

"You still could have told me I was eating a weed."

"Why?" She stood up to face him. "So you can

overreact like you're doing right now?"

"We have some wood sorrel, too," Mike lamely tried to change the subject, holding up a bundle of clover-like leaves.

"We're going to eat clover?" Cody snarled in Shel's face as he pointed at the sorrel. "What do you think we are, cows now? I need meat and I'm not talking about 'Stretch' over there either!" He pointed towards the fire.

Anger flashed in Shel's eyes as she glanced over to see the snake turning into a long strip of overly cooked jerky as no one had been attending it. Then she stormed off through the trees. Cody started to go after her but Mike grabbed his arm and pulled him back.

"Look, Cody, in case you haven't noticed, there aren't any grocery stores out here. Shel's doing the best she can and, if it wasn't for the things that she's learned, we'd all be lying next to..." his voice trailed off as he glanced at his wife then whispered under his breath, "so lighten up, would ya buddy?"

Cody turned and looked at Holly, letting what Mike had just said sink in, while Holly sadly nodded in agreement. Cody finally said, "You're right, I guess I'm just not handling starving to death very well. I'm on the edge man! Do you think I should...should I...go after her?" He stammered.

"Yeah, go," Mike, agreed.

After a half-hour of searching in vain, Cody returned to sit by the fire.

No one said anything for a long time then Mike ventured to ask, "Did you find her?"

"No, I've looked everywhere and can't find her. Where could she of gone?"

Having no answer, Mike continued working. He had boiled the plantain, cooled the liquid and was now putting it in a canteen for Holly to drink. He and Holly had tried to eat some of it and decided that it would be best as a tea. He was saving the sorrel for a kind of dessert, because after Holly had tried it she said it tasted like mild rhubarb or maybe more like tart lemonade and suggested they might eat it after they choked down the snake, if they ended up having to eat it.

"I can't believe I'm so stupid." Cody groaned, wrapping his hands around the back of his head and pulling it down between his knees, in frustration, "Where'd she go? Is she lost now, too?"

Holly sat up and put her hand on his shoulder but said nothing.

"She had her bow with her Cody," Mike said. "She's probably hunting, maybe she'll bring us something other than snake for breakfast."

They all turned and looked at the snake. "Oh, I do hope so!" Holly said, "I just can't bear the thought of eating old 'Stretch'." She smiled at Cody and he smiled back.

Shel ran for a while before she remembered that predators chase things that run. She stopped and whipped around, looking for anything that might be hunting her. Then she continued to walk quickly away from camp. She knew that Cody was right, greens just weren't going to cut it. They needed protein and they wouldn't be getting it from greens, not enough anyhow. Protein was the one thing that would help Holly's muscles to heal properly. They all needed it; to tell the truth, just to survive, to be able to keep moving each day.

Shel hadn't tried hunting with her bow yet, although they had seen creatures crossing their path from time to time along the way. They always seemed to catch her off guard, not giving her time to get her bow ready before the animal was gone again. And by the time they had stopped traveling every night, she was too tired to even think about tracking some beast through the woods for what might be hours.

This was actually the perfect time to try some hunting. They had to stay put for a while anyhow. And after her clash with Cody, she was sure she wanted to spend as little time with him as possible.

"Thank You Lord, for this opportunity to replenish our bodies. Help me to find something, so we can eat again today," she prayed out loud. Walking a little further, she saw a witch-hazel bush starting to bloom. She knew it was witch-hazel because it was one of the few bushes that bloomed in late fall and even on into the winter sometimes, but she had never seen one until now.

She stepped up to the bush, took out her knife and cut some of the flowering branches to bring back for Holly, just to lift her spirits, because yellow was her favorite color. 'The Color of Sunshine!' Holly always said.

The flowers themselves were really quite odd-looking, containing a bubbly brown center, from which the petals came out random looking more like long, shredded strips of yellow tissue paper that curled and bent in all directions. Up close the flowers were unavoidably, 'Ugly' but from a distance they were not bad looking at all. Shel laid the flowers aside and began to peel off some of the bark. "I can bathe Holly's shoulder with this, to bring the swelling down," she told herself as she worked.

Hearing something rustle in the bushes behind her, she quickly put down the bark and whipped out her bow, moving quickly and silently through the trees, then crouched down beside some big rocks and listened. She was close to whatever it was, but still she couldn't make it out. Suddenly Cody came crunching through the undergrowth, stomping like an elephant, walking right past the rocks that concealed her, and effectively scaring away whatever she had been tracking. She knew he was looking for her but she didn't care. She didn't have time to stand around arguing with him while whatever she was tracking got away. So she sat defiantly, waiting silently until he was out of sight.

When it was quiet again, she stepped out. Looking and listening, being careful not to make a sound, she couldn't see or hear anything except Cody shouting her name off in the distance.

"Shut up you moron!" She growled under her breath. She was about to give up the hunt when she saw a cleft in a rock and turned aside to investigate it. She slipped around behind some bushes and finding a cave, she went inside. It was a nice-sized cave, perfect for them all to hide in and it was hidden from view from the outside. "This isn't far from camp, maybe we can move here tonight," she said to herself.

She sat down for a moment to relax and enjoy the solitude of the cave, feeling content to know that if Cody were to walk by again she would be hidden from his view. It made her feel like she was a child again, playing hide-and-seek and she felt almost like giggling.

Then she thought, 'Why am I hiding from him? I should find him and tell him to find his own food from now on.' But she stayed put, as she replayed their argument over and over again in her mind. Planning out what she would say to him when she saw him again she thought, 'Lord why can't he just try and be nice? Why does he always have to be such a jerk? Why does he always have to be right? Why do I have to...' she knew as a Christian woman she was to be submissive to her own husband. But she couldn't help but feel rebellious towards that principle right now. "He's no better than I am, so why should I submit to him?" She grumbled to herself. Still she knew that the Lord wouldn't ask her to do something

He didn't have a reason for. "Ok, ok!" She said as she softened her tone and attitude. She would go back and humble herself, submitting to Cody, not because she wanted to, mind you, but because she wanted to be in submission to God and His will for her life. "As a sacrifice to you Lord!" She said. She was determined to do it, no matter what. "This is going to be hard for me Lord. Be with me and stop my tongue from saying anything that would be..."

She stopped abruptly as she heard a stick snap not far from where she now sat in the cave. She stepped out from behind the bush that covered the opening and immediately went into stealth mode, moving forward, low and silently. Coming up behind a bush, she saw a doe and it's two fawns. The fawns were almost as big as their mother and one was a button buck, with hairy bumps on its skull, where its antlers would be growing in next year.

'Sorry, Bambi, but it's your day to die,' she thought to herself as she nocked an arrow in her bow and pulled back, aiming at the fawn's heart. Swish! The arrow flew and hit its mark. All three deer jumped straight up and bounded off, the button buck only jumping twice before stumbling over its awkward long legs and falling to the ground. The fawn flopped its head back and forth as it tried to get back up. Its legs were moving with jerks as if it was still trying to run away. Shel stepped up and gently lifted its head, cradling it in her lap as she took her knife out and slit its throat. The fawn's lifeblood spilling out over her knees as it looked up at her. Its head twitched one last time and it was over.

Shel's thoughts went back to the days of the Old Testament, when the Israelites offered sacrifices for the debt of their sins, when the man of each family took a spotless lamb to the priest who would slit its throat, while the man held the animal's head. How the men must have felt the life go out of the small innocent animal as he stood there, like Shel had just experienced. Knowing that the lamb's blood had been spilled to cover his sins and those of his family. She thought of how devastated Cody would have been if he had lived back then. What a huge responsibility it was to be the head of a family. Shel felt the heaviness of her rebellion, her sin, and that sin could only be paid for, with death, by the spilling of blood.

"Sorry, buddy." She stroked the fawn's forehead, closing its big beautiful eyes, as she closed her own.

"Thank you Lord, for spilling Your blood for me, for taking my sins away with the sacrifice of your Son. Thank You Lord, thank You. Forgive me for being prideful; help me to be the wife that you want me to be to Cody." Her tears fell on the fawn's sinless, perfect face as she slowly picked it up and put it over her shoulders to take it back to camp. The sacrifice paid, so that the four of them might live.

She was surprised how far she had actually gone while tracking that fawn. When she finally got back to where she had left the witch-hazel, she put the deer down and rested. She was covered with the fawn's blood and a little of her own as she had brushed up against some black raspberry bushes, long bereaved of their berries. She decided she didn't want to get blood all over the flowers and bark so; she would leave them behind and come back for them later.

She started to pick up the deer again but it seemed heavier now somehow. *'I can't take all of this back to camp. It'd be better to keep the bloody mess out here anyways.'* So she knelt down and got started. It took her over an hour to clean the carcass but finally she threw away the entrails and the hide and picked up what remained, to go.

Hearing something fall behind her, she turned to see acorns scattered under a tree. The dirt was dug up in spots and there was a mud puddle nearby. As the air drifted towards her she scrunched her nose. "Ewww! Hogs are such disgusting creatures!" She stared at the acorns in the mud for a moment; wishing acorns were safe for human consumption. It was just as well, the thought of fishing them out of a hog wallow to eat sickened her. She pushed the thought aside, leaving the acorns to the wild pigs that would surely come back soon.

Wrapping the carcass in her jacket, Shel hoisted it onto her back. She immediately felt the difference in its weight compared to before. She brushed her hair out of her eyes and looked down at her hands as she felt the blood soaking through her shirt and onto her back. *'Oh gross! I'm definitely getting a bath tonight!'* She said to herself as she walked back to camp.

24
Wolves

Stay alert! Watch out for your great enemy, the devil.
He prowls around like a roaring lion,
looking for someone to devour.
1 Peter 5:8 NLT

When Shel walked back into their camp, covered in blood and carrying some kind of carcass on her back, the men jumped up and stared at her. She looked like a crazed wild woman with the skinned limbs of some long-legged animal splayed out behind her head. It had been hours and Cody was next to frantic when he started in on her.

"Are you ok? Where have you been? I looked all over for you and couldn't find you! Couldn't you hear me calling you?"

Mike stepped between them and shot him a look that clearly said, 'cool it buddy!'

Cody took a deep breath and started again calmly, "I'm sorry Shel, I know you're doing your best."

But she didn't look at him or respond.

Mike lifted the jacket with the carcass in it from her back. "Venison?"

"Yes, it is!" She said with a smile, as she turned to talk to Mike alone.

"Good."

"I found a cave we can stay in for a while, too."

It was obvious she wasn't ready to talk to Cody just

yet, so he kept quiet while she told what had happened. *'At least she didn't seem mad.'*

When Shel finished, she turned and looked at Cody for the first time and said, "I have to get a bath before it gets any later. Cody, would you like to join me?" He nodded and quietly stepped up beside her.

After walking in silence for a ways, Shel began to speak. "I'm sorry Cody; I was so distracted about finding ways to heal Holly that I wasn't thinking clearly."

"I'm sorry too, sorry I yelled at you. I had no right to blow up at the only one who seems to be doing anything about providing for us. Please tell me how I can help. I just can't sit around doing nothing any longer, I feel so useless and frustrated; I have to do something! I get so afraid for you when you go off alone. I feel compelled to protect you but you don't seem to want or need my help."

"I didn't know you felt that way," she said stopping to look at him. "I'll try to find things you can do and include you when I can. I know I get absorbed in what I'm doing and I don't think about anything else. I've always had a problem with that, I guess."

Shel was surprised at how their conversation had gone. She expected Cody to pick up their argument from where they had left off and had determined to bite her tongue when he did. But now she felt as if this might just be a turning point in their marriage. *'What had happened?'* She only knew what had happened to change her attitude. *'Was that all there was to it? Could it really be that simple?'* She didn't know but she was willing to humble herself, to submit a while longer just to find out.

She stopped and turned to Cody and he stepped forward to kiss her dirty face, wrapping her in his arms as if he didn't see the filth that caked her skin; the blood that she had spilled while searching for something that would satisfy their hunger. He didn't notice the stench of the serpent that lingered on her already stinking flesh. Then Shel knew that Cody was looking at her, like the Lord saw his bride, white as snow, spotless and without blemish. Tears slid down her filthy face and as he wiped them away, some of the dirt was wiped away as well.

When Cody and Shel returned, clean and happy, Mike already had the venison cut into smaller portions, and had the pieces lined up on big sticks, hanging over the camp fire, like huge shish-kabobs. He was dropping bones and bits of fatty meat, into a pan to boil as a broth for Holly, while eating some small bits of the raw meat as he worked.

The snake had been kicked into the flames and no one was sad to see it go.

The younger couple sat down joining Mike and Holly as they ate bits of venison. Cody had tried venison before but hadn't liked it. But this time was different, now it tasted like a tender rare steak, '*How could hunger change my taste buds so much?*' he thought as he chewed the tender meat, sucking all the flavor into his mouth before swallowing it.

Holly's suggestion of finishing off their meal with the wood sorrel was also perfect. Its clover shaped leaves were surprisingly refreshing as it cleansed their palates.

Cody put his arm around Shel and loudly "Moooooed!" in her ear as he kissed her cheek. She slapped his chest and pushed him away in mock displeasure but her smile gave her amusement away as they all chuckled at the joke.

The sun was getting lower in the sky and the couples busily readied themselves to head to the cave. Holly had insisted that they move because, even though she found waking up with her friend 'Stretch' exhilarating, she didn't like the idea of sleeping with one of his family members tonight. They decided that Mike would be responsible for getting Holly to the cave, while Cody and Shel cleaned up and moved everything else over.

Shel had taken off as soon as she had finished eating to get the witch-hazel, then marked the trail for Mike with some of it's yellow petals. That way he could concentrate on moving Holly and not waste steps trying to find the hidden cave.

When Shel returned to where she had left the witch-hazel, she collected the bark in one hand and squatted down to scoop up the branches covered with flowers, in her other hand. As she stood back up, a branch of the bush caught her hair and pulled some of it out. She slapped at the bush, pushing it away from her head, not realizing that she had lost her bright blue bandana. She just smiled as she walked away thinking about how pleased Holly would be to have the yellow flowers.

She walked towards the cave, picking a few flowers off of one of the branches and dropping them lightly along the way as Cody came up behind her, laden down with backpacks. The two of them went back and forth, moving everything from their old camp to their new campsite, including the firewood that was left. Lastly, they walked backwards with leafy branches, brushing away any sign of them ever being there and throwing handfuls of loose dirt (like skipping rocks on the surface of water) across the marks that still remained, making them disappear completely.

When they were finally finished, they set up their new camp for the night. It was getting dark quickly and Mike had already started a fire. The sky was striped with orange and the remaining blue that glowed faintly through the dark green trees stood out against its fading light.

Shel started to change Holly's bandage again and, as she pulled off the old bandage, Shel took in a sudden breath of shock. Mike and Cody rushed over to see what was wrong.

"Look at this!"

"What? I don't see anything!" Mike said staring at his wife's shoulder as if his eyes might fall out with fear.

"Look how well this is healing!"

He let out a sigh of relief and Shel turned to look at him. "Oh, I'm sorry Mike; I didn't mean to scare you." She then turned back to Holly. "This looks amazing Sweetie, it really does! How are you feeling?"

"I feel pretty good really, considering only yesterday I thought I was going to die! My shoulder hurts some and I'm tired, but not as tired as I thought I'd be after walking all the way here."

Shel finished dressing the wound and then Mike and Holly went to bed. It had been a long day. Mike would actually sleep tonight knowing his wife was on the mend. And Holly, even though she had slept repeatedly throughout the day, would sleep all night too.

As the sun went down, Shel took the witch-hazel bark and cut it up into small pieces, covering it with water, and began to simmer them near the fire. The smell was nice, making one feel like breathing deeply.

Cody and Shel took the first watch of the night, keeping the fire burning. Just as Shel was about to wake Mike, so that she could get some sleep, they started seeing eyes staring at them from the darkness and they huddled closer. Five or six animals pacing back and forth, their eyes glinting with the fire as they walked around the outskirts of their camp just beyond Cody and Shel's view.

Slipping out of the cave behind them Mike whispered, "What are they?" Startling them.

"I don't know, we just started seeing them."

"I hope you don't mind me leaving now," Shel said. "I can't just sit here and look at those things drooling over me, without having nightmares." She crawled into the cave with Holly, feeling glad to be out of sight. Covering her head, she could still see those eyes staring at her as though she was a tasty morsel, making it hard for her to fall asleep.

"Well, from the distance the eyes are from the ground," Mike mused, "I'd say they're wolves. They're not supposed to attack people, unless someone is maybe alone or wounded."

"You think they're after Holly?" Cody said with alarm.

"Oh, don't say that! No, they're more likely after the venison."

"Well, if we threw them some, would they just leave?"

"No, they wouldn't leave but instead, they would associate us with food. That wouldn't be good! But at the same time, they won't leave until the meat is gone either. And the meat will probably spoil in a couple of days if we don't eat it all. So I think what we need to do is cut it up in thin slices and dry it as best we can. It will probably last longer that way, and travel better for sure, then we can eat it like jerky or maybe we could boil it."

"It's already roasted!" Cody said with a puzzled look.

"I know, but we have to try doing something to preserve it." Mike reasoned, "We don't have any salt and we can't risk smoking it for days. It won't keep more than a day like this, in this damp air, I wouldn't think. And those wolves will follow us until it's gone, maybe longer, if they can still smell it on us."

"We need to get started then, we only have until morning. It's probably going to take us the rest of the night to dry it all," Cody said. "I'd like to keep the fire burning as long as we can," he nodded towards the wolves, "but it probably wouldn't be safe for us to let it burn all day. We were pushing it yesterday the way it was, burning it in the late afternoon like we did. Those men are sure to come back at some point."

"You're Right. We would have been sitting ducks. Hopefully we'll be able to think more clearly in the morning and not be so grumpy, having something in our stomachs." Mike smiled cautiously at Cody as if to make a point.

The men held each other's gaze for a moment longer before continuing to cut up the meat. Still, the eyes watched them intently, like dogs waiting under a table for someone to drop a morsel or throw them a chunk.

Mike was right, Cody thought, they didn't want those dogs following them around.

They cut as much of the meat as they could eat in a couple of days, saving aside some of the roasted meat for eating in the morning, then threw the rest into the fire, hoping there wouldn't be anything left for the wolves to munch on when they were gone. They didn't want them to make the connection that 'people' meant 'food'. But it may have already been too late for that. All they could do now was hope for the best.

While watching the wolves' hungry eyes, Cody started to think about Mark, chapter 7, where the Gentile woman came to Jesus to get him to cast a demon out of her daughter. He did it for her, but before He did, He tested her, to see her faith. '*Let the children be filled first, for it is not good to take the children's bread and throw it to the little dogs*'. He knew this story was about the Jewish people being His first choice but, then God extended the blessing to include the Gentiles that demonstrate faith. Cody thought to himself as he looked up again to see the wolves. Then he looked at his hands dripping with the juices of the meat as he cut it up.

He saw the wolves as being like the world looking

on at him as a Christian. If they're not drooling and licking their chops, maybe I need to ask myself, why not? Am I cutting into the meat of the Word, devouring it, taking it in, so that it becomes part of me? Do its juices drip off of me and its smells surround me? The meat of the Word lies in front of me every day and I'd rather read my newspaper. Cody scolded himself in thought, '*Lord, I'm sorry. I need to be digging into your Word. And like this meat, I need to cook it, smell it, and taste it; to eat it in its rawness and to enjoy its satisfying richness as it's gently cooked. I don't think I'm attracting those that are hungry, Lord.*' Cody had to admit to himself he didn't think anyone had drooled over his faith for a long time. He thought of the man in the cafeteria who had said 'Christians are such hypocrites'. In Cody's case he was right. But, of course hypocrisy is a human condition, he reasoned with himself, better known as lying, and deceiving. Men have always done it and still do today. Cody knew that he had been counted in their number. He knew he wasn't any better than anyone else. He knew he was supposed to try to be like Christ and he hadn't been trying very much at all lately.

After contemplating all of this, he looked over at Mike and said, "Mike, I'm sorry I embarrassed you at work the other day and that I gave Christianity a black eye."

"What brought this on? Those wolves setting out there waiting for us to mess up, so they can devour us?"

"Yeah, sort of, but that's a much shorter version of what I was thinking.

25
Ha Cha Cha

Likewise you younger people,
submit yourselfs to your elders.
Yes, all of you be submissive to one another,
and be clothed with humility,
for "God resists the proud,
But gives grace to the humble."
1 Peter 5: 5 NKJV

The men sat talking, while the wolves looked on, for the remainder of the night. Right before daybreak the wolves drifted off into the trees leaving the men finally feeling more at ease.

The sun was beginning to light up the sky overhead with a deep purple hue. The trees stood dark against a deep pink, as if the sun was peeking through trying to decide whether to uncover its head this morning or just roll over and go back to sleep.

Mike threw on the last log before allowing the fire to die out for the day. The fire made its last display of energy, snapping and crackling, throwing its sparks high into the air or spitting them out at the feet of those who sat nearby. Still small flames licked out from beneath the coals as if it knew it would starve in a couple of hours, fading gradually, glowing red, until it went out completely.

It was Cody's turn to sleep but Shel had slept so soundly that he was reluctant to wake her up. He knew there would be plenty of time to sleep while they waited for Holly to heal. So he sat watching the fire, while thinking about his and Shel's marriage. Finally he blurted out, "Mike, do you and Holly ever argue?"

"Sure we do. All marriages have their ups and downs, seasons of 'for better or for worse'."

"I don't think I have ever seen your 'for worse', I've only seen you two moving in harmony. You always seem to know what the other one's thinking, like there's some kind of antennas on your heads sending each other messages."

"We still have our arguments and irritable days, and also misunderstandings. We've just learned how to identify them and adjust to work our way around them."

"What kind of misunderstandings or argument?" Cody said with disbelief.

"Well, like a couple of weeks ago after work, I came home wanting spaghetti. I said to Holly, '*Oh, I was hoping for spaghetti tonight.*' I then sat down and ate the perfectly wonderful meal she had made, knowing full well she would make me spaghetti the next night. I had taken the last of the cheese to work, so I made myself a mental note to bring it back home the next day, because '*you can't have spaghetti without cheese!*' while she made a mental note to herself, that I (in my odd way) had asked her to make spaghetti and so the next night, she planned on making it for me. But, when she pulled out all the ingredients, she noticed we didn't have any cheese. '*You can't have spaghetti without cheese!*' she thought to herself. So she added cheese to her grocery list and forfeited the spaghetti idea for another equally good meal."

"When I got home, cheese in hand, and there was no spaghetti on the table, the argument started. '*Where's the spaghetti'?*"

'*We didn't have any cheese.*'

'*I had the cheese with me,*' I said, as I held it up.

'Why didn't you tell me you had the cheese with you?'

'Why didn't you ask if I had taken the cheese to work?'

"It was kind of humorous really, so it didn't last long. We've been married long enough to know that we would laugh about it sooner or later, so we might as well move on. We then sat down and ate what she had made, enjoying it fully, and we had spaghetti the next night."

"What? You call that an argument?"

"You didn't ask me how we used to argue, you asked how we argue now."

Cody sat deep in thought, not saying any more.

Holly got up and handed Mike the sleeping bag, then sat back in his arms. He wrapped the bag around his shoulder and up under her chin, then whispered in her ear, "How you feeling today, Sweetie?"

"I feel pretty good, a little shaky but the pain is leaving my shoulder. That's good, right?"

"That's very good," Mike said as he buried his face in the side of hers, planting a big kiss on her cheek.

Cody watched them, envying the achieved ease of their relationship. *'I don't want to go back home and have everything go back to the way it was before.'*

Mike broke into his thoughts, "There was a time when I had to make myself smile at Holly. I started to call her Button at that time, pretending that I was madly in love with her even though at times I wanted to leave."

Holly turned to look up at Mike, "Oh, I didn't know that! I liked the name Button, why don't you call me that anymore?"

"Ok, Button!" Mike gave her a smile and pulled her back into himself.

Holly looked back at Cody, "You know Cody, every day we get up, we either decide to work on our marriage, or to be jerks."

Cody blurted out, "I'm afraid I've decided to be a jerk more often than not, I'm ashamed to say."

"Amen to that!" Shel said walking over and sitting close to Cody, throwing her sleeping bag around them both.

"Well, you're no angel either," Cody shot back.

"You're right, I've been mean and spiteful and have enjoyed every moment of getting under your skin, but you..." her face was beginning to pull tight with anger as she stopped herself short.

"Okay guys, let's not start that again," Mike injected swiftly, then sat quietly for a second looking at them before adding, "do either one of you have any more questions for the old married folks? Because Holly and I would love to help you anyway we can." Holly nodded gently in agreement.

"Yes," Shel snapped out as if she had been waiting for the right moment to bring it up, "How do you know when you should be submissive to him?" her eyes fixing on Holly's.

Holly began to speak, "Well, always, really. Cody's the head that God has appointed over you, to protect you, to cover you and to guide you. You're precious to God, and He knows you're vulnerable; you're easily deceived because of the example that Eve set. Not that all women are exactly the same, but God's standard stays the same no matter whom you are. Women that have a strong will like you do, will naturally have a harder time submitting and being respectful. But God will reward the woman that decides to make that sacrifice every day as she lays down her own life, her flesh, to submit to her husband. Because in doing so she is submitting to God. I'm not willing to argue with God, to say *You don't know what You're talking about*. Are you?"

"No, not with God, but what if Cody's wrong?"

"Who determines what is wrong?"

"I guess I do?" Shel said shrugging her shoulders.

"If you have a disagreement, God asks you to submit and allow the chips to fall where they may. Cody's not perfect and he will make mistakes but it's not your job to rub his face in them. God's working in his life too, just like He's working in yours and you still make mistakes, don't you?"

"Yeah, of course." Shel said impatiently.

"Do you like it when he rubs your mistakes in your face?"

"No."

"You just need to learn to be quiet during those times and let God do what He will. Pray for Cody; you'll be surprised what that will do for you both. And Shel, on a personal note, you have to stop calling him a moron; that is so disrespectful. The Bible says that wives are to be respectful to their own husbands."

"Yeah, yeah we talked about this before." Shel pursed her lips, looking slightly irritated. "Well, what about women with abusive husbands?"

"Do you have an abusive husband?"

"No!"

"There are obviously marriage situations where this isn't going to work, but it's still the standard that God expects from us. I don't know if it will help an abusive marriage, but I don't think it could hurt. But, for those of us with normal marriages, respect and submission will make your 'standoff at the O.K. corral' marriage into the marriage you've always wanted it to be."

"Ok then, tell Cody what he needs to do now." Shel turned and glared at Cody.

Holly shook her head before saying, "That's not my job and it's not your job either; anyhow I'm pretty sure Mike has already told him what's what."

"Yes, he has!" Cody said.

Mike interjected, "Yeah, that's why he was so mad at me before we left on this trip."

"Tell her what you said about that scripture," Cody

said excitedly.

"What scripture?" Mike looked puzzled.

"You know, 'Ha-cha-cha'!"

"Oh yeah," Mike laughed uncomfortably, "well, when God handed out the curses to Adam and Eve, He told Eve that she would have a desire for her husband. What he meant by that was that she would want his position of leadership."

"That's one of the curses?" Shel asked.

"Yep, it sure is," Mike, added.

"Well, what's that have to do with 'Ha- Cha- Cha'?"

He laughed again nervously. "Well, it's just that the first thing men think of when they hear that she'll have a desire for him is... 'aaaahhh'."

"Ohhhh, that is dis-gus-ting!" She drew out the words, wrinkling her nose.

"I thought it was pretty good myself." Cody wrapped his arms around her waist, pulling her a little closer and kissing her on the cheek.

"Oh, stop it!" She squealed and slapped at him, which only made him laugh more.

"That's a man's dream woman, isn't it?"

"Yep." He made another attempt at the kiss as she pushed him away playfully.

Shel looked at Mike, "Alright then, why's it okay for you to talk about women and it's not alright for us to talk about men?"

"Are you kidding me?" Cody said with disbelief, "Holly just gave you all the do's and don'ts in one nice sweet little package and you want to hear what Mike yelled in my ear?"

"You yelled in his ear?" She said turning again towards Mike.

"Only a little, "said Mike.

"No, a lot, and the 'Ha- Cha- Cha' was the only nice part of the whole 'being taken out to the woodshed' experience. When I thought about it the next day, I had to find a place alone to laugh out loud."

Everyone got quiet as they all stared into the fire, smiling.

Shel turned to look at Cody. "Have you slept yet?"

"Not yet, I think I'll go do that right now," he yawned.

As he started to go he noticed that the clouds had turned a lovely peach color with a clear robin's egg blue behind them. The sun shone over the mountains, kissing the edges of the clouds with its golden light. It looked as if it was going to be a beautiful day. But that was all about to change.

26
Up a Tree

The wicked will not prosper, for they do not fear God.
Their days will never grow long like the evening
shadows.
Ecclesiastes 8: 13 NLT

Chuck and Leroy paddled the canoe across the river to where they had last seen the people they were chasing.

"I don't know why we're still trying to find them folks," Leroy complained, "I'm tired, I haven't been sleeping well and I've probably lost my job by now. We've been out here every day for a week. Can we just forget about this and go home? There's no way them folks are making it back to civilization, they're lost!"

"We'll have them before you know it, then we'll go home. And since you won't have a job, you can sleep all day if you like."

That didn't bring Leroy any comfort, but he didn't say any more about it.

The canoe slid onto the shore and both men jumped out and began searching in the opposite direction from the other day. Just as they were ready to walk farther upstream, Leroy saw some spots of blood on the rocks. "You got one of them," he said, leaning over with his hands on his knees. "One of them was bleeding pretty bad."

Chuck came over to see for himself. "Well, looky there, I got me one all right!"

212

The pebbles had been kicked around a little to cover their trail, but it was still clear which way the four had gone, just the same. And as the men moved further up onto the bigger rocks it became easier and easier to follow the trail. The blood on the top of some of the big rocks was smeared, where animals had tried licking them clean.

"I got one of them good! We'll be coming up on a grave soon!" Chuck excitedly exclaimed as they continued on up the hill. A huge rock stood in front of them as they climbed. Coming around the side of it, they saw the remains of what used to be a campfire and the overhang where the folks had most likely slept. The two men poked around for a while but saw no evidence of a trail leading off in any direction.

Chuck was getting angrier and angrier and was about to let go of a line of cursing that would have made the bars of hell shake, when they heard something off to the left of the abandoned camp.

"Let's go," he said to Leroy as he began running towards the sound. "That was too easy," he remarked, just before they crashed through the bushes and into a clearing.

However, there in front of them was something they hadn't expected and they froze in their tracks, finding themselves surrounded by a herd of wild hogs. The herd had been eating the bloody remains of some animal, while dragging its entrails around with them, as they grunted with pleasure amongst themselves. The male raised his head when he saw the intruders, concluding that they had come to take their meal away.

The boar charged them, squealing loudly, and striking terror in the men as they ran for the nearest tree. Slipping and sliding along the edge of the hogs wallow, pushing and jostling each other as they ran, they spotted a big tree with a low hanging branch. Chuck flew up first with Leroy following close behind, dodging Chuck's feet as they swung out, just missing his face. Chuck's gun caught a branch and slipped out of the back of his pants and fell, clunking Leroy on the head before clattering to the ground.

It stunned Leroy momentarily, giving the boar a chance to slash at his foot with its tusks swinging, catching his boot and sending it flying through the air to land in the wallow. Leroy's feet were knocked out from under him and he frantically wrapped his arms over the branch in front of him, managing to pull himself up onto it. He sat and rubbed his head as he fearfully looked down into the face of the ugliest creature he had ever seen.

The boar paced back and forth, and around the tree for a few minutes, then marked it and sat back on his haunches. It's ebony eyes flashed with fire showing his anger. His black and brown hairs poked out of his rough and filthy, dark hide. His fangs were a nasty crusted yellow that dripped with blood and drool, which then ran down the hairs that jutted out of his chin. Even though the men sat high in the tree, with a breeze blowing below, they could still smell the hog's stench.

After the initial relief of being out of the hog's reach had passed, Chuck and Leroy began realizing that they were stuck with no gun and no way to scare the family of hogs away. So they began to blame each other for their situation, shouting louder and louder, while becoming more outraged as they yelled.

The creature glared up at the intruders, grunting and pacing, slashing at the tree with his tusks and kicking up dirt with his back feet. He stood back and squealed so loudly that the men plugged their ears and then resumed their argument in hushed tones, finishing it - or rather ending it, knowing that neither of them were going to concede defeat.

The herd consisted of five piglets that scuffled around, fighting over the intestines of a remaining carcass, like kids playing tug of war, stretching them longer and longer until they would snap in two. The sow was seemingly unaffected by the battle that entangled her legs while the boar relentlessly guarded the tree.

After several hours of scuffling around and rooting up new things to eat, the swine began to settle into the wallow for their afternoon nap, making it painfully clear that they were not leaving any time soon. One of the piglets lay on Leroy's boot, sending it deeper into the mud, leaving only its toe sticking out, before the piglet fell asleep next to the sow.

The boar alone refused to nap but sat diligently staring up at Chuck and Leroy as they sat high in the tree, shifting around on the limb trying to get comfortable.

"What's that?" Chuck said as he pointed over Leroy's shoulder. There on the ground lay something blue, behind a bush with yellow flowers.

Leroy turned as he stood up on the branch so he could get a better look and at the same time regain some circulation in his backside.

"It looks like a blue bandanna." Leroy leaned back on the branch and, thinking for a second, said, "Doesn't Bo have a tracking dog?"

"Yeah, he does; if we ever get out of this here tree, we need to go get him to help us."

"How you going to do that without telling him what we're doing?"

"I'll think a something," Chuck said as he tapped his temple three times, suggesting that he was the thinker of the two of them.

Hours dragged on and it was starting to get dark when Leroy said, "Look at him!"

"What for?"

"Just look at him!"

Chuck turned to look at the boar. "What's the matter?"

Leroy in his best '*Three Little Pigs*' voice, sang,
♪ "Not by the hair of my chinny, chin, chin!" ♪

Despite Chuck's harsh exterior, he chuckled, just a little.

Eating the cold roasted venison and drinking hot witch-hazel tea the next morning seemed to lift the couples spirits. The tea had a burnt marshmallow kind of flavor to it and they sipped it contentedly.

"I think there's an herb or a root or something called 'marshmallow' isn't there?" Mike asked.

"Yes, there is, but I don't know much about it. I think it's like a Hibiscus, or maybe it's in the Hollyhock family, I can't remember," Shel said as she took another sip of her hot tea. "You know, somehow it just feels right to be drinking this tea by a campfire, don't you think?"

"Yeah," was all Mike said, continuing to caress Holly's hair as her head lay in his lap. Even though her face was pale, her cheeks were blushed as she slept peacefully.

"Is she running a fever again?"

"No, it's just the warmth of the fire." He touched her cheek tenderly. "Thank you, Shel, for saving her."

"It wasn't me, it was the Lord."

"Oh, I know but the Lord makes us into the tool He wants us to be and if the hammer isn't hard, it can't drive a nail when He picks it up to use it. You were willing to be made into what He wanted you to be, so you did have something to do with it, and so I thank you."

"I like that," she said.

"Ok, well you're welcome then."

Cody hadn't slept for long before he got back up. He drug his sleeping bag out with him to join the rest of them by what remained of the fire. He wrapped the sleeping bag around himself and sat down with his back to a rock.

Shel backed in between his knees and snuggled in, his arms welcomed her as he pulled the sleeping bag tightly around them both. She felt cold to the touch, so he busied himself with warming her, rubbing her arms and her drawn up legs as she sat soaking up his warmth. Her jacket had never completely dried out after she had attempted to wash the blood out of it last night, and now she was happy to have Cody to keep her warm. Even though Shel had been uncomfortable in her damp jacket, Cody felt that the Lord was keeping His promise to them; '*All things working for their good*', because they loved Him. Cody gave Shel a squeeze and heard himself whisper in her ear, "I love you." It sounded so foreign, but it felt good, like another wall had come crashing to the ground, a wall that had stood in their way for far too long.

The fire was slowly going out and they were sad to see it go, but die it must, if they were to remain invisible. The coals that hosted the golden red glow were white now and crumbling away layer by layer, true to the nature of wood. As the hot coals became smaller, some white ash gently flaked off and rose on the waves of heat, then being caught up by a morning breeze, floated away.

27
De-tailed

We are hard pressed on every side, but not crushed,
perplexed, but not in despair; persecuted,
but not forsaken; struck down, but not destroyed.
2 Corinthians 4:8-9 NKJV

"Did you slip a small Bible into one of the backpacks by chance, Babe?"

"No, I didn't, sorry. You have no idea how sorry I am about that." Shel sat up and pulled her backpack towards her. "I should have, it would have helped us a lot more than some of these things." She emptied her backpack out onto the ground and rummaged through some of the things they had yet to use.

"Oh, what I wouldn't give for a newspaper or a good book right now!" Cody said dreamily. The pile of papers that he had brought to use as fire starter was still back at their original campsite. Shel had packed a gallon zippy bag full of dryer lint, which was perfect for fire starter but a little harder to read than the newspaper. And at this point though Cody had already read the old papers, he would have gladly read them again, to pass the time and get his mind off of the worries of the day.

Shel continued to shuffle through the bottom of her backpack and found a small survival handbook and a Boy Scout manual that had worked their way down to the bottom of her pack.

"There you go. You said you wanted to learn more about how you could help out! I forgot all about these. I haven't had a chance to read either one of them since we left home; with all the running and hiding we've been doing during the daylight hours. And this would actually be a great time to do a little research." She handed the books to Cody, then sat back in his arms again as he held the books out in front of them.

"'A Boy Scout Handbook?'" Cody held the book up in disbelief to show Mike.

"Yeah, the young man in the sporting goods store said it would be interesting for me to read. I flipped through it when I first bought it. It has some basic survival things in it for the beginner. But of course, most of it seems to be dependent on a teacher or parent. Maybe there are more detailed books for a teacher out there somewhere, or maybe it was something every man knew, back then." She shrugged her shoulders.

"Back then?" Mike said as he took the book from Cody and flipped open the cover. "You make it sound like it was thousands of years ago. This book was printed in 1956."

"I don't care, either way I'm reading this one first," Cody said as he held up 'Wilderness Survival for Dummies'. Shel had stuffed it full of extra articles that she had printed off the Internet, which fell out as he opened the book. He recognized the three-tiered water filter that they had been using as the pages slid down the sleeping bag to land on the ground beside them. But he let them lay there on the ground as he began reading the introduction.

Mike flipped through the 'Boy Scout Handbook', and began to remember fondly, the season of his life as a boy with his Dad. It had made such an impression on him that from time to time he had taken in a boy who had never known the love of a father and tried to fill that need in their lives. Having no children of his own, working with the boys satisfied his desire to share and teach what he had learned as a boy.

In the last five years he hadn't worked with any boys, concentrating instead on the promise he had made to his dying best friend, to 'be there' for his son. He thoughtfully glanced up at Cody and smiled at the sight of his arms wrapped around Shel as they both read. Cody was going to be fine and perhaps it was time for him to start investing in young lives once again.

As he watched he prayed to himself; *'Thank you, Lord, for this time. Although it's been hard for us all and may even kill us in the end, I thank you for what it has done to strengthen our relationships and to perfect our faith.'*

Unexpectedly Holly sat up and said, "I hear voices!" then began pulling things back into the cave as the others sat frozen until they heard the voices as well.

Shel started to shove everything back into her pack, while the men kicked at what remained of the fire, spreading it out and covering it with dirt to stop it from smoking. Then they crawled behind the brush and into the cave, moving back into it as far as they could go until they sat motionless, listening to the sounds of men yelling, mixed with an occasional loud squeal or grunt.

"What is that sound? Pigs?" Holly whispered as she lay back down on Mike's lap, pulling the sleeping bag tightly up around her face so only her nose and eyes peeked out.

"It sounds like it. I'm going to go look and see what's going on," Cody said, beginning to crawl away.

"Cody, no. They have a gun!" Shel exclaimed.

"I'll stay back and hidden, Babe."

"I'm going with you then." She started to follow him.

"No, you stay here with Mike and Holly."

Mike reached over and clasped her arm, pulling her back to sit by him. As she sat back, he put his arm around her. "He'll be alright Shel, just trust him."

Holly slipped her hand out from under its cover and took Shel's hand, saying quietly, "It's time to submit."

Cody turned and came back to kiss her on the forehead, "It's going to be alright, Babe. Pray."

"I will."

"We will," Mike added.

Cody slipped out from behind the brush that covered the cave. He moved quickly, honing in on the sound of the men's voices until he realized that the men were no more than a couple hundred feet from the campsite they had left last night. As he got closer, he went down on all fours and crawled behind some bushes. *What are they doing in that tree?* He thought, trying to get a better look through the branches.

The men continued to yell at each other and as they did, a boar came into Cody's view and let out a loud searing squeal! The sound was so loud it shot through him, making him jump to his feet to run. But as he swung around, he saw standing in his way, a small piglet. It was chewing on something and didn't seem the least bit fazed to see him there. As the man and pig stood staring at each other another piglet rounded the bush and stood staring as well. Through the bush Cody could see the sow coming to investigate what her piglets were getting into. So he jumped over the piglet in front of him and ran as fast as he could, bent over so the men in the tree wouldn't notice him. When he was sure he was out of sight, he stood and raced the rest of the way back to the cave.

Cody hastily told the others how a herd of wild boar had treed the two men, and then exclaimed, "We should leave now!"

"Holly's not ready to move yet," Shel stated.

"We can go, I'm fine, really guy's. Let's go."

"No, you're not," Mike said. "We're staying right here, at least another night. We'll stay quiet and have no fire tonight but we'll be fine."

"What about those wolves we saw last night?" Shel questioned.

"We can use our long sticks if they get too close and maybe there's some kind of hedge we can make to keep them out?" Cody said, glancing at Shel.

Shel thought to herself for a few moments, then threw her shoulders up shaking her head as if to say, 'Don't look at me'.

"Come on Cody, we need to look around and see what we can find without using the hatchet. I'm sure we can find something." Mike turned as he stepped out of the cave. "You girls stay here," he stated firmly, with a finger pointed at them.

"What if the wolves scare off the 'three little pigs' over there?" Holly asked, seizing Mike's pant leg.

"Well, I guess we better pray that doesn't happen until we're ready to leave."

"Mike, I'm ok. We can go, really!"

"No, you're not! And getting a little farther away, only to be caught out in the open with wolves on all sides, is not a good idea. Here at least, we have the cave we can hole up in. We only have to defend one side."

"I guess you're right," she said slowly as she lay back down.

"We'll be alright, Honey; if God is for us, who can stand against us?" He gave her a quick, reassuring smile and walked away.

Shel laid her hand on Holly's shoulder and said, with a twinkle in her eye, "It's time to submit." Holly raised her eyebrows as they exchanged a smile.

The men searched long and hard for something

they could use as a barrier between them and the wolves but in the end they decided to string fishing line up between the bushes around the cave, tying in briers that would bite and tear at the wolves' flesh if they tried to get through.

Mike held the spool of line with a stick, and as Cody pulled the line out he reasoned to himself, '*I don't think they'll be able to see the lines, so if they try to come in, it will confuse them, weird them out as it catches them up. At least that's the way I hope it will work.*'

All night long those on guard duty watched for the wolves, but without a fire, saw nothing. The bushes around the cave from time to time shook and snapped but it was hard to tell from where they sat inside the cave whether the wolves, the wind, or just their own imaginations were causing it. Just before dawn they were awakened suddenly as resonant yelps and shrieks brought them out of their lethargy. It assaulted them, tearing away the peaceful night sounds that their ears had become so accustomed to.

When daylight finally came, Mike and Cody slipped out of the cave and found spots where the line was messed up and pulled free from the bushes. At one point in the tangled line there was what appeared to be the tail of one of the wolves. But under closer inspection Cody found it was just the fur off the tail. The line had wrapped itself up high around the tail of the wolf and when the wolf tried to free itself, the line tightened, until it cut through the fur and the skin. Then as the wolf pulled frantically, he skinned his own tail, down to the bone. Cody dropped the fur as it hit him what had happened. The thought of a wolf running around out there somewhere with only a bone for a tail caused a tremor to run through him.

Mike picked up the empty tail. "Well Cody, the fishing line was a good idea after all. I don't think that wolf will want to mess with humans ever again. We can only pray that he was the alpha male. At any rate, they won't be 'tailing' us anymore," he said with an ornery grin, shaking the tail in the air.

"Euuuuuuuuw, you are a sick man, Mike!"

28
Surprise

Thorns and snares are in the way of the perverse;
He who guards his soul will be far from them.
Proverbs 22:5 NKJV

The boar had kept Chuck and Leroy in the tree through the night and most of the next day. Finally, Leroy couldn't wait any longer, "THAT'S IT! I have to take a dump and I'm doing it right now." He stood between two branches, unfastened his pants and squatted down as far as he could without falling out.

Meanwhile, the boar sat back on its haunches, grunting and complaining about the sudden movement in the tree. When something fell out of the tree, he stood and meandered over to investigate the mysterious object. Cautious not to move too quickly he sniffed it, then reeled back and squealed in disgust, turning to kick dirt at the 'surprise' with his back feet. Then he walked about twenty feet away and began rooting along with the other hogs, clearly finished with the disgusting creatures in the tree.

Leroy had just begun pulling up his pants when Chuck dryly commented, "I always figured your stink could scare away wild hogs."

With his briefs up and his pants still down around his knees, Leroy took a swing at him. But as he leaned towards Chuck his right foot was pulled off of its branch. His arms swung wildly at the air as he fell, his pants catching on a branch, tearing almost completely in two, as well as a gaping hole in the back of his briefs. There he lay on his back, on the ground with the wind knocked out of him, his head only inches away from the 'surprise'.

The boar had turned to watch the screaming man fly out of the tree while the rest of the herd were scared off. It took a step forward and squealed loudly at Leroy who sprang up off the ground and ran, imagining the boar hot on his heels, ripping through the back of his legs with its tusks swinging wildly back and forth. With every step his torn pants tripped him up and he kicked and fought to free himself from their grasp as he ran towards the river.

The boar, in fact, had not moved from its spot at all. When Leroy was out of sight, it looked up at Chuck one last time, then walked off in the direction of the rest of the herd.

Chuck dissolved into laughter as he clumsily made his way out of the tree. Once safely on the ground, he picked up his gun and stuck it into the back of his pants. He then walked over and retrieved Leroy's boot from the wallow. With two fingers he slowly pulled it out, the mud refusing to let it go, making a disgusting sucking sound. The boot dripped with the stench of the hog as he carried it at arm's length.

Still laughing, he snatched up the blue bandana with his free hand while he passed the yellow bush, leisurely walking towards the river to meet back up with his friend.

As he neared the river, he could see Leroy pacing back and forth, mourning the loss of his pants, trying hard to keep the hole in the back of his briefs closed.

"That was the funniest thing I ever saw. I thought I'd fall right out of that tree from laughing!"

"That could've been you just as easy as it was me!"

"Then you'd be laughing instead of me."

"No I wouldn't," He thrust his finger towards the

trees, "I could have been killed out there, either from the fall or being ripped apart by that boar!"

"He never even moved, he just stood there with a puzzled look on his face, watching your naked back side slipping and falling as you ran like a madman, tripping all over yourself! I think he thought it was funny, too!"

"That's enough!"

"Oh man, when you landed right next to that stinking turd, I thought I'd die, right there."

"Shut Up, RIGHT NOW!" Leroy roared in his face.

"Sure, ok!" Chuck said, with a mock expression, throwing his hands up in surrender.

Leroy brushed himself off and straightened what remained of his clothes in an attempt to keep some of his dignity, some respectability. All he ever wanted was respect from people, for them to look at him and be afraid. That's the way he understood respect; being just a way to make people leave him alone. In truth, his rough exterior hid the wounded heart of a kitten.

His black hair hung limp over one eye while his pale face and large dark eyes gave him a youthful look. His arms and chest rippled through the plain white t-shirt that was two sizes too small in order to show off his muscles and tattoos. He worked out his upper body, twice a week, to maintain his forceful appearance. He usually wore blue jeans but now his white socks stuck out of the tops of his black combat boots, clinging to his scrawny legs as one strong arm hung across his slender backside holding his briefs shut. He was pacing back and forth, breathing deeply, in an attempt to regain a normal adrenalin level.

Chuck thought he looked like one of those kids' picture books that divide different kinds of people into three parts - head, chest, and legs. A preppy college kid's head, with a bodybuilder's torso, and thin hairy legs, complete with combat boots and a tutu.

There really wasn't a tutu, but Chuck imagined

that would complete his ensemble.

Chuck tried not to watch him in order to keep from laughing, deciding not to talk again until his friend had a chance to calm down. Leroy didn't get mad often, under normal conditions, but nothing about spending the night in a tree, fell into the category of normal.

"Man, it's hot out here," Leroy finally said as he wiped his free arm across his forehead.

"Yeah, it is. But I wouldn't think that would be a problem for you with your air conditioning and all."

"WHAT?" Leroy started towards him and Chuck winced at his mistake.

Now all Chuck had to do was stay out of his way for a while, just long enough for him to cool down. So he scrambled to his feet as Leroy swung his fist, catching him on the nose and sending him crashing back down. He quickly recovered and got to his feet before Leroy's fist flew again. This time Chuck dodged out of his way and he swung his own fist, popping Leroy in the left eye. Leroy's next attempt was fruitless too, as his big lumbering body moved as if in slow motion.

Chuck eluded another punch, but tripped over the canoe as he fled, unknowingly knocking it into the shallow current. Getting back up he turned on Leroy, enraged at being hit.

Leroy's demeanor softened when he saw the anger in Chuck's face. Now he shuffled around in an attempt to avoid being hit himself. Suddenly he froze in place, staring in shock over Chuck's shoulder, his eyes flying open as his jaw dropped.

Chuck, seeing Leroy's expression, stopped mid-swing and turned to see their canoe careening down the river. His wavy auburn hair standing up like flames on his head with twigs and dried leaves stuck in it, from their night in the tree. His eyes were quickly blackening and his nose was turning purple, but somehow, the purple seemed to match his auburn hair.

The canoe sped towards the rocks that the couple's rubber rafts were wrapped around as they still fought to get free. The water drove the canoe up onto the rocks, scraping across its bottom until it rolled over, flipped upside down and continuing down the river, spinning like a propeller winding down.

Chuck's face turned a bright red to match his hair. The veins in his neck looked like they were about to burst. His arms drew close to his side as they stiffened and his hands tightened into fists. He leaned forward, his arms ridged at his sides, as he roared with anger downstream.

But the canoe just continued careening out of control. He began to run along the shoreline after it. Smashing, stomping and striking out at anything that dared to stand in his way. Yelling at the top of his lungs, cursing God as he ran.

The water got more turbulent as the rocks got bigger and greater in number. The canoe sailed towards the rocks with increasing speed. Hollow, drumming sounds reverberated off of the water's surface as the old mahogany canoe struck the rocks in its way, bouncing off and then continuing on, inching its way ever closer to the opposite shore.

Chuck knew that there was little to no chance that the canoe would ever turn and come back to the shore he now ran down. So he stopped running and hollered once more, in an attempt to demand that the canoe bow to his control. "Get back here!!" He yelled until his voice began to fail him. Then instead of yelling, he began to pick up rocks and throw them as far as he could, watching the canoe as it disappeared over the falls. Defeated, he dropped to his knees; staring at the spot he had last seen his canoe go over the edge.

It was gone forever, so, after breathing deeply, he calmed down and rose to go. With his eyes still flashing, he spat out, "You're not going to stop me God. I'll just find another way." He pulled the blue bandana out of his back pocket and shook it over his head and said defiantly, "It's time to go talk to Bo about his dog." He retraced the path he had just taken, along the bank of the river, wading through the unfortunate grasses, bushes and branches that he had left in his wake; clutching the bandana in his fist as if he could make it cry out in pain if he squeezed it hard enough.

❖ ❖ ❖ ❖ ❖

Leroy had run off too, but towards the woods, in the opposite direction of Chuck. He was upset with himself for losing his temper. Nothing good had ever come of him losing his temper. He now ran through the woods, just far enough that he could be alone. If Chuck ever stopped throwing his tantrum and came back, he didn't want him seeing him crying like a baby.

He stopped running when he reached a clearing and dropped to his knees in the middle of a patch of bright red ivy. Turning his anger on himself he struck himself in the head with his fist over and over again. "You idiot, you idiot!" he moaned, groaning loudly. After a few minutes he stopped and hung his head until his chin touched his chest. His arms fell limp at his sides. He laid backwards, flopping down onto the ivy with his skinny hairy knees in the air. He cried quietly, not caring that the tears were running into his ears. His body shook with the tremors from his weeping, talking silently to himself, almost as if he were praying.

'What am I doing wrong? Why does everything always happen to me? How did I get myself into this mess? Why? Why? Why?' He pushed his hair out of his eyes with one hand then rested it on his forehead. He had no strength left after spending the last twenty-nine and a half hours in a tree with little-to-no sleep and nothing to eat. His energy was spent; he gave up and was soon fast asleep. There really wasn't any way for him to answer those questions, not now, maybe not ever. So why try?

Shel thought that Holly might be able to travel for a couple of hours today. The plan was to have her tell them if she needed to stop, when or if she got tired. Then, once she had a chance to rest, they would hopefully be able to proceed again and if she couldn't go on they would just camp there.

When Holly woke from her nap, they began to pack up only to be interrupted by the same angry voices and squealing they had heard yesterday. They rushed about but, before they could get everything together and tie the sleeping bags onto Mike's and Cody's packs, the voices began to move through the woods. They stopped, frozen in their tracks, straining to hear what was being said, struggling to know which way to go. They stood quietly for a moment like statues frozen in one position in a museum.

When the screaming and cursing seemed to surround them on all sides, it sent them diving back into their cave, dragging their things in with them as they did.

All of a sudden, a big man came crashing through the bushes with no pants on. When the man reached the center of a patch of red ivy, no farther than a hundred feet from where they were hiding, he dropped to his knees while the couples watched, wide-eyed from behind the bush in front of the cave.

"Where are his pants?" Mike questioned.

Holly whispered, "What's he doing?" as the man began hitting his own head.

"I don't know, but that man needs some serious help," Cody said, stating the obvious.

"Should we go help him?" Holly asked, turning to

look at Mike.

"No Button. We need to stay hidden here, and wait this out, whatever this is." Mike turned back to watch the man, then he began to pray out loud, "Lord, this man needs Your love. Draw him to You, Lord. Show him Your power to save. Change these men's lives, and protect us as You do. Give us wisdom to know when to move, how to move and if we should move. Amen."

They all said 'amen' in a mechanical way as they continued to stare through the bush that covered them from view. They could still hear another man off in the distance, screaming and cursing God even as the man in the clearing calmed down, then fell back into the ivy and began to cry.

Holly said, "Well, it looks like the Lord might be getting through to this one. But, I think I might have chosen a better place to pray than the middle of a poison ivy patch! But that's just me."

29
Mr. Itchy

For the wise can see where they are going,
but fools walk in the dark.
Ecclesiastes 2: 14 NLT

Leroy slept on the soft red ivy and found, when he woke, that it was already getting dark. He jumped up quickly and headed back towards the river, tripping on roots and rocks that were hiding in the shadows of the encroaching darkness.

As he stumbled along he grumbled to himself, *'I do wish I'd stop seeing Mac's dead eyes staring at me. I'll never get a decent night's sleep again.'*

When he reached the river, he found Chuck already asleep in the sand. He sat down beside him, feeling very alone. He took in a deep breath and sighed as he looked into the depths of the dark water before him. The autumn leaves were drifting down and gently landing on the water's surface. Twirling like so many pinwheels, spinning towards the shore where they ran into each other, fitting together like gears and grinding to a stop, then pushing up onto the bank where they, with time, would become one with the cool mud.

"God," Leroy began to pray out loud then stopped short as he turned to look at Chuck who slept on. Saying no more, Leroy began to survey the trees on the opposite shore. They stood tall and black against the deepening blue sunset, reflecting off the water as the sun abandoned the sky to the night.

The river rushed by Leroy with a constant roar as it crashed against the rocks in its wake. Even though the water was in upheaval, the sound of it calmed him and he lay down again for the night with his back to his friend.

When Chuck awoke the next morning cold and hungry, he found Leroy sitting by the water's edge washing his legs with the cool water, then rubbing them with damp coarse sand, moaning, "Oh, this is hell on earth!"

"What are you doing?" Chuck asked as he got up and approached him. "Oh Man!" he said, taking a sudden step back as he saw the poison ivy that engulfed his friend's neck, ears and legs with an angry red, liquid-filled rash. "What happened to you?"

"I don't know, I must a got bit by a swarm of skeeters or something."

"You must be highly allergic to them then, 'cause I got bit a mess a times, but nothing like that."

"I've got it everywhere, and I do mean everywhere. I'm fixing to start running and screaming any minute now!"

"Where'd you go yesterday? I called and called for you, but you didn't answer me."

"I went for a walk to try to clear my head," Leroy said carefully as he understated his meltdown.

"That musta been some kind a walk to keep you out there all day. I laid down to sleep a spell and when I woke up you still weren't back."

"Well, I laid down too. I was awfully tired after spending the night in that tree."

"I was about to go back to the truck without you," Chuck said with a scowl, "but it was getting too late to make it all the way back. So, I just laid back down here and waited for you but you never came."

As Leroy continued to scratch, he mumbled to himself, under his breath, "Well clearly I did come back." Then he sat thinking, giving Chuck time to cool down before saying, "You know Chuck, it kinda seems to me as if someone's been standing in the way of us getting them 'folks'!"

"You mean 'GOD' don't you?" Chuck spat out the word 'God' as if it tasted rancid in his mouth. "I don't care if He is standing in our way, we're not quitting and I don't want to hear another word about GOD! You got that? - Come on, let's get going," he said as he reeled around to walk upstream to where they left his pickup.

"I got to get me a shower as soon as I get home, this scratching isn't doing me a bit of good, in fact it seems to be making it worse!" Leroy mumbled, as he fell in line behind Chuck, forgetting about how important it had been yesterday to hold his briefs closed. Instead, he now appreciated the accessibility as he scratched his exposed backside.

They walked all morning and most of the afternoon. Leroy had taken the lead early on, moving almost at a run to get there sooner, while Chuck lagged behind enjoying the misery that his friend was in.

"Serves you right, running off and not coming back till dark. We could've been crawling out of our warm beds this morning instead of freezing all night. I haven't eaten anything for a day and a half! Oh what I wouldn't give for a full on breakfast with bacon, and," he paused then added, "and I ain't talking on the hoof."

"Look - I fell asleep, just like you did; I had to sleep in wet sand, just like you did. I'm just as hungry as you are... plus I'm itching like a dog at a flea convention. So just you be quiet! I'm trying to think of a way to stop this itching short of peeling my skin clean off. Can't we just get to your pickup and get on home?"

Chuck had parked his pickup on the other side of a bridge so when they reached it Leroy ran across. They had covered the truck up with branches to hide it from view of anyone passing by. It was hidden so well that when Leroy passed it, Chuck snorted with amusement. "You idiot, are you blind or something?" Leroy spun around and Chuck took one look at the spark in his swollen eye, then threw his hands up and stepped back, saying no more.

Leroy ripped the branches away from the truck and threw them aside, then jumped in. Chuck said nothing but joined him as the two of them started off towards town.

As they passed the first houses in the tiny town Chuck said, "I'll be stopping to get something to eat, what do you think you might want?"

"Are you kidding me? I just want to go home, I'm not fit to be seen out anywhere!"

"Well, I'm not going home till I get something to eat so you just sit there and starve for all I care." Chuck snarled, swerved off the road and up to a drive-up window.

Leroy frantically looked for something to cover himself but found nothing. In the end he sat: legs crossed, hands lying in his lap, trying not to be conspicuous in his briefs with his rash. But he could still feel the eyes of the teenage girl on him as she stumbled over her words.

"Welcome to Sally's b-big b-burger. How can I help yyyyou?"

Chuck looked over the menu as if he had never seen it before, slowly choosing, then changing his mind or adding to his order over and over again, thoroughly enjoying the awkward situation at both Leroy and the girl's expense. When a stern looking older man came back with his order, he paid for it quickly and then sped away.

"Did you see her eyes popping right out of her head when she saw you? You scared that little girl plum out of her wits!"

"What's the matter with you Chuck, are you insane? Can't you just once try and be a decent human being?"

"I am a decent human being, as you put it. You're the one sitting there in your knickers at a restaurant for crying out loud!" He was still laughing when he pulled into Leroy's driveway. "I'll be picking you up in the morning at about nine. We'll be going out to Bo's house to get that tracking dog of his. We're going to get them folks Leroy and nothing or no one's going to stop us," he paused to glare at him, "you got that?" Then he mumbled to himself as Leroy stepped out of the pickup, "I sure hope my mama ain't home, I can't take none of her junk today."

Leroy didn't say anything as Chuck peeled out; he just jumped back and went into the small apartment he called home to get his shower.

After showering, he put on a clean pair of blue jeans and a white t-shirt, feeling much better about himself until he looked in the mirror. He had known his eye was swollen from Chuck's punch, still it shocked him to see his left eye was purple and almost swollen completely shut while the rash devoured his face, pushing his other eye into just a slit.

There was one good thing about it though; his fine black hair was raised up slightly from the rash, giving it an interesting swoop, before it fell limp again over his black eye.

He sat down on the second-hand couch, which he found by the side of the road a year ago. As he dropped, the springs gave way then sprang back up slightly, leaving his mass sitting only inches from the floor. Picking up the phone he ordered a pizza and then lay back to rest and think while he waited for it to arrive, realizing that the tracking dog would find the people they were after and then he would have to shoot at least one of the folks they were pursuing, just to make Chuck happy.

"How can I get out of this, God?" He prayed under his breath. "Can you just let them get away somehow?" He couldn't catch his breath as his heart raced with thinking about shooting someone, but how could he get out of it? Chuck was meaner than a cornered badger and Leroy had already seen him kill one man with no remorse whatsoever.

Leroy knew that if he had to kill those folks he would be reduced to a babbling fool who begged on the streets for the rest of his life, not able to make sense out of the simplest of things.

"How can that be what you want for me God? I can't do this, I don't want to do it, but I'll have to. Please God, please if there's any way that you can change the direction I'm headed, could You please? Would You do that for me?" He stopped suddenly and added in a sedate tone, "No, I'm so sorry God, You got no call to be doing anything for me... not for me but for them poor unfortunate folks... do it for them."

He lay still for a moment listening, half-hoping to hear an audible response, but none came. He slid sideways, lying down on the worn-out, stained couch. Breathing deeply, he felt himself relaxing as the tension of the last couple of days faded away. His arm hung out over the edge, as there was no room for it on the shallow couch. The tattoo of a ravenous wolf baring its teeth looked up from his arm, as if ready to devour anyone who dared to come near him as he slept, or maybe it would decide to turn on Leroy as he lay there defenseless and alone, very alone.

30
Bon-bons

*No discipline is enjoyable while it is happening
-it's painful! But afterward there will be a peaceful
harvest of right living for those who are trained in
this way.*
Hebrews 12: 11 NLT

The next morning the couples sat inside their cave, without a fire, not knowing if the men were still out there somewhere. It would have been a horrible irony to be found, after hiding right under their noses for 24 hours. So they sat quietly listening, until the stillness of the forest convinced them that the men had moved on.

Holly was feeling more like herself, so as Shel changed her bandages, the two of them talked freely.

"Wow, I can't believe this is healing so well, already!"

"It's those amazing herbs of yours; I don't know what that stuff was but I'm feeling so much better."

"Do you think you might be able to travel a couple of hours today?"

"Oh yeah, sure," Holly said with a confident nod.

"We're planning on stopping for lunch and letting you take a nap, then if you still feel up to it we'll see if we can go a little bit farther. How's that sound?"

"That sounds good to me, I can't wait to get home again."

"I agree, the sooner we get back home the better! A hot shower awaits me and I think it's about time I discovered what a bon-bon is."

"I want a hot bubble bath myself and I think bon-bons are candies covered with a thin layer of chocolate. Personally, if I'm going to eat chocolates, I'd take a bowl full of truffles!"

"A bowl full of truffles? Exactly how big of a bowl?" Shel questioned.

"Any size bowl, I'd eat a large mixing bowl full of them right now if I had one."

"Not by yourself you wouldn't."

"Well, I guess I could spare one or two."

"Chocolate in any form or amount sounds amazing right now to me," Shel said as she finished wrapping Holly's shoulder.

"Mmm," Holly rolled her eyes in her head while lying back on top of the sleeping bag. "And a real bed to sleep in instead of a sleeping bag laid on hard ground."

"Yeah," Shel said as she lay down next to her friend, both with their knees in the air and Shel's blond hair overlaying Holly's red. "I'm having the hardest time trying to fall asleep on this rock hard ground." Shel slapped the ground with her hand. "Oh what I wouldn't give for an air mattress right about now!"

"We should've deflated one and brought it along, instead of leaving it behind. I would've carried it myself, if I had known what we were in for."

"No time, that's why," Shel reasoned.

"Yeah, that's true but stilllll", Holly drug out the word as she conceded.

"Well, I guess we could have thrown it into the water and paddled across the river on it!"

"Oh yeah, that would've been great too! Why didn't I think of that?" Holly exclaimed.

"Or we could of pulled it along behind us!"

"With the rope!"

"Now that actually makes more sense."

Both women sighed together as they lay arm in arm, gazing up at the ceiling of the cave.

"Let's get going girls," Mike said as he looked in on them, holding their backpacks in his hands. "Are you sure you want to carry this Honey?" He said. "We could divide it up and carry it for you."

Not wanting to burden her companions with the extra weight, Holly shook her head. "No Puppy, I'll be fine, really! I'll just carry it on my other shoulder or in my hand."

Knowing that Holly was feeling good made them all feel better about their situation. Telling a childhood story, Holly threw her arms wide to show the size of the cow that her and her brother had tipped. Then she went into great detail about how it jolted awake as it hit the ground, and jostled about as it tried to get back on it's feet.

They all laughed, but quietly Cody asked Shel, "Do you think it's alright that she does that with her arm?"

Shel threw her shoulders up, "I don't know. I was just wondering that myself. But, I guess if she doesn't mind it and she doesn't start bleeding or something, she'll be fine."

"I hope so."

Overhearing them, Mike turned and raised his brows in concern, nodding as if to say, "me too."

As they walked along, Shel stopped to examine some dried weeds. "Oh! These are wild carrots!"

Cody joined her, "It looks like old Queen Anne's Lace to me."

"Very good! You're getting the hang of this," she said approvingly as she took out her knife and dug the dirt out from around the plant. After she pulled it from the ground, she handed its long pale yellow root to Cody.

"Well it kinda looks like a carrot," he said, while raising it to his nose, "oh, it even smells like a carrot!"

"What we're looking for, Cody, are stems that are hairy."

Cody was still staring hard at the root.

Shel chuckled, "No Cody, not the root, the stem." She pointed at the fine hairs that stuck straight out from the stem. "If the stem isn't hairy leave it alone, because it's probably Poison Hemlock and you don't want to eat that! Also, if it is a wild carrot, it will have a blackish-purpley dot in the center of the flower. The flowers on these are done now, so we can't tell by that. But when the flowers of the wild carrot dry, they roll up into what looks like a little nest." She stuck her finger in the center of the nest to show him where a tiny bird might sit. "These are wild carrots, so we can safely eat them and they'll be good." She handed it back to Cody and then continued to dig the rest up.

The carrots themselves were only three to six inches long, the biggest being only about three-quarters of an inch thick. Once again the plants were too old and tough to eat. The taste was good but no amount of chewing could break it down enough to be swallowed.

With discouragement Shel forced herself to sound cheerful, "I'll boil them to get the flavor out, a nice little carrot broth would be good."

As noon approached Holly began to slow down more and more. When the others noticed that she seemed to be forcing herself along, Mike said, "I think we need to stop for awhile. We need something to eat and rest a little before looking for a good place to stop for the night."

Spreading out the backpacks, they all sat down as Cody removed the dried venison from his pack then thanked the Lord for providing for them before they began to chew. The venison was stringy and rubbery, much like chewing on an electrical cord but without the exciting zing that would follow. They also noticed that the taste was a little off, so they ate as much as they could then dumped the rest in the river before starting out again.

"Why is it that everything we want to eat is either too old or too tough?" Holly complained to no one in particular.

"Well, everything has a season that it grows, ripens, goes to seed then sets dormant," Shel began to monologue on her favorite topic, "unfortunately this is the season for most things to go to seed or lay dormant. What you're used to is walking into a grocery store and buying whatever you need whenever you want it. That's because man has figured out how to grow things out of season with green houses, grow lights, etc... we've engineered our foods to do what we want them to do. We have discovered ways of making them ripen on demand! We've left the ways of nature behind. We have abandoned the ways of our 'mothers that went before us.' The ways that they preserved foods for thousands of years: root cellars, growing winter crops, canning, pickling. Hardly anyone does any of that anymore and many times when they do, they use shortcuts."

"I remember my grandmother fermenting dill pickles and sauerkraut with a salt brine. But now, most of them are made with pasteurized vinegar. Yuk! I know there has to be other ways to preserve foods that we no longer know how to do. For instance if we had some salt we could have packed our raw venison in it to preserve it. You've heard of 'salt pork', right? Or if we had the time, we could have smoked it the old-fashioned way. I once had some smoked venison jerky that was just out of this world!"

"Oh, please stop!" Mike interjected. "My stomach

has already turned to devouring me alive. Please no more talk about food," he said as he raised his shirt and clasped his skin, void of its fat and shook it.

"Yeah, that was more of an answer than I was looking for," Holly said.

Mike smiled affectionately and joined his wife on the sleeping bags. Leaning to kiss her on the cheek, he said, "Ok Button, let's get that nap now." Then he and Holly laid down together.

Cody sighed as he and Shel walked off alone, pushing his hand into the cavity that was once his stomach. "Where's a Chick-fil-A when you need one? This 'barely having enough to keep us alive' is wearing me down."

"I could go for some chicken, I'd even settle for a rabbit, a squirrel or even a chipmunk right now."

"All this talking about food is killing me but it's all I seem to be able to think about, just the same. We should talk about things I don't recognize as food."

"You mean weeds," Shel said, with her hands on her hips in mock disgust.

"Yes, weeds – and please no more tree bark. I'm sure it's full of 'all things good' that will keep me alive. And I must admit none of us seem to be terribly weak yet. But the hunger is still there and I need something in my stomach."

"What if we try some fishing?" Shel offered.

"Ok!"

The two of them walked down to the river's edge and looked around for a good place to sit. Kicking off their shoes and socks, they sat up against a big rock where small pebbles and sand mixed. As Shel sat letting the water lick at her toes, she fumbled through the fishing tackle box. Cody stood gazing at the water, noticing movement on the other side of the river. He put his hand out to quiet Shel, "shhh."

Shel immediately stopped grumbling about Mike getting the fishing lines all tied up and came and stood beside Cody. "What is it?" She whispered craning her neck out to see.

Cody crawled up onto some boulders, extending a hand down to his wife to help her up, until they both stood looking, staring down into the water. "It's fish spawning, but it's out of reach," he whispered.

"How can we get some?"

"We can't, we're on the wrong side. Even if we could swim across, they'd all swim away by the time we got there."

"What about the fishing line?"

"No, all we have is line and hooks and small sinkers. We may have been able to cast that far if we had a rod and reel - but," he didn't need to say anything more to make his point.

"Oh, Cody it's not fair!" She sat down hard on the boulder overlooking the river. "I just can't take it anymore! Why can't we just wake up from this nightmare?"

"Shhhhhh, it's ok, Babe, I feel the same way." He sat down next to her, pulling her in with his arms, drawing her head in to rest on his chest.

"I just want to go home now!" Her voice was so small and vulnerable that it pulled on Cody's heartstrings. He wanted to fix it, but he couldn't make this trial go away. "It's going to be all right, Babe. It's going to be all..." he stopped abruptly.

"What?" Shel stopped to look at him.

"SHH!" He stood to look, his eyes catching movement in the water near them.

"What?" She asked breathlessly, becoming quiet and alert, standing to turn in the direction that Cody was looking. "What is it?" She whispered.

"The water is moving behind that big rock! Get your line out." He flapped his hand frantically towards the tackle box.

Shel dropped to her knees and began to untangle the line, while Cody stood high on a boulder watching the water. "I have it!" She said.

"We need a bug," Cody said as he slid down from the boulder and both of them searched the surrounding area.

"Over here, here's a bug!" Shel called quietly motioning for him to come quickly.

Cody carefully picked up the long-legged bug. "Perfect!" He said as he drove the hook through its tiny body. Shel cringed and turned away, moving cautiously towards the boulder and peeked over it. There in the water along the shore was a large female brown trout, flapping her tail to dig a trench where she would lay her eggs. Gently setting the hook on top of the rock Cody let out the line and slid it slowly down the side of the rock and into the water. The dying bug wiggled as it went into the water; its long legs kicking anxiously, not wanting to let go of life. Immediately a male trout that they hadn't seen before took the bait. Cody snatched it up while the female darted away. There now hung the most beautiful fish they had ever laid eyes on.

"I never thought a raw fish would make my mouth water," Cody said. "I'm feeling a little like Gollum right now; any moment now I might bite into this fish, 'Raw and Wriggling'." He shook his face as he did his very best Gollum impersonation and Shel snorted with delight.

❖ ❖ ❖ ❖ ❖

Mike and Holly had just rolled up their sleeping bags and were resting against a rock when they saw Cody and Shel coming with the fish.

"Should we start a fire?" Holly asked.

"No," Mike said, "it's too early to start a fire, we need to get farther today if we can."

"Unless you're not feeling well enough to keep going?" Shel questioned Holly with concern.

"Other than starving, I feel fine. And I'll eat that fish raw if it means we can get closer to home."

"Well it's time for sushi then!" Mike said. "Let's eat!"

After they had stopped for the night Mike took the fish hooks down to the water to try his hand at fishing while Shel went off to set the snares.

Looking through the survival booklet Cody found the directions for a small bird's snare, and got to work whittling the sticks he would need.

Holly thought it was about time that she started pitching in again so she built the fire. She then sat back and watched as the smoke rose to mix with the mist that already hung heavy in the air. A gentle breeze blew, pushing it aside to make room for the next cloud to form and roll away.

If those men were still looking for them, they wouldn't be able to find them by following the sight of smoke. Not in these mountains where the clouds settled on them like smoke.

31
The Phone

It shall come to pass that before they call, I will answer;
And while they are still speaking I will hear.
Isaiah 65: 24 NKJV

It was late afternoon when Shel walked off through the trees and Cody went looking for her, finding her up on a large boulder holding Holly's cell phone over her head.

"Is there any signal?" He asked as he approached her.

"Once in awhile, it comes and goes."

"How many bars?"

"Just one most the time, but sometimes it flashes two."

"Did you try and call anyone?"

"Yeah, my mom, but I don't know what good it would do even if I did get through to her. She's not going to know where we are... we don't even know where we are! I didn't tell anyone and I know Holly didn't either, we had no idea where Mike was dragging us off to."

Her words were bitter but Cody overlooked them and said, "Here, let me try something," as he crawled up onto the boulder and sat down beside her.

"I don't know Cody, I've tried to find a signal every morning since we started running but it's just too weak. How in the world do people communicate out here?" She slapped her hands down on the rock in frustration. "Or maybe the phone's broken. I thought maybe trying it later in the day like this might make a difference, but it doesn't. Do you think maybe it's broke?"

"No, it's not broke. We've been traveling in a valley following the river, surrounded by mountains. There won't be a signal out here unless we're standing directly under a cell tower or on the mountaintop. I'm sure once we're closer to a town we'll be able to call someone."

"Well, what good is that? We need help NOW!"

"Did you say you got two bars?" Cody asked, focusing on the phone.

"Yeah, but only flashes of two."

"Have you ever gotten three bars while we've been out here?" He stood up raising the phone over his head as she stood behind him.

"No, never. This is the first time I've even been able to get two bars."

He turned and looked at her, "Oh, but that's good! That means we're getting closer to a town or maybe a cell tower."

"Oh good!" she said as she wrapped her arms around his waist from behind and tucked her chin up over his shoulder to look on at the phone's small screen.

"You're too cute!" He kissed the side of her head then said, "Maybe if I can get a little higher, I might be able to send out a text. That is if it will hold two bars." He held it up and spun around.

Shel stood beside him and asked, "To whom would you send a text to?"

"Will. He and Julie were going to come over when we got back from camping, to talk about our trip."

"What! Will is coming over when we get back, after what you did to his wife?"

"Yeah, he wanted Julie to have some time to heal before I apologize to her."

"When were you going to tell me this?" Shel's anger stung her voice.

"Shel, can we please not do this right now? It's not really important is it?"

She bit her tongue, forcefully reminding herself to be submissive and respectful.

Shel had known Julie for years but had never quite made a connection with her. As she thought about it she could see how Julie would need time to sort things out. She glanced over at Cody and realized it was a show of strength on his part, that he was willing to deal with his sin head on, and she admired him for it. "I'm sorry Honey, you're right."

Cody was still focused on the problem at hand, "I can't remember if it's been eleven or twelve days that we've been out here. I think we're supposed to be getting back either tonight or tomorrow night. Will's the only one I told where we were going. Well... the general area we planned on going. And he's expecting us to be back before he and Julie show up at the house in the evening... tonight? I think? No one else I told is even going to realize we're missing until Mike and I don't show up for work on Monday morning."

"Someone will probably miss us at church on Sunday."

"Yeah, but they'll probably just think we decided to sleep in after our trip. I sure hope Will recognizes Holly's number."

"What are you going to say?" Shel said as he helped her down off the boulder.

"Just 'HELP'."

"Just 'Help'? Is that enough? Shouldn't you tell him about the men chasing us, or Holly getting shot?"

"No Babe, the more information you send, the harder it is for the message to go through, and with only two bars it may not go through anyhow. We have to keep it as short as possible."

They walked over to a rocky cliff overlooking a deep ravine and Cody spotted a tree at its edge. Climbing up as high as he could, he pulled the phone out of his pocket and held it up to see first one bar, then two, then back to one, two. It continued to flash back and forth so he decided to type in the message and hit 'send' the next time it flashed two bars. He did so and as he sent it the phone momentarily flashed three bars. He stared at it for a while to see if three bars appeared again, but they didn't. "Well, that was weird," he mumbled to himself. "Is that you Lord?" He asked as he closed the phone and stuck it back into his pocket.

Before coming down he decided to make the most of his vantage point. So, as he slowly scanned the horizon, he saw off in the distance what looked like a cell tower or possibly a silo or smoke stack. "I see something! Look, over there!" He pointed towards it.

"What is it? I can't see anything." Shel yelled back.

"Some kind of tower or something."

"Can we go that way?"

"Yeah, it looks like this ravine will take us right to it," he said as he worked his way down out of the tree. "Of course, you can never tell where we may end up if it bends and twists its way through these mountains."

By the time he reached the ground, Shel was practically jumping up and down with excitement as she peppered him with questions, "Did you send the message? Do you think it went through? How far does the ravine go? How far away is the tower? Can we go that way tomorrow? Do you think there's a town?"

She was still chattering and not giving him a chance to answer when they walked back into camp, knowing that she didn't really expect any answers, she just needed to voice her questions out loud. Cody simply smiled and kept walking, thinking to himself that tomorrow promised to be an interesting day.

"Are you sure Cody said they'd be home tonight?" Julie asked.

"That's what he said, they want to get things put away then have the weekend to relax before having to go back to work."

"Well, they're not here."

"I can see that," Will said with concern in his voice.

"You think something's wrong?"

They got out of the car and walked up to the Wiley's house and knocked on the door. "I don't know Julie, it's not like Cody to say one thing and do another. I guess it's possible that they had car problems?"

"Don't you have Cody's cell number in your phone?"

Will pulled his phone out and scrolled through his numbers. "Cody Wiley." He pressed 'call' and waited.

Inside the house he could hear a phone ringing. "He left his phone here, great! Do you have Shel's number?"

"No, but I think I can get it from May." She dug her phone out of her purse and hurriedly messaged May and received her answer back within seconds. Then she dialed Shel's number.

Will walked around the house, peeking in the windows.

Following Will, Julie found him at the back of the house with both hands cupping the window. "There it is I can see his phone."

"There's no one answering Shel's phone either. Did you hear it ringing?"

"No, I didn't. Try it again."

She pressed 'redial' and from somewhere in the house they could faintly hear a phone ringing.

"Ok, Shel's phone is in there somewhere and Cody's is setting there." He pointed at the nightstand closest to the window.

Julie flipped through her numbers. "I don't seem to have Holly's number, either."

Will scrolled through his numbers and after finding Mike's number, called it but with no more luck than the other two.

"Let's swing over to Mike and Holly's before calling again."

When they arrived at the Hilbert's house they saw Mike's phone lying next to the charger in the kitchen but no sign of Holly's phone.

"I've never seen Holly with a phone. Maybe she doesn't have one."

"She has one, I know Mike's called her before."

"I'll call the neighbor, she's taking care of Mike and Holly's animals for them." Julie dialed and waited a moment for someone to answer.

"Hello Mirah, I need to call Holly but I don't seem to have her number. Do you have it?" - "Oh good." She jotted it down and handed it over to Will, saying, "thanks, have a nice day!"

Just then, Will received a text. He raised his phone to compare the numbers and his breath caught, the numbers were the same, then wordlessly he showed Julie the message: *"HELP!"*

"You two look like a couple of Halloween ghouls," Bo said as he sat on the ground washing his tracking dog in a tub full of tomato juice.

"Well, I wouldn't trade the way I look for the way your dog smells!" Chuck reached up to pinch his nose for emphasis, but then thought better of it. His nose still hurt too badly for him to be grabbing it right now.

"I'd trade the way I feel," Leroy muttered, patting Duke on the head as the dog wiggled excitedly, from making a friend, "Cause if I don't get me a hot shower every three or four hours, I feel like peeling my skin clean off."

"So, you're tracking some folks for the law, is that it?" Bo said with disbelief.

"Yeah, we got us a contract to bring them on in," Chuck lied.

"Now let me get this straight. You and the Chief of Burt have some kind of an agreement, where he wants you to track down and bring in, someone that he wants to see in jail worse than the two of you? Is that what you're saying?"

Chuck and Leroy didn't say anything.

"Well, they must really be bad then!" Bo paused. "Oh, come on, you gotta be kidding me. Y'all must think I'm a real idiot or something!"

Chuck just glared at him as Duke began to shake, spattering tomato juice and stink on them all.

Bo yelled at the hound then did a little shake of his own, wiping his face with the back of his arm. "Duke, you stupid dog! I'm not doing this again. If you go and scare up another polecat I'll shoot you dead rather than going through this again."

"He's done this before?" Chuck asked, glad for the chance to change the subject.

"Oh yeah, this stupid dog's done it three times this summer. I'm not given him another bath like this one, either. I've used all the tomato juice my wife put up last month already. And I'm telling you, she's none too happy about that either."

Bo pulled Duke out of the tub and hooked his chain onto a post by the pump. He pushed the handle up and down until the water came out in a rush that poured over the dog, rinsing off the tomato juice as he worked his fingers through the dog's short hair. "Ok boys, I don't care what you're up to. Duke and I need us an outing and maybe if he runs around a little he'll stop chasing after them Polecats. We can't go 'till tomorrow, though. So, if y'all come back 'bout ten tomorrow mornin', Duke and I'll be ready."

❖ ❖ ❖ ❖ ❖

In the truck on their way home Leroy said, "You know Chuck, I been thinking. What if those people have one of those new cellulite phones?"

"Oh you idiot, that's the wrong word. They're not calling them that."

"Yeah they are, they have them cellulites up in the sky and their phones can call anyone-anywhere."

"But, that isn't what they're call them," Chuck sneered.

"Well, what do they call them then?"

"I can't remember right now," he turned to look at Leroy thoughtfully, then added, "but I'm pretty sure it isn't 'Phone'."

32
An Alliance

"And whenever you stand praying,
if you have anything against anyone, forgive him,
that your Father in heaven may also forgive you
your trespasses. But if you do not forgive,
nether will your Father in heaven
forgive your trespasses."
Mark 11: 25-26 NKJV

Will and Julie went to the local station to report that Mike and Holly Hilbert, and Cody and Shelly Wiley were missing. The officer listened, looked at the text then put them in contact with Detective Samuel Trusty, close to where their friends had gone missing.

Will described over the phone what Cody had said about the area they planned to go to, and that they were to meet them when they got back, but they never showed up. Then he told him about the odd text message he had received from Holly's phone.

Plans were made and Will and Julie ran home to pack their things so they could drive down and join the search for their missing friends.

Julie fell asleep for a couple of hours while Will drove. She was awakened by the sound of Will humming to himself. "What are you humming?"

Will answered by singing:

♪ *"Where, oh where, are you to-night?*
Why did you leave me here all alone?
I searched the world over,
and I thought I found true love,
you found your pillow and
thttt' you were gone!" ♪

Julie smiled, although at times she acted irritated with him for changing words to songs to suit what ever it was he wanted to say; but secretly over the years she had grown to like it. Scooting to the middle of the bench seat, she lifted his arm and slid in under it, next to his chest, laying her head back onto his shoulder.

He happily welcomed her by kissing her on the top of the head.

"You are aware that the words are 'You met 'another' and 'thhttt' you were gone'?"

"Yeah, but it didn't fit the situation, did it?"

"Huh!" She shook her head in disbelief as another smile curved up the corners of her mouth. They sat quietly for a bit until Julie asked, "Will, tell me again, exactly what did Cody say?"

"He said, 'I'm sorry Julie, please forgive me, it will never happen again.' You caught that he called me Julie right?"

"Do you think he meant it?"

"What, that he thought I was you?"

"Oh very funny!" She said sitting forward and shaking his arm off her. "You're just so hilarious."

"Thank you, thank you! I would like to thank all those that have helped me to get where I am today," he said pretending to take a bow over the steering wheel.

Julie didn't smile this time but moved over and peered out the window into the darkness.

"I'm sorry, Honey, come back here."

"No. Can't you be serious for once? This isn't a laughing matter!"

"Come on Sweetie, I was just kidding, come on." He put his hand on her arm. "I'm sorry! Come here."

"Will, I just have to know. I want to forgive him, but every time I think about what he did, I feel this terrible fear rise up, and I'm afraid when I see him I'll just run away."

"Sweetheart, how many men do you know that say they're sorry about even the smallest things, that fast, without being prompted? Well, besides me, of course," he said with mock arrogance, rubbing his knuckles on his chest.

"Will, I appreciate that you're trying to make me laugh, but that's not what I need right now."

"Alright, yes, I think he meant it, he had obviously been repeating it over and over to himself, using your name to be able to apologize to you. He wouldn't have called me Julie otherwise, we don't look all that much alike you know," he smiled in her direction.

"Do you really think he meant it though?"

"Yes, I think he definitely meant it, and I respect him for making a point to come over so quickly and ask for your forgiveness. Even if he was sent over to get the tent, he didn't have to repent, he wanted to. And as a Christian man he should be able to lay down his pride for the benefit of his sister in the Lord. Confessing his sin was an act of submission to God. You don't have to be afraid of a man that is in submission to God! He will make mistakes for sure, but he will always repent, if he's a man that can swallow his own pride."

Julie knew all about submission, as a married woman she was to submit to Will, and she was glad that most of the time she saw instant results of her efforts. But, now she saw that men must have it harder. Submitting to God didn't always bring results right away and many times men had to figure out what it was that God wanted from them before they could respond in submission to Him. Although she could imagine that if a man knew he was being submissive to God, that he would also have that same contentment, and even the peace, like she felt when she was being submissive to Will. It must have been humbling for Cody to confess and ask forgiveness of Will, but it was obvious to her that Will respected him now for it.

Julie turned to look at her husband in the dark and finally said, "Thank you, "as she moved back over next to him. He gently pulled her into a one-arm embrace as she wrapped her arms around his middle and said, "I love you."

"I love you more."

Ignoring his cutesy attempt to again make her smile, she sat in silence for a moment and then asked,. "Will, where do you think they are? What do you think happened to them?"

"Oh, I don't know! Could be Mike's SUV just broke down, or maybe they got lost. I'm sure the detective will be able to find out. He'll know the best ways to look for them, I'm sure."

"Do you think they're okay though?"

Will was quiet for a moment longer. "Yeah, I think they're all right," he said, unsure of his own comforting words.

❖ ❖ ❖ ❖ ❖

Will had been trying to sleep with his head leaning against the car window. He had nodded off a few times for a little while but he found that it was hard to sleep with his brain vibrating and his teeth clanging into each other.

As Julie saw him attempt to sit up she said, "Will, I was telling May about this thing with Cody and she was saying..."

"You told May that Cody made a pass at you?" He

259

snapped upright and looked at her intently.

"Yeah, why wouldn't I tell her? She won't tell anyone."

"Why'd you tell May?"

"She's my best friend; boy you sure wake up grumpy! Anyhow she wouldn't let me go until I told her what was wrong."

"You told May? That Cody Wiley had made a pass at you?"

"Will, stop yelling at me! She won't tell anyone!" She looked over at him, her eyes pleading for an answer to why he was so upset with her. "Yes! Why?" She finally answered his question.

He sat looking at her for a second then said quietly, purposefully calming himself down, "Julie, you can talk to your friend about things you're going through, but in this kind of situation, you don't want to use people's names or details. It's not good; you have just caused May to form an 'alliance with bitterness'."

"What are you talking about?"

He put his hands on his face and slowly pulled down in a frustrated attempt to find the right words to explain what he meant. He then interlocked his fingers and bit the knuckle closest to his mouth as he closed his eyes and took a deep breath.

"Julie, don't you remember the lady at the park?" He turned around to look at her, bending his left leg up and sliding his knee up onto the seat as he put his arm up over the back of the seat and laid his hand gently on her shoulder.

"Yeah, what about her?"

"You told May about that too and now she hates that lady, and she doesn't even know her name." He paused, then added, "You went back to that woman and apologized, and she to you. Even though things are good with you and her now, May still hasn't let it go. Knowing May, she'll probably take that bitterness to the grave with her."

Julie got quiet as she looked out the windshield at the road before her. It was starting to get light out; the black-silhouetted trees flew by as the sky turned a beautiful shade of deep blue. It wouldn't be much longer until they were in there.

Finally she said, "Why does she do that anyhow? And what do you mean by an 'alliance with bitterness'?"

"She does it because she's your friend and ally, she's on your side and she thinks that means calling judgment down on anyone who hurts you. She'll stand by you like a loyal dog, growling and chewing off the leg of anyone who comes near you." He paused then continued, "Jesus told a story about a man who owed a great debt to the King. The King called the man into his court and told him to pay his debt now. The man fell at the King's feet and begged for mercy. Then the King felt sorry for the man and forgave him his debt. Do you remember this story?"

"Yeah."

"Well, the man then went out happy and forgiven. But as soon as he saw a fellow servant who owed him just a little money, he went to the man and said, 'pay me what you owe me now'. The fellow servant then fell at his feet and begged the man for mercy, but instead of extending a hand of mercy, like the King had done for him, the man threw his fellow servant into prison until he could pay his debt."

"What's that have to do with May?"

"Well the point is, when you're forgiven, like we are as Christians, we aren't supposed to seize a 'fellow servant' as in 'a fellow Christian', if they are repentant, like Cody is, and throw him into a prison of our own making, holding him there until we find it in our wretched hearts to forgive him."

"If we don't forgive," Will continued, "we're saying to God that there is sin that is unforgivable, and we're right. The sin of unforgiveness is unforgivable to God. That is the unpardonable sin that Christians are always looking for. The God of forgiveness is not going to allow unforgiveness into heaven with Him; He has given everything to forgive you, to forgive me and to forgive Cody."

He then paused before asking; "Now think about the rest of the story, when the King heard about the fellow servant being thrown into prison by one He Himself had forgiven, what did the King do?"

"He threw the man he had forgiven into prison and released the fellow servant."

"That's right."

She looked at him for a long moment before saying, "So what you're saying is, if May doesn't forgive Cody, but instead holds him responsible for his sin forever, even though he repents, she's in danger of being thrown into prison for eternity? Even after Cody has been released?"

"Yes, that's right, we can't just push this scripture aside and say it's not for me, when we see this same kind of story told over and over in the Bible. You just can't build a gallows for one of God's people without being hung on it yourself, instead. No matter who May thinks she is, she is not God and she doesn't get to decide who receives God's forgiveness and who doesn't."

When Will and Julie finally arrived at the department, in eastern Tennessee at the foot of the Appalachian Mountains they went in and introduced themselves to Detective Trusty. His light blue eyes smiled back at them as he shook their hands. His light blonde hair hung limp over his forehead. He was tall and he looked Will in the eyes as they spoke. His skin tones being darker than his hair, made his eyes stand out all the more.

He pointed the couple in the direction of a huge

map that hung on the wall, so they could look it over before setting out. Scanning the map together they settled on the most likely location to start their search. They would work their way south, then into other counties if they needed to.

The patrol car took the lead as Will and Julie followed close behind in their own car. They stopped at every turn off on their way up into the mountains. After several hours of stopping and searching at each turn off, they found what looked like drops of blood and possible drag marks on the ground. Detective Trusty told Will and Julie to stay in their car, until he and his men had a chance to check things out thoroughly.

Finding a dark green SUV, Detective Trusty ran a check on it and found that it belonged to a Michael R. Hilbert. The stench of death was rising from a nearby gully, but he didn't say anything about it to Will or Julie, only mentioning that they had found Mike's SUV.

The deputies walked slowly down the gully, following the smell. When they found the body of a badly decomposing man, they stopped. One of the deputies began to take pictures as the other deputy continued down the gully to investigate further.

As he moved along he found two sets of men's footprints that were soon replaced by two scuffmarks sliding down the gully the rest of the way. At the bottom of the trail he found an abandoned campsite and looked around briefly before returning to the body.

The deputies all together bagged the body then lifted it, to carry to the top of the gully. Detective Trusty unzipped the bag slightly and peeked inside, then looked over at Will and Julie still waiting.

Julie fell to the seat weeping as the detective approached their car, then asked Will if he would come and take a look to see if it was one of their friends. Will felt sick and had to stop before he got to the body. Putting his hands on his knees for a second, to keep from passing out, he then continued on towards the body bag.

"Are you sure you can do this?" The detective asked him.

"Yes, just give me a second to..." Will gagged, then lifted his shirt to cover his nose and finished with, "Ok, let's do it." The detective unzipped the bag again and Will looked at the badly decomposing face of a man. His hair did look like Cody's, but his face at this point was unrecognizable. It had been somewhat eaten by marauding animals. Maggots rolled out of the man's nose, mouth and eyes, causing his flesh to look like it was moving. And the body was bloated, making the buttons on his shirt pull tight and even pop off in places. Despite Will's attempt at not breathing, the stench was unbearable, the sight was so gruesome that he reeled around and threw up on the ground. He couldn't tell if it was Cody, but he didn't think it was. He didn't know why he didn't think it was exactly, but maybe he saw something that wasn't quite right or possibly, he just didn't want to admit that it could be his friend. But when the detective asked him if it was one of his friends, he shook his head 'No', and then moved with speed away from the stench and back to his car.

Julie had sat back up and was looking out the window of the car as the detective unzipped the body bag. From where she was, all she could see was a man's golden straw-like hair. She felt sure she was looking at Cody, as her tears streamed down her face.

When Will crawled back into the car, Julie was staring expressionless out the window opposite of where the corpse lay on the ground, less than a hundred feet away. "Is it Cody?" She asked blankly, not looking at him.

"I don't think so Sweetie."

"Oh Will, what if it is? Where are the rest of them?" She wheeled around, throwing herself into his arms and wept bitterly.

33
Messenger

"Therefore, angels are only servants-spirits sent to care for people who will inherit salvation." Hebrews 1: 14 NLT

There was a strong sense of excitement as they woke the next morning. They were in clear sight of a tower of some sort, which possibly represented civilization, and, if they could make it there without being seen or shot at, they felt as if all would be well once again. Even the fact that there wasn't anything to eat couldn't dampen their spirits as they hurried towards the tower.

Moving down towards the river, they followed the shoreline downstream and into the ravine's mouth. The sides of the ravine rose higher and higher, taking them deeper and deeper into a confined area, which offered no escape, but it was beautiful and for some reason held no fear for any of them.

A small stream ran down the center of the ravine, and as the water passed over smooth rocks it filled the air with a soothing gurgling sound. Ferns and wetland grasses grew in patches around the stream and the sides of the cliffs were decorated with vines, bare roots and bramble bushes. Above them the trees leaned as far as they could as if to shade the visitors that passed below.

The cool morning mist hung low in the sky and, as

the sun rose, the mist caught its golden hue sending its warm glow into a new day. As they walked through the mist it swirled around them feeling shockingly brisk on their faces. Breathing it in was as refreshing as the hope of finally finding their way home.

"So, you're feeling good today?" Shel asked Holly as they stumbled over the small rocks along their way.

"Oh, look at this!" She swung her arm around and over her head. "See, I hardly feel a thing."

"Wow, I can see you are feeling better but please be careful, ok? I'm not sure what's going on inside your shoulder, but I don't know what else I can do if you re-injure yourself. I would like to say, though, it looks from the outside like it's completely healed. And I can't see any reason why when you get home, you shouldn't be able to take that bath you've been talking about."

"Oh! I can't wait, I've never felt so disgustingly cruddy in my entire life and I never want to feel this way ever again." She paused for a moment before she tossed in for good measure, "God willing."

"Amen to that!"

Duke ran beside the river's edge sniffing everything along the way as he went, while the men paddled downstream in Bo's canoe following the hound on shore.

Duke's long ears nearly touched the sand and stones as he relentlessly moved towards his goal. His master had tied Shel's blue bandana around his neck so he wouldn't forget her scent. As the dog walked along, the late morning light played across the length of his auburn body, interrupted only by the black saddle on his back, the white tip of his tail, and the black and white that mixed across his muzzle. His head moved back and forth, across the surface of the ground, as his tail swiped at the air like a flag snapping in the wind. His white underbelly reflected light onto the pebbles below. Lastly his lazy shadow was pulled along behind.

Bo kept his eyes on his dog, watching for the slightest change in his behavior, behavior that only he knew how to detect. "Well, one things for certain," Bo observed, "these folks don't seem to know where they're going and from what you've said, they've went from river to creek and switched back again. Where they'll end up, only Duke here can tell."

"What keeps him from just running off?" Chuck asked.

"He isn't going to run off. He's been trained to stay near me, unless I tell him otherwise."

"What if he scares up another polecat?"

"He isn't going to find one of them during the day. They're nocturnal. Anyhow, he likes tracking and he hasn't been out for a while. Just look at him, he's excited to be out and about."

"Well there are plenty of other stinking things he could get into."

"How about you mind your own business, Chuck? While I mind what my dog is doing! He has the scent now and he's keen to find whoever wore that bandanna."

"Hey, I'm just saying, what if he stirs up some stink somewhere along the way? I'm not riding back with him if he smells bad."

Bo drug out his response with irritation, "That's just - fine - with - me."

"What's that suppose to mean?"

"Look Chuck, Duke and I have an understanding; if he tracks anything stinking, he's going to get his butt kicked over his shoulder. Now you just stop fretting, 'cause if I hear one more word from you, I'm going to smack you upside the head with the butt of my gun. Then you can take a nap the rest of the way there, for all I care," he said with stinging disdain.

Bo sat behind Chuck in the canoe so he didn't see

Chuck when he sneered.

The couples continued moving along the ravine floor until late in the morning when they all decided it was time to rest and sat down one after another on big rocks or amongst the sun-warmed pebbles.

"I'm starved," Cody complained, "there has to be something to eat down here."

Holly stood and began to turn over rocks in the stream. "Come here little crayfish, we won't hurt you too bad! We just want to chew on you for a while." But no one laughed at her attempt at lifting their spirits.

The other three just sat rubbing their ankles and feet as Holly came and sat down again by her husband. They had been walking on rocks all morning which either jabbed at them through their increasingly worn shoes or turned their ankles this way and that, leaving their feet aching and their spirits low.

"I could eat my own hand if I didn't need it to rub my poor tired old feet," Mike said.

"Oh Honey, please!" Holly complained, slightly disgusted at the thought.

"I can't go on without something to eat." Shel's arms hung limp at her sides as she leaned against a big rock.

"I'd like to try out the small bird snare I've been working on," Cody said, with a tone of expectancy as he touched the snare that stuck out the top of his backpack. "But first we need to stop for the night." He looked around and added, "and this is not a good place to camp."

Shel lay her head back on her rock and let out a sigh of resignation. "I never thought I'd say it, but if we found some grub worms right now, I might just cook them up and at least try one."

"Eeeeuuwww!" Holly groaned remembering the

way their little fat pale bodies had looked in that pan, slowly crawling over one another. "This conversation is getting…" she stopped abruptly and a smile spread across her face as she jumped up, squealing excitedly, "It's a dog! It's a dog! We're saved!"

As Duke walked along the shore with his nose to the ground, the canoe sliced silently through the water. They had only been on the water for an hour or so before Duke sat down to await his master's command. Bo made a throwing motion and the dog took off running deep into the woods, like the beam of a flashlight on a dark night, searching for something lost.

"Where's he going?" Leroy asked.

"He's going to check out the scent we've been following, he'll be right back to let me know what he found."

Chuck let out a frustrated sigh as Leroy said, "He's a purdy smart dog."

"I think we're going to have to pull over and walk now," Bo said.

Chuck and Leroy turned the canoe towards shore, and as its nose slid into the sand, Chuck jumped out and began to pull the canoe out of the water, with the men still inside.

"No!" Bo shouted, but it was too late. As the canoe came up onto the bank, it tipped over, dumping Bo and Leroy out into the cold shallow water.

"You idiot!" Bo yelled as he jumped up out of the water, dripping. "What do you think you're doing?"

Leroy just stood up with his arms out to his sides as he watched the water run off of his fingertips, seemingly in shock at what had just happened.

"I didn't know that would happen, I swear I didn't!"

"I don't believe you Chuck Atteberry. Do you

expect me to believe that you're that stupid?" He yelled as he stepped out of the water.

"Sorry, it's really not that big a deal, you'll dry off before it gets cold out again," Chuck reasoned.

Leroy spoke up, "Chuck, it's not exactly hot out here today, and being wet's not going to make it any warmer."

"Oh, stop being such a baby!" Chuck snapped, brushing his comment off with his hand.

With that, Bo grabbed Chuck and pushed him out into the water with such force that he went all the way under, then sprang back out of the water like a cat. "AAAAhhh!" He yelled in rage. The anger twisted his face as he gritted his teeth so hard you could almost hear them cracking.

"Well there you go; we can all dry off together now!" Bo said, with his arms folded across his chest, before turning to walk away.

Chuck stood, hands clenched into fists, his eyes big with hatred as Bo casually took off his shirt and wrung out the wet hem. Chuck's hand shot around behind him, reaching for his gun.

Seeing this, Leroy stepped in front of him. "Now Chuck you asked for that and you know it. So, don't you be thinking about getting even. Anyway, you still want to find them folks, don't you?"

At that Chuck slowly replaced his gun and stepped out of the water.

Duke came bounding back and sat before Bo who patted him on the head. "Good boy, ok, go!" He made a hand motion and the dog was off and running again, but instead of running back into the woods, he started running along the river's edge, turning into a ravine.

They all stood to their feet to listen and heard the sound of a dog coming from behind them.

Holly began to jump up and down, holding them

all in turn as she danced around with excitement. "We're saved, we're saved!"

But Mike stopped her abruptly, his face was grave; his eyes big with the realization of what he had feared all along. "They're tracking us!" He whispered.

Holly's face fell, "Oh no, what do we do now? What do we do?" She turned around, looking in all directions, only to see steep cliff walls and no end to the ravine. "There's no way out, no place to hide!"

"What are we going to do, Lord?" Mike prayed out loud as he also turned, looking for an escape. Clutching Holly's hand they began to run farther into the ravine, leaving the younger couple still standing in shock.

Realizing he hadn't heard a word from Shel, Cody turned to see her frozen in place, her eyes big with fear and her face pale. She had always been afraid of dogs and now her worst nightmare was coming true. Cody took her hand and pulled her into his arms. "It's going to be ok, Babe." But she still stood rigid in his arms as he whispered, "Lord, show us what to do." Behind him he heard a voice say, "Go around, then up." He turned to see who it was, but no one was there.

"What'd he say?" Shel asked abruptly.

He turned back to her, "What did who say?"

"The man!"

"The man?"

"The Messenger!!"

"What Messenger?"

"Cody, stop repeating me and just do what he said."

He didn't understand what was going on, but the barking was getting closer by the second. He knew one thing and that was that they needed to run, so he seized her hand and ran after Mike and Holly who were ahead of them by several hundred feet, anxiously looking for a way out.

Cody mumbled to himself as he ran, "Go around, then go up; go around, then go up." He kept looking for something to go around, but there was nothing.

34
Bad Dog

Pull me from the trap my enemies set for me,
for I find protection in you alone.
Psalm 31:4 NLT

Mike and Holly suddenly stopped in their tracks by the dead remains of what was once a deer, as Cody and Shel caught up with them. The stench hit them hard, making them all want to turn and run the other direction, if that had only been an option.

When Cody heard himself repeating, 'Go around, and go up', he pushed through the stink, dragging Shel behind him. There was nothing to go up except an old gnarled tree, so he cupped his hands and put them down for Shel saying, "Go up!" The smell of the carcass filled his mouth as he said the words causing him to gag. He tried not to breathe but he could still smell the rotting corpse regardless of the amount of oxygen he took in or didn't.

The leaves rustled loudly as Shel pushed her way through the twisted branches above her head and started to climb.

Mike and Holly, seeing what they were doing, approached at a run. Cody put his cupped hands down for them. He opened his mouth again to speak but "Go" was the only word he could get out before he started to gag again, tasting the rot in the air as it entered his mouth.

Once in the tree, Mike turned and pulled Cody up. Cody scrambled as fast as he could into the tree, finding that it was perfect for climbing. He passed Mike and Holly, then hand-over-hand he reached the top, leaning back into the tree's smaller branches, he pulled himself up onto the grassy bank that over hung the cliff. He collapsed to the ground at the top, closing his eyes for just a moment, drawing in a deep breath and enjoying the taste of fresh air.

When he saw Holly's hand coming up, groping to find something to get ahold of, he grasped it and hauled her up. Between attempts to catch her breath she whispered Mike's name as she and Cody peered over the edge. Mike was tiredly pulling himself up the tree but was farther down than either of them liked as the sound of the dog's barking and men's yelling grew dangerously close.

"Come on Puppy, just don't look down," Holly encouraged him quietly.

Cody quickly slipped off his glasses and held them in his hand so they wouldn't slip off his sweaty nose and drop over the edge. He could hear the scuffling of feet on the rocks as he dove for the edge and Mike's hand touched his. He began to pull while Holly reached down and grabbed Mike's belt to help. Between the two of them they managed to hoist him out of sight as the dog and the men came into view.

Holly yanked one last time on Mike's belt as he swung his dangling leg up and onto the grassy overhang. And as she did his hunting knife that was sheathed on his belt fell out and sailed down. The butt end of the knife hit a branch of the tree making a deep 'thunking' sound, before it careened back into the air and stabbed into what remained of the carcass's back leg.

"Oh Lord no, please!" Holly whispered, but there was nothing they could do but pray that by some miracle, the men wouldn't see it.

The men ran along behind Duke following as closely as they could. Every so often the hound would stop and sit down; waiting for his master to catch up, sometimes stopping to sniff the ground before he bounded off again. When at last Duke began to sniff the air, Bo knew they were getting close.

"It won't be long now, we'll be coming up on them folks real soon," Bo said, translating the dog's movements.

Suddenly Duke lifted his head and lunged ahead, "AARROOUUWW! He bayed loudly, AARROOUUW!"

Leroy took off, following Duke closely, as the other two men fell behind. Finally the dog slowed, carefully approaching a decaying carcass of an animal next to an old gnarled tree.

Leroy watched as Duke began to move towards the old tree. Suddenly he heard a 'thunk' sound overhead, as something dropped from the tree. Lifting his eyes alone, he saw a man's leg swing up and over the top of the ravine and for only a second a man's wild hair and eyes appeared at the top of the cliff. Leroy took in a sudden breath which he instantly regretted as he gagged on the taste of rot in the air. He must have imagined it, the face he saw appeared to have been Mac's...which was impossible, because Mac was dead. Once again he willed his eyes to look up, holding his shirt tightly over his nose, but this time he saw nothing.

Duke ran back to the carcass trying to pick up the scent of whatever it was that had been dropped. Leroy cautiously strolled over to the carcass and found a hunting knife stuck into the deer's upper thigh. After only a moment's hesitation, he stepped closer and pulled out the knife. Hiding it behind his back, he wiped the blade clean on the leg of his jeans, and then quickly slipped the knife into the back of his pants.

Calmly he walked over to the tree and popped the dog in the nose as Duke jumped up to sniff at the trunk.

"No, Bad Dog!" Leroy whispered sharply. "Lord," he began praying under his breath, "them folks haven't done nothin' wrong, please help them to get away."

"What'd you say?" Chuck said as he walked up, holding his shirt over his nose.

"Oh, just that this has to be the right way."

"Why's this have to be the right way?" Chuck said impatiently. "That dog's been sniffing out stinking things again, that's all."

"I can't understand it!" Bo began to say as he approached the dog. "Duke, what are you doing? This doesn't smell like the bandana around your neck does it? I could do a better job, with my nose to the ground than you're doing right now! Bad dog!"

The dog dropped his head in shame and glanced over at Leroy, raising one eyebrow and tilting his head slightly as if to ask, "why?"

Cody peered over the edge of the ravine to see where the knife had landed, but saw nothing but the shape of a man moving back as a hound sniffed around the carcass. Dropping out of sight, Cody slipped his glasses back on as he listened to the conversation below. As he prayed quietly to himself he realized that Shel wasn't with them. He shot up, frantically whispering, "Where's Shel?"

Holly carefully crawled over Mike to the edge, and looked down into the ravine through some branches. Then she turned and shook her head 'no'.

Cody dashed away to look for her, as Holly stayed with Mike, who was still trying to catch his breath and to steady the panic that made him feel sick and shaky inside.

Cody hadn't gone far when he began to hear quiet

sobs. As he rounded the trees where Shel sat, she jerked in fear then promptly began to cry again, burying her face in her hands. He slid in beside her and put his arms around her, "It's okay Babe; we're all safe. The dog is in the ravine and there's no way he can get up here. It's going to be alright, Honey, I promise you." But nothing he said seemed to help as she continued to sob.

Over the past couple of weeks Cody had learned to lean on Shel as her strengths had seen them through time and time again. Now it was time for her to lean on him, he knew that what Shel needed right now was for him to simply hold her. So he sat and drew her close, pulling her head to his chest, under his chin, kissing her hair as he spoke comforting words in her ear.

Shel's fear of dogs had always seemed kind of ridiculous to Cody, but up until today he hadn't realized that everyone had their own fears and Shel's just happened to be of large dogs. He was ashamed that he had belittled her before and was determined to cover her fear, to protect her and to lift her up, instead of tearing her down. What he really wanted, more then anything, was for her to feel safe in his arms once again.

All of a sudden, a sharp "Yelp!" caused Shel to jump and bang her head hard into Cody's chin. It didn't hurt badly, but he tasted blood as he continued to hold her. "Shh, it's alright Babe, it's going to be alright."

❖ ❖ ❖ ❖ ❖

"Bo, that dog of yours is as dumb as dirt," Chuck grumbled as he followed him and his dog.

"Chuck, I told you to shut up and I mean it. This isn't any of your business."

Chuck quieted down but he was still mad. He had put up with more than his share of 'junk' today. At least that was the way he saw it. So as they walked out of the ravine, he started to finger his gun again. Then he said to himself, '*No, I guess I still need him.*' He remembered that Bo had said; '*I'll kick that dog's butt over his shoulders if he scares up anything stinking.*' But Bo hadn't done it, so Chuck hauled off and kicked Duke hard on the butt.

Duke let out a high-pitched 'Yelp!' and jumped sideways as he began to limp.

Bo turned and stood nose-to-nose with Chuck and asked in a low menacing voice, "What'd you do to my dog?"

"Oh, sorry, I must of stepped on his foot or something, so sorry!" Chuck said throwing up his hands while trying his best to look remorseful.

Bo stared at him for a moment then turned around and continued to walk while Chuck sneered at him from behind.

Just then Leroy came running up alongside Chuck. "So we're headed back then?"

"Yeah."

"That's good, but what happened to Duke?" Leroy questioned, noticing the dog's limp.

"I couldn't say." Chuck said coldly as he glared at the dog that still walked in front of him.

35
What Man?

And when they had come to the place called Calvary,
there they crucified Him,... Then Jesus said,
"Father, forgive them, for they do not know
what they do."
Luke 23: 33a- 34a NKJV

Cody held Shel in his arms as they sat, leaning against a tree, it felt so good to be there for her, loving her once again. Pride and rebellion had almost destroyed their marriage before. He knew now that it wasn't all her fault but his as well.

Sitting there he remembered what his Dad used to say, "Pride is the opposite of humility, repentance is a byproduct of humility and without repentance there is no forgiveness of sin, not from God, from others, or even for yourself."

"Shel," he finally managed to say, "Shel, I'm so sorry I've never supported you in the past. I'm sorry I haven't always been honest with you, and I've dishonored you in public and in private." He paused and added pleadingly, "I'm so sorry, please forgive me. - I love you."

She looked at him and smiled gently, "I forgive you. I haven't been a saint either, you know." She laid her head back down on his chest.

Cody knew that better than anyone, but he held his tongue from agreeing with her. He was dealing with his own sins, which was as it should be.

After a moment, she wrapped her arms around his waist and said simply, "I'm sorry too for not being respectful."

She lapsed back into silence, enjoying the closeness she felt with her husband, her covering. She silently thanked the Lord for the changes she saw in both him and herself. She was so quiet that Cody thought she had fallen asleep. Then, suddenly alert, she put her hand on his chest, looked him in the eye, and asked, "Cody, who was that man?"

"What man?"

"The man who talked to you."

"I didn't see a man."

"You didn't?"

"No."

"He talked to you though, right?"

"Who?"

"The Man."

He said slowly and methodically, "You actually saw a man?"

"Yeah, didn't you see him?"

"No!"

"Didn't he say something to you though?"

"I heard a voice say, 'Go around then go up'."

"Around the dead deer and up the tree?"

"That's what he meant, I guess? But he didn't go into any detail."

"Oh?" She lay her head back down, deep in thought.

"What did you actually see?" Cody said after a pause.

"I saw a man standing behind you. He smiled at me then leaned in and whispered something in your ear. You turned around and looked right at him. Are you sure you didn't see him?"

"Yes I'm sure, I did not see him. What else did you see?"

"Well, when I asked you what he said, you turned back to face me again and he walked away, following Mike and Holly as if to lead us in the right direction, glancing back at us, or me I guess, since you didn't see him."

"Then what?"

"I turned and looked at you, then back to see him again and he was gone."

All Cody could say was, "weird," with a puzzled look on his face, as if he was trying to reason it away.

"I heard you praying for help Cody." Shel looked a little put out that he didn't believe her. "So why are you so shocked that God sent an angel to help us?"

Just then Mike and Holly rounded the tree they sat against.

Holly asked, "Did I hear you say that God sent an angel to help us?"

Shel excitedly told the whole story again. The corners of Mike and Holly's mouths turned up into astonished smiles.

"Did he glow or have wings or something?" Holly's eyes were big with excitement.

"No! He looked like a normal guy – big and strong, yes; but he was just wearing blue jeans and a flannel shirt, like..." She looked around at the clothes they were all wearing. "Like us."

Holly smiled and said, "God spoke to you both; Cody to hear and you Shel to see. That's the way He often works with men and women. It's when we think we have the complete picture that we get in trouble, not listening and not seeing the other half of the story."

"That's true Button," Mike paused then said, "it seems to me as if the Lord's not finished with us yet." A knowing smile broke on his face. "We stayed behind and listened to the men tracking us. They thought their dog took them on a wild goose chase. Apparently, the dog likes things that stink. The cool thing is that the Lord knew this was all going to happen before we even came out here. He knew that we would need those men to not believe in their dog's tracking ability. And from the beginning of our ordeal He has been working all things for our good. And now He's sent us an angel to bring us out of danger."

It got quiet as they all just sat and thought, considering it all.

"Can we stay here for the night?" Holly asked, "I feel so weak and tired. And hungry!" She said with emphasis, her arms wrapped around her shrunken mid-section.

"Yeah," Mike answered, "I think we should. We need to eat something, anything! I'd also like to take some time to think about what just happened."

"It's going to take those men a couple hours to get back to the river, then back to wherever they came from. They won't be back tonight at any rate. So let's have a fire."

Shel's face was etched with concern as she asked. "Do you think they'll try to track us again tomorrow?"

"I don't think so, Babe," Cody said as he pulled her back into his arms. "But if they do, I have a feeling that it will be to no avail. God has His eye on us."

"I don't understand why God doesn't just have those men fall in a hole somewhere or break a leg or something," Shel spat out. "I mean," she started again, slightly taken back by the venom she recognized in her tone, "I just want to stop running and concentrate on getting home."

"We don't have a choice but to run from those men, Shel," Mike stated. "But at the same time we need to be willing to forgive them. Even while they're shooting at us! It's an important thing to God that we learn to forgive. He's put us in this situation so that we will pray for our enemies. If we can pray for them and forgive them, then we can consider ourselves Christ-like."

"I don't know about that," Shel snapped back, "most people don't ever seem to forgive. Even after years of holding a grudge they still don't forgive, even those who claim to be Christians fail to act Christ-like as you put it."

"Yeah, but can you honestly think of one of those unforgiving people that you'd want to be like, by following their example?"

She thought for a moment then said, "Yeah, if they're right."

"Shel, it's our sin nature that makes us want to hold a grudge against someone. The old man, the dead man's eyes that call to us to come back and walk in the path of death. When someone hurts us, or someone we love, we think it's our job somehow to make sure that they're punished. It's a form of self-righteousness really, holding others up to a standard that we choose."

Cody saw the dead man's dark blue eyes flash before him once again and realized how much like his own eyes they looked. He began to see that this whole trip for him had been about putting down the 'old man', 'the flesh'; 'the dead man' if you would. He was glad that he had turned around and was no longer walking down the path of death.

Holly quietly began to speak and Mike gave her his full attention. After years of marriage he had learned to recognize wisdom in her. Sometimes he missed the things that were obvious to her.

"Maybe it's because we don't have faith to believe that God will see the sinner as we do," she began, "that He might just forgive that person without our consent. Or maybe we think He needs our help to make sure that person remains miserable. We think it's our job somehow to make sure the world knows the sin that has been committed. You know, like the Pharisees when the harlot was washing Jesus' feet with her tears and drying them with her hair. They said, 'He wouldn't let her touch Him if He knew who she was'."

"But, He did know who she was. In fact, He was the only one who seemed to know who she really was, because He could see her heart. And she walked away that day happy and forgiven, while the men that pointed their fingers at her remained angry and unforgiving. And I'm sure, they acted hateful towards her the rest of her life."

"You're right, if I'm unforgiving it always makes me feel angry," Shel admitted, "and I'm unforgiving in other areas of my life, too." She paused, then added, "I heard once that, 'not forgiving is like drinking deadly poison and expecting the other guy to die.' It's true too, I think. Holding a grudge 'never ever' makes me feel good, but still, I catch myself doing it all the time. Somehow, I think that my bitterness is going to hurt that other person."

Holly stared blankly into the distance and said, "I've seen whole families be devoured because of unforgiveness towards someone. Every time they see that person somewhere, and she's happy, they grow more and more bitter. The hatred they feel for her keeps building until finally they stop going to all the places he or she goes, just so they can still act like everything's okay while they're rotting inside."

Cody added, "I can see what Mike's saying, too, about being Christ-like. If you think about it, Jesus forgave the Roman soldiers while they were beating him. He forgave them when they pulled out His beard, blindfolded Him and hit Him with rods. He forgave them when they drove a crown of thorns on His head, and when they put a purple robe on Him to mock Him. Then after the blood on His back and sides had a chance to coagulate and stick to the robe, they pulled it off. Still He forgave. They drove spikes through His wrists and feet, and hung Him up to die, then stood back and made fun of Him once again. And still, He forgave them each and every step of the way."

Holly added, "The only thing that the men chasing us want to do is to shoot us."

They all chuckled a little before sinking back into thought.

Shel sighed, "True, we always think 'I'm so glad that Jesus forgave *me of my sins.*' But we don't think of it as Him setting an example for us to follow, in forgiving others, no matter what they do or have done to us."

Holly then said quietly, almost inaudibly, "I sent a letter once to some people years ago, saying 'forgive me for the sin that I committed against you, in my past. And that I forgave them too for the sins they had committed against me'. Some called me and said, 'Thank you for forgiving me and of course I'll forgive you.' Some didn't respond at all, but one said, 'I have no idea what you're talking about'."

"I had humbled myself in asking him to forgive me, when we both knew full well he had been the one that had sinned against me. That hurt me a lot."

Holly's face and voice got sad; tears welled up in the corners of her eyes as she continued, "It made me angry at first, then the Lord reminded me that I had forgiven him. And I had, for the first time in my life, felt free. I felt a peace. So I asked the Lord to help me to forgive him again. And I felt the peace that passes all understanding wash over me once more."

"I had confessed and repented. I had done what the Lord tells us all to do, and so, no matter what happens outside of my relationship with God, I was free! I love being free; free of the hatred and the anger that I had felt hanging around my neck, for as long as I could remember; playing the offense over and over again in my head. I had never known this kind of peace. And I never wanted that unforgiveness back again. The Lord then prompted me to pray for that man. And, He gave me a love for him that even when everyone else had forsaken him; I still felt compassion for him. Because he doesn't know peace, he's trapped, he's lost."

She paused and everyone remained quiet, except for the sound of the birds singing in the trees that were oblivious to the tears that were being shed below. Holly finished with, "I really don't understand why that man has sacrificed everyone in his life for fear of being found out. Fear is such a demanding god that takes everything from you and gives nothing back in return."

Silence covered them like a blanket as they sat soaking it all in.

"Thanks for sharing that, Button." Mike drew her close and kissed her forehead as she scooted in close, laying her head back on his shoulder. They all knew enough about Holly's background not to ask any questions. But, they had heard her say time and time again, throughout the years, "We are the sum of our experiences and we choose what we do with them for good or for evil."

As Mike kissed the top of her head yet again, he prayed aloud, "Lord, we pray for the man Holly's talking about. Open his eyes to see that he needs Your love. And Lord, bless the men also that are trying to kill us. We don't know what's going on in their lives. We don't know the battles that they face each day. So we just pray that You will work on them wherever they are. And protect us, Lord, as You call to them. In Jesus' name, Amen."

36
Drum Stick

When I had lost all hope,
I turned my thoughts once more to the LORD.
Jonah 2:7 NLT

Both couples had given up on finding the tower, feeling as if aiming for something they couldn't see was leading them off in the wrong direction. When they heard the sound of water to their right again they felt certain that they were back on track.

In spite of their early start, by mid-morning no one seemed to have the energy required to go any further. With each passing day the pattern of hunger, weakness and despair had grown stronger, causing them to take more breaks for longer periods of time, and stopping earlier and earlier each day.

As the others slumped to the ground, Shel made an effort to pick some dry grasses and roll them into a tinder ball. Gathering up some small sticks, she stacked them tee-pee style on the ground. Sliding the tinder ball underneath she struck the magnesium bar several times, throwing sparks that could ignite the little bundle. Eventually the tinder caught fire and she then added larger sticks, nursing the small fire into a proper blaze.

Mike and Holly went in search of bigger pieces of firewood, talking as they worked. "We'll need to build some kind of shelter, so keep that in mind as we look for firewood. We don't want to burn something that's going to save us from having to chop any more wood than we have to."

"We each need to find a way to contribute in finding something to eat, too, Puppy. I don't know about you but I'm getting so weak and discouraged. I don't think I can move on if we don't find something to eat soon. I just don't know what I can do to help."

"I'm not ready to give up just yet," Mike said bitterly, mostly to set his own resolve. "It's okay if you need to just rest by the water for a while, Button."

Walking towards the river Holly sat down, as Mike continued to collect firewood. *'Something's not right here'*, she thought to herself as she stared at the water.

They had been walking within earshot of the water for days, making it easier for themselves, over land instead of rock. Going down to the river only when they needed to, then back to wherever they had camped.

Holly's sense of direction wasn't the best or even good, but still she somehow felt certain that they had been walking the wrong way today. "Hey Mike, why is the river so narrow? Which direction are we supposed to be headed?"

He stopped and looked at the water and his mouth fell open. Dropping his collected load of sticks, he mindlessly pointed upstream.

"Mike, aren't we supposed to be traveling *down-stream?*"

Mike fell despondently to his knees and said nothing as he looked this way, then that and mumbled, "How long have we been following this creek?" His eyes got big with fear, and then fell in resignation as the declaration he had just made floated away like a weight-less feather on the breeze.

"Mike, are you alright? - Mike? - Puppy, please don't..." She came and wrapped her arms around him and cried as Mike shook himself free from his trance of despair.

"Oh, I'm sorry Sweetheart." He held her for a moment before saying, "We need to get back with this fire wood."

When Mike and Holly came back, Mike said, "Cody, come help me drag a big log I found back to camp."

"Sorry man, but I'm going to be no good to anyone until I get myself a nap."

It may have seemed to everyone else that Cody was being defiant to Mike, but Mike knew that Cody had pulled guard duty, night after night; sitting up longer than any of the rest of them and now his body was demanding that he rest.

Mike wasn't sure he was ready to tell him they had been traveling the wrong way for at least a couple of days. He decided to let the man have a sound nap before dashing his world on the rocks, so he just nodded.

Cody pulled a sleeping bag towards him, untied it and laid his shoulder and head across the roll. The roll flattened under his weight as he closed his eyes. "I can't stay awake another minute. I'll help you with that when I wake up," he said, accompanied with the monstrous yawn that followed.

The sun shone down, warming him as he slept. The leaves rustled in the trees as the wind blew gently, releasing them from their bonds on their respective branches to drift to the ground where they slid along its surface, until they came to rest next to Cody. Meanwhile the shadows of the quivering trees played happily around him, he lay motionless. The air was brisk and the birds sang as they flitted overhead. Cody dreamed of catching them all and having a feast as his stomach growled in vicious protest to the lack of validity of the dream's truth. He gave a restless sigh but the wind shushed him, urging all that surrounded him to be still.

Shel had wandered off by herself earlier to try and find something for them to eat, while Mike and Holly started to build a shelter but they were soon exhausted and stopped to take a rest.

Mike picked up the fishing gear and slowly moved down to the water to see if he could catch a fish. Holly just lay limp on the dirt next to the fire, staring blankly into the flames, not caring that the other sleeping bag lay within inches of her reach.

It was late afternoon by the time Cody finally woke up and helped Holly to her feet so the two of them could finish the shelter.

Mike had already laid out a pile of branches, so Cody started to cut lengths of twine. He and Holly then began to tie the four long branches together, joining them on the corners to make a square frame. Then they added more branches to form a grid, fastening them in place. Cody hammered the four strong sticks into the ground with the butt end of the hatchet, two tall ones and two shorter ones. The shorter ones only being about six or seven inches long after being hammered into the ground. The frame sat up against the short sticks and leaned at an angle to rest in the Y at the top of the long sticks. The long sticks were about three-and-a-half feet tall and when the frame was tied into place, it formed the lean-to they would be sleeping under tonight.

Together they covered the frame with branches, leaves, and tall grasses; basically whatever they could find easily, layering them from the bottom to the top of the frame. Holly finished by lining the floor with dried leaves and grasses for them to sleep on

When Holly was finished she came and sat across from Cody by the fire. "Hey, did you know we've been going the wrong direction for a couple of days? We're not even following the river anymore, we're following a creek upstream."

He looked at her for a long moment, with no expression what so ever. Questions formed in his mind but they were pushed over and crushed by the despair he felt engulfing him. Not saying a word, he looked down and began to poke a small stick into a hole in the side of his blown out shoe.

"Cody did you hear me?"

"I heard you." He looked at her again. "I just can't," he shook his head, looking down again. "I just can't... I have to..." he muttered before going silent.

He pulled Shel's knife out of the front of her backpack and began to whittle the little pieces of his small bird snare, until he got them all just right. When he had finished, he took the snare far enough from their camp to attract curious birds, driving the stake into the ground and setting up the snare.

Almost before Cody could settle back down by the fire, a little bird came and landed on his snare. The rock he had selected as a weight, ended up being too heavy, so when the bird tripped the snare and the rock fell, it ripped off one of the poor little bird's legs.

The bird then squawked franticly as it flew off lopsided into the trees, leaving Cody with his mouth hanging open in horrified shock.

Holly quickly gathered herself and said slowly, "Okaayyyy who wants a drumstick?"

Cody winced before walking back over and replacing the heavier rock with a much smaller one and resetting the snare. Before long he had caught a whole bird and then several more.

Holly hardened herself as she quickly killed and cleaned their tiny bodies. "Sorry little guy, but we're starving to death," she explained apologetically as she worked.

Shel returned, discouraged and empty-handed, but when she saw five birds and a single leg, cleaned, skewered through, and roasting over the fire, she was amazed. The birds looked like bite-sized chickens with no heads and their twig-like feet still attached.

"That smells delicious! You actually got it to work! That's really cool!" She laid her things down and moved closer to inspect his work.

"Yeah, cool." He added half-heartedly, "I caught one after another and I basically just sat and watched."

"What happened here?" Shel said as she pointed to the lone leg.

"You don't want to know."

Shel sat down. "Ok, well, I set some snares. Lord willing, we'll have something bigger to eat in the morning."

The three of them sat watching as the fire seared the flesh of the tiny birds. Mike also came back into camp empty-handed, having lost all faith that they would ever get out of this alive. "What's that? I'll eat anything."

Cody wanted to be excited about his snare, but knew these songbirds were inadequate to keep them alive for long.

Holly just sat despondent as Mike plopped down beside her.

Then Shel began to speak, "I'm so discouraged, I just wish I knew more about what we could eat out here," she paused and then continued more to herself than to the others, "Well, I guess I do know quite a bit, but I'm just not able to identify anything without their leaves; and what good are they anyhow, out of season as they all are?"

The other three looked at each other wondering which one of them would tell her about going the wrong way. But, the fact that she still wanted to try, made them feel like they may have a chance to get one last breath before giving up and drowning in despair, so no one said a word as she rambled on.

"As for finding mushrooms, they're everywhere," she threw her arm out with a wide sweep before dropping it helplessly to her side. "But, I don't know anything about them except if you eat the wrong ones you'll get sick and die. I'm just so frustrated. I'm tired, I'm hungry, and I'm cold... I just want to be done with this."

Cody noticed that her teeth were chattering, so wrapping his arms around her he pulled her in close. She sobbed quietly, but still no one had a word of encouragement for her. So they all just sat staring blankly into the fire as it flashed, snapped and popped, sending sparks into the air, like fire flies: moving away as their glowing backsides went out, only to reappear somewhere else before extinguishing altogether.

Breaking the silence, Cody said, "How can just staring at this fire be so captivating? This is better than TV." Silence fell for a moment before he spoke sedately into Shel's ear, "We need to get one of those metal fire pit thingies, to put on our patio, Babe."

Holly mumbled as if she might just fall over again with exhaustion. "We have a brick fire pit, but we hardly ever use it. We need to start using it more."

They ate the tiny birds slowly, being careful not to drop even a morsel, since that's all they were anyhow.

When they were done, they still felt hungry. After chewing on the tiny bones they dropped them into the pot of water that was left boiling over the fire. It made them feel like more dinner was coming along at any moment. And although the marrow may indeed have given them a little more nutrition, the truth was that they were all growing weaker by the day and would soon have no strength left to find their way home, it had already impaired their judgment. But they thanked the Lord for what He had provided just the same, at times a little begrudgingly, but never the less in obedience and in thankfulness to God.

As Mike looked at those around him, he hardly recognized them with their gaunt, hollow cheeks, dirty and discouraged skeleton-like faces. Cody's mug was overgrown with whiskers. Mike reached up and touched his own chin, not recognizing what he found there. The shadows that the fire cast played a vile game of twisting and turning their already gaunt expressions into faces of death.

Mike's forehead furrowed as his mouth and nose drew into a knot, pulling his bearded chin up with them. The mere thought of them all dying had just become overwhelming to him. Mike felt guilty for bringing them all out here. But he had to stay strong no matter what. He must not show fear or weakness in any way. He had to be a rock but he wasn't sure that was possible for him anymore. The days had slipped into more than he had the energy to count, while their endless nights held only unquenchable fatigue.

Soon they all crawled off to the lean-to and lay down together, covering themselves up with the open sleeping bags. None of them cared or had the energy to stand guard tonight. They had little hope left, so they all just slept.

The sun gave up the day, with one last blink before closing its eye on them, and the fire snapped and flashed until it too stopped caring, slowly starving to death, fighting for its life, then fading and going out, leaving the night dark, cold and still.

37
Not for Me!

The path of the upright leads away from evil;
Whoever follows that path is safe.
Proverbs 16: 17 NLT

Bo and Duke jumped out of the back of Chuck's pickup when he pulled up in front of Bo's house. Walking over to the passenger-side window Bo said to Leroy, "I'd like to get an earlier start tomorrow. I'll be needing Duke to try one more time so I can figure out what he's thinking, before I go and have to retrain him all over again. I can't figure out what he's doing, why he's been sniffing out stinking things. He definitely scented something there along the river before he took us off on a wild goose chase. So, I'm thinking we'll need to start by the river and go downstream until we find them folks."

"Ok, we'll plan on picking you up in the morning then," Leroy said, glancing over at Chuck.

Chuck said nothing, continuing to stare straight ahead as if he hadn't heard a word that Bo had said. It was clear he had no intention of speaking or making plans with him for tomorrow's hunting trip.

Leroy wasn't sure if the silence meant that Chuck didn't want to go with Bo and his stupid dog or, if it simply meant he had no intention of being civil when he did. Either way Leroy knew it was best not to ask. So, turning back to Bo he said, "We'll see you tomorrow then, as early as we can get here." As the truck peeled out Leroy waved out the window in embarrassment over Chuck's rude departure.

The two men drove back into town in silence, Chuck seemingly focused on his driving while Leroy sat quietly, not wanting to know what else might be running through his head.

Leroy stared at the itching, bubbling rash as his arm rested on the edge of the open window, thinking about the people they had been chasing. Something always seemed to be standing in the way of getting to them. He knew if Chuck found out he had been a part of helping them get away, he'd likely kill him. He glanced over to steal another peek at Chuck then back again before the angry man noticed. He had never seen Chuck like this before and he had known him most of his life.

When Leroy was ten, his father left home leaving him with a grandmother that looked on him as if he were a nuisance, a mosquito sucking her blood. That was when Chuck had latched onto him and they had been 'friends' ever since. Like Leroy, Chuck had never known his father and had been left to the abuse of several stepfathers, which had made him hard and angry. For the first time Leroy wondered who he was really angry with? It seemed the harder and longer it took to find those people, the angrier Chuck seemed to get - not at them so much as at the God who was protecting them.

Leroy was sure that the hand of God was helping them as he reminisced about a young Christian family that he had lived next to, when he was a boy. His mouth drew up into a smile; they had taken him to church and vacation bible school and he had never forgotten some of the things he'd learned that summer. Crawling into their station wagon with their kids had given him a sense of belonging and gave him the opportunity to see the way a Christian family operated. He thought of the boy that was his age, 'Zeekers' and wondered if they still called him that!

His smile then faded as he remembered Chuck finding out about that family, and from then on making sure that the two of them had something else to do on Sundays and during VBS. He would pull out an old moldy army tent every summer and they would go 'camping'. Of course their camping trips only consisted of setting the tent up just inside the woods on the outskirts of town, close enough to the small market, Sally's Big Burger and the laundromat. They went swimming in the nearby river most of the week, staying out of sight of those 'goody two-shoes' as Chuck called them. He wanted to make sure no Christians found his weak-minded friend and convinced him to come along with them and 'give his life to the Lord' as they put it.

It always made Leroy feel a little sad to go 'camping' instead of going to VBS. He secretly wished that he could have lived with a family that loved him; like that Christian family had that summer, long ago. Even though Chuck had put an end to him forming any attachments with them, he felt such a sense of loss when they moved away. He longed to relive the way they loved each other and to feel that love shared with him again. He could see that Chuck also needed that kind of love. If he would just stop resisting, long enough, to see that love was what he lacked.

Leroy thought to himself, *'How did I get here? I had a chance for a happy life. Instead, I've let Chuck call all the shots. Now, I'm sitting in a pickup with a murderer and he wants me to murder too.'* He closed his eyes while he faced the side window and lifted up a silent prayer, *'God, save them folks and save me from having to kill them. I don't know why you'd do that for me because I'm no good. But they're good folks, so do it for them, please!'* He felt that *'please'* was a better word for him to use, a pleading, begging, groveling word. While the word *'Amen'* felt like a privileged word, a signature if you would. The final word to a contract, which only those that loved God had the right to use with their Lord.

Chuck dropped Leroy off at home then left. Leroy went into his apartment and flopped down on his couch. The silence was more than he could handle so he got back up and walked to his kitchen to get something to eat and switched on the small AM radio that sat on the counter. His favorite bluegrass station came on, playing a song he was familiar with, and usually liked, but today it grated on his nerves so he quickly changed the station.

The radio squeaked and whistled as he turned the knob. Then amongst the static he heard "In the name of Jesus." He swiftly turned the knob back, then listened, "If you've been feeling like the man the pastor was talking about today, you can give your life to the Lord, too. There is no end to God's love for you; nothing you've done is so bad that He can't forgive you for it." Leroy turned the radio off, put his hands over his face and began to cry.

"If only I could believe that was true!" He sobbed remembering all of the horrible things he had done throughout his life: the bullying of kids in school, the times he had beaten men up over some stupid thing. The stealing, lying, cursing, rage... and a few things he wished more than anything he could just forget. But he couldn't, instead those things just kept eating him up inside. "No, You can't forgive me! - IT'S NOT FOR ME!!!" He yelled, turning to a drawer in the kitchen, he pulled out a small handgun. Then, with his back against the cabinet, he slid slowly down to the floor next to the refrigerator. The old, faded and cracked linoleum, held an ever present puddle from the worn out refrigerator that had been leaking for as long as

Leroy had lived in the run-down apartment.

He sat staring at the gun. He wanted the pain to stop, all the years of guilt and shame, but somehow he couldn't make himself do it. He whimpered as he rubbed the barrel of the gun on his temple. "I'm such a coward, how can I be such a coward?" He wondered why he had always done exactly what Chuck had told him to do. He always did it, not wanting to make his 'friend' mad. He still was... tomorrow he would most likely have to kill someone for Chuck, maybe even all of them. "NO!!!" He shouted as he put the gun in his mouth and quickly pulled the trigger.

Instead of going directly home, Chuck went to a bar. After he had himself a couple of beers along with a burger and fries, he headed home feeling sorry for himself. He had never had any friends, except Leroy and now Leroy felt more like his prisoner than a friend.

"Why can't I get him to see how important it is to kill them folks?" He mumbled under his breath as he got up and left the bar.

As he walked to his truck and climbed in, he was thinking he didn't trust Leroy anymore, afraid that he was about to leave him like his father had done before he was even born. His father hadn't even cared to know him. Maybe his father didn't know his mom was pregnant... "It doesn't matter!" He wailed, "I HATE THAT MAN!" slamming his palm into the steering wheel.

There didn't seem to be any way to escape the anger and hatred that pulled his face tight, reflecting the condition of his insides as they twisted with bitterness.

When Chuck pulled into his mom's driveway, she stood waiting for him at the door; as though she knew he was on his way. She said to him as he walked up to the house, "Where have you been? I haven't seen you for days; what's going on with you boy? Did you bring home any beer or smokes?" She was still talking as he swung into his room and closed and locked the door behind him. He kicked his shoes off one by one as hard as he could, making sure to send them flying and smacking into the back of the door, where his mother still yelled on the other side.

"Now don't you go and put another hole in your door. Pretty soon you won't even have a door to put a hole in."

Ignoring his mother, he threw back the covers and crawled into his bed. Reaching for his used earplugs that already held a generous amount of earwax; he quickly shoved them deep into his ears. He pulled the covers up over his head with one movement, rolled over, and fell fast asleep.

"AAAHHHHHHHH!!!!" Leroy screamed in rage when the gun failed to fire. He threw the gun and it bounced across the floor before sliding through the living room and into the opposite wall. When it hit the wall it fired and the refrigerator next to him began to hiss. He chuckled a little as he looked at the mortally wounded white box. "Well, the manager did say he wasn't going to replace the old fridge until it was completely dead. Well, it's dead now! Chuck would be proud of me, I killed something."

He got up, and picked up the gun, and put it back in the drawer. Then he opened the refrigerator and pulled out a cold pizza, still in its cardboard take-out box. It was dried out and crusty, so he ate around the bad spot until he decided it was all just one big bad spot. He threw the piece he had been chewing on back into the box that was now lying open on the counter. Empty beer cans were strewn everywhere and dirty dishes overflowed the sink.

Wading through the dirty laundry that cluttered the floor of his bedroom, he made his way to the bathroom. When he finished taking a hot shower, he waded back through the mess and then he paced back and forth before sitting down on a hard chair. Leaning forward he pressed his face into his hands. "I can't get away from what we did, even when I'm asleep," he said thinking once again about the gun in the kitchen drawer, yet knowing he wouldn't have the guts to pull the trigger again. "I can't do this anymore God, please help me!"

He closed his eyes and laid his head on the back of the chair, rolling it back and forth over the carved hardwood, and as he did he had a vision:

(He saw himself standing on a narrow path, his back to a small door that was open. He knew he had the choice of turning and going through the door, or continuing on with the thousands of people who were now walking past him, as he stood still and alone. He saw glimpses of anger, sadness, fear, pride and rebellion on the faces of those that were walking into the darkness.

He then noticed a few ghost-like figures moving towards him; they were white and glowing, as if lit from within. They were passing through those in darkness, lighting up the small spaces that surrounded them. When one of them grew closer to him, he could see that the man was happy and was intently focused on the small door, which stood open behind Leroy. Then reaching Leroy, he stepped right through him. Leroy's eyes followed him through the door and as he turned, the man that had been just a glowing mist came into focus. Leroy continued to watch him as he walked towards a bright light that seemed to open it's arms to him and embrace him warmly, until the man and the light became one.

Turning once again, Leroy watched as the

thousands stumbled blindly into the growing darkness, while a black and heinous cloud lashed out and pulled those in that had chosen to walk in its way. It extracted screams of searing pain and horror, as all of its victims were locked in its grasp.)

A shiver ran through Leroy as he jolted up from the chair with a gasp. If he hadn't been awake he could dismiss it as a confusing dream or nightmare, but as it was he stood there shaken and frightened. He thought about it for a long while, but couldn't figure it out. "Maybe it will make sense in the morning," he said to himself. "I just need some sleep." So he crawled into his bed and willed his eyes to close, but instead found himself staring up at the ceiling for hours.

At some point during the night he did fall asleep, but peace evaded him. What he had seen in the vision disturbed him, but at least it had replaced Mac's ever-present dead eyes!

38
Polecat

"But I say to you who hear:
love your enemies, do good to those who hate you.
Bless those who curse you,
and pray for those who spitefully use you."
Luke 6: 27- 28 NKJV

Shel had set some snares last night in the hopes that 'something' would step into at least one of them and unwittingly feed them for a day or more. But when she checked the traps she wondered if Mike's statement that he would eat "anything" meant he would eat skunk.

Hurrying back to camp, which unfortunately was only about fifty feet from the snare that now held the striped villain, she spoke in a hurried whisper as she began stuffing their things into the backpacks: "We have to go now! I snared a skunk and it's only a matter of time before it freaks out and sprays everything around it and that includes us."

They all flew into a clean up mode, except for Mike. "Wait, I've heard that if you shoot a skunk in the back of the head, it doesn't spray."

"Who told you that?" Cody snapped with disbelief as he kicked dirt on the fire.

Mike paused then said, "Ok, I admit it was Guy who told me but..."

"Are you crazy? Guy Childers? Are you kidding

me? He probably told you that just to see if you'd be dumb enough to do it some day! He's the jokester that the jokesters are leery of! And he'll be the one who laughs the loudest if you come back smelling like a skunk. The skunk probably raises its tail and sprays you in your face as it's going down!"

"Maybe, but..."

"But what?"

"But my Dad used to tell us a story about his Mom boiling skunks for their oil. And how one day my Granddad came in, and not knowing what was boiling in the pot, took a big piece of the meat. He had already started to eat it when my Grandma came back in and told him what it was. He said 'it was the best meat he had ever eaten' and wouldn't give it back to her."

It was quiet for a moment. They were all so hungry. Their stomachs had of late made up their own languages. All four of them had their own dialect of course, but the message they were communicating was the same. 'We're starving, feed us!'

Mike continued, "I can't remember my Granddad ever smelling like a skunk. So there has to be a way to kill them without them spraying. Or how did my Grandma 'always'," he threw up his hands to strike quotation marks in the air, "boil them for their oil?" he said impatiently.

"Was your dad a jokester as well?" Cody asked sarcastically.

"No, he was a very serious and stubborn man."

"That explains it," Cody's voice still dripped with disdain as he continued, "Ok; let's just say it's possible. Do you think you could get close enough to shoot that skunk in the back of the head with the bow?"

"No, I couldn't, but maybe Shel could." Mike then turned towards Shel. "Well, what do you think?"

They all stopped what they were doing and turned and looked at her, as she now stood with her mouth hanging open. "I don't know! Maybe."

Mike spoke quickly, "I think if the Lord provides meat for us, then we need to thank Him for it no matter what it is. Didn't we just say last night that we'd eat anything?"

"You did," Cody grumbled under his breath.

After a long pause Shel sighed, "Oh, all- alright." She took up her bow and she and Mike headed off towards the skunk.

As they were leaving, Cody told them, "We're going to move everything out to the trail, just in case." He and Holly picked up the four backpacks and headed off towards the creek they now followed down stream.

When they were about a quarter mile away from where the skunk had been caught, Cody asked, "Why would anyone want to use skunk oil? And for what?"

"I don't know, but I'm pretty sure it's not the stink spray they were after. If his Grandma had to boil the skunk to get the oil out, it must have been more like the fat, you know - like lard - they wanted."

"Oh yeah, that makes more sense I guess. Still, why skunk oil?"

"That I couldn't tell you. But whatever the reason, it must have been worth the risk of getting sprayed," Holly said with a skeptical shake of her head.

Mike and Shel moved quietly towards the snare from opposite directions having agreed that Mike would distract the skunk giving Shel a clear shot at the back of the head.

The skunk was frantically trying to free itself from the snare when it heard Mike moving loudly through the bushes. It watched the bushes intently trying to get a glimpse of whatever it was that was stalking it.

It seemed to Shel as if it took Mike forever to get the skunk into position, as she sat behind a big rock waiting. *'If that skunk sprays like Cody said, I'm the only one that's going to get hit with it'.* She prayed breath-lessly, *'Lord, this isn't fair, this was Mike's bright idea after all!'* But it was too late to change her mind now and hand Mike her bow, while saying: *'here ya go buddy, he's all yours, have fun!'* No, she had no choice but to go through with it now.

Mike was almost in place, she could hear him in the bushes across from her. She raised herself up without a sound, brought the bow up to her ear and pulled back on the arrow. With perfect aim she let go, just as a dog barked. Shel jumped as the skunk turned towards the sound, and the arrow hit the side of its neck. The small black and white animal spun around with a streak as the force and weight of the speeding arrows struck it. The skunk started to spray halfway through its spin. When Mike heard the swish of the arrow, he stood up to see if his idea had worked. His eyes popped open and he roared "NOOOOOO!" as the spray hit him full in the face. He doubled over and dry heaved. His eyes watered and his nose ran as they dripped off onto the yellow stomach acid on the ground. In desperation he ripped off his shirt and tried to wipe the spray off his face and tongue, then he began to run, aimlessly at first, then down to the creek where the others waited for them.

From where Holly and Cody stood waiting on the game trail, they could hear the sound of a dog barking in the distance. *Were they being tracked again? Or were they getting closer to civilization?* Their attention suddenly shifted when they heard Mike yelling. They turned and looked at each other with puzzled faces as the smell drifted on the air in their direction.

Holly sniffed the air with a sour expression, "Well, I guess it didn't work."

The sound of barking was getting closer and they

could now also hear men's voices. But, Cody and Holly just stood there as Mike came running down the trail with Shel following close behind.

Holly threw her finger up, to hush them. "Shhhh, a dog!" Her hand quickly covered her nose. "What are we going to do?" Her words were muffled.

They all fell silent and listened to the voices, as they stood frozen where they were. They didn't have the strength to run anymore. There was nothing any of them could do. They had no choice but to face whatever may come, but for some reason they didn't seem to care anymore.

As the smell hit the men's noses they all stopped cold. "Oh no! Are you tracking that dang polecat again Duke? What's the matter with you? How many times are you going to do this?" Bo shouted at Duke as he dropped his head in confusion and shame.

Chuck swore under his breath, pulled out his gun and shot the dog.

Leroy and Bo froze in stunned silence and after a moment Bo growled. "What do you think you're doing? Why'd you shoot my dog?"

Chuck shrugged. "You said you'd shoot him if he tracked a polecat again," he said casually, with an arrogant smirk.

"HE'S MY DOG! You don't shoot my dog! If my dog needs shooting, it's my job to shoot him, not yours!"

Chuck snorted and turned away as Bo reached into his coat.

BANG! Chuck spun around with surprise as he held his hand high on his chest then fell, groveling on the ground before suddenly going still.

Leroy ran to Chuck and, dropping to his knees, he yelled out, "BO! What are you doing? You shot Chuck!"

"Look Leroy, I got nothing against you, so you just keep your mouth shut about this and get yourself out of here. Move away, start over, you're free to do whatever you want to now. He's not here to tell you what to do anymore." He kicked Chuck's foot before adding, "Me and my Abby, we'll be headed to California. We been thinking about it for some time now, she has it in her head to be an actress and now that I've killed Chuck, it seems the perfect time to be getting out of here. I hear in Hollywood they shoot each other all the time, every day! No one's going to care about me only shooting one no-good, worthless man." He turned to go.

"Bo, take your dog," Leroy said with a catch in his throat.

He came back, pushed Duke with his toe and said, "He's dead too, you get rid of him, or don't; I don't care either way. Because, I won't be needing a tracking dog with me in Hollywood." Then he turned and walked away, towards his pickup; thankful that today he had driven his own truck.

The couples listened in shock as the gunshots set their nerves on edge. They all had their mouths covered, both to quiet their breathing and to try and lessen the smell of Mike's new cologne.

It was quiet and all they could hear was the gentle gurgling of water and the sound of the wind in the trees accompanied now with the sound of moaning.

They cautiously crept forward to get a better look, then Holly unexpectedly stepped into clear view of the remaining man. As the others gasped in horror, she walked over and put her arm around his shoulder as he sat hunched over his seemingly dead friend.

"Honey, can we help you?" She said.

Leroy sat up and stared at Holly as the rest of them followed her out into the clearing.

"You're them folks! You're that family we've been chasing."

"I guess so, more like friends though," Holly said, with a smile and a tilt of her head.

"But why would you want to help me?"

Shel walked over and picked up her bandana as it lay on the ground in front of the dead dog and tied it back in her hair. "I wondered where that bandana went to," she said.

Leroy watched her for a second longer before saying, "You're them folks from McClure's Diner. I thought ya'll looked familiar." He then looked down and examined their feet, and reaching behind him, pulled a knife out from the back of his pants.

Holly fell back, but he just sat holding the blade with his fingertips as he offered it to Mike. "Is this here your knife?"

"Thanks! But how did you know it was mine?"

"I recognized your shoes. I saw one going up over the top of that ravine." As Leroy spoke a puzzled and frightened look passed over Mike's face.

Shel knelt down and checked for Chuck's pulse. "He's still alive." She pulled back his shirt to look at the wound. "But we'll need to get him to the hospital right away."

Leroy took off his over shirt and handed it to Shel who pressed it into Chuck's wound, as he knelt down beside her, pulling Chuck's keys from his pocket. He stood up next to Mike, then while looking at him exclaimed, "ya stink!"

"Oh, you noticed," Mike said with a nod and a smile as he went down on his knees to check out the dog. "This dog is pretty bad off," he said. "We're going to have to get him to the vet." He patted the dog on the head. "Hang in there Fido, we'll get you some help."

"His name is Duke," Leroy volunteered.

"Is he your dog?"

"No, his owner ran off thinking he had killed Chuck there. He thought the dog was dead, too. He won't be coming back for him."

"Shel, can't you do something for this poor dog?" Holly turned to look at her as she still held back, looking on.

Shel was stricken but still she pulled herself together and began to move towards the dog, then stopped. "Will he bite me?" She asked.

"I wouldn't think so but I'll tie his mouth shut just in case." Mike pulled a shoelace out of one of his shoes and looped it around, loosely tying it around the dog's muzzle. "There - it's safe."

Shel pulled off her bandana and slowly pressed it into the wound in the dog's side.

He whimpered a little but still he didn't move. "Oh, I'm sorry little guy," she cooed as her heart went out to the poor pup. And a smile seemed to turn up the corners of Duke's mouth.

"Do dogs smile?" Shel said in shock. "Because I could swear he just smiled at me."

"No, dogs don't smile," Mike said as everyone chuckled at the thought of it. She thought of all the greeting cards she'd seen with dogs smiling huge goofy grins with human teeth. So she pushed the thought of Duke smiling at her aside.

Cody and Leroy lifted Chuck gently, carrying him, while he weakly complained and cursed them both under his breath. Mike picked up Duke's limp, unconscious body and followed.

Mike lay the hound in the back of the truck, then helped Cody and Leroy put Chuck into the back, laying his head on Shel's lap, so she could continue to try and stop his bleeding.

Leroy jumped into the driver's seat while Holly slid into the middle and Mike sat in the passenger seat. "It's a small town, won't take us but a bit to get there."

Leroy had the worst case of poison ivy that Holly

had ever seen and the stench that was coming off of Mike was overwhelming. But nevertheless there she sat between Mr. Stinky and Mr. Itchy as they headed off towards town.

39
Stink Off

And he said, "Who are You Lord?"
Then the Lord said,
"I am Jesus, whom you are persecuting.
It is hard for you to kick against the goads."
Acts 9:5 NKJV

As Leroy drove them to the hospital, in the back of the truck Shel tried to stop Chuck's wound from bleeding, but even though it had slowed down considerably, it refused to stop altogether. He was weak but slightly more civil and Shel took advantage of this by first asking him about the black eye and the knot on his head that were now varying shades of green and yellow and then continuing with: "You know Chuck there was once a man named Saul, who hated Christians as badly as you do. He chased them down and killed them just like you wanted to do with us. The Christians then were very afraid of him and so they hid out. Now, I know that the Lord prompts us to pray for our enemies from experience, and so I feel certain that there were Christians then that were praying for him, just as we were praying for you."

"You were praying for me? I didn't ask you to do that!" He snapped at her.

"No, you didn't but we did it anyhow."

Chuck said no more but stared at her trying to sort things out.

She continued, "One day when Saul was on the road to find more Christians to kill, the Lord struck him blind with a white light and spoke to him saying, 'Why are you hunting Me down to kill Me'?"

A puzzled look passed over Chuck's face.

"See," Shel said, "that's what he thought too. So he asked, 'Who are you Lord?' And the Lord said, 'I'm Jesus.' Then the Lord told him to 'get up and go into town'. Now at about that same time God told another man to meet Saul in town and pray for him to receive his sight. Now this man was afraid of Saul but he went anyhow because the Lord told him to. A long story short, Saul gave his life to the Lord and went on to be a powerful Christian, and one of the men God used to pen the Bible that we read today."

Chuck's eyes narrowed when he realized he had been listening to a Bible story. "You really believe that garbage?"

"Yes, I do."

He snorted, turned his head away from her and said no more.

❖ ❖ ❖ ❖ ❖

In the front seat, Mike was content just to have the fresh air blowing over his face as he leaned out the window. Holly was leading Leroy to the Lord as he listened and responded with marked interest.

As soon as Leroy pulled up to the hospital, Cody jumped out of the back of the truck and ran in. briefly explaining Chuck's condition. Two men ran out with a gurney and quickly wheeled him into the emergency room.

Chuck wasn't happy that he had been caught or that the witnesses to his crime were still alive to tell the tale, but he was too weak to do anything about it now. Of course, that didn't stop him from cursing and swearing as they wheeled him away.

For over a week now, the urge to scratch had consumed Leroy's every waking moment, compelling him now to commit himself into the hospital for treatment. He knew that it would probably end in him being arrested but he was certain jail couldn't be as miserable as this poison ivy had been.

Shel pulled her wallet out of the front pocket of her backpack, then the women made a beeline for the tiny cafeteria, expecting the men to follow them. The small room consisted of a few mismatched tables and chairs that stood near a line of vending machines. The women passed over the chips and sodas and went directly to the sandwiches. After putting in their money they made their selections, and just like magic, there in their hands were complete meals; meat, cheese, bread and greens.

"I can't believe how easy this is," Shel remarked as she tore through the plastic wrap to get at the sandwich inside. "No wonder we're a nation of obese people." She spoke through the food stirring around in her mouth. "Food is so easy to get, no hunting and gathering, no having to clean and prepare it, it's just there waiting and ready. All we have to do is open our mouths and shove it in." With that, she took another monstrous bite out of her sandwich barely managing to choke it down before she stepped over to another machine to select a drink.

"Well I'm sure glad for that right now," Holly expressed as she frantically resorted to ripping at the plastic packaging with her teeth before proceeding to eat her sandwich with the same ravenous animal imitation that Shel had been doing. "Where are the guys?" But her words were unrecognizable as part of the English language.

A nurse, seeing two un-kept women stuffing their faces, watched with big eyes for a second before reporting them to the security guard as two homeless drifters.

Holly and Shel had no idea how they may have looked to others. They had just been focused on where they could find something to eat. So when they heard a voice behind them, they were both startled.

"Excuse me ladies, but you're going to have to move on, there's no loitering allowed in the hospital."

They turned to see a security guard standing behind them with his hand resting on his club and a holstered gun on his belt, looking as if ready for trouble.

"Why?" Shel asked but then she caught her reflection in a large plate glass window and it became clear why they were being asked to go. She turned and looked at Holly who had obviously seen herself as well and they began to laugh.

"I'm sorry ladies, but you're going to have to leave now." He reached up and took their arms to escort them out. As he walked them down the hall they told him the abbreviated version of their story. And when they had finished, they found themselves standing at the nurse's station near the front door.

Behind the counter, the nurse's mouth was now hanging open as she insisted that Holly be admitted or at least checked by a doctor before leaving. Holly protested, but the nurse just wheeled around on her office chair and made the call over the intercom for the doctor to come immediately.

Holly just shrugged her shoulders as if to say, "All righty then!"

The security guard pointed them to the chairs in the waiting area then proceeded to call the local chief. Within minutes an officer came flying into the lobby. Holly turned to Shel and said in her best Leroy voice, "It's a smallll ta-oown." They both laughed heartily.

The chief checked in at the desk and as the nurse pointed him in their direction he turned and came towards them. He was an older man of about seventy. His hair was white and cut extremely short like he was an ex-marine, it stood straight up all over his head looking like a halo as the daylight from the door shown through it from behind him. He was thin and wiry, with gray blue eyes that seemed smaller than they really were, peeking through his old black horn-rimmed glasses. And as he approached, he put his hand out in front of him, saying simply, "Howdy, I'm Police Chief Burt."

Holly took his hand. "Holly Hilbert," she said, "and this is Shel Wiley. We don't know where our husbands got off to."

"Ma'am; Ma'am," he nodded his head towards them both in turn as he shook their hands. "Pleased ta meet ya. I understand a crime has been committed?"

Mike had been stopped at the entrance of the hospital, before he could even step inside the door. Cody stayed back with him as a nurse came out and handed him a recipe for: 'Stink Soup' then directed them to some fishing cabins outside of town.

Mike crawled into the back of the pickup and said a little prayer for "Fido", as a male nurse swept him off down the street to the veterinarian. Cody drove Chuck's truck to the store, leaving Mike in the back while he ran in and bought the ingredients for the stink soup - tomato juice, apple cider vinegar and a couple of large potatoes. He also picked up a scrub brush, some strong soap, several beef jerky sticks and four extra-large candy bars, and even found a nice bible for Leroy. He already had one of the candy bars shoved in his mouth when he handed Mike his share of the food and they were off again.

The cabins weren't far but by the time they reached them Mike had one candy bar gone and he was ripping into the beef jerky wrapper with his teeth. The salty beef filled his mouth causing him to moan with contentment, certain that nothing had ever tasted this good.

Mike took a shower first, then ran a tub of hot water and spent the next several hours scrubbing his flesh until most of the smell was gone. Truth be told, he felt that most of his skin had gone down the drain with the stink, leaving him feeling slightly sore.

Meanwhile, Cody went back to the hospital in hopes of talking to Leroy. He knew that he was most likely in custody by now, but he still had some questions he wanted to ask him.

Shel stayed with Holly until the doctor finished looking her over. He wanted to keep her for 24 hours but Holly refused saying, "I'm fine! Just a little hungry and tired that's all." Her dirty face and unkempt hair said that there was a little more to her abrupt refusal than met the eye. The truth was she had no intention of sleeping in an uncomfortable hospital bed and being woke repeatedly through the night by someone poking and prodding her, on her first night back to civilization. In any case, there was no bathtub in a hospital and that was unacceptable to her.

Shel also took a shower at the prompting of a nurse who brought her a towel.

"You know ma'am, I think you saved your friend's life out there. I've never seen anything like it before. Of course the doctor won't tell you that, you know. Well, I have to get back. You enjoy your shower now, you hear?" The nurse dashed off down the hall as fast as she had come in.

Holly had fallen asleep long ago. When Shel came out of the shower, she was still fast asleep; so Shel decided that this would be a good time to find out what happened to Cody and Mike. After asking the hospital staff for help, Shel eventually located her husband in Leroy's guarded room.

40
Warriors

*"Enter by the narrow gate; for wide is the gate
and broad is the way that leads to destruction,
and there are many who go in by it."*
Matthew 7 : 13 NKJV

Cody gave Shel an affectionate smile as she entered
and motioned for her to join him and the police chief
as they questioned Leroy.

Leroy had been explaining what had happened,
answering all questions Cody and the Chief of Police
Burt threw his way, his halting story suddenly being
interrupted by a call on the police chief's radio. "Have
we seen them? Yeah, they're standing right here. They
came in a couple of..." the police chief's words were
abruptly cut off as he stepped out into the hall, closing
the door behind him.

The couple listened intently to Leroy's account of
events with enthusiasm. They were overwhelmed by
how the hand of God had been working on their
behalf. From what Leroy had been saying, every event
had fallen into place, like the pieces to a puzzle, one
piece fitting perfectly into the next.

Cody looked thoughtfully at Leroy, now realizing
that God had purposefully put Chuck and Leroy into
their lives. At the time, Cody had seen them as his
enemies, but still - out of obedience to God he had,
with the encouragement of his friends - prayed for

them. And now he was blessed to be spending time with 'an enemy' turned 'new brother-in-the-Lord'.

The police chief stepped back into the room, interrupting Cody's thoughts. "Well, it seems as if there's been search parties out looking for ya folks. They're on their way here now to question y'all."

"Oh, OK," Cody said with surprise, not wanting to think about what that meant right now, he pushed it aside and turned back to Leroy, giving him the nod to continue.

"You know, that polecat saved your lives. If it weren't for that stink you'd all be dead right now. And I'd probably be dead too, since I wouldn't of shot you like Chuck wanted me to."

Shel smiled, knowing that it had been God's plan all along for them to meet up with that skunk. She could almost hear Mike saying, '*If the Lord provides, you just thank Him, no matter what comes along.*' She knew that God was the author of time and had most likely planned for Mike's Granddad to eat that skunk meat so long ago, so there would be the story that Mike could tell, in order to save all of their lives years later.

She smiled as she watched Leroy, reflecting on their first encounter with him in McClure's Diner and how she saw such a difference in the man then and now. The old man had obviously been done away with.

"Can I ask y'all something?"

"Sure you can," Cody said.

"Well, last night before I went to bed, I closed my eyes and I saw something I just can't shake off!" He told them about what he saw: the small door and the thousands of dark figures walking away from it and the few white souls that walked through the door and into the light. Then he asked, "What do you suppose it all means?"

Cody and Shel stood staring for a second then

glanced at each other and said, "Wow!"

"You had a vision!" Shel exclaimed, turning back to him.

"A vision? Is that good?" He said with a worried look.

"Yeah, that's real good," Cody said. "God was speaking to you about getting saved, how you were headed in the wrong direction and needed to turn around."

"Yeah, it kinda felt like I was going in the wrong direction."

"Well, the scriptures talk about that," Cody said. "Matthew 7:13 and 14 says *'You can enter God's Kingdom only through the narrow gate. The highway to hell is broad, and its gate is wide for the many that choose that way. But the gateway to life is very narrow and the road is difficult, only a few ever find it'.*"

"Wow, I'm feeling so envious right now," Shel said, "I've never had a vision."

Leroy just stared up at the ceiling. "I haven't ever done a good thing my whole life, I feel like I don't deserve His forgiveness." A tear rolled down his cheek.

Cody put a hand on his shoulder. "The Bible says that *'All have sinned and have fallen short of the glory of God'* and *'Our righteousness is as filthy rags'*. We're all dirty Leroy, but God sees us as being clean when we give our lives to Him. He knows what He wants to make us into and He works on us until the day when He comes to take us home to be with Him. You're never going to be perfect except in God's sight. Of course there will always be consequences here on earth, for the bad things you do, but God's going to use those things to perfect your faith. And you will be able to reach people that I could never reach, because I haven't had the experiences that you have."

"Well I've always been a follower of something or other, a coward I reckon. So, I guess I can be a follower of Jesus now."

"No, Leroy you're not a coward, you're a brave man. That's where the world gets it wrong. They think we're all taking the easy road, but it's hard to be a Christian. Sinning is the easy way. It comes natural to us. But everyday that you get up and make a decision to follow Jesus, you can count yourself as being a brave man. Christians are warriors; you are a warrior now, with a flaming sword." He handed Leroy the Bible he had bought for him. "You will do battle with the devil every day. While those that walk in the darkness don't fight him at all, in fact he lies to them and traps them, until it's too late. Then he sucks them into hell, like in your vision."

Shel added, "As Christians we're an irritant to the world. Like a grain of sand stuck in a clamshell, the world works and works like the clam does to get rid of us. It starts to cover us with a hard calcium deposit in its attempt to quiet us. Yes we feel the slime of this world touching us. We feel at times muffled by the world covering us. But when the Lord comes to get us, He's going to open that clam's shell and pull out the most beautiful pearl. That pearl is you, Leroy. You're very valuable and precious to God."

Tears began to run freely down Leroy's face.

Cody continued with, "The Bible says, *'so let's not get tired of doing what is good. At just the right time we will reap a harvest of blessing if we don't give up'.*"

Leroy smiled, and somehow even though he was lying down he seemed to be a little taller, like he was relieved of a heavy weight that had been pressing him down. He looked at the Bible in his hand and said, "A flaming sword?"

"Yes, believe me, this is a flaming sword." Cody smiled as he took up the Bible and opened it to the book of John, then laid it back in his hands. "Start here, this is your foundation," he said as he tapped the page with his finger.

Chief of Police Burt was still in the room and listening intently. But neither Cody nor Shel felt like he was buying the whole conversion thing. He had known Chuck and Leroy their whole lives and wasn't about to let go of the judgment he had already formed about them both. They knew the chief of police wouldn't be doing Leroy any favors, simply because of what he considered to be some kind of show.

Just then Will and Julie walked into the hospital room with Police Detective Trusty, who extended his hand to shake Police Chief Burt's hand first, introducing himself; Cody's next, and then he nodded his head towards Shel. "Pleased to meet you, Ma'am."

Julie had already wrapped herself around Shel and it seemed as if Shel wouldn't be shaking her off anytime soon.

Will put his hand out to Cody who took it and pulled the tall man into a hug accompanied by manly slaps on the back.

Then the detective began to talk, "We've been looking for you all for several days now. We found your SUV and campsite first, then worked our way through the area. When I received the report from a chopper that they had found a couple of rubber rafts, wrapped around some rocks in the middle of the river, we thought you might have all drowned. Then today we got the call that you had been found. Apparently you folks picked the roughest spot in all of this area to go through. I'm surprised you're even standing here today, truth be told. Whether you know it or not, that's the hand of God on your lives."

Police Chief Burt snorted quietly as Cody and Shel looked at each other. "Oh we know!" Shel said.

"Now I have something to ask you. Can either of you by chance, help us with the name of the body we found in a gully near your campsite?"

"I got that," the police chief said, and then led the detective from the room, leaving the friends to talk alone.

"Oh man, it's so good to see a familiar face!" Cody said.

"We were so worried when we found that dead guy near the place you camped! Are you all ok?" Will asked inquisitively, not seeing Mike or Holly in the room.

"Well, Mike got sprayed by a skunk; they wouldn't even let him into the hospital. They stopped him at the door he smelled so bad. And Holly got shot..."

Julie took in a sharp breath as the color ran out of her face.

"No, she's all right," Shel quickly reassured her as she could feel her shaking. "She's just resting. They wanted to check her out that's all. She's more tired than anything else. They'll be done with her this afternoon." She glanced up at the clock that hung on the wall. "Just a couple more hours now and she should be free to go."

Julie sighed with relief, as Shel kissed her on the forehead. "We're all ok, Sweetie!"

"So Mike's not here?" Will asked as he walked over and sat down on a chair beside Leroy who had finally succumbed to the antihistamine the nurse had given him an hour ago and was now resting peacefully for the first time in over a week.

"Nope, Mike's at a hunter's cabin scrubbing his hide off in a tomato juice bath."

"And, who's..." Will nodded towards Leroy as he snored lightly.

"He's one of our pursuers."

Will and Julie both snapped their heads back to stare at Leroy, their faces asking many questions that couldn't be put into words.

The door opened as Detective Trusty entered the room followed by the chief of police, "I'm sorry, we're going to have to ask you all to stay in town for another day or two."

Police Chief Burt added, "I've reserved a couple of rooms at the local motel here in town until we get all y'all's statements, you'll be staying there. It's real nice!"

"That sounds good to me, we'd like to head over there right away if you don't mind," Cody said, noting the exhaustion in Shel's face.

Chief Burt said, "Well I can see y'all have had more than enough for one day. All y'all just come by the office in the morning and we'll try and have the paperwork ready for ya ta sign," he gave them one last nod before leaving the room.

Detective Trusty put out his hand to Will then Cody as he asked, "You know how to get there then?"

"Yeah, no problem, thanks so much for your help." Cody had already passed the motel three times since he had been in town and found everything to be within comfortable walking distance.

"Well, I'll see you tomorrow then, you all get yourselves a good night's sleep."

"Thanks again detective," Cody smiled.

"You're quite welcome," he smiled back and nodded to them all before leaving the room.

"You didn't happen to bring Mike's SUV and our stuff did you?" Shel asked Will.

"Yeah, we did as a matter of fact! We found his 'hide a key' and we packed up all your gear... minus the contents of your cooler." Will scrunched his face.

"That's alright." Shel put up a hand then continued, "All I really want right now is a clean change of clothes. And if we could find something to eat, that would be even more than amazing! I'm starving!"

"I saw a burger joint on the other end of town!"

Cody said. "How about Shel and I get cleaned up and meet you two there in about an hour?

Friendly banter passed between them as the waitress came and took their orders, then left again. The smell of burgers and fries wafted on the air.

Cody knew he was going to have to apologize to Julie soon and his heart was pounding hard as his stomach rumbled with hunger, as if protesting. He kept glancing over at Julie but she had been avoiding making eye contact with him. Everyone got quiet all at once. But just as Cody was about to say something, Will and Julie began to ask questions and Shel excitedly started to tell them the whole story, adding in what they had heard from Leroy. Will and Julie sat listening intently as Shel talked while Cody occasionally interrupted to add a lost detail or add a comment.

When their food came, they prayed together and began to eat as Shel told them about Leroy's vision and how they had had the privilege of interpreting it for him.

When they had finished eating, Cody slid his hand across the table towards Julie, to get her attention. Then he pulled it back again when she made eye contact. The room went silent and they all held their breath as they sat waiting for what was to follow.

"I'm sorry Julie, please forgive me, it will never happen again."

Everyone looked at her as they awaited her response. Julie looked around the table at their faces, in shock that even Shel seemed to know what he was referring to. Her eyes filled with tears as she turned back to Cody and choked out, "I do forgive you."

Will pulled his wife into his arms and as she yielded to his embrace, he kissed her on top of the head. Glancing over at Cody, a tear rolled down her cheek as the tension that she had felt following her around for over two weeks, got up and left, along with its baggage.

41
Eyes for You

For the wages of sin is death,
but the free gift of God is eternal life
through Christ Jesus our Lord.
Romans 6: 23 NLT

When Mike had finished trying to scrub his skin free of the stench of the skunk, he walked back into town. Stopping at the hospital he found that Cody and Shel had left shortly after the police chief, and Holly had been admitted for a short stay. He was directed to her room where he watched her sleeping peacefully. Her skin was clean and her hollow cheeks carried a pink blush while her lips parted slightly as she breathed in and out. Her wet corkscrew hair lay damp on her pillow and Mike couldn't help but lean over and kiss his wife on the forehead as she slept. He sat down next to her bed for a moment before he decided to try and catch up with Cody and Shel.

Stepping out onto the street he strolled down the street towards the police chief's office. Looking around at the storefronts and quaint shops he saw a picture-perfect small town. Soon he was stepping into the police chief's office, extending his hand and said, as an older man stood from behind his desk, "Hi, I'm Mike Hilbert, I'm one of the group that was lost out in your mountains here."

"Oh yes," the older man took his hand. "I'm Police

Chief Burt and this is Police Detective Samuel Trusty." He motioned to a young man in his mid-thirties who had been looking over a map that hung on the wall.

The police detective stepped towards him. "Mike, was it?" he asked as he took his hand.

"Yes sir, and you are Samuel?"

"Sam will be fine. So how can we help you Mike?"

"Well, I was just wondering where to find the rest of my group, that's all. I saw Holly at the hospital, she's sleeping but the others were said to have left soon after you did."

"Oh yes," Chief of Police Burt said. "I got them signed into the motel down the road. I reckon' they'll be there now unless they found themselves something else ta do," he chuckled.

Mike didn't want to bother his friends at the motel and he had noticed that Sam had been drawing some lines on the map behind him. "So Sam, have you figured anything out on that?" Mike joined him over at the map.

Sam turned around. "Well Mike, best we can figure, you folks did good for awhile, but when you backed away from the river, you started to wander off. The rivers and creeks snake their way around these mountains, and if you had stayed close to one of them, you would have found your way into one of the small towns in the foothills. Sorry to say but my trackers have found signs of you being here, here and here." The police detective scanned the map, pointing at a river, a creek, and then backs to the same river.

Sam continued, "That's as far as my search teams got before you came into town on your own. But we were told you took this ravine right here. That tower you were trying to get to was on a neighboring mountain." He paused, waiting for Mike to catch up. "Cody said you traveled for several hours, which would put you about here." He circled a spot on the map and added slowly, "There are no huge old trees in that ravine I'm told." He paused as if trying to figure something out. "Well, finally it looks like you may have walked in circles, until you started following this creek up the mountain, and here is where Leroy McCoy said he found you."

Mike stood speechless for a moment before asking, "How did we not know we were going back up the mountain?"

"Well to be fair Mike, you were all weak and every step you took, whether up or down, was labored. You folks were literally starving to death, so your judgment was a little impaired. Plus, these mountains as you well know, heave up and down, this way then that, no matter which way you're headed."

"True," Mike said, then said no more.

The stepbrother of the deceased was called in to identify the body, and Maclean Robert Ferrell was now officially pronounced dead. Police Detective Samuel Trusty volunteered to inform the Ferrell family himself, as he had very little to do until the next morning, when the Hilbert's and Wiley's would be coming in to fill out their reports.

Police Chief Burt compiled a list for him; along with several family members was the girlfriend of the deceased. The police chief explained how he thought that she should be told also, as he put it, "She's been frettin' about him bein' missin' for over a week now." Then Chief Burt handed the list to Detective Trusty who gave an understanding nod and turned to go.

"Ya know, I'm gonna be retirin' soon," the chief said as he followed the detective out, "and this little town could sure use a good man like yourself. Things get a mite slow around here but there's a lot to be said for that, 'course it would mean a pay cut for you, I'm sure."

"Hm-mm, I might just do that, I'll definitely pray

about it."

Police Chief Burt grunted at that and took a step back. In his experience, 'I'll pray about it' was just a polite way of saying, 'No thanks'.

Detective Trusty stepped off the curb and walked around to the driver's side door of the patrol car. "You know, I don't think I'd mind a pay cut. I like it here, it's quiet like you said and it beats looking at dead folks every day." He paused to look around at the small town. "You never know - I might just take you up on that offer."

With that, Police Chief Burt smiled.

Detective Trusty looked at the list in his hand and, after he took a deep breath, he opened the car door and slid inside.

The first stop was a nursing home on the outskirts of town that housed Maclean's grandmother. But it soon became clear that she had no idea what he was talking about, and very possibly had no idea what a grandson even was at this point. After several painful minutes he left and, pulling out of the parking lot, he said to himself, "Well, I guess there is an upside to having Alzheimer's."

He then visited the stepsisters who had already heard the news from the stepbrother who had identified the body. They seemed more bored and unmoved, than hurt.

Last on the list was the girlfriend that lived in the back of the local diner. As he drove back into town he prayed, 'Lord, it's sad to think of a man spending his whole life on this earth, and when he's gone no one cares. Didn't he have anyone who loved him?' he asked himself as he looked again at the address on the slip of paper. 'Still,' he said, 'as disturbing as that is, it has made my job easier, thank You Lord for that, I guess.'

Easily finding the diner he pulled up, stepped out of the patrol car, and walked to the front door. A little bell rang over his head as he stepped inside and a smile spread across his face. Inside was the cutest little retro diner he had ever seen.

"Hello?" He said loudly. Not receiving an answer he walked towards the jukebox at the end of the room to admire its cathedral shape. He slowly slid his hands over its smooth, peaked, hardwood top that curved as it sloped down. "This is absolutely beautiful," he said to himself. Then hearing a sound behind him, he turned around to see who it was.

Standing there was the most adorable little, old, lady he had ever seen. She gave him a toothless grin, her white hair was loosely pulled back while some of it had escaped the bun and now floated lightly, framing her face with a kind of sunburst as her eyes danced with delight.

"My husband and I purchased that jukebox second-hand in 1952. We bought new 45's for it every year for about twenty years then we just stopped tryin'. Can't stand me none of that there rock n' roll stuff. Of course the kids stopped hangin' out here soon after that, I can't say I minded that too much either." Her eyes twinkled, "now they just come in, buy their sandwich or ice cream and move on. And if they do decide ta stay with their rough talk, I just have ta start playin' one of the oldest songs in the old girl ta get them ta get along." She patted the old girl as she called it, then went on with, "only the older folks come in ta sit now. And they like to play her and just dance." She smiled as if she could see them dancing. Then, sliding her hands over the jukebox, she gave a satisfied nod: "Nice people with respect for other folk's stuff."

She slipped her hand in her apron pocket and pulled a quarter out. Then she punched in three selections that she knew by heart. Turning towards the detective, she put her hands out, palms up and said, "Shall we dance?" He took her hands nervously as she jested with him. "Now you mind yourself officer, if ya try anything, I'll gum ya to death!"

He had to laugh as she flashed her gums at him in mock chewing. And he relaxed a little as she took the lead. It was clear that she was remembering a dance from long ago so he gladly fell in line. As they swung around the floor, he watched her cheerful steps with surprise, being shocked to see this little old lady dancing so spryly.

"Now tell me officer, why do you think you came in here today?"

He took a second to process that question and then said, "Well, I'm looking for a Kate McClure. She lives here right?"

"Oh, she sure do! Alright young man, what's your name?"

"I'm Detective Samuel Trusty, ma'am."

"Are ya a Christian Sam?"

"Yes I am, I go to church regularly." He smiled, feeling like he was playing some kind of game with the jolly old lady.

"Are you single?"

"Am I single? May I ask where these questions are going?" He added as he raised an eyebrow with a slight smile.

"Relax Sam, I'm not interested in a young'un like you, at my age." She looked at him, tilted her head to one side, then raised her eyebrows and nodded as if to say, 'well Sonny, I asked you a question'.

"Alright, let me help you out a little," he said. "I'm forty-one years old. I have never been married. I am looking for a nice Christian woman, but I haven't found her yet. No offense." He smiled at her again.

"Good! Now you're goin' ta want ta know somethin' about my Kate."

His smile faded as he stopped dancing and stepped back. "I'm here to give her some bad news ma'am, that's all."

"Now Kate," the old lady continued, ignoring him, "she grew up in church but she wandered away for a while, lookin' for love ya know. Of course she can't find it that way, but she do try. Now, I been prayin' for her since she were born, her mama done died and her papa left her with her Granddaddy and me. Her Granddad died nigh onto eight years ago now. And I ain't gonna be livin' much longer bein' just a mite over twenty nine, myself. Now the good Lord done told me he'd be bringin' someone ta love my Kate afore I go, and in ya come."

She was quiet for a little bit but then added, "Now you'll be needin' time to be prayin' on this a mite, I expect. I'll leave ya here, until Kate gets back. She done stepped out for a minute but she'll be back real soon."

The old lady began walking then she wheeled around and said; "Now I ain't sayin' that ya are the one, just that ya fit what I've been prayin' for, ya hear?" She turned back around and disappeared through the door that led to the back of the shop, with a knowing smile on her face.

Sam stood speechless; trying to process what had just taken place. He wanted to run but he still had to deliver the message to Kate that her boyfriend was dead. *'I can't leave, she may be the only one in this world who cares that Mac is gone,'* so he stayed put, setting down at a booth near him, pushing the thought of running aside, and began to concentrate on the music. The song ended and the jukebox selected a different 45. He slid back out of the booth and walked towards the jukebox as it began to play. While a piano played softly, a singer sang smooth words about his love:

♪ *'I On-ly Have Eyesss Forr Youuuuu Dear...'* ♪

Sam didn't know that there had been such a song...

334

his thoughts faltered. He had only ever heard his Aunt say, *'And, I've only had eyes for your uncle, all my days.'* He had always liked the way that had sounded, so he had adopted it as his prayer for a wife. His heart jumped in his chest, *'what if God is trying to tell me something? No, no – no; I can't think like that now, not now.'* He leaned in to read the label on the record behind the glass window as it spun around and around, still not believing his own ears, but it only made him dizzy.

"Hello, my Granny said you wanted to talk to..." Kate stopped speaking mid-sentence as Sam spun around. He was tall and trim and his mouth hung open, making him look a little slow. Kate's heart started to race and she blushed as he stared at her. All of a sudden she was very conscious of what she must look like to him. She nervously brushed her hair out of her eyes as she looked up at him shyly.

When Sam saw her, his heart stopped, he took her in with one quick glance. Her cheeks pinked as she brushed a dark curl aside that had been hanging over one eye. Her green eyes sparkled as she looked back at him. He felt like he couldn't breath as he said, "Ka- Kate- Kate McClure?"

"Yes! That's me," her chin lifted a little higher in recognition of her name.

"I'm Detective Samuel Trusty ma'am," he smiled, and then he stepped forward and took her hand.

Character Reference

Mike and Holly Hilbert: husband and wife, fellow campers and mentors to Cody and Shelly.

Cody and Shelly (Shel) Wiley: husband and wife, fellow campers and friends of Mike and Holly.

Will and Julie Salamon: husband and wife, friends to main characters, Julie works with Mike and Cody.

May: Julie's friend from work.

Chuck Atteberry and Leroy McCoy: the bad guys, Chuck is the driving force of the twosome and Leroy is the reluctant follower.

Granny McClure: wise elderly woman, Kate's grandmother, owns the family's diner / ice cream parlor.

Kate McClure: Mac's supposed girlfriend, works with her Granny at the family diner / ice cream parlor.

Mac Ferrell: Man found dead in the gully wash.

Bo and Duke: Bo, the owner of a tracking dog named Duke.

Police Chief Burt: the law enforcement in the small town of Ponder.

Police Detective Samuel Trusty: in charge of investigating the disappearance of the campers, the Hilbert's and Wiley's, along with the murder of Mac Ferrell.

Reader's Study Guide

1. At first, how did you feel about Cody and Shel's relationship?

2. Could you see how they were both being selfish?

3. What were they each doing to expand the chasm growing between them?

4. Do you identify with Cody, and/or Shel, in their struggles?

5. Is there anything you can see more clearly now about how your partner thinks?

6. What can you do to change your relationship?

   (Cody, Shel, Mike, Holly, Chuck, Leroy)

8. In this story, is there a certain character or characters that you identify with, and why?

9. Discuss the fears each character dealt with and how they compare with your own.

10. Does God forgive saint and sinner alike, and what does He expect of us when our brother or sister falls?

11. Holly told how she wrote a letter of repentance and forgiveness to those who had hurt her, and whom she had also hurt. Do you think you could ever be that selfless?

12. What does forgiveness look like to God, and how does our view often differ?

About the Author

 When Peggy isn't caught up in the world of writing, she is working on half a dozen other projects at the same time. Included in these projects could be all manner of art, decorating ideas, murals, or even plays. Asking her husband about her many projects he said, "I love it! She's like 'Alice in Wonder Land'; she comes up with six impossible things before breakfast. At least they seem impossible to me, until she manages to do them all!"

Along with her husband of 40 years, Peggy has raised three children and has seven grandchildren. She is a graduate of both the 'Self Confrontation' and 'Inductive Bible Study' courses.

She has always been an observer of people and while dealing with personal trials, Peggy launched into writing in an attempt to try and sort things out for herself. Her stories jump off the page sparking a sense of adventure as well as believable relationships.

Peggy said, "In todays world we are constantly being bombarded, with dysfunctional relationships as though they are the norm, but in God, they don't have to be that way. Forgiveness, for one, is something the world knows nothing about. I wanted to show not only the trials of the characters, but also help the reader to apply this story into their own lives. Seeking the Lord we can begin to see things through His eyes."

Other Books include: Part 1 & 2 of 'HIS Eyes' series

Books 1, 2, and 3 of the 'Ash' trilogy

And 'Opposite Intent'

Made in United States
Troutdale, OR
06/29/2024

20804323R00196